JEZEBEL

Eleanor de Jong is the daughter of academics and grew up in Europe, America and the UK. She studied history and politics at university, and is now settled in London with her partner.

Also by Eleanor de Jong

Delilah

ELEANOR DE JONG

Jezebel

AVON

AVON
A division of HarperCollins*Publishers*
77–85 Fulham Palace Road,
London W6 8JB

www.harpercollins.co.uk

A Paperback Original 2012
1

First published in Great Britain by
HarperCollins*Publishers* 2012

A catalogue record for this book is
available from the British Library

ISBN-13: 978-1-84756-255-5

Set in Minion by Palimpsest Book Production Limited,
Falkirk, Stirlingshire

Printed and bound in Great Britain by
Clays Ltd, St Ives plc

MIX
Paper from
responsible sources
FSC
www.fsc.org   FSC° C007454

Acknowledgements

Although this telling of Jezebel's life is fictional, the characters, the setting, and the political issues are real. In a novel it is impossible to do justice to the complexity of Jezebel's situation, or indeed to stand back far enough to consider the full consequences of her presence on the historical stage. Interested readers might though like to seek out Lesley Hazelton's excellent biography of Jezebel in order to explore further the life of this fascinating woman in thoroughly researched and thought-provoking detail that draws on the contemporary world and ancient language to build a compelling factual narrative.

As ever, four allies stop the invasion of hostile forces – you know who you are. Much love and thank you. Thanks too to LB, who reminds me that service to the whim of others is not a bad place to start. At Working Partners, Michael Ford built the vats and then threw out the rotten snails. Charles Nettleton generously provided the biscuits this time.

And Kate Daubney was a valued research assistant once more.

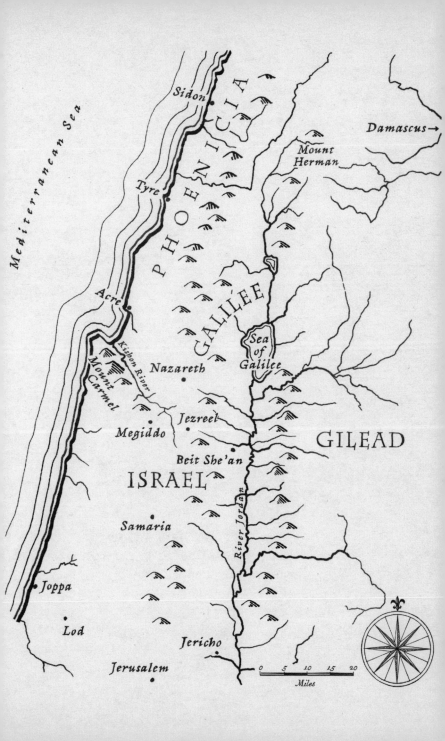

872 BC – Girl

Chapter One

Salt spray glistened in the stallion's mane and stung Jezebel's cheeks. She leaned close into the neck of the horse, urging the animal on through the low waves. Ahead, the city of Tyre rose up out of the lapis blue of the Great Sea, the white walls of the Royal Palace and the temples like the crest of a perfect wave just ready to break.

As Jezebel reached the causeway that climbed onto the lower reaches of the Tyrian island, Shapash the sun Goddess had already begun to draw her heavy head towards the soft shoulder of Yam, the God of the sea. Jezebel knew she should turn south at the city gates, towards the Palace and the stables. Rebecca, her maid, would be waiting to tut and sigh at how the young princess had surrendered her carefully arranged elegance for the dishevelled disarray of any other fifteen-year-old girl let loose for an afternoon.

But Jezebel couldn't resist one last whip of the wind in her hair and instead turned north, daring the horse faster and faster round the city walls. She galloped out along the narrow stone promontory, built on the orders of her father to protect the harbour from the heaving discontent of winter seas. For a moment, she felt like she was flying, until the stallion tensed beneath her, his ears pricked and eyes wide. He shuddered to a halt. Jezebel grabbed at the harness to steady them both, her knees digging hard into the saddle cloth. 'Steady, boy!'

The promontory fell away steeply on either side, the sheer walls plunging deep into the natural well that Tyrian ships called home. For a moment she felt dizzy, as though the tide was rising fast to meet her, and she laughed in spite of the unexpected rush of fear, and patted the horse's neck. 'Don't you dare tell Father I brought you out here.'

She glanced back along the wall but they were quite alone up here. A large crowd had gathered below on the wooden docks that nestled into the curve of the harbour, their attention entirely on a wedding party disembarking from small redwood boats. Snatches of pipe music and laughter drifted up. Jezebel spotted a girl of about her own age stepping off the boat, her hands taken up by a young man. They both wore the plain linen tunics favoured by fishing families, but the young man wore a second overskirt, a *shenti* in rich Tyrian purple. Jezebel's older brother Balazar wore the same type of garment – if somewhat more bejewelled – every day as he strutted the enclosed gardens of the Royal Palace. Jezebel guessed this young man must be one of the fishermen whose rare right to wear the purple cloth came from the back-breaking daily grind of harvesting the precious sea snails that gave up the dye. His bride was lucky to marry such a man, for if she could ignore the terrible smell of the rotting snails he must endure to make the dye, and if he could rise up steadily from fisherman to trader, perhaps one day he

4

would sail her in a much larger boat down the coast to Ashdod or even as far as Egypt.

The crowd cheered as the young man draped a fine purple veil over his bride's hair, and beneath Jezebel the horse grew restless. She shivered and glanced towards the setting sun.

'Father will be expecting us,' she said quietly.

She turned the horse around where the wall widened and let it trot back into the city. But she could not resist a last look down at the wedding party. The dock was now edged by the sparkle of shell lamps. The girl looked so happy as her husband fastened a purple-edged cape at her throat. Jezebel's hand reached absently to her own throat and the fat Red Sea pearls that rested on her skin. Perhaps Rebecca would know who the happy couple were, perhaps they were young cousins of hers and she would be able to tell their story. The island was full of faces Jezebel recognised and who would smile respectfully when they saw their princess ride by, but whose names only Rebecca could know.

Though when she sees me like this, Jezebel thought, *I doubt if she will ever speak to me again.*

Chapter Two

There was indeed a faintly frosty welcome when she returned to the stables, not from Rebecca but from Hisham, one of her father's senior courtiers.

'I must be in trouble if Father has sent you to find me,' she said as she handed the harness to one of the stable boys.

Hisham's lips barely curved. 'His Royal Highness has been waiting two hours.'

'I suppose Balazar has told on me. Otherwise, how would you have known where to find me?'

'The King had also hoped to ride this afternoon, Your Highness.'

'Oh.' Jezebel winced and glanced at her father's favourite stallion, now being rubbed down by the boy. 'I don't suppose I have time to change my dress either, do I?'

'I believe there will be time for that in due course.'

Hisham turned neatly on his sandalled feet, and led Jezebel through the Palace to her father's retiring room at a ridiculously stately pace considering the apparent urgency.

'You look a mess,' said Balazar from where he lay on

the couch beside her father's marble desk. King Ithbaal was sitting at the desk studying a scroll of papyrus that rustled crisply as his fingers worked across it. He did not look up at the sound of his son's voice and Jezebel chewed on her lip. The desk was piled high with scrolls, some of them papyrus, others of vellum, and a neat pile of engraved clay tablets stood on one corner. Jezebel tucked her loose hair behind her ears.

'At least I've not just been lying around.'

'Don't we have boys to exercise the horses?' yawned Balazar, twisting his black hair between his short fingers. 'Anyway, you should not go out on your own like that. I could see you racing along the beach from up here. It's not safe.'

'Or seemly?' she asked. 'When was the last time you even stepped out of the Palace? In all your seventeen years, have you ever *been* across the causeway?'

'I have no need to go down there. Anyone of note comes to us, Jezebel.'

Ithbaal let the scroll close around his hand. 'And did you see anyone of note on your ride today, my dear?'

She walked to the desk and kissed his cheek. 'I'm sorry. Will you forgive me? You should have told me at lunch that you wanted to ride. We could have gone together. I would even have let you saddle your own horse.' She maintained a pious expression for a moment, then smiled, for her father's dark eyes sparkled with amusement.

'Actually, we could have ridden out together to meet the Judeans,' he said. 'I am surprised you did not see their retinue on the Sea Road.'

'I thought they weren't coming for a few days.' Jezebel

pushed back one end of the scroll which her father had been reading. The angular letters were neatly inscribed, but they were so tiny and ran on and on. But still she read, lowering her head towards the scroll: *Tax on goods in transit—Contribution to maintenance of the King's Highway—*

She let the scroll go. 'Are you asking the Judeans to pay for the upkeep of the northernmost stretch of the Highway? They surely will not agree to that. It is the furthest stretch from Judah, and also the furthest from here, and the part of the Highway in which both kingdoms have least interest.'

'Are you calling Father a fool?' asked Balazar lazily from the couch.

'Jezebel is right. Strategically it appears to make little sense.' Ithbaal looked down at his son.

'Then it makes little sense,' repeated Balazar, his cheeks ruddying.

'Unless you think that Ben-Hadad of Damascus has ambitions to seize that piece of the Highway,' explained Jezebel. 'It borders his land of course. Should it fall into his hands traders would be at his mercy. That does neither Judah nor Tyre and Sidon any good at all.'

Ithbaal nodded, but his attention had fallen from her face to her dress. 'I presume you have something else to wear for dinner. One of your very best outfits. And perhaps that engraved amethyst pendant I gave you for the Spring Festival.'

'You want me to meet the Judean officials?'

'They're absolute barbarians,' said Balazar. 'No culture, no art, their food is bland, and that awful brown land—'

'I suppose I'll seat you between the King's son Jehoshaphat and *his* son Jehu,' said her father to her, resting his hand on her shoulder. He spoke casually, but she felt the weight of his touch. 'I am sure you will show them both the very best of your hospitality.'

Jezebel's heart banged hard in her chest, and she held her breath to slow it down. 'Of course, Father.'

Her father stood and walked away without another word and Jezebel could only watch him go, as dizzy now as she had been up on the promontory.

'You know what he means, don't you,' said Balazar slyly, 'sitting you next to—'

'I know.'

She ran past Hisham out of the retiring room and up the grand stone staircase to her room, flinging back the heavy drapes and darting across the corner of the room to the small shrine to the great Goddess Astarte beside the east window. But the stone plinth was already heaped with grapes, and the redwood circle carved with Astarte's manifestations was wound with fresh tendrils and leaves of the vine.

Jezebel glanced frantically around the room, for Astarte's shrine was only ever dressed for festivals and for weddings. At the foot of the bed stood Rebecca, her hands clasped at her waist, her eyebrows arched knowingly beneath her greying hair. Beside her was her youngest daughter, Beset, a year older than Jezebel and in Palace service at her mother's side. The girl smiled at Jezebel. Jezebel tried to speak, but her throat was tight and she could only sink down onto the white kneeler at the foot of the shrine. At a nod from Rebecca, Beset filled Astarte's ceremonial bowl with water and gave it to Jezebel. She drank it down gratefully.

'What did Father tell you?' she whispered, looking up at her maids. 'You must know something, else why would you have dressed the shrine?'

'So that Astarte will guide you,' said Rebecca.

'I will have to marry one of these Judeans to secure the safety of the Highway,' gulped Jezebel. She'd been expecting this day for two years – not many royal daughters remained unmarried in their sixteenth year. 'Has he told you which one?'

'The Palace is full of gossip—' whispered Beset.

'Then which?'

'It won't do us any good to speculate,' said Rebecca, frowning at her daughter. 'We have made our offering to the Goddess, so we must allow her to take care of you.'

Jezebel shook her head. 'It would surely be better if I did not understand what is at stake, then I could just do as I am told without thinking about it.'

'When have you ever done as you are told?' said Rebecca. 'Now come and bathe and then we can dress you. You must look your best for your future husband, whomever the Fates decide upon.'

Chapter Three

Later that evening, Jezebel entered her father's crowded chambers for the ceremonial dinner, her heart feeling tight in her chest. Two courtiers held the pleated train of her finest silk dress, and she kept her eyes fixed on her father rather than glancing around at what form her future might take. Ithbaal stood to escort her personally to the couch opposite his, signalling the respect which she was to be accorded by the visitors. Jezebel lowered her gaze to the tables, groaning beneath golden bowls piled high with cooked grains and meat, fruits and nuts.

'You look wonderful,' whispered her father.

Jezebel concentrated on keeping her shoulders drawn back. Standing so, she was almost as tall as her father. Her shoulders were bare, and almost brushed by the amethyst pendants of her earrings. Rebecca had wanted to whiten her skin, but Jezebel hated being pasted with make-up, especially when it was liable to crack as the evening wore on. She settled for a pearlescent shimmer dusted across her collar bones. Her lips were painted vermillion, using one of her mother's recipes learned from the Egyptians.

'I had always thought it like the cool of a midnight sky,'

11

said a voice to her right, 'but in truth it is more like the heat of a glorious sunset.'

'I'm sorry?' said Jezebel politely, turning. The accent was not like any she had heard before.

'Tyrian purple,' said a young man settling on the couch next to her. From Balazar's dismissive description, Jezebel had imagined the Judeans to be as dull and ugly as their lands, but this fellow was as handsome as any of the young men of Tyre. His jaw was a little squarer and his eyes had a dark knowing about them that Jezebel found oddly cool in their attractive setting. From his unlined face, he might have been only a couple of years older than her, perhaps even eighteen, but his body was certainly a man's. She blushed at how intently he studied her in return. His eyes caressed her shoulders, then took in the folds of fabric that draped across her body. 'The cloth I've seen dyed with it in the Jerusalem markets has a rather bluer hue to it,' he continued, 'but your dress is quite rich and red in comparison.'

There was a moment's silence before Jezebel realised he was expecting an answer, but when she tried to speak, no words would come. The Hebrew he spoke was guttural but soft. She coughed, her fingers covering her mouth, and the young man quickly reached for a bowl of wine and offered it to her.

'Thank you,' she whispered, furious with herself for being so struck by his looks that she had forgotten her poise and her manners. She drank some wine, and swallowed hard. 'I'm afraid that the colour you are describing isn't true Tyrian purple, but *tekhelet*.'

'I don't know this word,' he said, 'what does it mean?'

12

Jezebel swallowed some more wine, its richness surely flushing her cheeks even more. 'Tekhelet is the colour used for our ritual clothing.'

'And that makes it different?'

Jezebel lowered her gaze. 'I am quite sure one of the officials will be able to tell you about the technical processes if you wish to know.'

He leaned closer to her and she smelled the sweet almond oil on his hair. 'It can be very boring,' he whispered, 'listening to a lot of officials droning on. But I'm sure the Princess Jezebel can make even a dead snail sound interesting.'

'It seems you know more about me than I know about you,' said Jezebel. 'I'm afraid I don't even know your name.'

The young man lowered his head and hesitantly offered his hand, palm up, in the traditional Phoenician greeting. Jezebel lowered her palm onto his in response, the calluses at the base of his fingers catching on her own smooth soft skin.

'I apologise. A soldier's hands are not as soft as a princess's,' he said. 'I'm Jehu, the youngest in the Judean line. My father, Jehoshaphat, sits to your left. My grandfather Asa sits between your brother and your father.'

Jehoshaphat had turned towards the sound of his name, and she offered her hands for the greeting. The father's jaw had the same hard contour as the son's but his mouth lacked fullness and his eyes were hawkish. He glanced contemptuously at Jezebel's hands, then turned his attention back to Balazar. King Asa was a small man with bright eyes and just a scattering of hairs across his liver-spotted scalp. Most of his fingers bore thick gold rings, and he

13

threw a mischievous smile towards her, as if to say 'Were I a younger man . . .'

Jezebel darted a glance at Jehu, but he made no apology for his father's rudeness, or his grandfather's lechery, only staring at the back of his father's head. She fumbled for her golden platter to cover her embarrassment at being snubbed, selecting fruits and meats from the table.

Jehu began to do the same, hurriedly saying, 'I have spent little time on the coast. I had not imagined Tyre would be so striking.'

'Thank you,' said Jezebel rather formally, staring at her plate. 'I am sure there are many attractive towns and cities on the Judean coast.'

'Perhaps. But I have never seen them for the Judean army have never had to defend our nation from armies of mermaids and seahorses.'

Jezebel glanced up in spite of herself, and found Jehu grinning shyly at her, his eyes gazing deep into hers. She smiled and broke his gaze, but he quickly spoke again.

'Your officials were talking of a city called Mog'dor, where the Tyrians own great yards for turning the snails into dye, but I cannot imagine what such a place is like. Is it not far to the west, beyond the end of the Sea Road?'

'But not beyond the end of the sea,' said Jezebel allowing her eyes to be drawn back to his. 'Where feet might fail, a boat will always sail.'

'Give me a horse instead. You are not at the whim of the winds on a horse.'

'I love to ride too,' she answered, glad of something in common. 'But a boat can carry far more cargo and will bring you more by return. The King's Highway, the Sea

Road, these roads will always stop where the sea begins. But the sea crosses land by way of rivers—'

'You make it sound almost beautiful.'

'The sea is beautiful.'

'But I think only you could make it sound so.'

Jezebel blushed deeply but she held Jehu's gaze as he offered her his plate of food to share, the light of the shell lamps glistening on his dark curly hair. She tentatively reached for the plate, her fingers settling on a bunch of grapes in the middle, and she smiled to herself as she picked them up.

Perhaps Astarte is watching after all, she thought.

Chapter Four

In the sharp morning light, Tyre looked almost more beautiful than at sunset, its white buildings sparkling. Up on the roof of the Palace the light breeze caught Jezebel's dress and her headscarf fluttered behind her. Beset had stayed with her long after Rebecca had gone to bed last night, and they had spent considerable time choosing the outfit, giggling softly between them at how Jehu might admire the flattering cut of one against the pretty hues of another. Their efforts had been worth it, for Jehu had hardly taken his eyes off her since he and Jehoshaphat had followed Ithbaal up to the roof for the best vista of the city. Indeed he now grinned foolishly at her as he rubbed his palms vigorously on his bare arms. This morning he had shed his formal robes in favour of a rough tunic strapped with a leather belt and knife sheath. His strong calves were laced into leather riding boots, and he looked very much the warrior he claimed to be.

'Are you cold?' asked Jezebel.

'I'm not used to the sea wind. It is cooler than when I'm galloping through the valleys.'

'I prefer to ride along the beach.'

'It isn't good for a horse to run on such soft ground. They waste their effort and their hair gets clogged with sand.'

'I agree with you, Jehu,' said Ithbaal. 'And I would advise you never to let Jezebel ride one of your horses for both of them will return muddy and exhausted.'

Jezebel smiled but avoided looking at Jehu. The young man was even more handsome in the sunshine, taller and broader than she had realised, like one of the heroic Temple statues with his feet wide, his arms crossed, and the black curls on his head kissed lightly by the breeze. So she turned away, containing her attraction, for the negotiations were the purpose of this visit and not merely the prelude to a suitable marriage. Ithbaal had watched her during the banquet last night with that glimmer of amusement she loved so much, and she had glowed to know she was making him proud. It didn't harm, of course, that her dinner companion had been charming, and it made up for Jehoshaphat's less engaging disposition.

'Women should not ride,' said Jehu's father as he peered across the city's roofs. 'They cannot keep up with men when the going is fast, they're easily scared by the dogs, and they turn feeble when the blood of prey is spilled.'

'Spoken like a true huntsman,' said Balazar, who was lolling against the parapet.

'Surely you don't allow your women on the battlefield?' asked Jehoshaphat of Ithbaal.

'I find their wisdom more valuable than their physical strength.'

'Hmm.' Jehoshaphat sneered. 'In Judah, women have no contribution to make except in the home.'

'Then on that perhaps we differ,' said Ithbaal. 'Phoenicians

17

constantly seek harmony with each other, with our surroundings, and with our Gods. For example, this very island is a partnership between land and sea. Indeed, it was a great feat of construction to put land back into the sea to build the promontory, not to mention a mastery by Melqart, the God of Tyre, of Yam, the God of the sea. I admit I sacrificed a good number of bullocks the night before the building began.'

'So many Gods to satisfy,' said Jehoshaphat dryly.

'Tyre reminds me of Jerusalem, my home,' said Jehu quickly, looking at Jezebel. 'It is built on a plateau in the mountains that sticks out into the valley below, rather like this island. I think you would like it. And it does no harm that you have to cross Israel's ugly plains to get there for it sits like a jewel in a headdress compared to their heathen encampments.' At that he turned to Ithbaal. 'I was surprised to hear you mention concessions to the Israelites at dinner last night. They're not worthy of your consideration.'

Jezebel glanced at her father, but it was Balazar who caught her eye, gleeful at the prospect of an argument.

'The difficult history between your peoples is well known,' said Ithbaal, 'but Phoenicia's own history is one of exploration and friendship. We have long sailed the Great Sea in search of trade, and such exchanges are always defined by difference. Besides, as Israel are our neighbours it is neither practical nor wise to exclude them—'

'But with your superior knowledge of the Sea,' insisted Jehu, 'and an agreement between ourselves on the King's Highway, we could control the north–south routes to both sides of Israel and exclude them altogether. It is no more than they deserve.'

'Jehu, mind your place,' said Jehoshaphat. Jezebel held her breath. For all his fairness and wisdom, her father was not used to being interrupted, or disagreed with.

A light cough broke the silence and Jezebel saw Hisham standing at the top of the stairs. 'Your Highness,' he bowed to Ithbaal. 'Your visitor has arrived and is waiting for you in the courtyard.'

Jehoshaphat looked down over the parapet, then jerked around angrily. 'That is the headdress of an Israelite official. How dare you invite them to join our negotiations!'

Jehu strode across to join his father and peered over the edge. 'From his unsteady gait on the horse, I'd say the intruder is Ahab's aide, Obadiah.'

'I believe King Ahab of Israel is as entitled to be addressed by his rank as your own grandfather,' said Ithbaal patiently. 'Obadiah isn't party to our discussions, but as I explained, it isn't in the interest of my own kingdom to build relations with only one nation at a time—'

'I will be consulting with my officials about this,' snapped Jehoshaphat, barging past Hisham down the stairs.

'Balazar,' continued Ithbaal, 'please invite Jehoshaphat and his staff to join you on a tour of the Silk Halls. He is sure to find the beauty soothing, and the merchant opportunities extremely lucrative.' Ithbaal turned to Jehu. 'You are very welcome to accompany your father on the tour.'

'Perhaps I will await the outcome of your discussions with Obadiah before I accept,' said Jehu coolly. 'It would be foolish to become intrigued by goods that were no longer available to me.'

'You may slay a man with a single thrust of a knife,' said Ithbaal, 'but to build a partnership takes more than one passing of hands.'

Jezebel watched her father and Balazar walk away down the stairs, then she glanced at Jehu. Perhaps he was still cold, for he shook, and his shoulders were tense beneath his tunic.

'Come down to the gardens,' she said suddenly, surprising herself. 'They're far prettier than the Silk Halls, and we'll be out of the wind.'

Jehu raised his chin. 'I apologise. You must think I've insulted your father.'

'I've argued with him just as fiercely.'

'But not with so much at stake.' He looked towards the stairs. 'And now my own father is angry with me too.'

'You were only defending Judah's interests.'

Jehu shook his head and sat down on a stone bench. 'If he trusts me to know what they are. My father would rather have brought my older brother instead, but my mother is the second wife—'

'And she has more influence than the first?' Jezebel couldn't help but laugh. 'You must forgive me now, for I don't understand the purpose of these ranks of wives and children.' She sobered her face. 'But clearly it troubles you.'

'I've much to prove if I'm to rise to my proper place in the Judean Kingdom.'

'If what I hear is right,' said Jezebel gently, sitting down on the bench beside him, 'you have little to worry about.'

Jehu glanced at her. 'What do you mean?'

'Rival kings might argue but their servants always gossip happily together. I'm told you are thought of very highly in your household.'

20

'How would you know what the servants have been saying about me?' he enquired, his mood abruptly lightening. 'Have you been asking about me?' he asked, teasingly.

Jezebel blushed. 'I too have a proper place in my kingdom, to listen to what others say.'

'I am quite sure there is more to your talents than that,' said Jehu reaching for her hand, not in greeting this time, but lifting it carefully from her lap, his thumb delicately stroking her palm. 'I confess there are some attractions to this Phoenician custom of openness.' His eyes locked on hers, so dark and deep, and she felt his breath warm against her lips as he leaned in towards her.

A gull screeched loudly as it landed on the parapet beside them and Jezebel jumped. 'You noisy bird,' she laughed.

'I suppose there are even Gods in the birds who look over you,' muttered Jehu, leaning towards her again. But this time Hisham's discreet cough interrupted them and Jezebel stood up abruptly, smoothing down her skirt.

'Yes?'

'Jehoshaphat is asking for his son,' said the attendant.

Jehu straightened himself and strode towards the stairs without another word. And Jezebel turned her back on Hisham and looked down the coast towards Judah.

Chapter Five

She was late to the banquet that night, having spent such a long time choosing what to wear that even Beset had lost her enthusiasm for the game. 'You are as choosy as a child sometimes,' Rebecca had said. 'I'm sure that your Jehu will notice only those beautiful eyes of yours.'

'He isn't *my* Jehu yet,' Jezebel had replied, but that light retort echoed rather dismally as she approached her father's chambers. For Jehu was not on any of the couches, nor was there any sign that he was expected. Instead Jezebel's couch was drawn tightly between King Asa and Jehoshaphat, who was already loudly criticising the Israelite visitor, Obadiah.

'How can I possibly endure an evening of that?' muttered Jezebel, her shoulders sagging.

'Are you all right?'

Jezebel looked into the shadows. 'Daniel?' A tall slender youth a year or two older than her emerged from behind a pillar, his dark straight hair tucked behind one ear. His brown eyes narrowed as he peered into the room, and his face was taut with concentration. 'What are you doing here?'

'Eavesdropping for my uncle,' he murmured, moving close beside her. He smelled of the sweet medicines of the herb garden, rosemary and sage.

She glanced around the walls of the dining room, where a number of both Phoenician and Judean officials were silently watching on. 'Is your uncle not here?'

'He is with the other priests giving thanks to Dagon, so the Gods might bless the grain negotiations. But he sent me to find out whether tempers had improved since Obadiah's arrival.'

'Do you know why the Israelite has come?'

Daniel only shrugged.

Jezebel sighed. 'Well, he is making everyone feel bad. I came down for dinner but now I don't feel much like eating.'

'Shall I make you a warm drink? Menes was teaching Eshmun and I only last week about how mint can help soothe the stomach. Go up to your room and I will bring it straight away.'

Jezebel squeezed his arm and headed for the staircase. But as she reached the corridor outside her room, she found Beset waiting for her, her face flushed with the delight of a secret.

'I don't know what you're looking so cheerful about. Jehu was not at the dinner. Perhaps his father is keeping him out of affairs.'

'He's not at the dinner because he is waiting in your chamber,' whispered Beset. 'Mother's gone off for the evening to see her sister.'

Jezebel's heart leapt and she fussed with her beaded belt. 'What is he doing here?'

Beset gently touched her shoulder. 'I believe you should find that out for yourself.'

'But Daniel is on his way up.'

'Leave that to me.'

'Does anyone else know Jehu is here? If my father finds . . . if *anyone*—'

'You know you can trust me,' said Beset, giving her a gentle push into the room.

Jehu was standing at the window, his outline lit softly by the glow from the lamp nooks in the wall. Jezebel glanced back but Beset had already let down the heavy curtains over the door.

Jezebel ran her fingers over the neck of her dress. But Jehu didn't turn from the window. *He must be as nervous as me.* She hesitated, watching him, her breath quick and shallow, then she slid off her sandals and crossed the room in her bare feet, drifting silently to his side like a moth settling on a night-scented flower.

Jehu slid his arm around her waist without breaking his gaze from the sky, and Jezebel entwined her fingers into his, hoping he couldn't feel how hard and fast her heart now beat beneath her skin. She felt giddy as he lifted his free hand and pointed to the sky.

'The stars are just the same here as they are in Jerusalem. My favourite, Kesil the archer, his belt across his waist. And above him, Ayish the red star—'

'We call that Baal's star,' murmured Jezebel, 'though it is also the eye of the bull who thought my ancestor, the Princess Europa, so beautiful that he stole her away to be his lover.'

And finally Jehu looked down at her. 'Is that what I must do? Steal you away?' His head lowered towards her face and she smelled the sweet almond oil that made his hair glint in the lamplight. Their eyes met for a long moment but Jezebel could think of nothing but how it would be to kiss him, to feel all his body against hers. And then, at last, his face lowered and his mouth found hers, firm and full at first, then as he drew her into him, his fingers sliding beneath the folds of her dress, his lips parted and as he drank the breath right out of her, she knew she would give herself entirely up to him.

Jezebel measured the following days in two parts: the hours she was with Jehu and the hours of waiting. During the days she would catch sight of him now and then, through a balustrade, or from a window, as he accompanied her father, her brother, or other officials on various tours of the city or to meet persons of interest. But she could see from the way his face occasionally drifted from his companions that his mind was elsewhere.

With Beset's help he came to her room each night after dark, and left before the sun rose, either climbing along the outside sea-facing wall, or sneaking through the corridors. He would joke about the boredom of the visit as they lay in each other's arms, feeling the sea breeze trail its delicate fingers over their skin. And after they had sated their desire, they spoke of the future. He admitted that the diplomatic life was not for him, and longed to be away from the watchful eyes of his father and grandfather.

'They're never quite sure what my role is,' he said one night. 'I don't even know where to stand half the time.'

'It's the same for me,' said Jezebel. 'My brother seems to think I interfere where a woman's voice isn't needed.'

They had other things in common. Both had lost their mothers – Jezebel's had never recovered from a chest problem when she was ten, and Jehu's had died in a difficult childbirth when he was three; the child hadn't survived either. He could not even remember what his mother looked like.

They spoke of their love of riding, of the different breeds in Judah and Tyre. Jezebel suggested they could elope, steal two horses and gallop along the river road, and make camp in the mountain passes like soldiers, hunting food and cooking over a fire.

'I think you'd make a good fighter,' Jehu said.

'What makes you say that?'

'You like to be in control,' he said.

Jezebel rolled on top of him, giggling, and pressed his arms above his head. A thin scar snaked across the top of his chest, white against his bronzed skin.

'How did you get this?' she asked, tracing it with her finger.

'When I was twelve,' he said. 'I was running with a ceremonial sword from the smith to give to my brother Jehoram. I slipped.'

'Where is Jehoram now?' Jezebel asked.

'My father left him in Jerusalem. He doesn't travel well over long distances.'

'That's cryptic.'

'My brother is clever,' he said, 'but he has never been strong.'

Jezebel sensed she was touching a nerve and changed the subject.

'Did it hurt?'

'Not as much as my wounded pride.'

Jezebel smiled and kissed the scar. 'Boys are silly,' she whispered, feeling Jehu's manhood stir beneath her. 'Always playing at soldiers.'

Chapter Six

Jehu held his hand out to Jezebel as she stepped onto the royal galley, but she was far steadier on her feet than he was. He looked pale beneath that bronzed skin, and his hands were clammy against hers. Gone was the assured lover whose body she had enjoyed night after night in her chamber, the sleeping couch now so strongly scented with him that she thought she would never know other fragrances again. But here on the edge of the harbour, the west wind was sharp with salt, and Jezebel felt as though she had woken up from a deep sleep to find winter had turned to spring.

Certainly that was their reason for being on the galley, to open the water festival of Yam in gratitude for seeing the fleet through the harsh winter. She released Jehu's hand quickly, so no one could mistake his courtesy for intimacy. The ceremonial redwood boat was in position beyond the harbour, piled high with the carcasses of all the boats that had foundered in the previous year. The whole pyre would be set ablaze as the sun set, but first there was the inspection of the merchant fleet by Ithbaal, raised up in the prow of his galley.

'Why must it roll around so much?' muttered Jehu as he stood beside Jezebel behind Ithbaal.

'Because Yam breathes just as you do, only in the ebb and flow of the tide.' Jezebel longed to reach out and steady Jehu, slide her arm around his waist, feel the muscles across his abdomen tauten at her touch.

She suspected that the cordiality between kingdoms remained only between herself and Jehu. There hadn't been a banquet for almost a week and negotiations now only took place between lower level officials. Ithbaal had invited Jehu to the ceremony as a last gesture of faith, but he admitted to Jezebel he thought the son just as stubborn as his father and grandfather. They would not concede on the point of taxation of exports to pay for the military patrols on the King's Highway, and there was nothing more to be done about it.

Earlier in the day, as the galley was rowed out, Jezebel felt torn. She wanted to tell her father that Jehu's passion could be useful if it was properly directed. She was desperate to explain that Jehu was not blindly holding on to his family's principles but could reason as thoughtfully as he could make love to her. But as she cast a subtle look at him, whose hands gripped the rail of the boat, she guessed nothing but an enforced declaration of marriage between them would bring the nations together.

'It will be calmer in deeper water,' she said as the vessel pushed past the first of the great trading boats, its prow carved into the rearing head of a sea serpent.

He didn't answer. He stared wide-eyed across the water, his teeth gritted and jaw set.

'Don't be afraid,' she murmured. 'Yam won't swallow you up when I'm with you. He wouldn't dare.'

'My people are meant to walk the earth, Your Highness,' he said eventually, his voice more brittle than usual. 'We fear the sea because, just as you say, it might swallow us up. Only our prophet Moses could control the sea, and even he didn't sail upon it but parted it so that my ancestors could walk on the land beneath. Our priests tell me that we are a people destined to walk the land forever in search of a home.'

'Then you will only ever walk in circles,' said Ithbaal from the prow. 'This is your opportunity to change that, to break with the narrow vision of your father and grandfather, to lead your nation forward to exceed the very history that still confines you. Do you have the courage to do so, or will you stand rigid on this deck forever, pretending that the wooden boards are a little piece of earth beneath you?'

'Well said, Father,' cried Balazar from the other side of Jezebel. But she could only exhale quietly and try not to look at Jehu. If that was not an exhortation to him to marry into the Tyrian royal family, then what was?

So it was with considerable joy late that evening after the festival that she watched Jehu walk alone from her father's retiring room towards the guest wing in which the Judean delegation were staying. He didn't look up at her window, but she couldn't expect that he would. Appearances had to be maintained until the announcement was made. Besides, there were still two hours before Jehu would climb the tree outside her window in the dark and creep into her bed, and Jezebel was desperate to hear what her father had said to him. She was considering casually going down to her father's chambers when Beset knocked on the open door and parted the inner curtains. She glanced quickly around the room, no doubt fearful that Jehu was also there, but kept her voice steady.

'His Highness the King is here to see you. Shall I ask him to wait?'

'Of course not.' Jezebel came away from the window. 'Father? Come in.'

Beset drew back the curtains fully and gave a low bow as Ithbaal entered. He looked around him at the cosy space, soft with couches and cushions and the yellow tones of the oil lamps, and for a moment, Jezebel was sure he would notice Jehu's distinctive almond scent in the room. But he merely gave a nod of satisfaction and sat down on a couch beneath the window. Jezebel smiled to herself. At least if Jehu scaled the tree, eager to give her the news of their engagement, he would see that her father had got there first!

'You have made these chambers very comfortable for yourself. You have your mother's eye for beauty.'

'Thank you, Father.' Jezebel sat down beside him.

'At least you can take all these fancy pieces with you when you move, and recreate this room exactly as it is elsewhere. It won't be the same, of course.' He paused, and Jezebel looked eagerly at him. 'What I'm trying to say is that I will miss you when you are gone, but the time has come for me to let you go. The negotiations have been completed and you are to be married.'

Jezebel gasped, her hands flying to her cheeks to smother the flare of delight. 'Just as you wish, Father.'

'In three days you will travel to Samaria to marry King Ahab of Israel.'

Jezebel sagged on the couch, all her giddy joy suddenly dispelled. Her hands turned clammy in her lap as she stared at her father, panic rising fast in her chest. 'What? I don't understand. King *Ahab*?'

'It has been a far more difficult negotiation than with the Judeans, if that could be possible, and I don't believe that Obadiah came here prepared to give up anything at all in exchange for you. But it is the right outcome for Tyre.'

'But the Judeans have been here longer.'

'What sort of reason is that?'

Jezebel scrambled to order her thoughts. 'Then settling with Israel is the less ambitious choice, they are our immediate neighbour, they open no new land routes for trade, and Jehu was right, the King's Highway and the Sea Road together would secure—'

'Jehu's arguments are persuasive only because of the passion with which he delivers them. Just because a man shouts loudly does not mean that what he says is right. He is thinking only of Judah whereas I'm thinking of Tyre and all the Phoenician kingdoms.'

'But Jehu is a better match—'

'For whom?' demanded Ithbaal, standing up. 'For you or for Tyre? You have enjoyed a life utterly without responsibility, Jezebel, and though you are more than intelligent enough to understand the issues, you know nothing of what sacrifices must be made for the good of the kingdom. It is time to put aside your personal wishes and become a true princess of Tyre. You are to marry Ahab and there will be no further discussion about it.'

He strode across the room towards the doorway and Jezebel sucked hard on her cheeks, trying to control her tears until her father had left.

But at the doorway he suddenly stopped, steadying himself on the doorframe as he turned.

'Perhaps I haven't presented this to you very well. Perhaps if you had seen Obadiah for yourself, if you had witnessed both sets of negotiations, you might have understood better what I've had to consider myself. And perhaps if I had seen matters through your eyes, I might have understood that the presence of a handsome young man, however misguided, is always going to be more attractive than the proposition of an absent stranger. But Ahab is a sound ruler.'

'And what is the point of owning two great ports,' sniffed Jezebel, 'if you cannot safely navigate the sea between them? We must protect all of the King's Highway, not just the top and the bottom.'

Jehu didn't see the arrangement that way at all.

The dish of nuts left his hand and smashed against the wall and Jezebel flinched. 'Your father had no intention of ever sealing a deal with us!' he yelled.

She went quickly to him, smothering his body in her arms. He remained rigid, trembling with rage. 'Don't be angry, please. If there was any other way . . .'

'He kept us hanging on here for days while he waited for Obadiah to make up his mind,' Jehu muttered.

'It's not like that—'

Jehu pushed her away. 'Isn't it? I've been a fool.'

'We love each other! What's foolish about that?'

'Love? Is that what you call this? Sweetening me night after night so that I might go back to my father every morning with fresh reasons for us to stay and negotiate.'

'Don't say that!' cried Jezebel, stepping back. 'Don't say things so hurtful when I know you don't mean them. I must go to Israel and marry a man I've never met instead of the man I love.'

'So you say!' His voice cracked on the words, and she could see his face holding back his tears. The boy who had seemed so grown up now looked very young.

'I'd never given myself to a man before you came to Tyre.'

'You want me to believe you learned those charms in my arms? Surely a people as travelled as yours have learned a thing or two along the way.'

'Oh!' Jezebel fell back on the couch, unable to hold back her tears. Had this monster, who even now was kicking over stools and hurling cushions across the room, lurked always beneath that tender exterior? As he grabbed the ceremonial bowl from Astarte's shrine, she threw herself at him, trapping it between them.

'Don't dishonour us both,' she whispered urgently, 'don't call down the rage of the Gods on us for what has happened.'

She clasped his face, now wet with tears of anger and disappointment, and wiped them away, then she kissed her fingers so that she might taste his misery and know

34

it as well as her own. 'Don't blame Astarte but pray with me that our love might last for all eternity.'

Jehu's head fell against her shoulder, and Jezebel felt his body shudder against her in a great heave of despair. 'No God will protect that.'

'Then at least believe in me. Stay with me tonight, one last night, so that we can seal our love—'

But Jehu pulled away from her, drawing out of reach. He turned his back on her and laid Astarte's bowl back at the foot of her shrine. 'I won't lie down with the wife of the Israelite king. The God I share with him would forbid it.'

'Jehu!'

He shook his head and strode from the room. Jezebel watched the curtains sway in his wake, felt the last sweet draught of almond-scented air brush her face, then she sank sobbing to her knees.

Chapter Seven

'Hail, Hail!' cried the crowd at the head of the causeway. 'All Hail to Jezebel!'

Jezebel glanced at Beset, who stood beside her in the Palace courtyard. But the young maid was staring at the huge gathering of Tyrians who lined the path linking the promontory to the mainland, her eyes wide with her own nervousness and anticipation of her future responsibilities at Jezebel's side. Beyond Beset stood Daniel with his horse, the beast saddled up with his medicinal chests and rolls of clothes and blankets. Her friend smiled at her and puffed out his cheeks – there weren't really words for occasions like this.

Barely a month had passed since Jehu and the Judeans departed the city, but it seemed like longer. Everything had changed, and Jezebel felt as though she'd been snatched up on a whirlwind of preparations which would carry her away from Tyre to a new and strange life.

Before the retinue stood an enclave of priests, all dressed in the same long linen robes, led by Daniel's uncle, Amos. He held aloft a great wreath of sacred branches which he would shortly break apart and spread on the first few steps of the journey. The offering to the Great God El was to ensure safe passage south to Samaria.

Finally, ahead of Amos in the arch of the Palace gateway stood Ithbaal, with the wine bowl of Kotharat, the Goddess of marriage. The King raised the bowl high, then he turned to face Jezebel and summoned her forward.

'Go in safety, go in peace, go in contentment,' he intoned. 'May your journey through life be rich and fertile, and may it please the great pantheon of our Gods.' He drank from the bowl then handed it to Jezebel. It sat heavily in her palms, steadying their tremor. She looked uncertainly at him, then lifted the bowl and sipped from it, the wine sweet in her dry mouth.

He leaned forward to take the bowl from her. 'I will miss you,' he murmured softly. 'But you will become a great emissary for our kingdom. And every one of our people gathered here to see you go believes that too.'

Jezebel looked around her at the Palace officials, at Rebecca sniffing proudly into her apron, at the fishermen, the traders, the priests and all the families of Tyre clustered together, each of them perhaps holding their breath just as she did, uncertain of the future. She swallowed hard, and gave the bowl back to her father, then straightened herself as she knew she must, her bead-edged scarf rippling over her shoulders, and looked out across the causeway towards the land.

'To Samaria.'

It was a long walk down through the crowds that lined the road, their cheers rolling around her like the waves on the beach. But she knew as she crossed the causeway that those same crowds would ebb away quickly enough too. Her city would forget her. In the days since Jehu had left, she'd prayed to forget him too, just to escape the pain of the memories. The almond sweetness was fading from the cushion on which he had lain, now tucked safely into the carriage behind her, but his image was stubborn and resolute in her mind. The love which had made her feel afloat above the petty concerns of trade and borders and politics now lodged deep in her stomach like nausea on a rolling sea. She doubted it would ever leave.

As soon as she reached the shore, Jezebel paused, waiting for the retinue to swell up around her and regroup for the journey, first along the coast and then inland. Priests, diplomats and officials clustered into their groups, all watching her intently. But it was not until the stable boys arrived that Jezebel spoke, tilting up her chin as she strode through the crowd.

'I will ride from here.'

'Your Highness?' said Philosir, the senior official sent by Ithbaal to Israel. Beneath his headdress, his forehead was lined with all the wisdom of the kingdom, and those sharp blue eyes that had seen so much observed her shrewdly. 'Your carriage would be more comfortable.'

'I want to ride.'

'It is very warm this morning,' said Beset, 'and we have a long slow journey ahead of us all day. You'll want to look your best when we arrive tomorrow.'

'I won't hide away among this delegation,' said Jezebel. She paused, trying to still the fear in her voice. 'It is my place to lead it as any Phoenician princess should.'

Philosir and Beset exchanged the briefest of looks, then Philosir clapped his hands. A horse was brought forward with a mounting block, and Philosir offered his hand to Jezebel to mount.

'I understand you very well,' said Jezebel as she took it, settling herself side-saddle in all her finery on the horse. 'But I must begin as I mean to go on.' However that might turn out to be, she thought to herself.

Philosir bowed his head, his grey hair curling at his shoulders, then he released the harness so that Jezebel could trot out of the group. She saw Daniel urge his horse forward to join her, but she shook her head and broke into a canter to put space between her and the group. Too far and they would canter to catch up with her. But a small gap should allow her the solitude she craved.

It had been a small argument with Philosir this time, but she knew that would surely be the last of such victories. From now on, she must do as others wanted, from the diplomatic orders rolled up in parchment in Philosir's chest, to the rituals of Amos and the priests, and not least the wishes of her husband-to-be. Rebecca had explained to Jezebel and Beset that Ahab wanted her as his second wife to give him a son, as those his first wife had provided had all died shortly after birth, leaving him with just one daughter. As she thought of this, Jezebel couldn't help but remember Jehu on the roof of the Palace talking of first and second wives, the shame and impotence of being born a strong man to the wrong woman. She shivered a little and cast a brief look at Tyre, now receding against the shimmering blue of the horizon, its people attending to their own business again, their princess no doubt already a fading memory. Then she rode on, aware of the dull murmur of the retinue dragging behind her, trying to picture a bed she had never slept in, a lover she had never seen, and a future she could barely imagine. While miles ahead Jehu was probably forgetting his loneliness in the soft arms of some other girl.

The mountains had been a soft smudge on the horizon for a while, like dirty clouds belched by Shapash from her yellow sun. The land had none of the sparkling purity of the sea, and Jezebel had felt suddenly frightened when she glanced over her shoulder and realised she could no longer see the coast at all. The light was draining quickly across the dusty foothills around them as Daniel rode up beside her.

'We are making camp for tonight because there is a spring just over there and soon it will be too dark to ride safely any further. Shall I bring some water to wash your face and hands?'

Jezebel looked past Daniel towards the well. It was a ramshackle wooden construction, dilapidated from use and with none of the elegant mosaics of shells that celebrated the carefully pumped water on Tyre. Some distance away were the huts and tents of a small Israelite settlement, as brown as the land around. But she knew appearances were deceiving. The land here concealed vast underground reserves of water.

'Let's get you off that horse. You should eat something and rest.'

Jezebel shivered. 'I'm not hungry.' She rubbed her belly. 'I feel sick with nerves.'

Daniel smiled gently. 'I'm not surprised. But some food and wine will settle you down and help you sleep. Even you have never spent a whole day in the saddle.'

Jezebel laughed ruefully and guided the horse to the rapidly assembling encampment. Tents were being erected and wood piled up for a fire, and she could hear the rhythmic evening chants of the priests. The land grew dark even as she looked at it, and she suddenly felt weary. As she dismounted she couldn't even work out which way was home, and she stood alone on the edge of the busy group, watching them prepare everything for her just as she would expect it, so they might all pretend that this was still a little piece of Phoenicia. But there was nothing familiar in all this industry, not the nervous murmurings of her staff nor even in Daniel's soft plucking of his nevel, tuning the twelve strings so that he might play soothing songs of home. Even the air smelled strange and dry, and Jezebel rocked back her head to breathe in from the sky and not the land. And there, far above her, sparkled Baal's star – Ayish, as Jehu had called it – and there, as she traced the patterns in the sky with her finger, Kesil, his twinkling archer.

Where are you, my love? she wondered. *Do you look towards Tyre as I do, and remember?*

41

Chapter Eight

The next morning it was not the unfamiliar light that woke Jezebel, nor the strange soft breaths of the horses against the walls of her tent, but the awful heat in her skin and the lurch of sickness in her stomach.

'What is it?' said Beset, sitting upright in her bed on the floor beside her.

Jezebel clamped her hand over her mouth, her tongue bitter with bile. Beset emptied a water bowl just in time and held her as the sickness heaved through her, drawing her hair back from her face and resting cool damp cloths against her neck and forehead.

'You rode too long in the sun yesterday,' the maid said. 'I'm calling for Daniel.'

Jezebel didn't have the strength to disagree, and soon she lay still while Daniel gently felt her face and then carefully touched the skin around her belly.

'Was it the food? The water in that well might not be good so far inland,' suggested Beset.

'No one else is sick,' said Daniel standing up from where he had knelt beside the couch. But he was frowning, and he was slow to soak the cloth from Jezebel's forehead in the bowl of cold water. 'How long have you been feeling like this?'

'Just today,' she replied weakly.

'But you said you felt sick last night.'

'I remember.'

'Have you woken like this on any other morning recently?'

'Daniel?' said Beset in a warning tone. Jezebel shivered, not from feeling so awful but from the strange atmosphere that was building in the tent.

Daniel bowed his head but his expression was confused and he frowned over hidden thoughts Jezebel couldn't decipher. 'What is wrong with me?' said Jezebel, suddenly afraid.

Beset took Jezebel's hands in hers and gestured to Daniel with a jerk of her head that the two young women should be left alone. He glanced at Jezebel, his face creased with worry, then he slipped out of the tent.

'Am I going to die?' whimpered Jezebel.

'No, no. Well . . .'

'What is it?' Jezebel felt sick once again, but purely from fear. She tried to sit up on the couch and Beset piled cushions behind her, never once letting go of her hand. Then the young maid knelt down on the ground beside Jezebel, looking up at her mistress. Jezebel was comforted by the shadow of Rebecca's sensible comfort in her daughter's face, but Beset suddenly looked so grown up that Jezebel felt her eyes sting with tears at how their worlds were surely changing.

Beset, thinking her mistress understood, nodded with relief. 'That's right. You are with child.'

Jezebel shook her head in bewilderment. 'I don't understand.'

'I thought you had guessed for yourself.' Beset chewed her lip with worry. 'Those nights of intimacy you shared with Jehu. He has left his seed in you and you are now carrying his child. The early sickness is very common, it does pass, but in eight months or less you will give birth to his child.'

Jezebel grabbed Beset's hand, gripping it hard as she tried to get up off the couch, but her head was spinning. 'But I'm not yet married to Ahab. When I give him a child that isn't his own he will . . .' Panic surged through her. He would certainly cast her out, and she'd be lucky to escape with only exile. Death would be swift for the child. And where could she go then? Her father's anger would be implacable, the shameful stain on the kingdom too great. She wouldn't be welcome in Tyre, the soiled princess, and foreign kingdoms would view her as nothing but a pariah. She could only shake as if Baal Hadad's godly roar shuddered through the skies in anger at her foolishness. 'Oh, dear Gods, what have I done?' she wailed.

'Shh,' murmured Beset, sliding her hand around Jezebel's shoulders. 'Daniel?'

The young physician returned to the tent, his face taut and pale in the shadows. He looked almost as wretched as Jezebel felt but she could no longer bear to look at him. When Beset stood up to confer, she curled into a ball, drawing the covers over her head. She didn't want to hear their fears for her future. She'd known, she supposed, that it could have ended like this, but in those blissful nights it hadn't mattered. Jehu was going to be her husband and any children would be legitimate. It would have seemed perverse to curtail their passion, churlish even. Now those desires looked very reckless indeed.

Beset tugged the covers aside, leaned again over the bed, her long black hair dangling against Jezebel's cheek. 'All is not lost,' she said. 'Daniel can make you a special drink that will end your worries.'

'But I've never concocted such a thing before.' Jezebel could hear the desperate concern in Daniel's voice and she pressed her face further into the pillow.

'If you take the life of the child then you are saving Jezebel's in return,' Beset replied.

'I trained as a physician to save all lives, even the ones who haven't yet known this world.'

'But you do know *how* to make the drink,' said Beset.

'It goes against everything I believe—'

'But you believe in Jezebel. Surely you believe in the role she plays for our kingdom?'

Daniel sighed and after a moment Jezebel heard the creak of the lid as he opened his small medicine chest, and with these strangely comforting noises she sat up on the bed and faced him. She lifted her eyes to look at his and saw not judgement, only a sad understanding.

'I'm so ashamed,' she whispered. He nodded, silently drawing together powders and dried leaves and mixing them with wine. Then he came to the bed and offered her the bowl.

'This will purge the child. It will make you sick and you will bleed. You should ride in the carriage and not on the horse today while you take this treatment. But perhaps that is for the best.' He smiled ruefully. 'For you

45

cannot ride into Samaria as though you are going to conquer it.'

Jezebel took the drink from him. 'I don't know how to thank you—'

Daniel cut her off with a wave of his hand. 'No one need ever know.' He closed his chest, picked it up off the floor and left.

Jezebel watched him go, then she glanced wretchedly at Beset. 'He's angry with me.'

'He's afraid,' said Beset.

Jezebel looked down at the bowl, the sweet red liquid cloudy and bitter with the poison that would tear Jehu's baby from her. She thought of the sky beyond the roof of the tent from which last night Kesil the archer had looked down on her. Soon the stars would be the only reminder she had left of the nights she had shared with Jehu. Slowly she lifted the bowl to her lips but the smell made her wince and she retched, the bowl shaking in her hand.

'Probably best just to drink it in one go,' said Beset. 'That's what my mother always told us to do with medicine when we were little, do you remember?'

Jezebel nodded. 'Then could you bring me more wine? This smells so awful that I'll need something to wash it down.'

'I'll come straight back.' Beset disappeared through the tent flaps, and Jezebel let the bowl sink into her lap. Her hand felt beneath the covers for her stomach. There was nothing there yet, no bump, no sign of the baby's presence except in the sickness in her throat. But she knew in that moment that for all the good intentions of Daniel and Beset, for all the dreadful fear of what would happen if Ahab found out, she could no more end the life of the child than she could put a stop to her longing for Jehu.

She snatched up the bowl and poured the liquid away in the corner of the tent out of sight. Then she curled up on the couch and cried.

Chapter Nine

'This city was built to keep strangers out,' murmured Jezebel under her breath.

The carriage lurched and she clung on to Beset, not daring to look out at how the slopes fell steeply away. They had been travelling for much of the day across the undulating foothills but the city of Samaria now towered above them on a great flattened mountain as if all the Gods had chosen this as their table round which to sit and feast. The city was barely visible from down here, though as the long Phoenician entourage twisted and turned its way up the steep sides of the mountain, Jezebel glimpsed the dull yellow corners of buildings and shallow reeded roofs. The sun was already low in the sky and the air grew colder with every step of the horses' hooves.

Finally the carriage slowed and Jezebel peered out at the looming city walls, a last defence against any determined invader who had made it this far. She could hear Amos and Philosir up ahead presenting their credentials to the gatekeepers, and a moment later a soldier appeared at the carriage window, his face creased from months of defending this harsh landscape, his hair long and greasy.

'So you're the Phoenician bride?'

Are you expecting any others? she wondered. She chose to ignore the word he'd used for 'bride'. Rather than kingly consort, its meaning hinted at a brood-mare paired with a stallion. 'I'm Jezebel, Princess of Tyre,' she answered.

He stared at her as one might a strange sea creature beached on the shore. They'd paused before the ascent for her to assume her best purple travelling cape and the modest cap of the betrothed bride.

A shout went up at the head of the procession and with a great creak the gates were opened and a bugler played a single solemn note that sounded more like a peal of bad tidings than a welcome. The carriage lumbered forward once more and the procession dragged into the city. But there was none of the warmth and joy of the departure from Tyre, none of the cheering or the wash of the sea. Instead the city was flat with the clop of hooves on stone as they travelled among the walls within walls, deep into the heart of the city. Jezebel caught a glimpse of what was surely the King's Palace, a huge stone edifice that rose up in the middle of the city, its sheer walls pockmarked with windows and wooden shutters. The Israelites who passed the carriage met them with cold curiosity, drifting begrudgingly apart to let them pass.

It wasn't quite the warm welcome Jezebel had expected. She felt Beset's hand link with her own beneath the cape.

The carriage jolted to a halt and the doors were snatched open. A pair of soldiers clad in leather armour stood on each side. Neither offered a hand.

Jezebel climbed out of the carriage as elegantly as she could, shaking out the heavy travelling cape over her dress. The procession had stopped at another closed gateway and Jezebel realised they were outside the Palace, for the great walls soared above her, pale against the dusk sky. In one of the high windows she thought she saw a woman looking out across the city, but when she looked again the figure was gone. Her gaze fell to the stony street beneath her feet and she shivered. Philosir appeared at her side, Amos behind him, the priest's normally tranquil demeanour tainted with worry.

'I apologise, Your Highness,' said Philosir rather more loudly than was his usual custom. 'I do not know why we are being kept here outside the Palace gates like tradesmen.'

Because it is a trade, thought Jezebel. *And someone wants me to remember that.*

After a short wait the gates yawned open and through them emerged Obadiah, the Israelite envoy who had arrived in Tyre the day after the Judeans. He wore a black robe over his tunic, embroidered at the edges in pale thread, but his head was bare and he looked rather scruffy next to Philosir. He had also dispensed with the permanently obsequious smile he had worn in Tyre and he looked humourlessly down his long narrow nose at Jezebel. She wondered fleetingly if her father had been deceived by the courtship of negotiation, like a maid duped at market by a flirtatious farmer. Nonetheless she took a deep breath and bowed while Philosir offered his hands to the other official in the traditional Phoenician greeting.

But Obadiah ignored them both, instead asking his

soldiers, 'Why have you brought them here? Escort them to the rear gate.'

Philosir asked sharply, 'Is there to be no formal welcome?'

Obadiah raised his brows. 'Before the wedding?'

'This is a meeting of kingdoms, not just a marriage of convenience.'

Obadiah gave a dry laugh. 'There will be a dinner this evening.'

'Before or after the wedding?' asked Beset. 'Should Her Highness wear the wedding gown or—'

Obadiah waved a hand. 'I will have someone see the girl to her chambers. The rest of you should follow the walls around to the far side.' And then he strode off into the Palace compound without a backward glance.

Jezebel glanced at Philosir but the diplomat was himself exchanging angry whispers with Amos. So she took a deep breath and walked through the Palace gate after Obadiah, lifting her cape so that it would not drag in the dirt. She could feel every eye on her. Stopping, she turned around.

'Well?' she said in a voice so loud and clear it surely didn't belong to the girl who was shaking so much inside she could hardly breathe. 'Which of you will take me to my chambers?'

Her momentary courage was lost in a rattle of horses' hooves and a spray of dust as a rider cantered round the Phoenician party and into the courtyard. The soldiers suddenly stood to attention and rapped their staffs into the ground, one of them dashing forward to take the horse's harness as the rider dismounted.

'From the look of you, I assume you are Ithbaal's

daughter,' said the rider, a tall lean figure in a dirt-streaked tunic and leather jerkin. Greying hair fell in a tangle around his shoulders. He must have been twice Jehu's age, at least. His nose was narrow and his eyes small and very dark as they watched her. A deep scar ran beneath his mouth and along his jawline. 'They told me you were beautiful, although I would suggest that striking is a more accurate description.'

At least my face isn't scarred, and my clothes are not filthy.

'Your Highness?' asked Philosir hesitantly.

Jezebel's heart sank. *Ahab?*

'And you must be the diplomat,' replied the rider. 'We will meet more formally later.'

He strode off through a courtyard, slapping the dust from his tunic, and Philosir moved quickly to Jezebel's side. 'I wish it could have been more auspicious a first meeting,' he murmured.

'I wish he could have been less rude,' muttered Beset.

But Jezebel could only stare after him. *And I wish he weren't such an old man!*

Chapter Ten

The chambers she had been allocated were a pleasant surprise. Not only would they furnish comfortably with all the cushions and couches she had brought with her from Tyre, but they commanded an excellent view far across the land towards the west. Across a narrow corridor outside her room was a long balcony above one of the internal courtyards, thick with climbing plants, though their flowers were barely in bud due to the relative cold up here. In her memory, Tyre was already so low and small, and even with the spectacular view she couldn't see the sea along the line of the setting sun.

And somewhere to the south, on another mountain sat Jerusalem, and Jehu.

A snap of barking cut the evening peace and Jezebel shuddered. Down below a group of wild dogs strained on chains as they dragged a pair of soldiers around the castle walls, their mottled coats rippling over their muscular limbs, their mean faces wrinkling up over sharp yellow teeth as they howled up through the shadows towards her.

'They can smell the infidels.'

Jezebel twisted away from the window. A woman stood

behind her. The voice had been so low and hard she'd thought it a man's. The face was hard too, and her hair was scraped back into a brutally tight twist. She looked as old as King Ahab, as old even as Jezebel's own father, her skin lined like the layers of rock that formed the mountain beneath Samaria.

Jezebel gave a cordial nod of greeting but the woman made no effort to respond, so Jezebel said, 'I'm afraid I don't understand what you mean.'

'The dogs. They know Yahweh isn't your God.'

Jezebel felt her politeness grow taut with impatience at the woman's tone. 'He is one of the pantheon of Phoenician Gods. He is the son of El and the brother of—'

'He is the only God. And those dogs down there defend His Name. They can smell your corruption. Be wary of them.'

She just means to frighten me. Perhaps she is the King's sister and disapproves of him marrying someone so young.

'Mother?' A girl barely a couple of years older than Jezebel appeared in the curtained doorway, dressed in a simple ochre dress that shone against the swathes of black worn by the older woman. The girl glanced at Jezebel, looking her up and down, taking in the cape which Jezebel still wore like a protective shield. 'That purple is such a beautiful colour. I envy you—'

'Of course you envy her,' spat her mother.

Jezebel gave a friendly smile to the girl. 'I have another one like it if you would like to borrow it. I imagine it gets very cold here in the winter, being up so high.'

'That's true. Last winter—'

'Esther!' snapped the older woman.

'Mother, please. It's not her fault.'

'What isn't my fault?' asked Jezebel.

Esther's face creased into an awkward smile. 'Don't you know who we are?'

'I've only just arrived. My name is Jezebel. I have come from Tyre.'

'We know all about you,' said the older woman.

'Then you have the advantage,' said Jezebel. 'I've already been here long enough to know I'm not welcome, but I cannot defend myself if I don't know who hates me.'

'We don't hate you,' said Esther quickly.

'On the contrary,' said the older woman, 'we bid you great welcome.' She bowed low and swept her hand almost to the floor as Esther watched, wretched with embarrassment.

'I'm afraid I've been told very little about the family of the King,' began Jezebel, but Esther interrupted her.

'Please, it doesn't matter, it really isn't your fault. We none of us wished for—' Her words ended in a shriek as the older woman slapped her face.

'Do not speak for me!' snapped her mother. 'When you have been used up and thrown away as I have, then you can speak for me!'

Esther tried to reply but her words were choked with tears and she ran clumsily away.

'What riches I have brought the House of Omri,' said the older woman bitterly. 'May your reign be as long and as happy as mine.' And with that she swept out of the room.

Jezebel sank down on the nearest couch, her hand resting on her flat belly. *She must be Ahab's first wife,* she thought. She frowned, trying to remember the name Beset had told her, but she was so weary from the journey, and the late afternoon gloom seemed only to cloud her thoughts still further. *At least I won't be alone,* she thought, trying to imagine how the baby lay within her, but it was little comfort to know that she had brought her own trouble to a Palace that had already made her so unwelcome.

The room was little better now the shadows were falling, for no servant had yet appeared to make up the fire or light the lamps. *I can't stay in here forever,* she thought, so she wrapped her cape tightly around her and went out to the balcony, seeking the warm glow of braziers that filtered up from the courtyard below. The dusk hung like a *tekhelet* canopy across the sky, and Kesil had not yet shown his sparkling bow. But Baal's star glimmered faintly as though he was keeping half an eye out for Jezebel, and she wandered slowly down a wide stone staircase into the courtyard. The whole place seemed deserted but three braziers burned fiercely around a circle of benches in the centre of the courtyard and Jezebel sat down on one of them, holding her hands up to the flames to warm herself.

With a sense as keen as the dogs' out in the street, Jezebel abruptly realised she was not entirely alone. She turned as gracefully as she could manage to find Obadiah standing behind her, his narrow features starkly lit by the glow from the braziers.

'I would not go wandering around the Palace if I were you. Not everyone welcomes you here.'

'That is because they don't know me yet,' said Jezebel, irritated by all the hostility.

'I did not agree to the marriage because I liked you.'

'That's fine, because I'm not marrying you.'

'You have no idea how difficult it will be to become Queen of Israel,' said Obadiah, moving into the shadow of the brazier. 'You're just a child.'

'I am quite sure that is not why King Ahab wants to marry me.'

'What makes you think he wants to?'

'What are you chattering on about, you little fool?' A reedy voice cut across the courtyard and a tiny elderly woman swathed in layers of silks hobbled between the benches, her gown glistening with pearls, her hands glimmering with gold and precious stones. 'Ignore him, my dear. Ignore all of them. Politics has made every last one of them a little soft in the head. And none more so than Obadiah, who has spent so long listening to his own voice that he believes every word he says.'

Jezebel swallowed her laughter, and rose to greet this extraordinary woman whose bright beady eyes now shone in her wrinkled face.

'By your youth and your beauty, I assume you are Jezebel of Tyre,' continued the old woman. 'You must be missing your home so let me tell you a little about mine.' She glanced at Obadiah. 'What are you waiting for? Run away and bore someone else.'

Obadiah gave a curt bow and vanished into the shadows.

'Ours is a marriage of inconvenience, you might say,' said the old woman, watching Obadiah's departure.

57

'Neither of us can dismiss the other, nor can we ignore them. Each of us is wedded to the King by duty and a certainty that we are his best adviser. Such are the trials of the Queen Mother and the Chief of Palace Staff.'

Jezebel bowed low, cheered enormously by this tiny woman, so humorous and spirited. 'Your Highness.'

'Never mind that.' The elderly woman linked her hand into Jezebel's arm. 'Would you see me to my room, my dear? That way, you will always know where to find me.'

'Of course, Your Highness.'

'Call me Raisa. After all, I am mother to the man you have been dragged down here to marry, and we are to become family.' They set off across the courtyard, between elaborate statues and ponds that shimmered in the lamplight. 'My son is a good man – don't let that shaggy haircut fool you into judging him otherwise – but he takes little care of his appearance because he spends too much time thinking. Not all of them useful thoughts, but I'm probably the only one in the Palace who is allowed to say so.'

Raisa paused beneath a lamp that lit the foot of another staircase and clamped her bony fingers around Jezebel's chin. 'Hmm. Not enough to see you clearly by, but you have a strong face, a good straight nose, and a nice figure on you. I think you will do very well in the House of Omri.' She patted Jezebel's cheek then began to climb the stairs, leaning heavily on Jezebel's arm.

'Not everyone seems to agree with you,' said Jezebel. 'I met the King's first wife.'

'Leah sought you out already, did she?' Raisa chuckled. 'Then you'll know you have nothing to compete with there, not least in temperament, for you look to me to have a good heart. Bad-tempered people, the Judeans, impetuous angry souls with a born sense of entitlement, and Leah is no exception.'

'She's from Judah? I thought—'

'We were sworn enemies?' Raisa smiled. 'All the more reason to attempt such an alliance. The marriage was brokered while my husband was still alive. I'm afraid, as so often with these arrangements, there was never much affection between man and wife.'

Jezebel tried not to wince, but she obviously didn't completely succeed.

'I'm sure it will be different for you two,' said Raisa. 'Leah never showed any wish to make it work.' The old woman waved her hand, as if to shoo the subject away. 'I've tried to influence Ahab in the way he raised Esther, of course, but one can only hope.' Raisa took a step back from Jezebel and peered at her with sparkling dark eyes. 'Of course, your people have recently endured a long visit from the Judeans so you know what I'm talking about. Leah's brother is Jehoshaphat.'

'So she is Jehu's aunt?' said Jezebel.

Raisa frowned. 'He's the child of the second wife, isn't he?'

'Yes,' said Jezebel, colouring. 'He accompanied Jehoshaphat to Tyre. I do see a certain family resemblance.'

Raisa laughed. 'You are an intelligent girl for your years. You think a lot and don't say too much. That will help you with Ahab but . . .' She paused. 'Well, you'll work it out.'

Jezebel wasn't sure what Raisa had been about to say,

59

but as Obadiah had already stated, clearly not everyone was as happy with the match as her mother-in-law. She knew well enough about the long period of distrust between Israel and Judah. Since the kingdoms had separated in the bloody civil war after King Solomon, outright hostility had been avoided, because diplomacy was preferential to antagonism, and both sides found common ground in their homage to Yahweh, their one true God. Jezebel had not realised that Ahab's first wife was a daughter of Judah, and could see that failure to produce an heir and heal the wounds under the auspices of Yahweh would carry heavy disappointment for Leah and those who had arranged the wedding.

She and Raisa walked together in silence to the top of the stairs, where Ahab's mother reached up and cupped Jezebel's face in her hands. 'I hope you produce many children for my son and for Israel. That is what you have come here to do and so I bless you in the name of the God we share. It will be good to hear children running through the Palace.'

'I am sure that in the daylight I will learn to appreciate its beauty.'

'My husband, the former King, built it. His House, the House of Omri, should continue to prosper with you here.'

Jezebel thanked her for her kindness, and the old woman disappeared through a curtained doorway, leaving Jezebel alone once more. *Surely there must be more than half a dozen people living here*, she thought, but though she strained to hear sounds of life, she felt as alone once more as one of the tiny stars in the great firmament above.

She looked around her, trying to get a sense of the layout of the Palace, but as she followed the balcony round, searching for her own room, she found only a wall and another corridor leading off in a different direction. She wandered along it, looking for a stairway so that at least she could return to the garden level. But it was all so confusing in the shadows and she felt a little sick. She leaned against the balcony and put her hand on her stomach, but she immediately let it fall again, for someone like Obadiah would surely seize on such a gesture. For though the baby had not yet begun to swell in flesh it was already growing in her mind, and around it such intense thoughts of Jehu that she was sure anyone who knew him – his aunt Leah, for example – would somehow see them reflected there. And what of Ahab, tonight, in the marriage bed?

She gazed up at the sky, looking for Kesil once more, but her attention was caught by a quiet sobbing somewhere below. She peered down into the small courtyard and identified the shadowy outline of Esther in a corner.

Jezebel walked swiftly along until she found a staircase, then she padded down it, her cape dragging behind her. Esther sniffed and glanced up, her eyes shining with tears. 'You shouldn't stay here. Mother will be furious.'

'I've no wish to get you into more trouble. But you shouldn't be out here in the dark. And besides, if we're all going to be living here together, we can't really avoid each other.'

'Obadiah has seen to it that we should. Mother and I have been relocated to this wing.' She nodded towards the small courtyard. 'I apologise for the way my mother spoke to you. She hates being in Israel and she has always hated the Phoenicians too. She says you sacrifice people and not animals.'

'No wonder I've had such a hostile reception,' laughed Jezebel nervously. 'It's not true, I promise you.'

'And she says your Gods are so malicious they will sink foreign ships if they sail in your waters.'

'Without charts and plans of the coast, the sea can be dangerous. But that could happen to even the most experienced sailor, whatever kingdom they come from.'

'She despises you.'

'Look, Esther, I'm only here because my father and your father agreed that it was in the interests of both our peoples. It is what young women like us must do.'

'I hope it never happens to me.'

Jezebel chewed her lip. It felt so strange to be making friends with this girl, almost the same age, when in just a few hours she would be lying down in a bed with her father. Perhaps Esther sensed that too, for she stood up.

'If Mother goes back to Jerusalem, as she keeps threatening to do, your life here might be a bit easier. It's a shame though, because you seem so nice.' Esther smiled shyly then she glanced up at the balcony. 'I must go before Mother misses me.'

'Of course. But maybe we could take a walk together tomorrow? You could show me round the Palace?'

'Perhaps,' said Esther uncertainly. 'Your wing is that way.' She pointed through an archway lit with torches. Then she set off quickly across the courtyard, her fingers sketching a wave.

Jezebel walked back towards her room, listening to the

strange sounds of the Palace around her as it slowly came alive in the dark, to the distant barking of the dogs and the calls of the servants behind hidden doorways. She smelled the roasting of meat and the stewing of fruit for the wedding banquet in her honour, and heard a lonely bugle call drift into the night sky. But it was of the sea she thought, that faraway kingdom of her own that she carried in her heart. And of the child that grew in her before its time.

Chapter Eleven

In the light from flickering lanterns, the young woman stared back at Jezebel, haughty and refined, almost arrogant in the way her eyebrows arched and her eyes stared, rimmed with the blackest kohl. Her skin was fashionably paled with the most expensive of the ground powders but it looked like a mask, taut and still, concealing every thought within. Only the mouth curled faintly, reddened with dyed wax. But if her face was mesmerising, it was merely an opal in the most elaborate of settings, from the headdress of sculpted gold through which her hair was delicately woven, down through the rich swathes of silken gown edged with hundreds of tiny shimmering pearls, to the jewelled sandals and sparkling ankle bracelets which tinkled musically as she walked. She was the richest of offerings in every sense.

'I hardly recognise myself,' said Jezebel.

Beset lowered the bronze hand mirror, its panel etched with a scene from the abduction of Princess Europa by the lovesick bull. 'You look like a queen.'

Behind the facade and the armour of a bride, Jezebel's heart thudded with fear and her hands sweated, and she prayed that the paint on her face would not smudge and smear. It was well after dark, and she'd heard the dining party gathering for some time.

'I hope the King has made such an effort,' murmured Beset as she straightened the train of Jezebel's gown one last time. And then the maid stepped back to admire her work and sniffed, quickly wiping a tear from the corner of her eye. 'Your father would be so proud.'

Jezebel lifted her chin to swallow down her own emotions and the wide gold neckband rubbed against her throat. There was something to be grateful for in these ceremonial outfits for they made you stand tall and proud even when you wanted to run away to curl up and hide. And perhaps Philosir understood that, for he didn't make her walk any slower than she could bear to on the way to the banquet, giving the Israelites that clustered in the Palace corridors enough time to notice her but not to weigh her further with their disdainful fascination.

She passed beneath the grand archway to the dining hall. Over the silence that followed the pronouncement of her name, she heard dozens of indistinct whispers. There was not another woman to be seen among the diners, and their garb was so drab she felt their disrespect in all their dullness. Even Ahab, sitting imperiously on a raised platform at the head of the table, looked plain in a long grey robe that sparkled with silver thread. He rose slowly to greet her, perhaps as overwhelmed as she was by the trophy Obadiah had won for him in the negotiations.

'Please, sit with me, Jezebel.'

At the moment she sat down on the smaller throne

beside his, three Israelite priests stood from their couches and left the room. Ahab reddened.

On the opposite side of the table Amos, who was standing in dutiful expectation of his princess, turned towards Obadiah, who sat on Ahab's other side. 'You were never shown such contempt in Tyre,' he said.

'Priests here don't bow to the King,' said Obadiah, 'and certainly not to a wife.'

'Especially one so gaudy,' said the other remaining Israelite priest. 'They must grow gold in Tyre, from the look of her. If that is any indication, perhaps the Phoenician lands will be more fertile to farm than Judah's,' he added.

So her suspicions and Raisa's aborted warnings were confirmed. Jezebel sensed Ahab tense beside her. He was staring at her, his cheeks flushed with embarrassment and his eyes bright with rage, their chestnut brown so vivid against his hair and gown. She felt sorry for him, and guilty for being so elaborately dressed, as though the effusion of all her riches had somehow made everything so much worse. But why hadn't he challenged his priests? In spite of all her own awkwardness she held his gaze in hers and smiled at him. As he studied her, probing deep beneath the mask of betrothal, she thought she saw a half-smile pass his lips in response, though when he spoke his voice was brittle with suppressed fury.

'Would you like wine?' asked Ahab.

Philosir had told her that women did not normally drink wine with the men in Israel and indeed there was a slight pause in the chatter around the table when Jezebel nodded and took the drinking bowl. And then she realised that this was in itself a small act of defiance by Ahab, and she sipped from it.

'This vintage comes from my vineyard at Jezreel, a city north-east of here,' said a nobleman sitting between the priests and Obadiah. He was a round fellow with a cheerful face, rather less lean than the other Israelites who still gawped at Jezebel, and his hair was curly, and as grey as Ahab's.

'Ever the merchant, Naboth,' said Ahab dryly.

'We grow most of our vines there for the valley is fed well by the river that runs through it.'

'Is it not too cold?' asked Philosir, his voice strained with enforced politeness.

'The winds are weak so far inland,' said Naboth. 'The Winter Palace is there too.'

Jezebel had heard already of the city of Jezreel several times. During the coldest part of the year, the royal court left Samaria and travelled inland for the warmer climate. Although most of what she'd heard of the fortified city was grim.

'The wine is very nice,' she said.

Naboth gulped from his bowl. 'I told you they would like it, Obadiah.'

'You also told me there were mermaids in the sea,' said Obadiah. 'But I didn't see one.'

'There are many extraordinary riches in the Great Sea,' said Philosir, 'and it is on such discoveries that we have built our prosperity, just as you have built yours from the land.'

'Israel isn't as it once was,' said Ahab, passing his own gold plate piled high with food to Jezebel. The gesture touched her, subtle as it was.

'Our land is drying out,' he continued, 'and the crops didn't flourish this year. What you see here is the best of it, and I'm not ashamed to ask our Phoenician neighbours to help us survive.' He turned to Philosir. 'We need engineers to help us extract the water from our springs if we are to survive another summer.'

'The land isn't drying out,' said the first of the priests, 'but our farmers have lost their faith that Yahweh will provide. And is it any wonder?'

'When you understand the intellect of our Phoenician neighbours as well as you claim to understand the souls of our people, then perhaps I will concede your point,' said Ahab. 'But for now even you must admit that we cannot provide all that we need by way of cloth or metal ores, not to mention knowledge that can help our people live comfortable lives.'

Jezebel picked up a flatbread rolled with cheeses and olives, and chewed tentatively at the corner. With all the butterflies in her stomach she hadn't realised that she was hungry and she'd eaten very little since being sick this morning. The food wasn't bad at all, though rather blander than she was used to.

'His Highness is right,' said Naboth, the nobleman. 'We need to expand our horizons if we are to make the most of what land we have.

'When the springs north of Samaria are properly dug out,' Naboth continued to Philosir, 'I will be able to plant a new vineyard. There is an excellent curve in the foothills which faces full south and will catch the sun all day.'

'Perhaps it would be better to plant on a west-facing slope,' said Jezebel absent-mindedly, picking up a fig. 'If the vines have too much sun they will be sweet enough, but without cool autumn mornings the wine will lack acidity, and won't have sufficient finesse.'

Her mouth turned dry and the fig hung from her fingers. Without turning her head at all she knew every Israelite in the room was staring at her, some of them with expressions of utter disdain, while her own people stared at their plates. Jezebel felt her face burn with shame beneath the mask of white powder and she lowered the fig to the plate. And then, unexpectedly, Ahab roared with laughter from beside her.

'That is the best advice you have ever been given, Naboth,' he said, 'and I suggest you take it.'

Chapter Twelve

Jezebel tried to sit still on the couch in her room as Beset unpinned the long tresses of her hair from the headdress, but she was far too anxious to maintain any repose, and she simply grabbed the last few pins and yanked them out herself.

'You are bound to be nervous,' murmured Beset as she lifted the headdress off Jezebel's head and laid it down in its cedarwood box. 'The first night with your husband is an important occasion and will set the tone for your marriage.'

Jezebel wriggled off the couch and went to the window, her hand resting on her abdomen. 'It's not that.'

'You did the right thing,' muttered Beset, stroking her arm.

Jezebel sighed and couldn't look into Beset's eyes. Instead she turned up into the dark sky, searching for Kesil's constellation. But the night was shrouded with thin cloud and she saw nothing to comfort her.

'Jezebel?' said Beset. 'You did drink the purge, didn't you?'

She shook her head a fraction. 'I couldn't kill the child,'

70

she whispered. 'It was a betrayal of all that Jehu and I meant to each other.'

'But what about the King?' hissed Beset. 'He isn't a fool. When the child is born before nine months are over, he will know anyway.'

Jezebel sat down on the deep window ledge, looking out to the north-west, towards Tyre. 'Perhaps I will be lucky and he will only send me home in disgrace.'

'Amos told me you received a very hostile welcome at the banquet. When the priests find out about the baby—'

'Then they will certainly do worse than send me home.' Jezebel shivered and moved away from the window, turning to the shrine to Astarte that Beset had already set in the corner of the room. 'The best I can do is to be honest with Ahab. Besides, he will know after tonight that he isn't my first lover.'

Beset huffed. 'That, at least, is easily taken care of. A man's pride is fragile, yes, but easily fooled.' She went to the shrine and fiddled around in a box in the base, pulling out a small metal vial. 'Chicken blood. It will pass for a broken maidenhead if you spill it when the time is right.'

'How did you—'

But Beset put her finger quickly to her lips. A steady tread approached along the corridor. 'I pray that Astarte and Kotharat will look after you. But you must have faith in them.'

Beset leaned forward and kissed her charge on the cheek, then ran through a curtain to the side of the room and into her own quarters beyond. Jezebel looked at the bed, then at the couch, trying to decide where Ahab might most want to sit down next to her, but her heart was beating so fast that she couldn't hear herself think and could only wipe her damp palms on the delicate folds of her sleeping gown. *Do I defy you, Kotharat, if I remember making love to Jehu when Ahab lies down on me?*

But if the Goddess was listening she sent no sign, for in a moment the curtain was pushed back and Ahab entered. He was dressed as he had been at dinner, but the silvered gown now hung undone about his shoulders. He glanced around him, taking in the shrine, the well-stuffed Phoenician couches beneath the window, and the luxuriant blankets and sheets on the bed, all unpacked during the banquet.

'Your maid has made it very comfortable for you. I'm glad. I want you to be happy here.'

'Thank you, Your Highness,' whispered Jezebel, far less sure of her voice now than she had been at the banquet.

Ahab smiled, the creases around his eyes catching deep shadows in the lamplight. 'There's no need to be so formal. That's for my advisers and my nobles, not for my wives. Although you'll have noticed that not everyone treats me with the same respect.'

'I will do my best to honour you, and will defer to your judgement at all times.'

'That isn't what I've been told.' Ahab sounded rather fierce and Jezebel couldn't help but wrap her arms defensively across her. 'I frighten you, I'm afraid. It isn't surprising, but I'd hope you will soon learn what sort of man I really am.'

He crossed the room and stood very near to her, delicately fingering the long curls of hair that framed her face. He was a head or so taller than Jezebel, but he didn't loom over her, only looked down rather sweetly at her.

72

'My mother has already taken a great liking to you,' said Ahab, his breath fragrant with wine.

'She is a fine woman.'

'You have no mother of your own, I understand.'

'She died several years ago.'

'I hope you will come to enjoy Raisa's wisdom as I have, not to mention her comfort. For when our first son is born you'll know not only my pride but the pride of my late father, for the future of the House of Omri will be assured.'

Jezebel couldn't meet his eyes any longer.

Ahab slid his fingers beneath her hair to the nape of her neck, stroking the skin so lightly that his hand might have been made of feathers. Jezebel felt herself quiver with bewildering delight, and when he drew her to him and began to loosen the clasp of her gown, she found herself reaching for the neck of his tunic to unlace it. His kisses were soft and delicate at first, as if he were still afraid of frightening her, but she quickly found his passion beneath his restraint and she was already breathless with anticipation when he finally drew off her gown. She couldn't help but notice that his body was not sculpted and strong like Jehu's and he caught the way her eyes lingered on the scars on his arm and his shoulder as he lifted her up and laid her down on the bed.

'This body has lived a little, I'm afraid,' he murmured as he lay down beside her. 'But the men who drew my blood did not live to see the wounds heal.'

In Jehu's voice such words would have sounded terrifying, but Ahab's was as soft and thoughtful as his manner with her. He touched her with such tenderness

73

that she knew his body wished to find its echo in hers and when he entered her she felt not the fear nor the repulsion she had so dreaded, but such an intense and unexpected pleasure that she barely remembered to reach for the vial of blood in time. While his head was buried in her shoulder, she flicked off the stopper with her right hand and felt the slightly warm liquid trickle over her fingers. She wiped them on the sheets, but Ahab made no remark, if he even noticed.

Afterwards, they lay in silence for a long while, the whole Palace so quiet that Jezebel could hear each of Ahab's breaths as they caressed her hair. She felt his eyelashes brush her forehead each time he blinked, and beneath her fingers his chest pulsed with the beat of his heart. There was such intimacy in the way he held her that she already felt his renewed stirrings of desire in herself. And yet it was infused with such guilt that made her cheeks burn, for it was Jehu's arms she remembered being held by, his unshaven jaw that she recalled softly scratching her throat as he kissed her, the smell of his hair she missed so dreadfully.

She must have slept, for in the early hours, she woke to him stirring and leaving the bed. In the near darkness, he tied the robe at the waist, then leaned over the bed and kissed her once more.

'You will find your wedding gift at the end of the orchard,' he murmured.

When he was gone, Jezebel buried her face in her pillow and let the tears flow so they might flush out the poisonous turmoil in her heart and in her head.

Chapter Thirteen

In the light of dawn the Palace did seem more welcoming, its interlocking courtyards now easy to navigate. Guided by her curiosity, Jezebel rose early and wandered towards the walled gardens to the south. A pair of soldiers overtook her with watchful nods, the air was sweet with the smell of baking breads and honey cakes, and as she looked up at the colonnades and archways, she hoped it would not be impossible to make some sort of home for herself here.

It would never be Tyre, but what city was? And if Ahab was always as kind to her as the previous night, if he was as good a man as Esther said—

The nausea rose fast within Jezebel just as it had the previous morning, and she stumbled to the nearest tree, desperate not to be sick out here in full view of the Palace. But she couldn't keep it down and she staggered against the trunk, retching over and over until her body stilled and her mouth tasted sour.

'Perhaps you swallowed something you were not accustomed to,' said a cool voice.

Is that dreadful man following me around? she

wondered weakly, lifting her head to find Obadiah staring down at her, his eyes tracing her body as though he was imagining her first night with the King for himself.

'Or perhaps you don't find our food as palatable as the Judeans?'

An awful thought occurred to Jezebel. Could he know? Had he perhaps seen Jehu climb into her room in Tyre?

'Your water isn't as pure here,' she forced herself to say as she straightened up and moved away from the tree, 'nor the air you breathe.'

'You haven't spoiled the surprise, have you, Obadiah?' Ahab came striding down the gentle slope towards them, the regal gown of the night before dispensed in favour of a plain white tunic and a wide leather belt.

'Of course not, Your Highness. I would not dream of denying you that pleasure.' Obadiah lowered his head and moved away, leaving the King and Jezebel alone.

'Good morning,' Jezebel bowed low.

Ahab lifted her chin and kissed her on the forehead. 'I knew you wouldn't be able to wait to see your wedding present, and I woke up knowing I couldn't either.' He smiled and took her hand and led them between low clipped hedges across the gardens. 'Custom dictates I should wait until after the wedding ceremony, but I would much rather show you now without any of the pomp and nonsense that will be expected.'

At the far end of the gardens was a small wooden gate in the high wall which he opened to reveal a tangle of lanes sprawling down the gentle slope into the city. Ahab put his hand over Jezebel's eyes then she felt him turn her gently to the right before lowering his hand again.

'There! A little piece of Tyre in Samaria.'

A stone's throw from the Palace walls, nestled among wooden huts was a tiny round building with an angled roof, built entirely out of the white stone she knew from Tyre, not the local yellow rock. Above the entrance a star within a circle had been carved out of the stone, and around the pillars that flanked it were endless engraved doves in flight. Inside she could see a pristine white altar decked with stone sculptures of all Astarte's icons, the horse, the lion, the sphinx and the dove. Even in the morning light it sparkled as though Astarte herself had begotten the Temple from the night sky and Jezebel thought it the most beautiful building she had ever seen. It was a perfect size for her and her small cadre of priests to worship in and seemed to reflect the presence her father wanted her to establish in Israel – contained and discreet but still elegant.

'When I saw the shrine in your room last night,' said Ahab, 'I knew that I had been right to build this for you. I set the top stone myself. It has a hole carved through it so that your Gods may always look down on you.'

Jezebel's eyes grew wet and once again she wrapped her arms around herself, not in fear this time, but to contain the extraordinary surge of emotion that threatened to overwhelm her.

'I thought wives were expected to take their husband's Gods,' she said.

'And abandon their own?' said Ahab. 'Perhaps for some

people this is true, but my father never succeeded in doing so with my mother, and he was the wisest council I know.'

'And how will your subjects take this?'

'They are your subjects too. You are a long way from home,' said Ahab, 'not in distance but in difference, so I want you to know that this will always be yours, just as this city is now yours, and the Israelite people are yours too. They will learn to know you and love you just as you will them. But this is my personal gift to you.'

'Thank you,' she said quietly.

She didn't mention the soldiers who had passed her in the garden and who now stood on guard at the Temple entrance, spears in their hands and swords in their belts. Ahab was clearly not so confident of universal approval as he made out. *They are your subjects too.* It hardly answered her question. But voicing any further reservations would seem ungrateful, so instead she accepted Ahab's arm. As they walked back up to the Palace in silence, she prayed inwardly for Astarte's protection to reach this far into hostile lands.

Chapter Fourteen

A few days later, Jezebel stood in front of a polished obsidian panel set into one of the walls of her chamber, pulling her dress tight across her belly. In the reflection she could see Daniel fiddling around in his medicine chest, and Beset brushing an outer robe. Both were fully engaged in their business but the room was full of their silence and eventually Jezebel could stand it no longer.

'I wish one of you would just say something.' She saw Daniel look across the room at Beset.

'Are you sure you feel well enough to go out?' asked her maid.

'Of course,' said Jezebel. 'I always feel better by the middle of the morning.'

Daniel and Beset exchanged glances once more, then they joined Jezebel in front of the mirror-stone, all three of them staring at the reflection of Jezebel's abdomen. 'It barely shows,' murmured Beset.

Daniel didn't say anything, and not for the first time, she wondered if he disapproved. Since their time on the desert road, he had stayed close to her, giving her salts to overcome her sickness. But his face wore a permanent crease of anxiety, as though reflecting on the magnitude of their shared secret.

'I feel terrible lying to Ahab,' said Jezebel. 'He's been so kind to me.'

'You should be safe for two or three months yet,' said Beset, 'if we dress you properly and it is dark when you lie down with the King.'

But Daniel rubbed his chin, ran his fingers through his hair, and finally he turned away from the mirror so abruptly that Beset let go of the dress. Jezebel turned after him.

'At least say *something*?'

Daniel sat down alone on the couch. He linked his fingers together, stretching them to and fro, then he stood up again and went to the window. 'I don't think you should go out with Esther today, that is all.'

'She is the only friend I have here, apart from the two of you,' said Jezebel.

Daniel smiled a little at this, but his crease remained. 'Then at least stay in the Palace.'

'But she is going to show me the cloth merchants and the markets. She wants my opinion on which cloth is of the best quality and that at least is something I know a little about.'

'Does she talk to you about her mother?'

'Not really,' said Jezebel, now feeling Daniel's anxiety herself. 'Should she?'

'Perhaps she wouldn't anyway. Not given how things are.'

'I know it must be difficult for her now I'm here, but there isn't anything I can do about it.'

'You could ask the King to take down your Temple.'

'What makes you say such a thing?' asked Beset.

'I fear that if Ahab does not take it down then someone else will.'

'Leah?' asked Jezebel, perplexed by the turns of the conversation.

'Not Leah, but the priests who are loyal to her. Amos told me last night that there is a lot of anger among the Samarian priests that Leah has been displaced. The Judeans pray to Yahweh just as the Israelites do.'

'But surely they're angry with Ahab and not with me.'

'They believe you're seeking to influence Esther away from her mother. It's no secret that Esther is her father's daughter in temperament and intelligence, but you appear to be blatantly leading her away from Judah altogether.'

'But I've never taken Esther into my Temple—'

'Jezebel?' Esther's voice rang out, breathless, from the corridor. 'Are you ready to go out?'

Jezebel shot an urgent look at Daniel but he simply shrugged at her.

'I'm doing the best I can,' she hissed at him as she grabbed her robe from the bed. 'I can't spend the rest of my life locked in here!'

As Esther guided her through the narrow streets of the city, Daniel's warnings lingered. Jezebel found herself more than usually distracted by the people around her. Every eye watched her, every mouth formed around a judgement of her, even if many of these people wished only to be left to get on with their lives.

The cloth merchants treated her with a grudging respect when they realised she knew what she was talking about, and one even spoke with her in an almost friendly fashion about the difficulties of getting good red dyes to set in wool. But as they left the bustle of the market to return to the Palace, Jezebel noticed a group of priests gathering ahead of them, their dark murmuring shot with the light tinkling of tiny bells that hung from the hems of their blue robes.

'Let's go this way,' said Jezebel, pointing to a nearby lane. 'Doesn't this go to the jewellery quarter?'

'But this is the quicker route, even if we aren't going to the Palace,' said Esther.

'Then what's down here?'

'Nothing really.'

The priests had moved in very quickly and they encircled Jezebel in a swirl of bright garments. Their beards bristling with animosity, their tongues fat with insults. In a moment she was separated from Esther.

'Heretic!' one shouted.

'Phoenician harlot!' snapped another. 'You bring your false Gods to our land!'

Jezebel spun round, throwing furious glances at one priest after another, but there were so many of them, and like a swarm of hornets they seethed around her, driving her back against a wall without touching her at all. She stumbled on the uneven ground and grabbed at the wall to steady herself, but her voice quavered as she tried to control her fury and fear. 'I've nothing but respect for your God, so you can find the same for mine.'

'You deserve no such thing,' said another, spitting at her feet. 'And you,' they turned as one on Esther, 'you should save yourself while you still can.'

'Help us!' Esther called out.

Jezebel tried to see through the crowd of the priests' turbans but she could only see the top of Esther's head.

'You bring shame on your mother and on all the people of Yahweh by consorting with the infidel!'

And then Jezebel heard the clop of approaching feet and the clank of horse tack. The priests scattered like flies and in their absence she saw a pair of soldiers riding slowly from the opposite direction. She moved to Esther's side. 'Did they hurt you?'

'They should not have spoken to you like that,' whispered Esther, pale with shock.

The soldiers glanced incuriously after the departing priests.

'Are you all right, Your Majesty?' asked one.

'I think so,' Jezebel replied. 'We should be getting back to the Palace.'

Jezebel slid her hand around Esther's shaking elbow and guided her home. But once she had seen her safely through the main gate, she walked around the garden walls towards her Temple. Astarte would bring her much-needed peace and guidance to see her through this dreadful experience, she told herself, breathing deeply to calm herself.

Even before she reached the Temple she sensed that something was wrong. There were no guards at the entrance gate. As she turned into the lane she saw the two pristine white columns were smeared filthy brown with horse dung. She looked around, her chest contracting with panic, but the lane was completely empty. She swallowed down a few nervous breaths and entered the Temple.

She strangled a sob of anguish. The desecration of the

inside was far worse than the filthy pillars. Each of Astarte's beautiful statues had been smashed to pieces, and the walls were daubed with more dung. Worst of all, on the altar lay a dead dove, its throat cut.

Jezebel pressed her lips together and closed her eyes. She listened as hard as she could for the peace of Astarte's wisdom, begging it to fall like rain through the Temple roof and cleanse the dirt from the place and the anger from her heart. But all she could feel was the ground surely shaking with Baal's purest rage, and she turned and ran for Ahab.

If Jezebel wished for solace in Ahab's arms, she didn't find it. He pushed past her to see the devastation for himself, and emerged fuelled by the war Goddess Anat's burning desire for vengeance. He summoned the head of his personal guard and issued in the coldest terms the order to round up every priest who had openly taken issue with Jezebel's arrival, starting with the three who had left the wedding banquet.

'If you would just let me talk to them,' begged Jezebel as she stood before him in his private office, 'I could show them that I mean them no disrespect.'

'They won't listen to you.'

'Then I ask that you do. Exacting revenge on them will not solve this.'

'I won't tolerate their contempt for you, for it's nothing less than contempt for me!' he barked. 'I've put up with their petty disregard for the Judeans throughout my marriage to Leah, but now they turn that into some perverted loyalty to our southern neighbours, just so

84

that they may turn their malice on you. Priests of Yahweh occupy a privileged position within this kingdom – I tolerate their outspokenness, but outright rebellion must be quashed without mercy.' He strode to the wall and grabbed down a long sword which hung in its ceremonial sheath, yanking out the blade so quickly that it sliced the air.

Jezebel stepped back, shocked by how easily the gentle lover had been swallowed up by the ruthless ruler. 'What will you do to them?'

'Exactly what they would do to anyone who defiled their temples.' He raised the sword and pointed it over Jezebel's shoulder just as Obadiah strode into the office.

'Your Highness—' He stopped at the sight of Jezebel and gave an obsequious bow. 'Madam.'

'Well?' snapped Ahab.

'The girl is too young to be party to affairs of state.'

Ahab started to reply, but Jezebel saved them both the trouble by leaving the room without another word.

Up in her chamber she lay on the couch in front of the window, Beset beside her holding her hand, and they listened together for the inevitable resonances of Ahab's punishment, first the awful screams of the executed, then the dreadful thump of the bodies being thrown over the city walls. Twelve men in all met their deaths. Only as the sun began to cast its golden evening light into her room did they rise to look, still clinging on to each other, and saw the cluster of vultures swirling thick and black over the foothills to the east.

Jezebel sat for a long time in the window that night, staring out towards Tyre, to where her own Gods surely sat in judgement on her husband. While Samaria lay stunned in silence below her, not even a whisper or the bark of a dog disturbing the dark, news would soon break over the Phoenician border like a storm-swollen wave of the travesties inflicted on their distant princess. But Jezebel was politic enough to know that stories changed and shifted like sand-dunes. By the time her father heard of what had happened, the complexion of the events would no doubt be quite different.

Chapter Fifteen

The hot and barren summer did little more than stifle the tensions of Jezebel's arrival in Samaria, and she spent much of the season shut away inside the Palace, at first under Ahab's orders for her own safety, and then under Daniel's as her belly swelled with the child. She felt enormous, and was sure that Raisa would notice that she was bigger than she should have been. But as the eighth month came and went, she and Ahab only delighted in the prospect of the birth, so auspiciously soon after marriage, and Jezebel was left to pray with Beset that the child didn't resemble its true father.

Ahab had also been distracted by reports from the banks of the River Jordan, to the north-east, where the forces of Ben-Hadad of Damascus were gathering to threaten the fertile Israelite plains of Gilead. Ahab spent endless nights in his rooms consulting with his soldiers, and Jezebel, growing ever bigger, felt a fondness grow for him that she had never imagined possible. Despite the affairs of state, he made sure that they met every day to eat together, and she would listen as he talked with his officials about Asa, the King of Judah's continuing reluctance to join the

Israelites for war. Obadiah was ever present, like a dark shadow cast by the high summer sun, eyeing her in his way that made her feel dirty.

Eventually Ahab agreed with his advisers that Ben-Hadad couldn't be allowed to threaten the plains any longer and, at first light one late summer morning, with a storm brewing in the humid grey skies, the King rode out with his army to war, confident that his rival would be defeated before his longed-for son came into the world. Yet Jezebel realised the anxiety she felt was not only about the baby, but also about the possibility that Ahab would not return from the war. She had traced the scars on his body many times now, and she remembered well his words that first night they shared together, but still she offered up a prayer as he passed beneath her window, his eyes lingering on hers. *He's been so kind to me,* she thought, *please bring him home safe and soon.*

With his absence, and that of three-quarters of the soldiery, the city felt desolate. Jezebel too felt empty despite her huge belly beneath her gown. She tried to fill her time with daily rituals of her own, and one morning, almost three weeks after his departure, she waddled alone across the gardens to her Temple to pray for Ahab as she always did. She wanted to pray too for the baby. She knew Daniel was concerned that the baby was about to go beyond safe term, and though every day meant another day Raisa would not think the child born early, Daniel's anxiety made her nervous. The Temple had long ago been cleaned and new statues found for the altar, and though it had taken her a while to stop looking over her shoulder, she had drawn courage from the stillness that pervaded its walls. This morning though she felt too big to kneel to pray and instead she sat on a small bench and smiled at the statue of Astarte.

'You got me into this trouble,' she murmured, rubbing the mound at her waist, 'so you will have to forgive my lack of penitence.'

As if Astarte was in no mind to forgive her disciple, a bright flash lit up the Temple with a deafening crack, and within moments rain was pouring through the skylight and all over the altar. It was the first rain the city had seen for months but Jezebel was in no mood to celebrate it and she pushed herself up from the bench.

She'd barely reached the gates when she felt a sharp heave of pain and a great wetness between her legs. She wailed with the agony of opening the gate and fell to her knees just inside the garden. The rain soaked through her clothes and she tried to crawl but soon she curled howling into a ball, unable to do anything but cry, even her tears washed away by the intense rain.

Was this her punishment for lying to Ahab? Would she die in the storm with Jehu's baby still unborn? *Please, forgive me*, she begged Astarte.

She was so absorbed by the cascading pain that it took her a moment to realise that someone was leaning over her, talking to her.

'I saw you from the Palace. Is it the baby?' Daniel's taut face hovered above her.

Jezebel nodded weakly.

'Have your waters broken?'

'Yes—'

'I'm not going to leave you, and Beset is on her way

with help.' He bent over her, shielding her from the rain, and she felt his fingers draw her sodden hair away from her face. She made herself listen to his voice as he told her to breathe as deeply as she could. And soon she was being carried through the courtyard to her room, Daniel's hand in hers, Beset drying her face with a cloth, trying to think of anything but how much it hurt.

Upstairs Raisa was waiting with a bundle of linens and basins of water, the sleeves of her gown pinned above her elbows.

'You are so sad to see Ahab go that you have called his child forth to keep you company!' said Raisa. 'There now, lie yourself here. There are plenty of cushions.'

Jezebel could only do as she was told, and as another scream of agony welled up within her, Raisa bathed her forehead with warm cloths soaked in lavender water. A midwife bustled with cloths and bowls beside the fire, and Daniel stood uselessly by the bed.

'She will be well looked after,' Raisa reassured him. 'I've either borne or delivered every child in the House of Omri and this will be no different. Now go along and make sure the nursery is ready. The Queen will be perfectly safe with us.'

Jezebel gazed helplessly at Daniel. She hadn't realised that he wouldn't be staying with her and as the midwife brought a tray of wooden implements over to the bed, she clamped her eyes tight shut in terror. She felt Daniel squeeze her hand and then he was gone.

'An early child is always at risk, Jezebel,' Raisa was saying. 'Do you understand?'

'It will be all right,' said Beset gently, close to her ear.

'Chew on this liquorice root when you want to scream, it will calm you and stop you from biting your tongue.' Jezebel felt the rough twig slide between her teeth and she started to breathe through her nose, listening for the midwife's steady counting.

But the pain would not end and for hours she writhed and cried, the liquorice roots quickly shredding in her mouth without soothing her. In her delirium all Jezebel could think was that the Gods were so angry with her for deceiving her husband that they had decided she would be stuck forever with Jehu's child unborn between her legs. It was all she could do not to scream her fears.

But finally, as the sun began to set, and with one last dreadful holler that Jezebel would never forget, the baby was born.

'A boy!' cried Raisa. 'Yahweh has blessed the House of Omri with a boy!'

Jezebel released a great breath and opened her eyes. A tiny body hung from Raisa's bony hands, his eyes screwed shut and his feet wriggling beneath him. Jezebel's breath caught in her throat at the beauty of her child, how fragile he was and yet how strongly he kicked and cried with his first breaths. The midwife cut the cord, and Raisa handed her the baby.

'Bathe him quickly and carefully,' said Raisa, 'keep him warm and let Jezebel hold him. They must know each other immediately if this boy is to survive.' Raisa glanced knowingly across the room. Jezebel followed her gaze and realised Esther had joined them. But she stood apart from the others, chewing her thumbnail, and when Jezebel smiled at her, Esther turned and ran away.

'The legacy of Ahab's first wife isn't your concern,' said Raisa. 'The Judeans have chosen to turn their backs on us in our time of war, so I won't be surprised if Yahweh permits this boy to live, to confirm the new way forward for our people.'

'I heard the baby cry. It's healthy?' Daniel appeared in the doorway, his hair damp with sweat as though he had been the one giving birth and not merely worrying about it.

Raisa tutted and pulled Jezebel's gown down over her knees. 'I would have sent for you.'

The midwife handed Daniel the bundled child and after a brief inspection, he handed Jezebel her son and she nestled him against her breast. He had a shock of dark hairs damp from being bathed, and Jezebel couldn't help but think of Jehu.

'He even looks like Ahab,' said Raisa, stroking the child's head.

Jezebel looked up with surprise. 'You think so?'

Raisa laughed. 'You didn't expect him to be born with grey hair, did you?'

Chapter Sixteen

Jezebel recovered quickly from the birth and within two days was able to walk around the Palace, if a little tenderly. She spent most of her time in the rooms adjacent to her own, where a wet-nurse had been provided to look after the baby. But when the nurse went for her meals or to take a bath, Jezebel would lift the boy out of his crib and hold him to her breast and the child would suckle fiercely. The child had survived the crucial early days of what everyone but Beset and Daniel believed to be a premature birth, and with that apparent good fortune the priests had come to regard Jezebel with a certain cool acceptance, although she was under no illusion that the joyfulness across the city at the arrival of the longed-for son was still tempered by hatred of her religion. Amos had allowed the Palace priests to undertake all the Israelite birthing ceremonies, then he had secretly blessed the child in the Phoenician custom in Jezebel's room. And when the boy had made to scream, as though with the voices of all the Gods who fought over his protection, Daniel had simply held him and in a moment the baby had forgotten his discontent, gurgling at the physician and allowing the sacred water to be poured over his head, hands and feet.

Even Obadiah had accepted that Jezebel wandered freely round the Palace now, and that each afternoon she would go to Ahab's office in the hope that he had sent her another letter tucked in among the military dispatches from the battlefield. Two weeks had passed since she had written to inform him of the birth of her son, and she was growing both impatient and anxious at his silence. One afternoon she was so eager to discover if a letter had arrived that she did not realise the office was already occupied until she had thrown back the curtain to enter.

Obadiah was seated in Ahab's chair at his desk, flanked by a number of senior priests. But in front of them stood a tall man in military uniform, whose dark curls and sun-tanned skin, so recognisable yet so strange in this place, made Jezebel put her hand on the doorframe to steady herself.

She gulped down her gasp of surprise with an apology. 'I beg your pardon for the interruption,' she said.

Jehu turned at the sound of her voice, and his lips parted a fraction.

Jezebel, acutely aware of her appearance, felt her cheeks blaze with all the raw pleasure of seeing him again, and the embarrassment that their reunion had come in front of Obadiah. What was he doing here?

Jehu nodded minutely at last, but said nothing and strode to the window. He stared out, his jaw hard, his eyes averted from her.

'I was not informed that we had received a Judean

delegation,' she said to Obadiah, then felt immediately frustrated with her imperious tone.

'Your Highness has been occupied with your child,' replied Obadiah. 'I did not anticipate you would be interested in matters that concern the Kingdom of Israel.'

'Your solicitude is generous,' said Jezebel. 'But now I'm here, I'd be grateful to know what brings our visitor to Samaria.' She glanced at Jehu but still he ignored her.

'Jehu comes with news,' said one of the priests, a relatively young man named Enosh who had risen quickly in the Palace since the reprisals in the spring. 'King Asa of Judah has died. Jehoshaphat is now King.'

Jezebel crossed the office towards Jehu, memories of her lover displaced by sympathy. 'I'm sorry to hear of your grandfather's death.' She recalled the way his sparkling eyes had followed her throughout the visit. 'I remember him as being very spirited when he came to Tyre.'

Still Jehu didn't reply, nor did he turn to face her. After a moment's awkward silence, Jezebel bowed and left without looking at the priests. Clearly he would make no sign of their intimacy in front of the Israelite priests, but still his indifference upset her. Surely now he'd had time to reflect upon their parting, he understood that she had never meant to hurt him? Perhaps it was wounded pride, or shame at their shared passion. He'd probably found another lover by now – perhaps even a wife – just as she had married Ahab.

As she climbed the staircase to return to her rooms, her sandals slapped angrily and her fingers had balled into fists. Whatever his reasons for such dismissiveness, he hadn't even accorded her the respect her position here—

'You forgot your letter.'

At the sound of his voice Jezebel's breath caught in her throat. Jehu stood at the bottom of the stairs, the folded vellum in his outstretched hand.

'I suppose someone else has already read it,' she said.

Those should not have been my first words to him after all this time, not after our child's birth.

'You always were astute for your age.'

'It is no more than is necessary for the Queen of Israel. We are honoured by your visit, though it is unexpected.'

Jehu shrugged. 'My father thinks my skills of diplomacy in need of development.'

In that moment, seeing him so lost, so put upon, she had to fight to stop herself descending the stairs and taking him in her arms. Instead, she found herself uttering banalities.

'So now you are son to a king.'

Jehu stiffened. 'I hear a son has been born to Ahab also. Yahweh has seen fit to bless this marriage after all.'

Jezebel fought to keep composure in her expression. His words sounded bitter and yet he looked at her with that familiar intensity that burned right through her. Anyone who saw them together would surely know what they had shared, and there were bound to be officials near at hand, no doubt with the explicit instructions of Obadiah to eavesdrop on their conversation.

'I would say that all the Gods have been kind to us.'

Jehu moved to the balcony and looked out across the gardens towards the south-west. 'Even though only Yahweh is acknowledged here.'

Jezebel followed his gaze which was fixed on the roof of her Temple.

'Your Gods have a reputation for being malicious and fickle,' he continued. 'I hear that even on the day of Ahab's departure for Gilead the skies opened and drowned twenty of his troops. Was that not also the day you gave birth?'

'If it is Yahweh who has blessed me with a child then presumably He could have protected the men of His own nation from a force of nature,' said Jezebel.

Jehu glanced at her, and for the very briefest of moments Jezebel could see just how much he still yearned for her. Somewhere in a room behind them their child cried out. For a moment, Jezebel's hopeful spirit imagined leading Jehu by the hand to greet his son.

'You shouldn't have accepted Ahab's gift of a temple,' said Jehu.

The spirit of the past vanished in a haze of disillusionment. 'Considering little love is lost between Israel and Judah at the present time,' she said, 'you are well informed as to events in Samaria. Of course, if you knew Ahab as I do, you'd know that he retains a more open mind than many.'

'Such an open mind that he himself executed some of the priests whose only crime was to uphold their own faith in the face of an unbeliever. Your influence is remarkably corrupt.'

Jezebel was so shocked at his accusation, she was about to ask Jehu whether he thought himself corrupted by her too, when Obadiah appeared in the courtyard below, looking up at the balcony.

Behind her, the baby's cry had turned to a constant wail.

'I won't keep you,' she said in a hollow voice.

Jehu peered in the direction of the sound. 'My time here is brief,' he said. 'I've come to escort Leah back to Judah.'

'I see. Is Esther going with her?'

'No. She's chosen to stay with her father. And her new friend,' he said, drawing his attention back to Jezebel.

'Does Ahab know of Leah's departure?'

'I believe not.'

Jehu seemed to be about to add something, but instead he turned away and loped down the staircase to join Obadiah. Jezebel could not watch him leave, but went into the nursery and took her son from his crib. Had Ahaziah sensed his father's brooding presence? And what would Jehu have said if she had led him into this room and told him the truth? For while her cheeks flamed with raw anger and loss, her head rattled with everything she could have said but didn't. Such a course of action could only create discord and chaos. By the time the child had stopped crying, all that remained was a dull ache in her heart.

Chapter Seventeen

From the roof of the Palace, Jezebel could see the dust kicked up by the advance rider, and behind that the steady brown cloud of men and horses that moved across the plain. Before long the rider was driving hard up the steep mountain road and she heard his triumphant shout even before the gates were opened.

'Victory,' he yelled. 'Victory to King Ahab of Israel and his army!'

The bugle call went up as news surged through the city and soon the streets rang with cheering and shouting. Citizens jostled to get the best view of the army's ascent. But Jezebel stood for a long time alone on the roof in the cool autumn sun, watching the army approach, eager to see Ahab but terrified of what he would see in her child.

'I thought I might find you here,' said Beset behind her. Jezebel glanced at her maid, who was holding out a cloak of ochre wool. 'Don't get cold.'

'How is the baby?'

'He has suffered an endless stream of visitors, mostly the Palace priests, since the rider was first sighted. He received the first few in good humour, but when Enosh arrived he started screaming and even Daniel couldn't calm him. Raisa chased them away in the end. But they all had to see for themselves that the baby was still fit and well to meet his father.'

Jezebel nodded and turned back towards the sight of the approaching army. They'd be here soon and she could already make out Ahab in the lead from his distinctive black horse beneath him.

'I keep telling myself that if he doesn't notice it the first time he looks at the child, he won't see it at all,' she said.

'No,' said Beset, arranging the cape around Jezebel's shoulders.

'But if the resemblance is as strong as I've come to think it is then—'

'Do you love him?'

'Ahab?'

Beset smiled. 'Yes, Ahab.'

'I missed him much more than I thought I would, and his letters brought me great comfort. I know he didn't tell me much of significance, but it mattered to me that he was thinking about me, even when he was far away with a war to fight. He is the only one who welcomed me from the start.'

And does he love me? Could any man with more than one wife truly love any of them? She turned away from the parapet. Certainly, they seemed to have found a fondness for each other. He had her loyalty too. There were times in this dark and complicated city when she thought that mattered more even than the son she'd given him.

Beset stopped at the head of the stairs. 'It's been less than two months, but you have grown so much older since he went to war.'

'Is it the baby that made me grow up?'

Beset shrugged. 'You will make a good mother, I'm sure of that.'

Jezebel squeezed her maid's hand in gratitude. 'If I'm wiser too, then perhaps the baby will be the last mistake I make.'

Her stomach churned as she processed with the Palace priests down to the city gates to wait for Ahab's arrival. She was wearing the Queen's gown and headdress, formally given by Raisa after the baby was born, and the baby lay in her arms wrapped in a cloth edged with gold beads. Perhaps he sensed the significance of the occasion for he had not stopped wailing since the priests' visit.

Ahab dismounted from his horse and strode to meet them, ignoring all the pronouncements and ritual welcomes from Obadiah.

'This is the boy?' he said, looking deep into Jezebel's eyes.

'Welcome home, Your Highness.'

Ahab picked the baby straight out of Jezebel's arms, abandoning the ceremonial cloth. 'He looks strong despite being so young.'

'He was eager to see the world you have secured for him,' said Jezebel. 'He came a little early, as all your sons have done, but this one wanted to live.'

'Early indeed.' He studied the child's face for a moment and Jezebel's stomach tightened. A few steps away Obadiah was watching them and Jezebel knew that she must not show any inkling of fear or doubt.

'But blessed!' cried Ahab, swinging the child aloft so the crowd could see. 'I name him Ahaziah, and he will be heir to my kingdom!'

The crowd cheered and Ahab kissed the baby's forehead. Then he laid him tenderly in Jezebel's arms. His eyes held hers for a long moment and she relinquished the last of her fear, for he regarded her with such deep affection, such longing, that she knew not much time would pass before he came to her room.

In the early evening, having bathed and anointed herself with her favourite oils, she went downstairs to his chambers. She knew he had been talking with his officials – it was to be expected after he had spent so long away – but surely he would welcome her touch at his shoulders, easing away the aches and pains of so many days sleeping rough on the plains. They could eat together as they had before he left, and he could tell her about the campaign.

As she approached the office by the servants' steps, she heard raised voices and paused behind an arras to listen. The corridor was darkened with the dusk and she edged back the curtain and peered through. Ahab was standing braced at his desk, around him perhaps a dozen men, Enosh and several priests, and with them Obadiah and his diplomatic cadre.

'But you have disgraced Yahweh,' Enosh was saying angrily. 'To spare the enemy is an insult to the sacred rite of *herem*. Ben-Hadad and his army were defeated. You should have slaughtered them.'

'And what does Yahweh give our people in return?' demanded Ahab. 'Does He give me trading routes to Damascus and beyond to Assyria and Babylon? Does He give me preferential access to Aramean food that we so desperately need for our people?'

'*Herem* gives the right to take gold and silver for the treasury of Yahweh—'

'By that you mean your temples,' said Ahab.

'You defy the word of God,' argued Enosh, 'and in doing so you show yourself to be an infidel. Israel cannot afford to have a king who is an unbeliever.'

Jezebel found herself shocked once more by the power wielded by the priests of Israel. Her own father would have them flogged for such impertinence.

'Our neighbours will seize quickly on the weakness of a ruler who throws aside the principles of his God,' said Obadiah. 'Your heart must be a man's.'

'Why don't you speak your mind?' demanded Ahab, glaring at his most senior official. 'I don't believe I understood you properly.'

'It is well known that the ungodly principle of mercy you apply originated in the Phoenician pantheon,' said Obadiah, 'when their God named Baal defeated another named Yam, and wished to kill him. Their Goddess Astarte, to whom you built that inflammatory temple, apparently intervened and asked for Yam's life to be spared. Her seductive charms turned Baal's wrath into all the weakness of compassion, and Yam went free. Yet still his realm, the sea, lies uneasily against Baal's realm of the sky, and their conflict will never end.'

'I'm surprised you know so much about a religion you pretend to despise,' said Jezebel stepping through the curtain.

'She should not be present,' snapped Enosh. 'She has no place here.'

'Jezebel's place is by my side,' said Ahab, drawing himself up to his full height. His sword was still strapped to his hip and his hand fell to the hilt.

Jezebel's sandals scuffed loudly on the stone floor as she walked to Ahab's side, but she knew everyone's eyes were on Ahab. Would the warrior king be forced to shed blood at home as well as abroad? She pressed her clammy palms discreetly against her skirts.

'And yes,' said Ahab, glancing at his wife, 'I give Jezebel credit for reminding me that there is strength in compassion. Her wisdom means that I have secured supplies of Damascan grain for our people this winter while our own harvests have failed. Your pockets might have become heavy with Ben-Hadad's gold, but how would you have fed our people? The Assyrians won't sell to a kingdom that kills its neighbours and then asks for food.'

'You have led our King to betray his God,' said Enosh to Jezebel. A murmur of agreement swarmed through the other priests.

'And when Ahab named his son Ahaziah, he told his people that the child will always hold Yahweh close,' said Jezebel. 'That is what the name means, is it not?'

Ahab glanced at her again but the gratitude in his eyes was so fleeting and so private, she was not entirely sure she had seen it at all for he slammed his palms down on the desk.

'I am your King,' he bellowed, 'and while I am ruler of this kingdom and the lives of the people are in my hands, you won't question my—'

The heavy door to Ahab's office swung open with a deafening creak and a voice boomed out of the gloom beyond. 'The lives of the Israelites are in the hands of the one *true* God, Yahweh. As he breathed life into the first man, he can take it from us, leaving us as carrion for scavengers.'

The priests turned as one, then dropped to their knees. Even Obadiah stumbled backwards away from the door. Ahab shifted his weight beside her, but Jezebel could only stare as the dishevelled old man shuffled into the office, dressed in a ragged tunic and a rough shroud of animal skins, a tall gnarled staff of oren wood in his right hand.

'Do you defy your God?' demanded the intruder. 'How dare you let this whore speak his name!'

'Forgive us,' muttered Enosh from where he knelt.

Jezebel looked at her husband but he didn't say a word. For the first time since she'd met him, he looked afraid. She glanced down at his sword but his fingers now flopped against its hilt as though they did not know what lay in their grasp. He couldn't defend her even if he would.

'Are you speaking of me?' demanded Jezebel in a voice that made her throat burn. She walked around the desk to face the unkempt stranger. 'If you call me a whore then do so again to my face so that I may know you mean it.'

'Jezebel,' he hissed, his eyes glittering as they moved over her. His nostrils twitched also, sniffing the air like a dog. 'I know exactly who you are. You have opened your legs to corrupt the son of Omri and the product of his foul lust now corrupts the whole Kingdom of Israel, spreading like plague from your diseased sex.'

The curse stung but she would not be silenced. 'Then my reputation surely outstrips yours, as I have no idea who you are.'

'Jezebel . . .' muttered Ahab.

'Forgive us!' cried Enosh.

But the stranger lifted his hand to demand silence. 'Of course you do not know my name for you are not blessed

105

by Yahweh to do so. I am the prophet Elijah. I am the Navi, the one who is called by our God to defend His law.'

Jezebel looked belatedly at Ahab, as though hearing only now his fear for her.

'Why do you look to him?' asked the ragged man. 'A king's authority means nothing. Ahab has broken the law of Yahweh as only a weak man could.'

'He has shown wisdom in preserving the future of his people—'

'His people?' said Elijah, his voice shrill as he stepped further into the room. 'They are not *his* people!'

Elijah leaned in close to Jezebel, his eyes yellowed, his tongue darting over his cracked dry lips, his sour breath on her face. 'Your temptations wreak their own destruction, your debauchery flows like poison, woman of shit and plague.' He pointed to Ahab. 'The rivers run dry, *king* of men. My Lord's wrath has drunk them up and spat out dust into your eyes. Until you cleanse your kingdom, no rain shall fall. Your wells will echo with the wails of the thirsty. Your crops will wither and perish. This I promise you in the name of Yahweh.'

He drove the staff hard into the floor, cracking the tile beneath, then he turned on his heel and shuffled out.

Behind his priests, Ahab looked utterly broken. Even Obadiah had lost the supercilious gleam in his eye. The priests remained on bended knee until the prophet's steps could no longer be heard and then clung on to each other as they rose from the floor, wailing and moaning among themselves.

Jezebel returned swiftly to Ahab's side and slid her hand over his, but he didn't move and she felt a sudden desire to shake him, to shake all of them to wake them from their stupor. Elijah's words had been as foul as his mouth yet none of them had even stirred as the vitriol had sprayed from it. She suspected that the priests condemned her as Elijah did, if not in quite such vulgar tones, but she was stunned that they had accepted his verdict on Israel just as readily as his verdict on her. She patted Ahab's hand, desperate to bring him back to life. 'A drought began long ago in these lands—'

'Heralding your arrival,' said Enosh, hauling himself up on the corner of the desk. 'Yahweh must have foreseen the damage you would do to our people but we didn't heed His warning.' He turned to Ahab. 'Nor did you take note of it. You were so determined to put a son in the House of Omri that you made a pact with the infidels.'

'Enough!' shouted Jezebel, desperate to find a way to strengthen Ahab again, to give him something else to think about. 'The Phoenician engineers know how to extract the water from the underground springs, don't they?' Jezebel shook her husband's arm, who finally roused and nodded wearily at her. 'Then surely this land need not be dry even if it does not rain.'

She tucked her hand into Ahab's elbow and stroked his arm, trying to soothe herself as much as him. 'But the question is,' she said, 'will you accept their help to save yourselves, or will you die of thirst to prove the prophet right?'

Four years later

868 BC – Mother

Chapter Eighteen

'Yahweh has blessed the House of Omri once again!' cried Raisa, grasping the baby firmly. 'It's another boy!'

Jezebel gulped to fill the void left by the last agonising exhalation on which the child had been born, and looked wearily between her bent knees to where the baby was screaming its first cries of life. Her heart swelled with relief and joy that she had safely borne another son that lived and breathed, for her second male child had been stillborn two months early and she could not bear the heartbreak of another. Even if it was only a gift known to herself, Daniel and Beset, she so desperately wanted to give Ahab his own son.

The midwife cut the cord and then took the baby to the golden bath before the fire where Beset was waiting.

'Quickly now. It's freezing in here,' said Beset, lowering the baby into the warm water. The child shrieked, all but smothering a brisk knocking at the door.

'Is the child well?' called Daniel from his exile in the corridor.

Jezebel struggled onto the bed, dragging covers over her. Now the labour was finished, the sweat was cooling

111

on her face and neck. 'Come in, Daniel. The worst is over.'

'Stay where you are, young man,' said Raisa. 'She is not yet appropriately dressed.' She laid a down quilt over Jezebel. 'I've never known a winter like it,' she said. 'Such bitter winds for months and yet no snow. Imagine how cold the King must be in Samaria.'

Jezebel tugged the covers closer to her chin while she tried to imagine what Ahab was doing at this very moment. He'd left as soon as the snows on the distant mountains had melted, to take up residence at his main Palace for the spring and summer. The late winter days made it difficult to guess what time it was, as it seemed only light or dark. The unending grey stone of the Winter Palace at Jezreel must surely have been made from fallen clouds, for the whole settlement felt permanently enfolded in coldness. Samaria would be far worse though and Jezebel knew she should be grateful to be here.

Despite a generous dispatch of furniture and fabrics from her father in Tyre that first winter, Jezebel had never been able to make her chambers here as cosy as those in Samaria; this Palace was a military fortification first and a home second. She was woken daily by the clanging of gates, the hammering of weapons in the forges, and the frequent shouts of the troops that rang through the casement walls of the fort. Perhaps her sense of discomfort was exacerbated too by the barren lands stretching to each horizon. The drought had afflicted Ahab's lands just as Elijah had promised. Even with the ongoing irrigation projects run by Tyrian engineers, four summers of dwindling crops had left the kingdom wretched.

112

The wet-nurse peered round the curtain, and seeing the birth was over, she emerged with a little girl balanced on her hip, followed by a small boy wielding a wooden sword.

'I thought you would want to see your children before they go to bed, Your Highness,' said the nurse to Jezebel. 'Give your Mama a cuddle, Ahaziah,' she said, lifting the sword out of his hand.

The little boy jumped onto the bed and rolled into his mother's arms, causing Jezebel to swallow a squeal of discomfort. But she buried her face in the child's neck and he rewarded her with a face full of dribbling kisses.

'Bed now,' said Jezebel, and the boy leapt off again and disappeared through the curtain, hollering as he went. 'How is my darling little Athaliah?' she said, reaching out for the girl. 'Have you fed well today?'

'She has, Your Highness,' said the nurse, as Jezebel gave the child a quick cuddle. 'Has a name been chosen for your new son?'

'The King wishes to call his second son Joram,' said Raisa proudly as Beset carefully dried and swaddled the newborn. 'I will dispatch the messenger to Samaria myself. Ahab will be so pleased, Jezebel, you have done well.' She leant over the newborn and kissed its forehead, then returned to the bedside to squeeze Jezebel's hand. 'You have given my son a family, and the House of Omri is at last as full as it should be. But now you need some rest. Put the older children to bed,' she instructed the nurse, 'then you may collect the baby.' She swept out of the chamber with her usual stately vigour, pausing rather reluctantly at the door to admit Daniel.

'She is an extraordinary woman,' murmured Daniel as he drew a small couch up to the side of the bed.

Beset laid the baby in Jezebel's arms and held a silk scarf around her while Jezebel arranged the child at her breast. 'It is good that you have given Ahab a son of his own as well as a daughter,' she whispered. 'Now no one can ever say—'

There was a knock at the door. 'Jezebel?'

'Esther, come in. I'm fit for visitors.'

The young woman looked round the curtain, and seeing only Beset and Daniel, she entered. Daniel offered his chair to her but she smiled shyly at him and shook her head.

'I won't stay. Perhaps,' she hesitated, frowning a little, 'perhaps you might feel up to a walk tomorrow, or the day after?' she asked Jezebel.

'Of course. I have been lying down for days and will be glad to see something other than the ceiling!'

Esther laughed and glanced at Daniel, and Jezebel smiled to herself. She knew Esther thought Daniel very handsome, but it was no good fostering a romance between the two. Esther would always be a king's daughter and Daniel little more than a foreign servant in the Israelite kingdom. Besides, selfish though it made her feel, and despite the friendship that had grown strong between the young women, Jezebel couldn't imagine giving up any of the small coterie of Phoenicians who had stayed so loyally with her since they left Tyre. For while she had settled well into the role of Ahab's queen, she had done so by virtue of knowing that she was never alone among her new people.

But Jezebel knew it was not of Daniel that Esther wanted to speak in private. 'Why don't we go to the market tomorrow afternoon?' she suggested. 'I have a yearning for some of those dried Egyptian apricots and I'll get a good price if you are with me.'

Esther nodded with relief and left with another furtive glance at Daniel. Jezebel nuzzled the baby's head with her nose, and hoped it could not sense her eagerness to get out of bed and find out just what had been going on during the last days of her confinement.

'You look very well, considering,' said Esther, as she and Jezebel weaved slowly past the pottery stalls in the market square the next afternoon. The sky was a rare winter blue, but the sun was already falling fast and the air was sharp and cold.

'It gets easier,' replied Jezebel. 'I'm just glad the child has a strongly beating heart.'

'Father will be pleased.'

Esther hesitated, and Jezebel knew why. Rumours had circulated quickly with the death of the previous male child. It was said, in some quarters, that the ill-fate was her punishment from Yahweh for confronting Elijah. She lifted a black and white pot from the back of a cart, studying the design on the pot, then put it down, smiling at the merchant. Jezebel had no doubt where those rumours had originated. She turned back to Esther. 'I suppose that Obadiah and I will circle around each other once again as we always do, as he tries to find a snide way to congratulate me while concealing from me what Ahab is doing in Samaria.'

Esther glanced over her shoulder as they wandered on. 'Have you seen him yet?'

'He has been staying out of my way. Apparently he believes that women who have recently given birth have surrendered all their intelligence to their new baby and are incapable of sensible conversation.' Esther's smile was fleeting. 'I presume he's not been staying out of your way though,' added Jezebel, tucking her arm through Esther's. 'What has he been up to since I took to my bed?'

Esther waited until a pair of soldiers had passed them before she spoke in a low voice. 'As you suspected, that routine of his has grown quite regular now. He goes to the gate on the east wall every two days with a basket of bread and meat and a skin of water. One of the priests is always waiting for him there, and the goods are carried down the hill to someone waiting on horseback near the bottom.'

'Does he know you've seen him?'

'From the day of your confinement two weeks ago, he took to timing his delivery to coincide with my morning walk and yesterday he actually accompanied me all the way from the Palace to the east gate. For he doesn't seem to care that I see what he does.'

Jezebel squeezed her friend's arm. 'We've all seen the way he looks at you.'

Esther shivered and rubbed her hands together. 'I'm not so naïve that I haven't noticed it for myself. In fact, I admit I've been using it to my advantage.'

Jezebel winced. 'Nothing is worth that risk,' she said. 'I know you worry about your father—'

'But it's almost as though Obadiah wants me to ask

what he's doing. He has grown so bold with the King away in Samaria. Since he had your adviser Philosir sent back to Tyre, there's no one to hold him accountable.'

'Let that be my concern.' Esther steered her towards the apricot seller. 'What else have you seen?'

'The day before yesterday,' Esther said, 'a group of ten priests left the city, returning last night just after the birth was announced. I only found out they had gone because Amos was surprised how few priests were in Temple when he went there to tell them about the baby. The group returned while the senior priest was deciding what to do about the birthing rites in my father's absence. They were clearly alarmed to find Amos there and hurried him away.'

'They have such contempt for others,' muttered Jezebel, then she stopped in her tracks. 'They were away two days, you say?'

Esther nodded.

'Just like the food – every two days. Then whoever is receiving food and important visitors must be a day's ride from here. Near enough to get to the city, but far enough away to be safely out of sight. It has to be Elijah.'

Esther nodded. 'Ahab's absence from Jezreel gives the priests – and Obadiah – the perfect opportunity to communicate easily with him. Who else would command such attention?'

The apricot seller wrapped handfuls of the bronzed fruit in a square of linen and passed them over. Jezebel offered him some coins, which he refused with a toothless grin at her step-daughter, but Jezebel laid them down on the cart anyway.

'Clearly Elijah is not going to be allowed to suffer from the drought,' she muttered, as they turned back towards the Palace. 'But with all that food he is getting, he can't be alone.'

Esther was silent until they had reached the edge of the market. 'Amos told me last night that he had always thought that several priests involved in the desecration of your temple in Samaria had been helped to escape before they could be caught. The other priests speak sometimes of pilgrimages to Mount Carmel, and Amos is sure that is where the fugitives hide out.'

'It is the right distance away. They stay overnight and return the next day. It fits.'

'So Elijah is with them?'

'It seems likely,' said Jezebel, suddenly tired from the rush of anger. 'I wish Obadiah hadn't managed to convince Ahab to send Philosir away. I should've realised sooner that I need someone to help me keep a close eye on him – someone other than you.' She squeezed Esther's arm, but her friend's eyes fell to the ground. 'Is there something else?'

Esther would not look at her and Jezebel tugged at her arm. 'Come on. We don't know when Ahab will return and I can only keep up with Obadiah if I know everything he's been up to.'

Esther turned to Jezebel. 'It's not just Elijah. What Obadiah doesn't know is I saw him and one of the senior priests meet a Judean soldier outside the city gate a few evenings ago. They gave him some scrolls. I was standing on the city walls—' She blushed. 'I was waiting for Daniel to come back from his walk, he was late and it was nearly curfew and I thought I might, you see—' She tailed off in utter embarrassment, but Jezebel hardly heard her.

'Is there no end to his betrayal?' she said. 'If Ahab had known about Obadiah's aid to the priests, he would have slaughtered him too. To help Elijah is duplicitous but to communicate unsanctioned with the Judeans is treason. Especially when they have done nothing to help us through the drought.'

She strode up the lane, driven by angry purpose, Esther running to keep up. 'But what can you do? You can't confront him because he will just deny it.'

'I can be ready. I will watch him myself now, Esther, until he is sick of the sight of me.'

Chapter Nineteen

The energy of her fury abated during a sleepless night of worry, and the next morning Jezebel rose early in a contemplative mood and went to the small Temple to Yahweh on the north side of the city. Jezreel lay on a hilly plateau among the once-fertile plains of the Jezreel valley. The shadows of mountains rose up to the east and west. From the vantage point of the high fortified wall Jezebel could see the river snaking through the valley. The first winter she'd come here it had been a wide blue swathe, but each year the waters receded, and now it was little more than a narrow ribbon through the brown flatlands. The Phoenician engineers had built systems to pump water from wells up to the cities, but there was nothing to be done to help those who lived on the plains. It was easy to see why Elijah's prophecy had found such influence among the people.

She watched a woman draw water from a supervised well in the north wall. As the woman stowed the wooden lid on her pail she glanced at Jezebel, smiling nervously. Jezebel smiled in return and took herself away. It was easier for her husband. He could walk among his subjects, talking to the people, but she was all but confined to the Palace complex when she was in Jezreel. She had counselled Ahab to use his soldiers for the digging of new wells, at least to show he was working to alleviate the effects of the terrible drought. There was little that she herself could offer but prayer.

She had learned the rituals of worship of Yahweh, which weren't so different to those for the same God in Tyre. She slid into the darkened Temple and lit a lamp for the altar. Then she knelt and offered up thanks first to Yahweh and then to Yahweh's consort Asherah for the safe birth of Joram, and finally, silently in her heart, a long cycle of prayers to Baal Hadad, Lord of the Skies, for rain.

I must not lose faith, she thought to herself as she left the Temple, but she couldn't ignore how alone she felt, so far away from Ahab and all his familiar rituals, the same breakfast each morning, the mint tea they shared in the afternoon, how he would visit her in the evening while she was having her bath and talk over the day's dispatches from all corners of the kingdom. Perhaps it was time to go home, she thought, looking at the overcast sky. And then she found herself smiling, for she realised it was not of Tyre she was thinking, but Samaria.

She turned at the sound of a horse trundling along the street behind her, and found the vineyard owner Naboth riding on a cart beside his driver, a full load of wine jars stacked behind him. She stood to the side of the lane to let the vehicle pass, and as the cart drew near Naboth clambered down to join her.

'I hear congratulations are in order, Your Highness.'

'Good morning, sir,' she said.

121

'Another son! The King will no doubt be delighted.'

'You are very kind.'

'Will you ride with us to the Palace? I am surely one of many who will honour you with gifts to celebrate the birth.' He waved at the wine in the cart.

'I am content to walk, but thank you for your generosity. The King enjoys your wine very much.' They walked on ahead of the cart. 'I confess the children are not always as interested in the gifts as they should be. I had difficulty interesting Athaliah in a set of gold teething rings sent by one of the northern nobles for her birth. And Ahaziah is always more interested in the wooden sword the King made for him than anything else.'

Naboth grinned at her, his round face puckering with delight. 'That is why I only ever bring wine.'

'How are your plans for the new vineyard progressing?'

'The vines are in the ground, but the lack of rain has not helped.' He lowered his voice. 'I've been talking with one of your engineers about how we might divert water from the well systems towards my land. The Egyptians call it a *qanat*, they tell me, and it is a frightfully clever arrangement. It will be expensive of course, and I do wonder whether growing grapes is the most essential of harvests for our people at this time. I would be interested in your thoughts.'

'You're kind,' said Jezebel. 'I think you're probably the only person in these parts who cares what I might think.'

'You have always been wiser than others wish to acknowledge,' said Naboth, but Jezebel hardly heard him for Beset was running up the lane towards them, her head undressed and without a cape.

'Come quickly!' gasped her maid.

'Is it Joram? Is he ill?'

But Beset was shaking her head, her eyes wide. 'Ahaziah,' she gulped. 'He's disappeared.'

'Jump in the cart and we can ride back,' said Naboth, but Jezebel was already running up the lane with Beset.

'Where did you last see him?' demanded Jezebel.

'He was playing in the nursery while Athaliah was feeding,' said Beset breathlessly, 'but the nurse thought he had come to see you and I thought he was still with her. I've looked everywhere I thought he could be, but I can't find him!'

'He can't have gone far,' called Naboth trotting behind them, but Jezebel was far swifter on her feet than the stocky nobleman and she ran as fast as she could, Beset gasping beside her. Daniel was waiting for them at the Palace gates, Amos with him.

'Has he been found?' cried Jezebel.

'Not yet,' said Daniel, his face pale. 'Someone said he was seen up on the north wall—'

'But he knows not to,' said Jezebel.

'If he were to fall—' said Beset.

'Surely no one will let that happen,' said Amos. 'Beset and I will search the Palace room by room. Daniel, go with Her Highness and search the gardens and the stables. We'll send the household staff out into the city.'

The priest and the maid disappeared into the Palace.

'Let's try the stables first,' said Daniel. 'He's been talking a lot about horses recently.'

Jezebel nodded, trying to order her thoughts. At only four years old, her son wasn't allowed to ride without Ahab, but perhaps he'd just wandered off to look.

However, the stables were empty and Jezebel felt sick with panic. Despite being enclosed, the city now felt so big, its lanes and buildings so infinite and rambling. Daniel placed a comforting hand on her shoulder.

'Where can he be?' she wailed, gazing round the endless turrets, the Palace walls ringing with the howls of the dogs and the whinnying replies of the horses.

'The dogs! In the name of El, no!' Jezebel ran off towards the kennels. The dogs were barking in that snappish way that she had never forgotten from her first evening in Samaria, their deep dry cries so threatening.

She followed the din and found a cluster of dogs jumping and growling at each other round the kennel master in the yard, fighting over a piece of meat that he swung above their heads from the end of a child's wooden sword—

'Ahaziah!' screamed Jezebel. 'Ahaziah, where are you?'

The dogs turned, their attention snagged on her voice, their eyes keen and dark on her every move, their bodies piling over each other to see her better.

And then she heard a small voice pipe up.

'Mama?' Ahaziah peered around the legs of the kennel master.

'What do you think you're doing!' she shouted at the kennel master as she rushed forward. As soon as she took a step, the dogs turned as one, straining on hind legs towards her. Their barking and snarling redoubled, their muzzles snapped and drooled, their eyes narrowing to hate-filled glassy slits.

'I should stand back, Your Highness,' said the kennel master. 'They don't take kindly to strangers, whether they have royal blood or not.'

'Give me my son!' she shouted.

The kennel master shrugged, and lifted Ahaziah, pushing bodily through the wall of fur and fury without fear. He deposited Ahaziah in her arms. Jezebel seized him to her chest, but he was giggling.

'What are you doing down here?' she said angrily. 'These animals are wild, not like the horses.'

He stared at her, so surprised, his eyes wide and pleading, then he peered over her shoulder at the dogs who still whined after him.

'He's in no danger—' began the kennel master.

'Answer me, Ahaziah!' said Jezebel.

'Uncle Obadiah brought me down here. He said baby Joram was too little to play with, so I could play with the dogs instead.'

His voice, so innocent and uncomprehending, began to quell her terror. She cast a scornful look at the master of the hounds, and walked quickly away with Daniel at her side.

'My sword's back there,' said Ahaziah. 'I want my sword.'

Jezebel ignored her son. Until that morning, she'd thought Obadiah nothing but a thorn in her side. Now she saw he'd threatened her in a way that Elijah never had.

Chapter Twenty

The courtyard was already crowded with crates and chests as dawn broke a few days later. Jezebel stood to one side watching, the baby Joram cradled in her arms. Ahaziah and Athaliah had been carried down from their beds and lay, still half-sleeping, in one of the carriages, while Beset fussed over the other carriage in which her mistress would ride with the baby. A small corps of soldiers were tying their bedrolls in an orderly fashion to their horses, and somewhere out beyond the gates the dogs were whining and straining on their chains.

'I wish we didn't have to take those awful beasts,' Beset whispered to Jezebel as she helped her into the carriage. 'I'm almost too afraid to look at them.'

'I suppose that is the point,' murmured Jezebel, stifling a yawn. 'Hopefully any wild animals and bandits will feel the same way.'

'You look tired,' muttered Beset.

'I was awake all night wondering whether this is really the right decision.'

Daniel came to the window of the carriage. 'Are you

wrapped up warmly enough? I can bring you more blankets.'

'I'll be fine.'

'There are hot stones in the footwell.' He pulled his hood up over his head. 'The nurse and I will look after the little ones . . . but look, it isn't too late to change your mind. It is much too cold for the baby to be travelling so soon after its birth, and you are not yet fully recovered either.'

'I know the risks. Joram will be as safe as he can be wrapped up with me, and I can feed him whenever he needs it.'

Daniel shook his head disapprovingly and his fingers lingered on the door of the carriage for a moment before he went to join the older children. Jezebel ignored Beset's concerned look and they remained in silence until the retinue of carriages and horsemen had made its long slow way out onto the plain heading south. The flat valley lands were turning a dull gold with the rising sun.

She hadn't told Daniel the truth of why they were leaving – she was concerned he might try and confront Obadiah and that could only make things worse. He'd likely have guessed the reason though. She'd never taken one of his sleeping powders before, but the night after finding Ahaziah among the dogs, she'd known sleep would never come naturally. Ahab had wanted her to remain in Jezreel because of her condition, but there were other concerns now which outweighed such comforts. Whether Obadiah was merely asserting his power, or he actually intended harm, she couldn't take the risk in staying.

She could claim publicly that it was the long absence

from the King that prompted the journey back to Samaria, but she intended to tell him of her suspicions as soon as she arrived. While the drought lasted, his kingdom was as vulnerable from its own citizens as from the wandering malice of Elijah. Jezebel tugged back the curtain that enclosed the carriage and watched Jezreel shrink behind them. 'I feel like a soldier abandoning my post.'

'But you're not a soldier,' said Beset firmly, 'and Ahab has not asked you to fight for him.'

'I'm fighting for the safety of my children. Any accident that befalls them only looks like divine judgement on me.'

'Then by taking a newborn baby across the wintry lands you are surely playing into their hands,' said Beset.

Jezebel didn't reply. Instead, she tucked Joram even more tightly beneath her cape, feeling his tiny body snuggling against her breast.

The day passed in eerie quiet, for there were few other convoys on the road and the tents of the occasional settlements had their flaps down to seal in the little heat of their fires. The people of the kingdom seemed resigned themselves to whatever fate was in store, for they weren't ploughing the brown fields or tending their scrawny livestock.

As the party of carriages and soldiers drew up into a defensive circle at dusk in the southern foothills of Mount Carmel, Jezebel began to feel more settled. A meal of roasted rabbits and stewed berries did much to revive everyone's spirits, and there was an almost lazy mood around the campfires after the food had been served. Groups of soldiers were laughing with each other, and even the dogs were chewing in silence over the pelts and bones of the dinner. The horses were fed and watered, their shadowy silhouettes guarding the camp like ghosts from the God Melqart's underworld.

Jezebel drew her cloak around her and looked up into the dark. The skies had cleared as the day went on and a frost was crisping the air; she breathed deeply to revive herself from her stupor. Free of the carriage and far from both Palaces, there was freedom in standing alone in the middle of the land, the children under someone else's care, and she felt a fleeting guilty pleasure at the thought that she might steal one of those very horses tonight and ride off into the black, letting the horse carry her wherever it would.

An alarm bell rang from the perimeter of the camp. 'Enclose, enclose!' yelled a watchman. 'Horses approaching!'

The soldiers jumped up, snatching their weapons. The dogs barked and strained at their chains, and Jezebel ran to the tent where Beset and the nurse were watching over the children by twilight.

'What should we do?' asked Beset.

'Gather up the children and put them in the carriage. Neither of you is to leave them at all, do you understand?'

'What about you?'

Daniel ran over, a flaming torch in his hand. 'They're bringing a horse for the carriage. Can you drive it yourself?'

'Of course, but where to?'

'There are caves just over to the east. One of the soldiers will go with you.'

'I can't just leave.'

'Act like a queen for once and let someone else do the fighting.'

Jezebel's retort was lost in a sudden cacophony of barking and they looked towards the noise to see a great wall of torches racing towards them.

'Forget the horse, just get in the carriage with the children and don't move,' Daniel shouted. 'We'll try to drive them off.'

'Are they bandits?' asked the terrified nurse as Jezebel clambered in. Athaliah was crying, but Ahaziah was still fast asleep.

'There are too many of them for that,' muttered Jezebel, tucking Joram deep into her bosom as she peered out.

'Pull the canvases down,' squealed Beset. 'They won't be able to see us.'

The torches were spreading out in a wide attack formation, the hooves of the horses thundering in the ground.

'But then I won't be able to see them,' said Jezebel firmly. 'I don't want to be caught by surprise.'

But the carriage shook with the approach and Jezebel knew that if the carriage was surrounded there was nothing they could do. There was something very organised about the attack; the way they held their lines as they approached.

The commander of the Israelites brandished his torch ahead of them. 'Who goes there?' he shouted. The horses swarmed around them in a great rattle of swords and hooves. 'State your purpose!' demanded the commander, and Jezebel noticed that a small cadre of her foot soldiers was silently closing in around the carriage, reversing formation to protect her.

But she was temporarily blinded by a great swoop of fire as a horse cantered past, cutting through the cadre, and she was still blinking, trying to get her bearings, as the rider drew his beast up close to the carriage, dispersing her guards.

'Who are you?' he shouted.

Jezebel lifted her hand to shield her eyes from the glare, but her ear had caught on the rider's accent and she said, 'I can tell you are Judeans, and as you are on Israelite land you should identify yourselves first.'

The horse reared at the carriage and the nurse screamed, but its rider galloped off without another word and a moment later another rider cantered up to the carriage, pulling his horse in such a tight circle that dust blew up in their faces.

'Only the most headstrong Israelite queen would cross the plains in winter,' said a familiar voice.

'Jehu of Judah,' sighed Jezebel. She was relieved that the entourage were not hostile, but she felt vulnerable seeing him like this, far from the Palaces; from the places they usually met. Nor did she look her best, her hair and face dusty from the journey, and it was Ahab's newest son whom she clutched to her breast.

'Why are you riding across my kingdom in the middle of the night?' she asked. 'Anyone would think you were starting an invasion.'

'King Ithbaal did say it was late in the day to leave Tyre.'

'You've seen my father? On what business?'

Jehu grinned. 'You can come out of your hiding place,' he said, leaping down from his horse and grabbing open the door. 'Are your children in there?' Athaliah wailed in response.

131

He eyed the swaddled bundle she held close to her then held his hand out to help her climb down. 'And you have recently given birth to another.'

He whistled, and a number of his soldiers ran over. Jezebel could see her own guard jostling for superiority, and she handed Joram to Beset, telling her to let them escort her, the nurse and all three children back to the tent.

'Is your physician at hand?' asked Jehu. 'The one who plays the nevel.'

'You mean Daniel. Yes, he's here. Are you hurt?'

'One of my men took a fall. He needs help.'

Jehu strode away shouting for Daniel. Though he had been nothing but brusque since his troop had emerged from the dark, Jezebel felt her irritation at his swift command of the combined camp subside into reassurance at his presence. Perhaps she was the only one though, for it took a while for her own soldiers to settle down to the Judeans' presence.

It is up to me to show good grace, thought Jezebel as she sat down by the fire again and watched Jehu make his way around the camp, checking on his men. *My soldiers will surely be calmer if they believe I don't feel threatened.*

When Jehu passed within reach of the fire, she said, 'I'm sure your men must be hungry, and we have plenty of food to spare. You are welcome to join me here.'

'Dare I turn down the Queen of Israel?'

'I'm still Jezebel to you, surely?' she said more softly. 'Or have you taken your own queen-in-waiting?' She regretted her boldness as soon as she had spoken, but Jehu only snorted.

'I still ride alone.'

He strode off again towards his men and for a while she thought he wouldn't return. But soon he emerged out of the shadows and crouched down near her, just out of reach, his skin shining against the flames. His body had grown even stronger in the years since she had seen him last, and shadows lined the creases round his eyes. His hair was a little longer too, and it suited him. But he wore the same belt and boots of the warrior horseman, and as he sliced through the roasted rabbit with his knife, his fingers tearing off flesh, she thought him more at home out here on the plains than he had ever been on a banqueting couch.

As the memories blazed within her, they sat in strained silence. Jehu, chewing on his meat, seemed oblivious to her discomfort and she was relieved when Daniel approached.

'Excuse me, Your Highness. Sir, your soldier has broken some ribs but I've set them with straps and given him something for the pain.'

'Will he be able to ride tomorrow?' asked Jehu, still intent on his rabbit.

'As long as someone looks out for him. The drugs are strong and he may feel sleepy.'

'We will tie him on,' said Jehu. 'And now, having worked your magic, you can play for us on that harp of yours. I'm tired of listening to the whining of those dogs.'

Daniel glanced over Jehu's head at Jezebel and she nodded. *What must he be thinking, seeing Jehu again with all he knows of our past? And what of Ahaziah?*

'The rabbits are fat enough considering your land is

133

dying,' said Jehu as Daniel began plucking at the strings, a little way from the fire.

'Your fields must be barren too. I don't imagine the rain stops at the border.'

'You haven't learned any humility, have you?'

'I haven't learned to be afraid of bluster and bluff, if that is what you mean. Elijah is a fine orator with a good show in rage and rudeness, but he doesn't control the forces of nature.'

Jehu threw some bones into the fire, where they popped and crackled in the flames. 'I can't believe you're still so complacent.' He scuffed at the earth with his boot. 'You have a responsibility to this kingdom because you married into it and yet you choose to disregard the authority of this man chosen by Yahweh to be His emissary.'

'Do you really believe that to be true?'

'Yahweh sent flocks of ravens to feed Elijah in his cave. People speak of it from Damascus to Moab.'

'So I've heard,' said Jezebel, thinking of Obadiah and the smuggled baskets of food. 'But why would Yahweh see Elijah was fed when He allows His own people to starve?'

'Must you be so contrary?' said Jehu. He sat there picking at the meat, just beyond her grasp, the two of them alone in the dark while the rest of the world lurked around them in the shadows. She could almost see him bristling in the dark with frustration, and several times she thought he was about to speak, but he did not leave her side. Soon she could hardly breathe for the anticipation of what he would do next. She glanced towards the tent where his son lay sleeping. How would it change things if he knew? He might at least understand that the world was less simple than he thought.

Eventually, she had to speak, for she couldn't bear the last words between them to be his anger. 'The Gods I worship are in an eternal search for harmony with each other,' she said quietly. 'Even when El is in a fury and Baal and Mot are fighting, still they seek balance with each other. I find it difficult to understand how one God acting alone could take a people to the brink of destruction just to prove he can control them. Where is the compassion in that?'

'Elijah showed great compassion when he raised the son of the Phoenician widow from the dead. Even your father was talking of that.'

Jezebel was hardly surprised. Elijah – or at least the manifold stories about him – seemed to crisscross the kingdoms, spanning hundreds of miles. His peripatetic wanderings had more than a hint of myth about them. 'I haven't heard of such a thing,' she said. 'Why does Elijah tell such tales? If he wants to show his power, he could simply ask Yahweh to make it rain—'

'But unlike the Phoenician widow, you have not yet accepted that Yahweh is the one true God.' Jehu finally turned his gaze on her, his dark eyes pleading. 'I wish you would.'

Jezebel felt a great yearning spring unexpectedly from her, but it was not exactly as she remembered it in Tyre. In the few blissful nights they had spent together, he hadn't mentioned his God at all, but now his passion for Yahweh seemed all-consuming. She watched him, wondering why he had changed, but the shadows on his face confused her and she could bear no more. She stood up and bade him goodnight, not waiting for his response.

As she lay alone in her tent, she listened to him pacing round and round the fire, wondering if he would break the eternal circle and slip through the hides to find her beneath the blankets as he had just a few years ago; wondering whether she would welcome him if he did. He paced for so long she grew sure he would not come to her but suddenly she jerked awake, her heart pounding, certain she could hear the familiar rise and fall of his breath just beyond the tent. His name formed in her mouth. All she had to do was whisper it.

A barrage of shouting shattered the dark and the dogs howled. Jezebel heard the brittle exchange of coarse oaths between soldiers.

'Settle down!' shouted Jehu, his voice just outside the hides.

Jezebel held her breath, listening keenly. For a long time she was certain he didn't move and she heard the distant grumble of Israelites and Judeans insulting each other, the whine of the dogs, and the steady rise and fall of his breath in the cold night air.

He turned away, his boots scuffing away into the dark. She listened until she lost him in the rustle of the plains at night and then still she waited, wondering if he would return. But as the night grew colder, the shimmering glow of the fires made her weary and the shadowy place between memory and reality began to blur. Finally sleep caressed her confusion away.

When she rose at first light, her first sensation was one of disappointment, followed by guilt. She was married to Ahab, and yet she yearned for another. Now she felt foolish

136

too. Years had passed since those wonderful nights when he would sneak to her chamber in Tyre and the years had come with their burden of responsibilities and the complex loyalties which made a mockery of love. Even if they had overcome their stubbornness and uncertainty, even if they had found the pleasure of each other's body once more, the stark light of day would have chased the short-lived happiness away.

She tucked her hair in her hood, rinsed her mouth with water that had almost frozen in the pail by her bed. *Let our parting at least be on good terms,* she thought.

But as she emerged from the tent she saw that the camp was exactly as it had been when her Israelite convoy gathered in the dusk last night. The Judeans had vanished. She looked across the campsite but everyone was going about their business, preparing to leave, muttering good-naturedly to each other, their breath clouding in the freezing air. Beset emerged from her tent, followed by Ahaziah who ran around, waving his wooden sword. The maid half-smiled and raised an eyebrow in gentle, teasing enquiry.

Jezebel shook her head.

He left me again, she thought, *just like he always does.*

Chapter Twenty-One

She didn't dwell on Jehu's unceremonious departure for long. As the caravan of travellers approached the Samarian foothills she saw that in the last two months at Jezreel the land here to the south-west had turned almost black with drought, as far as the eye could see. There were far more people here too, farmers and their families clustered at the roadside trying to sell their unused tools in exchange for food, the occasional goat tethered to a rope, thin and bleating. And in every face the staring deep-set eyes of those who have not enough to eat and know who they blame. Jezebel shrank back from the starving gazes.

It was in sombre mood that she went to Ahab's office immediately on her return, Joram gurgling in her arms.

The King welcomed her warmly, kissing her forehead and caressing the baby's cheek. 'You should not have come though, the weather could have turned at any time.'

'I missed you. And judging by the state of our people, life has not been easy here.'

He sighed and shook his head. 'I've never known a winter as bad as this one. The grain silos are almost empty and there's simply not enough to go around. Supplies are taking too long to come from the north-east, they're often mouldy when they finally reach us, and the Judeans continue to refuse us help.'

Jezebel felt a hot surge of guilt. She'd been so pre-occupied with seeing Jehu again, she'd not even thought of pressing the case for assistance with him when she had the chance. 'Are they suffering badly from the drought as well?'

Ahab shrugged and sat down on the couch at his desk. 'I've no way of knowing. They barely acknowledge our existence, and Jehoshaphat has refused to meet any of our delegations.'

'Elijah must have great influence in Judah,' said Jezebel, 'if they can sacrifice their neighbours so readily. His advocates must be very powerful.'

The door opened and Enosh entered, garbed in the most elaborate of the priestly robes. He glanced at Jezebel, then at the baby in her arms.

'Ah, Your Highness,' he said to Ahab. 'I see your son has indeed arrived safe in Samaria. If you would like to bring him to the Temple we will perform the ceremonies for his birth. I understand the child was taken from Jezreel before they could be completed,' he added coldly, without looking at Jezebel.

'We will come along shortly,' she said.

'The Temple is only for worshippers of Yahweh,' said Enosh, glancing at her.

'I've been worshipping in His Temple in Jezreel,' said Jezebel, 'and He hasn't yet sent a plague of locusts against me.'

'Then you must be blind to the suffering He inflicts on

the rest of Israel while you pray,' said Enosh, clasping his hands smugly over his robes.

Jezebel was about to reply when she noticed how stained his fingers were. His beard too was dirty with crumbs.

'Have you been feasting?' she asked politely. 'No doubt in celebration of the birth of your King's son?'

Enosh brushed absently at his beard.

'I would like to see this feast, to be sure that it is sufficiently lavish and appropriate to the great blessing Yahweh has visited upon the House of Omri. No doubt you have breads and meats, and all the dried fruits of the Palace gardens, a feast fit for the son of a king.'

Enosh glanced at Ahab, but the King must have nodded, for he looked anxiously back at Jezebel. 'Your Highness?'

'Have you gathered many together?' asked Jezebel, marching out of the room, Joram still in her arms. 'Is this a gathering of all the priests in Samaria, or only the very fortunate?'

She didn't need to look over her shoulder to know that Enosh was following, for she could hear the frantic slap of his sandals in the corridor behind her, and the steady stride of Ahab to the rear.

She swept across the courtyard, out through the front gates to the Palace, and across the lane to the Temple which loomed over the gates. Servants, citizens and soldiers alike stopped and stared as the Queen marched among them, but she held her chin high and drew Joram a little closer. Within the Temple the few worshippers who knelt in prayer glanced up as she entered, but around the walls rang laughter from somewhere within, like a musical whisper. She followed the echo to the priests' chamber at the rear.

'Your Highness!' stuttered Enosh behind her, but Jezebel swept back the curtain and walked in. At least thirty priests were crowded round a table laden with platters and bowls, many of which now bore only crumbs and pips and chewed bones.

'This room is a sacred place!' bellowed one, turning to see Jezebel behind him.

'Women are not permitted here,' snapped another, 'let alone—'

'His Highness the King,' cried Enosh over the other voices, and the room fell to muted muttering. The priests shuffled back from the table, some lowering their heads, others just staring, and Jezebel stepped to one side to allow Ahab to stand beside her.

In Jezreel too, food had been rationed even for the royal household, and the sight of so much gluttony brought a feeling of nausea to Jezebel's stomach. 'I'm sure this meal is in honour of the birth of a new son to the House of Omri,' she said, 'but no child of this House will feed while his people starve.' She turned to Ahab. 'At least thirty families could have fed themselves for a week each on what was surely here an hour ago. Would food like this not be better distributed to those who need it, both inside the city and down on the plains? It does no credit to Samaria that some live so richly and others so poorly.'

'You let the infidel speak for the kingdom?' asked the priest whom Enosh had interrupted before.

'Salah,' said Enosh. 'The King is present.'

'Then he should listen to us and not his unbelieving

wife. It is our sacred right to break fast in the Temple of Yahweh.'

'You would gorge yourselves in the faces of the starving whom you lead to worship?' said Jezebel, feeling Joram stir against her chest. 'There are people on their knees out there whose faces tell me they have barely eaten in a month.'

'But we are Yahweh's priests, not the priests of the people,' said Enosh, glancing from Salah to his King and back again.

Several of the priests muttered in agreement, but Joram let out a miserable cry. Jezebel rocked him gently but he was growing agitated by the mood of the room and he would not stop wailing.

'You allow this foreigner to meddle in the politics of our land?' demanded Salah of the King.

'I do,' said Ahab, 'for it is precisely because she isn't one of us that she sees us so clearly.'

'That is for Yahweh to judge—' began Salah.

'Enough!' shouted Ahab so loudly that even his baby son fell quiet. 'I will give orders immediately that the supplies from which you draw your feasts be shared out among the people of this city and as far beyond as they will go. Your hoard will no doubt not feed many but it will feed some until one of our neighbours sees fit to help us. And until then, you too may know the hardship of our people, for you are nothing if you are not one of us.'

'You are defying your God,' said Enosh, 'and there will be consequences.'

'And I will pray that no one will die of hunger from

your self-righteousness,' said Ahab. 'Now which of you will perform the rituals for my son?'

There was a long awkward silence while Enosh glanced around his peers. Then he said quietly, 'We all will. Please wait in the Temple while we prepare ourselves.'

Jezebel gave her son to his father, then she took her leave of the room, but she was barely across the Temple floor when she heard Ahab call her. She stopped and turned, but his expression was almost invisible in the gloom.

'I'm sorry,' she murmured as he joined her, Joram gurgling in his arms. 'I didn't give you a chance to talk me out of it. But it made me so angry, so much greed when so many want for so little to survive.'

'They should all have known what to expect of you.' Ahab smiled. 'Unlike me you have remained the same throughout and not tried to appease your enemies.'

'They are not your enemies—'

'They are not my friends either so let us hope I still have one in the world at least. Please ask Esther to wait for me in my office. She should be ready to travel to Tyre.'

'You are asking my father for help?'

'If only he might give it without expecting something in exchange.' Ahab dropped his gaze from hers and Jezebel felt a sudden pang of sadness.

'You mean to offer Esther to marry my brother Balazar.'

Ahab was slow to lift his eyes to hers, and his guilt at the trade was such that Jezebel could hardly bear to acknowledge it. 'I only hope your father sees fit to help you,' he said, 'for who would blame him if he didn't want to help such barbarians as the rest of us? Esther is a

143

beautiful girl, she will surely make a fine wife and mother—'

'Tyre will have plenty of grain from Egypt and from Arabia too,' said Jezebel, struggling for some advantage that would cover her own sense of loss at her friend. 'My people always store enough to trade as well as to feed themselves.'

'I hope that the gift of my daughter is enough. For I won't give my wife back as well.' Ahab rested his fingers against her cheek.

'What do you mean?'

'You might so easily have been a bride of Judah, and I know that Jehu has been in Tyre again in recent days. I hope your father does not regret his choice.'

Jezebel turned her face into Ahab's palm and kissed it, then she leaned forward and kissed Joram on the forehead. 'Then you should know that I do not.'

Chapter Twenty-Two

The trees in the Palace courtyard were just beginning to bud, and smoke rose through the roof of the Temple of Astarte beyond the gardens. Jezebel inhaled deeply, the air tinged with the sweetness of the rosemary branches that Amos and the other Phoenician priests were burning in tribute for the coming of spring. She would go down later and lay her own garland of rosemary on the pyre, watch its pale blue flowers of winter turn black in the flames, and offer up the Prayers of Renewal to Astarte for the rebirth of the land. Hopefully, the Goddess wouldn't miss the sacrificial lamb that usually topped the pyre. Though Tyre had been generous with wheat to see Israel through the last of the winter, grain had been restricted to feeding people and many animals had been slaughtered for food instead of being milked.

Jezebel left the balcony to go to her room to dress, but the sound of Athaliah's terrible cough stopped her, and she hovered outside the nursery door, wondering whether to go in. Daniel had forbidden her from holding the three-year-old girl while she was still so sickly for fear that she would catch the infection too, but Jezebel ached to comfort her.

She peered round the curtain. Daniel was sitting on a low couch beside Athaliah's bed. He held a bowl before her nose from which steam rose, and Athaliah's tiny hands held its rim as she breathed from it. But now and again she would cough uncontrollably and Daniel would put down the bowl and rub her back until she stopped.

He has such patience, thought Jezebel. *He has left his home and his family behind to come here and care for me, for us, among strangers, and he has never once complained.*

'Drink,' cried Athaliah softly, tears welling up in her eyes. Her hand batted at her throat and Jezebel felt the pain in her own.

Daniel took the steam bowl from her and picked up a cup from beside the bed. Athaliah sniffed and took the cup in both her hands and drank it down, some of it dribbling down her front. Daniel mopped at it with a cloth, then put down the bowl and picked up Athaliah, setting him on her lap. He drew her into a cuddle and rocked her a little. 'Is it sleep time, little girl?'

He should be rocking his own child to sleep, thought Jezebel.

A strange twist formed in her stomach at the thought that she would one day have to give Daniel up for a life of his own. He had considerable responsibility in the Palace, often caring for the King now too when he suffered with minor ailments, and the confidence suited him. His hair still hung straight around his face, just brushing his shoulders, but the intelligence of his expression was attractive, and Jezebel knew several of the young women in the Palace household often took a detour past the

146

nursery, ostensibly to coo over the children, but really to catch a glimpse of their physician. But he wouldn't marry an Israelite, for he was too closely associated with the Queen to be acceptable to any father in Samaria. For a time she'd wondered if he had returned Esther's fondness for him, but she had been in Tyre for three months and her destiny as Balazar's bride had recently been confirmed by a message from Ithbaal.

'Praise be!'

A cry floated up from the street below the window, and Jezebel almost pushed back the curtain to enter the nursery. But Daniel had not stirred and Athaliah was snoozing against him, and instead she let the curtain fall back silently and went into her own chambers.

'Praise be! Praise to Yahweh!'

Had Baal brought rain at last?

Jezebel pulled back the shutters and looked up at the sky, but it was still a flat unbroken grey. She stuck her hand out but it stayed dry and she noticed people gathering in the street below, among them several of the Palace's priests. They were all looking along the street and Jezebel followed their gaze towards a shambolic procession that clustered around a donkey, on top of which sat a shabby old man.

'Elijah,' Jezebel muttered to herself. 'What brings you back to Samaria?'

'Praise be, the Prophet returns!'

Down below the priests were beginning to whip up the crowd, and cheers were already breaking out among the onlookers. The bustle around the donkey was growing and as the procession arrived beneath Jezebel's window the old man looked up, as though he expected to see her standing there watching.

Jezebel shrank out of sight just in time, but Elijah shouted, 'Douse the flames in the infidel Temple! Let Yahweh's flames burn in their place! Douse the flames of those false Gods for they are not your own!'

'Praise be!' cried the priests in the street, and a great cheer swelled through the crowd.

Jezebel snatched up her ceremonial wreath of rosemary and ran out onto the balcony and down the stairs, heading for Ahab's office. But when she got there she found a delegation of priests and advisers already with him.

'Elijah isn't welcome here,' Ahab was saying to the Palace priests. 'He does nothing but stir up bad feeling.'

'If he has come, it is because the people will it,' said Enosh.

'If he has come, it is because Yahweh wills it,' said Salah.

'If he has come it is because someone has told him that today is the start of the festival of Astarte,' said Jezebel, shaking her wreath. She looked at Obadiah who was standing at Ahab's side, his hands clasped across his midriff and said firmly, 'Elijah has been invited here by someone in this city to stir up trouble.'

'He has come because Yahweh has asked him to put out the flames in your Temple,' said Salah.

'Then perhaps he would be better letting them burn and hope they take the Temple with it,' said Jezebel. 'Surely if he despises my religion so much he would rather destroy it.'

'Only if it is Yahweh's will,' said Salah.

148

Jezebel looked at Ahab, trying to suppress the desperation she felt. She could sense trouble as surely as she could smell the burning rosemary now scenting this wing of the Palace. As she was trying to think of a way to cajole him into saying something in her defence, Amos entered, breathless and red in the face.

'Excuse me, Your Highness, I apologise for interrupting you.' He glanced at the others in the room. 'I thought you should know that Elijah has brought a crowd to the Temple of Astarte. I fear a riot.'

Ahab pushed his way through his advisers and marched through the gardens. Jezebel followed him, her panic rising. Her husband flung open the garden gate and found a great gathering of people on their knees in the street while above them on the steps of the Temple stood Elijah, ragged and dirty, his staff planted at his feet. Around him priests and citizens alike knelt at the Temple walls, banging the stone with sticks. Ahab picked his way across the lane but not one of his people rose to salute their King and among them a murmur quickly grew into a chant.

'Yahweh! Yahweh!'

'Be careful,' whispered Jezebel, but soon she and Amos were cut off from Ahab as Enosh, Salah and the other priests swarmed around them, adding their voices to those of their people, emboldened now by how Elijah stood on the steps of the foreign Temple glaring down at Ahab. The King was alone in this sea of fervour, waves of rebellion breaking against him. But his eyes blazed just as fiercely as Elijah's and he turned on the prophet, clambering up the steps to look him in the eye.

'Why do you not gather in your own Temple?' Ahab shouted above the din. 'You do not worship Astarte, yet you have these people bowed down before her.'

Elijah rammed his staff into the steps beneath his feet. The racket of banging stopped immediately and everyone looked at the prophet. He had defied the King with this gesture once before in his own Palace. Now he defied Astarte on the steps of her Temple.

'Yahweh has bid us take back this corner of the land of Israel,' he bellowed.

The crowd roared their approval.

'Then let Yahweh show Himself,' demanded Ahab.

'He shows Himself through me,' cried Elijah.

'How convenient,' said Jezebel, pushing forward among the prostrate people.

Elijah glanced at her as if noting her presence for the first time. 'You doubt me, woman of dung?'

Amos followed Jezebel. 'Astarte is not a jealous Goddess. Yahweh need not feel threatened.'

'Yahweh demands the respect of all in His kingdom,' said Elijah, 'yet you spurn him.'

'We respect all Gods by return,' said Jezebel.

'And where has your respect got you?' Elijah roared. 'Your crops are as sickly as your girl-child.'

Jezebel gasped, and thought again of Obadiah's prying eyes.

'But I have diverted water so that they will grow again,' shouted Ahab.

'Yet still the people starve,' said Elijah.

'I have brought grain to feed them.'

'The drought will not last forever,' said Jezebel, trying

to reach Ahab with her heart across the breach in his kingdom that lay before them.

Elijah's face split into a black-toothed grin. 'Perhaps not. When Yahweh wills it, the rain will pour.'

'Let Yahweh will it!' someone called.

'Let Yahweh bring us rain!' shouted another.

'I have brought you all the water there is!' bellowed Ahab.

But Elijah pointed north with his staff, towards the mountains. 'I lay down a challenge. Let the foreign priests come to Mount Carmel. Let them pit their Gods against Yahweh.' His eyes drifted over Amos, then rested on Jezebel.

'What sort of challenge?' she asked, nauseous with anticipation.

'A challenge of fire,' said Elijah. 'A test of power. If your Gods claim victory then they may keep their place of worship here, but if Yahweh wins then the whore of the House of Omri will submit to Yahweh and so will every one of her people in this land.'

Ahab studied Elijah, then his gaze tripped over the expectant faces of his subjects. Finally he looked at Jezebel and then at Amos. But his expression was empty. He shook his head. 'I will not speak for another,' he said.

'It is because you do not speak for her and because you do not speak for Yahweh that Israel suffers beneath your rule,' said Elijah.

'Then I will speak for myself,' said Jezebel. 'Our religions differ because our people, our lands and our lives differ.'

'You propose a competition that not even the Great God El could have conceived of,' said Amos.

151

'You refuse the challenge?' asked Elijah, eyes glittering darkly.

Jezebel looked across at Ahab, but for the first time her husband would not meet her eye. He stepped down from the Temple, crossed through his people and walked past her into the Palace gardens, only waiting for her at the gate. She glanced at Amos, and they turned together to follow him, but Enosh and Salah and the other Israelite priests remained behind with Elijah. As the garden gate closed a great cry rose up from the people, but Jezebel felt Elijah's stare burn into her, long after she had taken herself from his sight.

Chapter Twenty-Three

That evening in the King's office, Ahab sat at his desk, his head in his hands. He had enforced an early curfew and the city had fallen into an uneasy quiet. Though Elijah had reportedly left, Jezebel had declared that there would be no evening worship at Astarte's Temple. The Phoenicians had met instead in her rooms where they had marked the feast day in a subdued mood, burning a single twig of rosemary on the shrine in the corner of Jezebel's room and murmuring prayers for guidance instead of celebration.

Down here among the officials and priests, Jezebel felt the temporary tranquillity of the ritual subside into frustration. Salah and Enosh stood together with Obadiah on one side of Ahab's desk, their mutual allegiance clear to all. Obadiah had not joined them for the confrontation at the Temple and his face now was quite expressionless. He had not even looked at Jezebel when she entered the office, but she was sure it was the very absence of concern for the kingdom he served that revealed his true loyalty so well. Who else could have told Elijah about Athaliah's illness? She silently urged Ahab to see things as they were, right in front of him, but when he lifted his head, his voice was flat and resigned.

'Something must be done,' he said to Enosh.

Enosh glanced at Salah, who looked to Obadiah.

How can you not see their conspiracy? she silently raged.

'I can no more control Elijah than you can,' said Enosh. 'Besides, it would be a blasphemy to attempt it.'

'The wisest course of action is for you to allow the challenge to go ahead,' said Obadiah. 'I can appreciate that your personal loyalties to your wife and to your father's house make it difficult for you to reach a decision, so you should simply leave it to Yahweh to make the decision for you. After all, it is His challenge, not yours.'

'Will that bring peace to my kingdom?' asked Ahab, spreading his hands.

'Only Yahweh can decide that,' replied Obadiah, 'but if it is your will then it is surely His. And if the many Gods of Phoenicia overcome Yahweh, then Elijah has also been shown to be a fool.'

'Don't agree to this,' said Jezebel. 'They're trying to control you.'

'What choice do I have?' snapped Ahab, slamming his fists down on the desk.

Jezebel's face burned as though Ahab had slapped her. 'Then as your queen,' she said, 'my priests and I will do your bidding.'

It was still dark when Jezebel rose and dressed herself in the heavy woollen shift. It felt rough and unfamiliar and she struggled to wrap the shawl around her head so that her hair would be concealed, but there was no question of lighting a lamp if she was to leave the Palace unnoticed. In a few hours, Ahab would rise and join the Palace priests for the ride to Mount Carmel and Elijah's challenge. She had to get there first.

Jezebel glanced guiltily at the bed. Ahab hadn't come to her since their argument over the challenge some seven days ago. She'd lain awake that first night after he had dismissed her from his office, expecting, then hoping he would come, and finally accepting that he would not. But he didn't come the next night, nor the one after, and only then did she realise that something in her marriage had truly changed. If Raisa were here, Jezebel would have sought the older woman's advice, but she had chosen to remain in Jezreel for now. Alone like this, Jezebel could only listen to the spiralling doubts in her head.

She had to duck into a doorway as the nightwatchman passed her in the street, his torch spitting and hissing at the shadows, and near the city gates Jezebel found Daniel and Beset waiting exactly as planned, each already astride a horse. Jezebel mounted in front of Beset, her maid's shaking hands weaving through the folds of her mistress's cape. Jezebel passed the harness to Daniel, who wore a shabby goat-herder's hat, and let him lead the little convoy out through the gates, silent as he gave their excuse of a sick relative in the river plains.

No one spoke again until the horses had made their way safely down the precipitous mountain road lit only by a sliver of moon. The night crept into their clothes as they trotted through clouds of their own breath. At last, as they reached the plain, Daniel pulled his animal close to Jezebel's and drew back the scarf from around his face.

'Are you sure you want to continue?'

'You're always asking me that,' murmured Jezebel, smiling nervously at him.

'Because you always take such risks. I can go to Carmel alone, I'm Amos's nephew after all and I have every right.'

'It's my repentance Elijah wants. No one but me can ask him to change his mind,' said Jezebel. 'And if I have to get down on my knees then I suppose I'll do so.'

She kicked the horse hard and it took off towards the north-west. The route was easy enough, following the curve of the mountains to the coast, but they would have to ride some distance from the foothills if they were to pass unnoticed all the way to Elijah's encampment on the coastal side. Amos had warned them that the prophet had surrounded himself with renegades from Ahab's own army who would slay an intruder before they enquired as to their business. Jezebel would rather Daniel and Beset had let her go alone, but they'd both insisted on accompanying her. Now, in the chill of the dark, she was glad of the presence of her two closest confidants.

Several hours later, as the dawn turned the black sky to sapphire blue, the land began to slope away towards the sea. Soon they saw the tell-tale tracks of horses in the dusty earth. *We're close*, Jezebel thought. She slowed her horse and waited for Daniel to catch up.

'Don't tell me you've changed your mind now we are here,' he said.

Jezebel shook her head. 'I'm going on by myself. If Amos is right about the guards, it will be easier for one of us to pass than three. And it is me Elijah wants to see beg.'

'You can't go alone,' said Beset in her ear.

'Please,' said Jezebel, 'wait with Daniel. I will be back as soon as I can.'

Beset clung to her for a moment, then slithered down off the horse. Jezebel turned the animal away, unwilling to linger with their worries, and rode north following the tracks towards the foothills that were a dark shadow ahead, tainted faintly by the soft pink glow of the sun rising to her right. She urged the horse on, aware that the priests of both religions would already be gathering at the gates of Samaria for their own journey north.

The plain dipped ahead of her and the mountains reared up far larger than she had expected. Out of the dark crevices emerged dozens of huge men, gathering at the sound of her horse, their bodies glittering in the dawn with the blades of knives and swords. *It's an army*, she realised. *He means to fight with men as well as with Gods.* The horse shied as though it sensed some great dark danger beyond them, but Jezebel kicked again and the animal unwillingly trotted on, its head swaying wildly. The guards drew their swords as she approached and the wind sang on their blades.

'I wish to see Elijah,' she shouted, her voice small against the looming mountainside.

A huge fellow rose up from a rock near the fire. 'Who's asking?'

'I am Jezebel of Tyre and Israel. '

The giant drew his sword from its scabbard and as she rode past him he swung it, slicing through her harness. The horse neighed and its head reared up, but Jezebel was too experienced a horsewoman to fall off and she gripped hard with her knees, steadying herself and the animal.

'I will fall only at the feet of Elijah,' she said. 'Please inform him I'm here.'

The brute stared at her with a leering grin, then strode swiftly into the caves. Jezebel kept the horse moving in a wide circle around the men. She had no wish to linger within reach of any of them, but she had only completed one more circuit when the guard reappeared, and grabbed the neck of her horse with one hand to stop it.

'My master will see you.'

Jezebel dismounted, pulled her scarf away from her face and set off a step ahead of the giant towards the caves. The darkness was well lit within, shot with the yellow glare of lamps and brush torches. The rugged cavern roof was shrouded with smoke from the burning fat of roasting meat mingling with the torch fires, the bitter miasma catching in her throat as she inhaled, trying to steady her nerves. On either side of the well-trodden passage through the cave, men rolled up their beds of blankets and skins or ate from bowls of food, ogling her as she passed among them. Her status as their queen meant nothing here.

Another coterie of guards barred her way, and she tried not to look surprised when her eyes caught on a familiar face. Obadiah stood at the centre of the group, his Palace tunic exchanged for a rough woollen robe that brushed the ground, and a dark turban.

'They haven't seen a woman in a long time,' he said. 'Does your King know you're here?'

'I could ask you the same,' Jezebel replied, trying to sound bold though her voice quavered in the echo of the cavern.

He stepped out of the group, studying her scruffy robes

158

and windswept hair. 'You make an attractive offering to these men, even looking as travel worn as you do.'

'I've come to see Elijah,' she answered, peering past him. Fires glimmered far ahead, shadows dancing on the walls.

'You can't change anything now. It's much too late for that.'

A shiver ran up her spine. 'Ahab will execute you for treason, which he no doubt should have done before. '

'You are so sure of yourself,' said Obadiah. 'You have all the arrogance of the outsider and none of the humility. I counselled Elijah against seeing you.'

'Yet here I am.' She pushed past him, on into the depths of the mountainside. He tried to grab her arm, but she shoved him away. 'Why do you want to prevent us meeting?' she asked as she stumbled on, looking around for Elijah. 'Why have you shown yourself to me at all? You could have hidden out in the shadows, pretending still to be loyal to the King. Yet you fear me, don't you? You fear that just as I have poisoned Ahab's mind, so I might corrupt Elijah.'

'He fears Yahweh,' boomed a voice ahead. Jezebel shuddered as its echoes enveloped her, but she followed the smell of food and just around the next corner, she found Elijah, squatting before a fire, tearing at a piece of meat with his teeth. In an arc behind him there were at least a dozen priests, the fire casting their cloaks and turbans in giant shadows around them. Elijah looked strangely small crouched before her, his bony feet poking out from beneath his filthy cloak of skins, his hair spun in matted curls about his face, his piercing eyes rolled up to meet hers.

'I've come to ask you to leave Ahab's kingdom,' said Jezebel. 'Your presence is unsettling to his people.'

Elijah snorted and grabbed a drinking bowl at his feet. Still his eyes didn't leave hers even when the bowl covered most of his face and wine dribbled down his beard. 'I notice you don't claim them as your own people,' he said, wiping his mouth on his sleeve.

'Many of them have welcomed me as their queen.'

'And many have not,' said Elijah. 'They are the people of Yahweh and He suffers Ahab to oversee its order. But I am a prophet of Yahweh and therefore I have every right to stay in His kingdom.'

'Then at least call off the challenge. You already control these people because they have been deprived of water—'

'If I truly wanted to control these people I could command them to rise up as one and slay their King.'

'Then why don't you?' said Jezebel.

'Because Yahweh does not like to use His power unless He has to.'

'And yet He already uses that same power to starve His people into submission. There is no compassion in a God like that—'

'And where is the compassion in your Gods of fire and death, of war and strife, of storms and sea?' he said, rising to his feet. 'Why must you pray for fertility to give birth to children, or pray for harvests in order to feed yourselves? Your people prostitute themselves to any God who might give them what they want instead of submitting their will and their faith to the one true God. Your so-called religion is a disease, and you are its malignant root in this land. I will cure Israel of your Gods by any means.'

The cave reverberated with his fury and Jezebel realised that where reason had failed only begging might indeed now succeed.

She lifted her chin and looked into his gleaming eyes. 'Is there nothing I can do?'

Elijah walked round the fire towards her, firelight dancing down one rough cheek before vanishing in the mass of his dirty beard. 'Submission can take many forms,' he said quietly.

Even with the fire, Jezebel felt chilled, and in spite of herself she glanced at Obadiah, who was watching her intently, his lips parted a fraction.

Jezebel swallowed down the taste of bile that rose in her throat. 'Is it money you want?' she made herself ask. 'Ahab would pay for peace.'

Elijah stood before her now, his fetid stench soaking the air between them.

'And how much would *you* pay for this peace?' he asked.

Before she could answer, he raised a grimy hand, dragging his fingers across her lips.

Jezebel smacked his hand away, ducking out of his reach, and lurching past Obadiah back towards the daylight. Elijah's mocking laughter chased her through the cave and the soldiers jeered as she ran past them, her skirts tangling in her legs. The horse was whinnying at the entrance, and it darted towards her outstretched hands as she grabbed the scraps of harness and hauled herself up into the saddle. She kicked hard and they galloped away, glad of the sharp morning breeze to blow the dreadful smell of the caves from her skin and her clothes.

But all she could think, as she rode away, was that she had failed.

Failed her Gods, failed her people. And failed herself.

Chapter Twenty-Four

She couldn't reach the city before the processions of priests left for the challenge at the southern end of the Carmel mountains, so the only way to stop the challenge going ahead was to try to talk Amos out of participating. Daniel and Beset had pleaded with her not to return alone but Jezebel was insistent: they should ride along the mountain range and wait for her there. Either way she would join them at Carmel.

We can always go home to Tyre, she rehearsed in her head, breathless from the hard ride. Her father would know they had done what they could. Tyre had given Israel grain and the King his sons. If Leah could leave, then so could she.

Convincing Amos wouldn't be easy and her heart sank as she spied the dark smudge on the horizon heading north from Samaria. As she drew closer she could see two distinct groups, one fat and long of Israelite priests and many people from the city, the other a tiny cluster of her own priests, their white robes sparkling against the dusty land. Each group led a bullock, its horns tethered with chains, and horse-drawn wagons followed, piled high with wood.

But as she scanned the processions for the royal party, she realised Ahab was nowhere to be seen. 'They're deciding the future of your kingdom,' she muttered, 'yet you let them do it behind your back.'

There was some distance between the two processions and Jezebel rode ahead of them, then dismounted to wait for the Phoenicians. Amos bowed respectfully to the woman who waited with her horse by the roadside, not realising it was Jezebel until she spoke.

He stared at her in disbelief. 'I thought you had stayed in the Palace with the King.'

'How could you think such a thing of me?' she began, but Amos stayed her words with his hand on her arm.

'I was thinking of your safety,' he said, 'not that you would abandon us.'

'Then you know why I am begging you to turn back,' she said desperately. 'Please, Amos. If you fear for me, then you must fear for yourselves. I can't bear to see you hurt.'

'Baal will answer our prayers, Jezebel. Look to the west, see how he already musters his clouds above the sea for us.'

Jezebel grabbed his arms. 'There are dark forces at work here,' she said, 'forces that don't accede to the will of our Gods.'

'Do not abandon your faith,' said Amos gently, 'for that is what we are fighting for.'

'I don't want to fight,' cried Jezebel. 'I don't want to bring on a war just because Elijah calls for one.'

'Then trust your Gods,' said Amos. 'Let Baal decide the fate of all of us.'

He kissed his fingers and pressed them to her forehead, then he rejoined the group.

Every man, woman and child from miles around seemed to have made the pilgrimage up the slopes of the Carmel mountains. They stood in tight groups, robes and shawls pulled around them against the wind that swirled across the plateau. It whipped at Elijah's hair as he stood before them on a pile of rocks, two great heaps of wood stacked to either side, several cart lengths apart.

'Behold!' he cried. 'The sacrifice!'

Jezebel waited, anonymous among the crowd, her heart thundering within her. To the west the sea had lost its glint beneath the rolling grey clouds, and to the east the Kishon River ran in a flat dull line beyond the mountains.

Enosh and Salah led the Israelite priests in a roar of approval as Elijah drew a short knife from a sheath at his hip and clambered down from his platform. Jezebel didn't need to peer through the crowd to see what he was doing, for a dreadful shriek rose up from the bullock beside the pyre on the right as he cut its throat. The other bullock reared and squealed in fear at the fate of its companion, and Amos quickly put it out of its misery. Jezebel felt Beset slide her hand into the crook of her elbow. Her head throbbed, and she felt dreadfully weary in the face of this fervour that couldn't be stifled.

The bullocks were dragged up onto the pyres with ropes, their blood staining the wood, then Enosh and Salah climbed up onto their pyre too, large jars in their hands. Their feet were bare, Jezebel noticed, as they would have been in the Temple.

'Wet wood can only be lit by the hand of God,' shouted Elijah to the crowd. 'Entreat your Gods to do the same,' he shouted to Amos, as Salah and Enosh began pouring water onto the pyres. Jar after jar was passed up to them, and Jezebel watched as Amos and two of the youngest of her priests struggled to climb their own pyre, their robes caught in their feet, emptying as many jars over the bullock and the wood. Their robes became stained with the blood but still they poured water until Elijah climbed back onto his platform.

'Now call down your Gods!' he cried to Amos. 'Tell them to light your pyre.'

A sharp gust of wind blew across the plateau and Jezebel shivered. Out to the west the clouds grew darker and a blood-curdling shriek went up from the Phoenician priests. Jezebel glanced across at Daniel and saw his lips moving in echo of the ritual prayers called out by their priests. Jezebel moved with Beset through the crowd to get a closer look, though many around her were fascinated too by what must have been strange, foreign songs. Some even clapped in time with the intense rhythms of the divine summons, for its beat was infectious and mesmerising, but others laughed and turned away, wondering why they must wait for so long for the true spectacle to begin.

Soon Amos's feet were bleeding from dancing on rocks and stones instead of the smooth marble floors of the Temple, but still he chanted on, his gaze reaching ever further into the skies. But the clouds rolled no nearer and the air did not grow taut with the promise of fire as it might do on a hot summer evening. Jezebel shrank a little deeper into her robes. She added her own prayers to the priests', but felt the wind snatch them away like worthless things. As though Daniel could read her mind, he rested his hand very briefly on her arm, and she saw a terrible, desperate look in his eye. Late morning dragged into afternoon, but still Amos and the priests cried out, their voices growing hoarser and their pleas more shrill. Jezebel stood and watched, and surely Elijah now noticed her among the crowd for she was one of very few who didn't boo and catcall at the failure of her Gods to impress.

With a groan, Amos collapsed in a heap beside the pyre and the other priests staggered in their tracks, falling against each other, bewildered at being abandoned by both their God and their leader. Daniel pushed through the crowd to tend to his uncle, while Elijah rose slowly from where he had been sitting before his own unlit pyre.

'Do you surrender?' he demanded.

But the other Phoenician priests could only mumble at each other and look frantically at Daniel, as though he might now guide them.

'Surely you can see my uncle is sick,' he shouted.

'Then why do his Gods not heal him? Because they know Yahweh is the true God!' cried Elijah, driving his staff hard into the ground.

There was a sudden deafening crack from above and the ground seemed to shake beneath their feet. But it was the clouds that heaved apart in a single blinding flash, lighting up every face that gasped and stared into the sky. A great bolt of lightning struck Elijah's pyre as though a silver sword plunged deep into the heart of the land. People screamed as the wood ignited, flames surging up around the carcass of the bullock, and Jezebel shuddered as though Elijah's staff had thrust right through her.

'Behold your God!' bellowed Elijah.

But he looked not at the Phoenician priests but at Jezebel, and though her face stung with the shimmering heat of the pyre, her heart turned ice cold. Beset's fingers dug hard into her arm but she could not break his gaze.

A great roar flooded through the crowd around her, many falling to their knees, others reaching for the sky and calling for another strike of lightning. The Phoenician priests who had clustered around Amos were staring in awe at the flaming pyre, but their lips soon began to move once more in the chants to Baal, their faith revived by Elijah's apparent success.

'Are you all right?' Beset was whispering to her, tugging on her arm, but Jezebel was slow to look at her maid, as though struck too dumb to think. A great wind was swirling up again around them and she felt her scarf whipping against her face, as though Baal was trying to wake her up. She glanced at the sky.

It's just a coincidence, Jezebel told herself. *The clouds were gathering for a long time. If Amos had not fallen when he did then the lightning could easily have struck at his call—*

'Beg Him to forgive you!' cried Elijah over the chaotic din of people wailing, praying and crying, and the deafening crackle of the burning pyre.

With a second deafening crack from above, rain cascaded down on the mountain as though some celestial river had burst its banks and fallen to earth. Below, the plains were turning dark beneath the downpour and the air swelled with the choking smell of wet earth. The pyre fizzed and sizzled but still it burned and Elijah climbed back onto his platform, his hair plastered to his face in grey ribbons, his robe sodden against his bony shoulders.

'Do you and your kind submit to Yahweh?' he demanded of Amos, who still lay where he had fallen.

'Truly the skies open,' cried out Amos, 'for Baal has given this land the water it needs!'

'Will you submit to the one true God?' demanded Elijah again.

'We will not!'

'Then meet Him in repentance!' Elijah raised his staff and a great holler rose up around the plateau as his army of giant guards suddenly swarmed through the crowd towards the Phoenician pyre, their swords raised high. Jezebel recognised faces from the caves, their lechery and boredom turned into vicious masks as they barged towards Jezebel's priests, surrounding them quickly, their huge bodies shielding the Phoenicians from view.

'Daniel!' shrieked Beset, burying her face in Jezebel's shoulder, but her voice was lost in the roar of the crowd around them, the roar of bloodlust.

Jezebel was rooted to the spot, frozen by her own powerlessness. Elijah was far beyond reason, the soldiers too strong to overpower, the crowd too big to command even if she had the courage to climb Elijah's pyre and reveal herself as their queen. A great cry rose up from the soldiers as they set about their enemies with flashing blades. The crowd fell quiet, their jeering fractured by the dreadful grunts of the soldiers as they threw home their blows. And then, as the ground turned red with the blood of the priests, running freely across the stones, the crowd began screaming, falling back around her in panic, their arms flailing, striking her as they ran past her.

'We must go!' cried Beset in Jezebel's ear. 'They will kill you if they find out you are here!'

'But Daniel is with Amos,' shouted Jezebel, shaking off her maid's tugging hand. 'Save yourself! Follow the others down the mountain and get back to Samaria.'

'I can't leave you!'

'You must! Go!' Jezebel shoved her maid into the crowd and watched as she was carried away by the great tide of panicking worshippers that was now flowing down the side of the mountain, slipping in the rain, their feet red with the blood of the priests. Beset looked petrified as the crowd sucked her in but Jezebel soon lost her in the mêlée.

Carry her to safety, she begged Astarte as she scrambled across the slippery rocks to where Enosh and Salah stood at the head of their priestly cadre, their backs turned on the carnage that was still being inflicted by their soldiers just a short distance away. She pulled the shawl off her head and felt the rain beat into her scalp. Enosh jerked in surprise as he recognised her and even Salah took a step backwards.

'How can you condone this?' she shouted. 'We came here in peace!'

'Yahweh's vengeance is great,' said Salah coldly.

'So this is your sacred right of *herem*,' she spat. 'The victors slaughter the losers!'

'You can still save yourself,' said Enosh, though his eyes betrayed a fear that was not in his voice.

'You would tell the King you had butchered his wife to carry out your rituals?'

170

'He means that the treasures of the defeated become the property of the victors,' said Elijah behind her.

Jezebel turned to face him. 'Call off your animals,' she demanded. 'Or must they drink the blood of their enemies as well?'

'Because you don't hear Yahweh's voice, you do not understand His laws.' Elijah grabbed her wrist and dragged her body against his with staggering strength for such an old man.

Jezebel jerked to free herself but he only pulled her closer, his sodden beard brushing against her mouth. 'The golden treasure of the Phoenician priests becomes mine. And what treasure that is,' he breathed on her face.

'Leave us!' he shouted to his priests, sliding his other hand beneath her hair, his bony fingers gripping her head so that her face was almost touching his. She wriggled to free herself but her feet slid against the wet rock and his grip tightened.

'You would let your prophet defile such a sacred place as this?' she shouted out to the Israelite priests. But they melted away down the mountainside, the army in their wake, and she was left alone with Elijah on the plateau, the rain beating down on them. He looked around swiftly, then wrenched her across the rocks towards an overhang some distance behind the pyres. She screamed and wrestled with him, but his victory had given him unearthly strength, while the sickly stench of death soaked into her sodden skin. Elijah thrust her beneath the overhang, and she fell back on the rocks, struggling to kick him away as he forced himself against her.

'The people have witnessed a great sign,' said Elijah,

yanking at the folds of her robes, crushing her with his weight. 'Word will travel fast and soon you will find there is no one in Israel who will speak up for you. And when you finally submit to me, you will beg for Yahweh to forgive you.'

She felt his manhood grow stiff against her belly and as he tore back his own robe, she realised there was no other way out.

Forgive me, Astarte.

Jezebel gazed into his eyes and let her body go limp, then she slid her hands around his hips as enticingly as she could. But in one swift jerk she snatched his knife from its sheath, grabbing the hilt in her fists and driving it down hard and deep into his groin.

Elijah howled and lurched back, his hands grabbing for the knife but she only drove it in deeper before she pushed herself away and scrabbled to her feet.

'This treasure will never be yours!' she spat at him.

He groaned in agony, his back arched as he pawed at the red stain spreading across his clothing. Jezebel hitched up the saturated folds of her robes and ran across the plateau to the carnage surrounding the Phoenician pyre. The ground was a sickening mass of blood and flesh, some of the bodies so mutilated as to be unrecognisable.

She convulsed in a wrenching twist of retching and sobbing, slapping her hand over her mouth and nose, but her body heaved again and again.

Oh dear Gods. Amos. Daniel.

She looked up at the sky, breathing deeply of the rain as it washed the tears from her eyes. 'Mot has triumphed here today in death, but El will grant eternal life—'

'Jez . . . Jezebel . . .'

She gasped and looked down. Among the severed limbs and shattered bones a figure was moving, long straight hair thick with blood, clothes stained dark red. Jezebel shrieked, but grabbed blindly at the figure, hauling it out of the savagery.

'Daniel?' she sobbed. 'Oh Daniel! I thought I had lost you!'

The physician fell against her, stumbling out of the dreadful carnage, and Jezebel dragged him upright, smearing the rain against his face to clean it, pushing his hair out of his eyes.

'Is Amos—'

Daniel shook his head, swallowing hard. 'I tried to protect him . . . their swords fell fast.'

'But not on you?'

He showed her his arm, and she saw a slice through his sleeve, his blood melded with that of his uncle, but the wound barely longer than her finger.

'Then perhaps Mot didn't want you yet,' murmured Jezebel as she led him as fast as she dared down the slippery mountainside.

Chapter Twenty-Five

Ahab had been sitting on his bed, head in his hands, for a long time. His grey hair fell limply over his shoulders and his eyes were closed. His breath was so shallow Jezebel wondered if he had simply given up the will to live and surrendered himself to death.

Shock deadened the streets of Samaria. When Jezebel first rode with Daniel into the city, she thought Ahab had called a curfew. But, when she eventually found him in his chambers, she realised he was too stunned to think of such things as the safety of his people. She bathed, dried herself, then sat down on the bed next to her husband and waited. He barely acknowledged her presence. Perhaps the stench of blood and death still lingered on her skin.

All of her priests – all those loyal men who had left their homeland to follow their princess – dead.

The candles were burning low when Raisa pulled back the curtain some time later. Jezebel was relieved to see that the Queen Mother had returned safely from Jezreel. Raisa's face was dark with fury and so Jezebel joined her at the doorway, glad that Ahab had not even noticed his mother's presence.

'You should be in bed,' she whispered to Jezebel as she dropped the curtain behind them.

'Do you mean that I should not be at Ahab's side?'

'I think he is beyond helping himself tonight. He is wrestling with his own foolishness, Jezebel. And a man must fight his own pride if he is to admit such a thing.'

'What do you mean?' Jezebel asked.

'I think you know all too well, but are too wise to say it. You must have noticed one man who was absent from the mountain today, for I returned to find him lurking and fretting in the shadows of the Palace, wondering if his plot would bear fruit.'

'Obadiah,' growled Ahab from his room.

Lifting the curtain again, Jezebel and Raisa went to the King.

Ahab lifted his heavy-lidded eyes to Jezebel. 'You told me they were trying to control me. I thought you meant Elijah, Enosh, Salah, the priests.'

'You surround yourself with wise women and yet you ignore us all,' said Raisa. 'But what are you going to do about Obadiah?'

'No,' said Ahab, 'what am I going to do about Jezebel? How will she ever forgive me?'

He looked at his wife, his face riven with self-loathing. 'Everything you brought with you, everything you are has been eroded away by this hateful kingdom, and yet still you stand beside me. I would not have blamed you if you had turned north and gone back to Tyre.'

'I would not have left without saying goodbye to my husband or my children,' she said, remembering how she had thought of escaping. *Was that only this morning?*

'I curse myself for naming my sons and my daughter in praise of Yahweh,' muttered Ahab. 'His prophet has brought darkness to my kingdom and they will carry that burden their whole lives.'

'Nonsense,' said Raisa. 'If they learn to exceed the foolishness of their father, they will grow strong like their mother. But, my dear,' she looked at Jezebel, 'it would be as well for you to stay in the Palace with them for the next few months. Let the city settle. Let them see for themselves that you stand by Israel.'

'It is rumoured Elijah will move deep into the south towards Sinai with his followers,' said Ahab. 'It's better for us all that he stays there, and that you remain where I can be sure you are safe.' He reached for her at last, took her hand in his.

Jezebel wondered if she should tell them of Elijah's attack on her, but something stopped her. Had it really happened as she remembered? With the terrible cries of Amos and her priests, the roar of the soldiers, the heat from the fire and the cold shear of steel on steel . . .

'I should have come to Carmel today,' Ahab said, perhaps sensing the ugly shadow of memory in his wife. 'I should have stopped Elijah before he exacted his revenge on your priests. Instead I stood on the roof of the Palace and watched the sky go black and rain fall as blood on my kingdom. I promise I will never be deaf to your wisdom again.'

'And Obadiah?' asked Raisa. 'Jezebel won't be safe from him in the Palace. He has committed treason and should die for such a serious infraction.'

'Treason to whom though?' said Ahab.

'To his King,' Raisa replied, her tone cold.

'If you have him executed,' said Jezebel, 'then Elijah will seize on it and use it to hurt you further. Exile might be a more politic option.'

Ahab nodded. 'Then let everyone in this kingdom know you alone are responsible for sparing his life. That will haunt him far more than the prospect of his own death.'

And so at dawn the next morning Jezebel stood at the gates of the city, flanked by Ahab's personal guard as he watched her from his chambers above, and gave the formal decree of denunciation. Obadiah, manacled hand and foot, held her gaze while she read out his fate, then she tore his robes of seniority from his back, and snapped his ceremonial staff in two. She held out to him the lower piece of the broken staff, the sign of his betrayal.

'It was you who brought me to Israel,' she murmured. 'How that must sting you now.'

Obadiah set his jaw. 'I should have listened to your father when he told me that Ahab would get more than just a bride,' he said.

'You could have used your diplomatic skills to strengthen this kingdom rather than divide it.' She could feel the weight of Ahab's gaze down from his window, and she pressed the wooden segment into Obadiah's palms. 'May you never know the hospitality of the kingdom of Israel again,' she announced to the gathered crowd as Obadiah shuffled and staggered down the scree of the mountainside, forbidden from using the road as an outcast citizen of the kingdom. 'May her friends shun you and her enemies despise you and may you live out the rest of your life knowing that we will grow stronger without you.'

To herself, she added, *And may I never set eyes on you again.*

Eight years later

860 BC – Queen Consort

Chapter Twenty-Six

Jezebel shifted her weight on Ahab's throne. At least none of the assembled nobles could see how her legs swung beneath the table, too short to reach the ground. Daniel had advised, with a grin, that her own throne could be brought from the banqueting hall in the Jezreel Palace to the Council Chamber for the daily meetings, but Ahab had been insistent: if she were to run the Council in his place, she should sit in his seat. The long cedarwood table was more crowded than usual, for this was the monthly petitionary court, at which the kingdom's landowners gathered to request favours and loans from the Palace at whatever price Jezebel saw fit. The room was heady with the chatter of the murmuring dignitaries and landowners.

Jezebel stared at the papyrus scroll on the table in front of her while Yonah, a nobleman who owned land to the east of Samaria near the River Jordan, put forth his case.

'So,' she said, interrupting him. 'You want five new wells.'

'Yes, Your Highness, as I was saying—'

'And you expect this to increase your overall yield three-fold by the end of next year.'

'Possibly sooner if the wells are dug quickly. A team of

181

engineers are ready and waiting to begin digging, down at the—'

'And you want a loan of five hundred—' Jezebel consulted the scroll again, 'five hundred from the Palace to fund this?'

'Yes, Your Highness.'

'Then I will give you that loan in exchange for a tithe of ten sacks of grain in every hundred for the Samarian silos. You are responsible for delivery. We will recall the loan in three years, by which time your new fields should be well established.' She glanced at Tobiah, one of the Council advisers, who was scratching neat notes on a segment of scroll. He nodded and she slammed the marble gavelstone down in its bowl.

'Next!'

'Thank you, Your Highness,' said Yonah and moved to the far end of the table.

'Who is next?' asked Tobiah.

'I am, Your Highness.'

'Naboth,' said Jezebel, smothering the smile that always sprung to her face when she saw the cheerful nobleman. It was essential not to show favour in the Chamber, even among those nobles whose goods directly supplied either of the Palace households. 'What is your call on the Council?'

'I wish to buy the land adjoining the Palace farm here at Jezreel. Meir, the farmer who owned it, died recently with no direct heirs and by right the land will fall back to the King by the next full moon in two days' time. But I want permission to buy this land to extend my vineyard, at a cost of ten thousand.'

'Ten thousand!' muttered one noble.

'You more or less own the Jezreel plain already,' protested another.

'My lords,' said Tobiah, but the nobles paid no notice.

'Just because you supply the King's favourite vintage you think you make the only good wine in Israel,' grumbled Yonah.

'You have as much right as anyone to buy that land,' said Naboth to the first protester. 'But no one else is offering.'

'Because we cannot afford to.'

'Because we are not as greedy as you,' said someone else.

'Quiet down!' Jezebel banged the gavelstone down. 'You quarrel like my children over the last apricot.'

'With respect, Your Highness, it is far more important than an apricot,' said Yonah, pushing through the nobles to approach the throne again. 'Naboth will own more land in the kingdom than anyone other than the King if you agree to this. That isn't fair, nor is it in the interests of our people.'

'I provide work for more labourers than most of you put together,' said Naboth, 'and I train them well so that they can grow vines of their own. But at least one man around this table uses men to build for him but does not let them live in anything more permanent than a hideskin tent!'

A noble named Achidan pounded his fist onto the table and shot Jezebel a look of pure anger. 'Do you allow such insults to pass in the Council?'

Jezebel stood up. 'I'm calling an adjournment. You fight

183

among yourselves like dogs and you leave me no choice. I will consider Naboth's request and all other petitions still on today's docket, and reply at the next Council in ten days' time.'

'But that will be too late!' cried Naboth.

'What about my petitions?' demanded Achidan.

'I will decide on all petitions by then,' said Jezebel. 'And you would all be advised to attend in a more peaceable frame of mind.'

Tobiah leapt up from his stool and pulled back the throne with the help of Reuel, another of the advisers, and Jezebel swept out into the ante-chamber. Behind her the Chamber erupted into a barrage of shouting among the nobles.

Shortly, Tobiah and Reuel appeared clutching the scrolls.

'I think deferring was the right decision, Your Highness,' said Tobiah, straightening the wide cap he always wore.

'The problem is, they're all right,' said Jezebel, walking on towards her private office. 'Naboth does own more land than everyone but the King himself. Someone has to! He's a generous employer, but his wealth frightens the others.'

'Perhaps he would understand should you turn him down,' said Reuel, his youthful eagerness undimmed by the dull procedure of the Council.

'I will consult the King,' said Jezebel. 'I may sit in his chair but this is still his kingdom.'

'Is he much recovered?' asked Reuel, then reddened as Tobiah sent him a reproachful glare.

Jezebel smiled to show no offence was taken. The truth was that Ahab's illness had come and gone like passing clouds over the previous year, though the current spell had lasted several days. 'It's just better that he is spared the long meetings,' she said. 'They wear me out as it is.'

Reuel dodged ahead and pulled back the curtain to Jezebel's office. A fire was burning well in the hearth and the shelves were full of orderly piles of scrolls and slates. Reuel and Tobiah each had their own desk, and a third desk beneath the window was occupied by Boaz, the oldest and most senior of the advisers. He lived permanently in Jezreel and didn't travel to Samaria in the summer, and Jezebel was secretly most fond of him too, for he remained utterly unruffled by drama and was not affected by Reuel's naïveté or Tobiah's condescension. Ahab had made new appointments after Obadiah's denunciation and these three had become the most trusted of the cadre that now served Jezebel. They complemented each other well: the wise old dog, the sharp mind and the enthusiastic apprentice.

'Have they arrived yet?' asked Jezebel, trying to keep the excitement out of her voice.

'The delegation from Tyre have been sighted from the lookout, Your Highness,' Boaz replied. 'They should be here very shortly.'

Jezebel's heart lifted at the thought of seeing her father and Balazar again. Twelve long years had passed since she came to Israel to marry Ahab and, as befits marriages of alliance, she had never gone back to Tyre, for a daughter once given isn't expected to return. But even her father, she thought with gentle pride, could not have imagined how his daughter would rise to become the effective ruler

185

of their neighbour. With Ahab weakened by his malady and unable to complete a day's duties without retiring to his bed, it had fallen to his wife to run the affairs of the kingdom, and the people had mostly grown to accept the firm but fair hand of their Queen.

'Let's dispatch the remaining business of the day without delay,' she said, settling herself behind her desk. 'What news of Judah?' she asked Boaz.

'A messenger arrived today from King Jehoshaphat acknowledging the arrival of the Israelite troops to aid his border dispute with the Edomites.'

'He was grateful then,' said Jezebel, rolling her eyes.

'I'm sure of it, Your Highness,' said Boaz, inclining his head respectfully.

'And I suppose within a week he will want another troop. Does he send news of how he intends to hold the borderlands? I would rather he didn't actually go to war.'

'I regret not.'

'Very well. We will have to wait for their delegation and see what they have to say. Are they still expected today?'

'More likely tomorrow or the next day.'

'As vague as ever.' She looked at Reuel. 'And what of Ben-Hadad?'

'I meant to tell you before Council,' interrupted Tobiah, 'but there wasn't time. Our representative at court tells us that the Damascan King is extremely ill.'

'That concerns me,' said Jezebel to Boaz. 'We know little of his son, nor whether the new order will honour the old agreements.'

'But they rely greatly on food from Israel and metal

ores through the Phoenician kingdoms. It isn't in their interest to provoke a war.'

'And we wouldn't go into it alone,' said Jezebel.

'At least we hope not,' said Reuel cheerfully.

Tobiah frowned at his irreverence. 'There's a great deal more to diplomacy than you—'

The Herald's trumpet cut off the adviser's words, and Jezebel pushed back her couch. *Father!* 'Gentlemen,' she said. 'I go to meet the Tyrian delegation.'

'Your Highness,' they bowed as one.

Jezebel rushed through the corridors towards the main gate, the fanfares ringing off the stone walls around her. She could hear the horses entering the courtyard and she skittered to a halt in the main hall, pausing to check her hair had not loosed itself from its headdress and straightening her gown.

'Your Highness,' said the guard at the door. 'Shall I open the—'

'Yes, yes,' said Jezebel. 'Let them in!'

The huge oak door swung open and Jezebel tried to adopt a dignified poise to enter the courtyard. Two carriages were pulled up with a dozen or more wagons behind them, and a man was dismounting from a horse, his back to her.

'Father?'

'Good to see you too,' said Balazar, turning towards Jezebel's voice. He had grown quite stocky since she saw him last, his sharp chin softened by a roll of flesh, his lips more ample and his cheeks ruddy and round. His hair was thinner too and had laid a little more of his forehead open to the sun. He looked her over just as she did him, then he grinned and strode across the courtyard. He grabbed his sister and squeezed her tightly. 'You look beautiful,' he said. 'Quite the queen.'

'Good to see you too,' she smiled. 'Is Father in the carriage?'

Balazar's shoulders sagged. 'I'm sorry, Jezebel. He was too sick to travel.'

'He's unwell?'

'Who is unwell?' Jezebel turned to see Daniel and Beset entering the courtyard. 'Does someone in the party need help?' asked the physician.

'We are all fine.' Balazar grasped Daniel's arm, greeting him like an old friend. 'And even Beset still looks beautiful despite the foreign air!' he murmured, leaning towards the maid.

'While my brother has grown fat and happy on too many Tyrian delicacies,' said Jezebel as Beset blushed.

'Is Menes seeing to the King's health?' asked Daniel of his old teacher.

Jezebel sobered, unable to hide her disappointment at her father's absence. 'Is he very ill?'

'So many questions!' said Balazar, his hands flying up. 'Do you not want to see who I *have* brought with me?'

He went to the door of the first carriage and pulled it open, and out stepped Esther, her belly gently swollen beneath a beautiful woollen travelling robe of Tyrian purple. Her hair was dressed in elegant twists and curls, and the awkwardness of her early womanhood had been shed with the securities of motherhood and a confident husband.

'Oh!' cried Jezebel and ran across the courtyard to greet

her, kissing her on both cheeks and hugging her old friend. 'The loveliest sister a woman could have. Your father will be so pleased to see you! What a wonderful surprise for him.'

'I've four more surprises like that one,' said Balazar. 'Our youngest son,' he gestured to a baby Jezebel could now see in a nurse's arms inside the carriage. 'And our three older children,' he waved at the carriage behind and three faces peered out, twin girls and a boy, all of them under five years old. 'They each have two names so I will explain them to you after lunch. For now, they all answer to Children!'

'Yes, Father!' the children cried.

'You see?' said Balazar proudly.

'Mama?'

Jezebel looked round and found her own children clustered in the doorway. Ahaziah looked grown up for his eleven years, his arms folded, his feet spread in a combative stance, and his wooden sword shoved into his belt. Athaliah stood shyly behind him, her dark hair loose on her shoulders, still a little girl for all her ten years. Young Joram was the least interested in the visitors, pushing a wooden horse on the ground and making neighing sounds.

'Here are your cousins,' said Jezebel, 'and your uncle Balazar. And you remember Esther, Ahaziah.' She looked at her dear friend. 'Our family has grown complicated, has it not? My husband's first daughter now my sister!' She sighed. 'But I do wish Father were here too.'

'He regrets not making the trip,' Balazar said. 'Has the Judean delegation arrived?'

189

'Not yet,' said Jezebel. 'There'll be time for business later.'

'I need to speak with Ahab in private,' said Balazar.

'I handle the kingdom's affairs now,' said Jezebel. 'I'm sure my last message to Father made that very clear.'

'But I must speak to your husband.'

'Then you will have to wait,' she said, fighting to keep her smile pasted on. 'He sees visitors in the early evening before dinner. And I'm sure that Esther and the children will be more welcome than the prospect of diplomatic demands.'

'I'm not an entirely ungrateful guest,' said Balazar, seeing that he needed to lighten the mood. 'I've brought you bolts of silk and jars of the best olive oil, and a jar of the best Tyrian honey just for you. I haven't just come to do business.'

'Judging by the size of you,' said Jezebel, regaining her smile, 'you have only come to be fed.'

Chapter Twenty-Seven

But that afternoon, Balazar insisted on a private audience with Boaz, Tobiah and Reuel, and Jezebel found herself relegated to duties of hospitality. It was no hardship, though, to guide Esther round the gardens at Jezreel, introducing her to all the exotic animals that had been captured and given to the King as gifts: a lion from Sinai, a crocodile from the southern reaches of the River Jordan, and monkeys from Egypt. And in Raisa's company too, there was much to laugh about. The Queen Mother now walked with the help of a gold-embossed stick, but she was far more sprightly than her son and drew great energy from her younger companions.

'If only your mother had proved as fertile as you,' said Raisa as they studied the colourful fish in the water gardens, 'she might have been less unhappy here. I regret her misery.'

'She missed Judah,' said Esther with a surprising frankness. 'But no one was to blame for that.'

Across the orchards, Ahaziah ran, pulling Esther's three older children in a row behind him, laughing as they went.

'It is wonderful to hear the Palace full of the laughter of children,' said Jezebel.

'That is what these palaces were built for,' said Raisa. 'But until you and Esther began to have children of your own they were prisons.' She reached for Esther's cheek and caressed it. 'I hope you too weren't unhappy here.'

Esther took Raisa's hand and kissed the back of it. 'What I learned here has given me the courage to become a princess of Tyre. I hope I've done you both proud.'

'Oh nonsense,' said Jezebel. 'Balazar is lucky to have you for a wife and I shall make sure he knows it. Your marriage and these wonderful children are one of the few good things to come out of those dreadful years of drought. If my father had not seen fit to help us with grain—'

'Or to accept the gift of a beautiful girl for a daughter-in-law in return,' added Raisa.

Jezebel nodded and smiled, but she was unwilling to finish her thought aloud, for she was sure they no more wished to mention Elijah than she did. A cool was settling on the garden and she looked up at the sky, dotted with clouds, the sun already halfway down. 'It will turn cold as the sun goes down. We should go in.'

She linked her arms with the other women and they set off for the Palace. 'I think Balazar has grown very plump on your contentment,' she said to Esther as they passed through the courtyard and turned the corner. 'I don't want to watch when he climbs back on that horse— Oh!'

Jezebel stopped. Ahead of them in a doorway stood

Daniel and Esther's nurse, their arms entwined, kissing deeply.

Raisa gave a soft snort of amusement, and they broke apart, pressing themselves against opposite sides of the arch.

'What are you doing here?' Jezebel said. 'The King needs your attention, Daniel. And what about the baby in your charge?' she snapped at the nurse. 'Have you entirely abandoned your responsibilities?'

Daniel moved swiftly into the Palace, his face flaming with embarrassment. The nurse curtseyed.

'Go on your way,' said Esther gently. The nurse obeyed and scuttled off too.

'It's all right,' said Esther to Jezebel. 'Baby Hiram always sleeps in the afternoon, and one of the maids will be looking after him.'

'That isn't the point,' said Jezebel, for some reason blushing herself.

'No,' said Raisa with amusement, 'that isn't the point at all.'

There was an awkward silence, then Esther said, 'Don't you remember what it was like to be young and in love? You forget yourself and everything seems wonderfully strange.'

'That was a long time ago,' said Jezebel, rather more brusquely than she intended. Indeed memories of Jehu had grown thin and distant and she had never felt that intoxicating desire for Ahab that Daniel had shown just now. She distracted herself by helping Raisa up a step into the Palace.

'Besides, I always thought Daniel was rather handsome,'

said Esther shyly as she walked down the corridor ahead of them, 'and I'm not entirely surprised that other girls think so too.'

'I can't see it myself,' said Jezebel.

Raisa tugged on her arm and rolled her eyes. 'If that is true, then I'm Queen of Egypt!'

Chapter Twenty-Eight

'Come away from the window,' said Beset. 'You will catch your death.'

Jezebel gazed out across the shadowy contours of Jezreel towards the setting sun, her silk bathing robe fluttering in the cooling breeze. The faint sounds of Esther's children laughing with her own echoed through the Palace, and a huge bundle of dried lavender stems brought from Tyre sat in a fat bouquet before Astarte's shrine, sweetly scenting the room. There was great peace in this part of the day, after the business of the court and the Palace, and before she donned the gown and jewellery for the formal demands of dinners and banquets. She'd grown accustomed to the weight of it all, but sometimes she wondered for whom she was dressing these days, when she mostly ate alone with Ahab, increasingly at his bedside.

To the west, the city trumpeter gave three fast high notes and one long low one, the dusk call to warn the citizens of Jezreel and those on the mountain path that the gate would soon be closing for the night.

'I cannot dress you if you don't tell me what you want to wear,' said Beset.

'I don't care, it's only family, anything will . . .' She tailed off, her attention snagged by a second trumpet call, the Herald Welcome. She frowned, listening as it was repeated. 'Perhaps that is the Judeans,' she said to Beset. 'Could you dispatch Reuel to meet them? I'd given up the idea of them arriving today at all.'

'Only if you promise to choose something to wear before I get back,' said Beset as she left the room.

Jezebel pushed back the shutters and waited. Soon a horse came trotting from the gates along the street beneath the window, its rider dirty from the ride. She leant out. The lone figure looked up at the high walls of the Palace and Jezebel's breath caught in her throat.

'Jehu,' she murmured.

He smiled, his eyes bright amid his filthy face, taking in the way her hair fell loose over her shoulders, the tight wrap of her bathing gown across her breasts.

Jezebel's heart jumped, but her voice had dried and she couldn't speak. How was it that the sight of him still made her tremble after all this time?

'Jehu of Judah,' Reuel's voice piped up from the other end of the street, 'may I bid you welcome to Jezreel.' The young man ran down the street, his skirts flapping against his knees, half-bowing as he went. Jehu turned the horse and glanced up at the window as he did so. But Jezebel stepped back out of sight before her adviser could see her and she sat down on the couch, weak at the knees.

A one-man delegation from Judah again, thought Jezebel. Perhaps the King and his brother were engaged with the border dispute. *Or perhaps they think so little of*

196

Israel now, that the second son is all we deserve. That would be humiliating for Jehu. *Or perhaps . . .*

She picked up her old bronze mirror and ran her fingers over the engraving. Europa was still dancing through the waves, one hand on the horns of the bull who loved her so much that he abducted her rather than live without her.

Or perhaps he chose to come here himself.

She laid down the mirror on the couch and went to the chest in which her clothes were stored, selecting the most elaborate of her dresses and the most jewelled of her headdresses. At least Beset would be pleased she had made a decision.

Jezebel was late to the banquet and she found Daniel in the ante-room, mixing powders in a drinking bowl. Normally she would have peered over his shoulder to see what he was doing, but instead of his usual welcoming smile he glanced away as soon as he saw it was her.

'I apologise for interrupting you,' she said coolly. 'Is the King feeling unwell again?'

Daniel didn't look up, but she could see his cheeks burning in the lamplight. 'He has a headache.'

'He seems to have a headache every day now,' said Jezebel, cross with Daniel for being so formal and with herself for minding.

'He does.'

'Is it a permanent feature of his illness?'

'Possibly.'

'Your Highness,' said Zebulon, Chief Steward of the Palace, entering from the banqueting hall. 'Your guests from Tyre are already seated, and the Prince of Judah is expected shortly.'

'See to the King with special care this evening,' said Jezebel. 'I know that he wants to be with his daughter but these formal affairs drag on and I don't want him getting overly tired.'

Zebulon bowed and retreated to the hall, and Daniel turned to follow him, the bowl of medicine in his hand.

'Daniel,' said Jezebel, sounding more desperate than she would have liked. He stopped, his back still to her. 'About earlier . . .' she began, feeling for an apology in the hope it might clear the air.

Daniel spoke without turning. 'Her name is Hemen. She isn't only Esther's nurse but also a friend of my sister, we knew each other long ago in Tyre.' He hesitated. 'We liked each other once—'

'You can be friends with whomsoever you choose,' she said, striding past him. 'I would just prefer not to stumble across your *friendship* in the Palace gardens.'

She walked into the banqueting hall towards her couch at the far end. Balazar and Esther were already seated on one side, Esther close to her father, her attention fixed on him. Ahab was dressed in a white tunic underneath his old silver threaded robe, but he had grown so thin it sat loosely on his shoulders. His hair had grown so fine and white, his beard wispy, and his eyes seemed cloudy, even in the sparkling lamplight. As she strode down the room, Jezebel found herself almost embarrassed at how the table glistened and groaned with food and gold tableware, when her husband was so frail and distracted.

If Jehu weren't here, we could have done this informally in his room, she thought guiltily as Daniel knelt by the King's side with his bowl of medicine.

She settled on her couch just as Jehu pushed back the curtains. He had bathed and put on clean clothes, but his skin had grown darker than ever from years of riding in the hot desert sun. While all others seemed to wane around her – Ahab, Balazar, Raisa, even Beset – Jehu seemed unchanged, like the stars in the night sky. He stood in the doorway, drinking in the sight of her until she felt compelled to gesture to the table in order to break his powerful gaze.

Zebulon made to pull out the empty couch opposite Balazar but Jehu simply straddled it and sat down, planting his elbows on the table.

'Welcome to Israel,' grinned Balazar. Jezebel flinched at her brother's gauche informality. It should have been Ahab who greeted the guest. 'I hope you're hungry,' Balazar continued, draining his bowl in a gulp, and reaching for the jug beside his plate. 'I made a start on the wine. You should try some.'

Zebulon placed a jug beside Jehu's plate then poured a bowl for Jezebel.

'Welcome to Jezreel,' said Ahab from the other end of the table, coughing as Daniel took away the medicine.

Jehu jerked to his left, apparently caught unawares by the presence of the King. He half stood, knocking the plates at his place, and gave a stiff bow. 'Your Highness,' he muttered.

'There, Father,' said Esther offering her father a plate of food. 'Try to eat this. You are too thin for my liking.'

'You remember my wife, I'm sure,' said Balazar to Jehu. 'Your cousin, I believe?'

'Tyre has been blessed,' said Jehu.

'Still got that lovely black stallion of yours?' asked Balazar, grabbing a leg of meat and carving from it onto his plate. 'Marvellous beast.'

'I rode him here,' said Jehu. 'My father wanted to take him to the Edom border but I stole him away before he could.'

'Sounds like something Jezebel would do,' said Balazar, stuffing his mouth with fatty flesh. 'Stud?' he asked, chewing. 'The horse, obviously, not Jezebel.'

'Balazar,' Jezebel frowned at her brother's lewdness.

She felt Jehu's eyes on her but when she turned to meet his gaze he looked away and tore at a flatbread. 'The horse's line has been ensured,' he said. 'I'm rearing four colts and a mare in our stables.'

'Then your enjoyment of riding is assured for years to come,' said Jezebel, anxious not to be excluded from the conversation. She turned to Balazar. 'I hadn't realised Tyre kept such good relations with Judah since the death of King Asa.'

'Old Jehoshaphat isn't so bad once you get to know him,' winked Balazar, draining his wine cup again. 'Especially when he sends a wise emissary such as his son Jehu to do the listening. But he can't seem to get on with the Edomites, can he?'

Jezebel looked at Jehu expecting an answer, but again she only fleetingly caught his eye before it turned away. 'I think,' she said, hoping he would look at her properly, 'that the Edomites are nervous at the recent incursions by bandits from the tribal area to the south.'

'Small fry,' muttered Jehu, reaching across the table to spear a chicken with a knife from his belt.

'Then why does your father fear them so much?'

'Who said he feared them?' Jehu tore meat from the breast with his fingers.

'He certainly feels threatened by them if he asks for troops from us.'

'The Edomites are blocking trade from the Red Sea through Eilat and into Judah, and the Arabu tribal leaders are helping them do it. By the way,' said Jehu, looking up at Balazar, 'your father will want to know that his assessment of the price of grain from the southern lands was exactly right.'

'My father is a very experienced trader,' said Jezebel. Jehu just picked up his wine bowl and buried his face in it.

'What of the kingdom of Aram-Damascus?' asked Ahab weakly from the other end of the table.

Jehu lowered his bowl and gave a half nod to the King. 'Ben-Hadad has died. A messenger intercepted me today as I rode along the river.'

'He was not old,' said Ahab, rather wistfully.

'How did he die? Choking on the breast of an Aramean maiden?' Balazar laughed.

'I think Esther has the weaker end of the bargain in your marriage,' observed Jezebel.

But Balazar waved his hand. 'My skills as a diplomat—'

'Diplomat!' scoffed Jezebel.

'Very well, my skills as a negotiator are entirely true to generations of Tyrians before me. Know your opponent's weaknesses as well as his strengths, know what brings a smile to his face as well as down on his knees. Ben-Hadad was always much more easily persuaded when he had spent the night surrounded by young women of biddable dispositions.'

'At least there is no doubt in the succession,' said Jehu.

'His son Ben-Hadad takes the throne?' asked Ahab, rubbing at his forehead.

'It seems likely.'

'And what of him?'

'He has developed an aggressive reputation,' said Jezebel to her husband. 'I understand he saw his father's negotiated settlement with you over Gilead as unforgivable weakness. I doubt we'll be as lucky if the situation occurs again.'

'Then let us pray it doesn't.'

'Praying may not help you,' said Jehu. 'Ben-Hadad may have Yahweh on his side.'

Jezebel shivered and lowered the date she was eating to her plate. Ahab's eyes had grown sharp in his pallid face and Esther was looking at Jezebel with pure fear in her expression. 'That is a familiar phrase,' she said.

'Elijah has been seen near the city of Damascus,' said Jehu.

'That's a long way from Sinai,' said Jezebel to Ahab.

'We couldn't have expected him to stay in one place for long,' said her husband. 'He needs allies, he must move around—'

'Because no sensible person will give a home to such an agitator,' concluded Jezebel. 'He cannot have very many followers, because in numbers they would draw attention to themselves. Besides, Ben-Hadad the son will be wary of sharing his new-gained power with a prophet. He'll keep Elijah in check, I'm sure.'

'I'm glad to see you still say things as you see them,'

said Balazar, raising his drinking bowl to his sister in toast. 'She has a clear line of sight,' he added to Jehu.

'I think her view may be clouded by the arrogance of power,' replied the Judean.

'I beg your pardon?' said Jezebel.

'Ignoring Elijah's influence is foolish.'

'He is a troublemaker.'

'He strikes with Yahweh's hand.'

Jezebel held his gaze in hers, daring him to speak of the mountaintop at Carmel. But when he said nothing, she said, 'He manipulates people's basic fears for their lives and their deaths while doing nothing to improve their lot in either respect.'

'Those who follow Yahweh will find they're taken care of according to His will.'

'Elijah isn't a leader, he doesn't build nations or rule them with compassion and intelligence, he merely races from mountain to plain, writing his own myths—'

A wine bowl smashed on the floor.

'Father!' cried Esther.

Ahab was slumped in his chair, one side of his face sagging, his arm dangling limply.

Jezebel ran to his side. 'Zebulon! Get Daniel, and bring one of the flat couches in from the Council Chamber so the King can lie down. We will need men to carry him upstairs too.' She crouched beside him, cradling his distorted features in one hand, desperate to hear the sound of breath passing his grey lips.

Daniel came running in and dropped to his knees on the other side of Ahab. 'Did you notice any other signs?'

Jezebel shrugged, guilty for how absorbed she had been in her disagreement with Jehu.

'He kept rubbing his forehead,' said Esther. 'He had trouble putting food in his mouth so I thought he wasn't hungry.'

Daniel pressed his fingers against the King's neck. 'He is very weak. We must get him to bed. Quickly now,' he said to the servants who were hovering in the doorway with a couch.

Jezebel stood back while Daniel oversaw the King's safe passage out of the banqueting hall, and she slipped her hand around Esther's shoulder. 'Go and be with him. I will come by in a little while.'

Esther touched her swollen belly with shaking hands. 'We were going to call this baby Ahab.'

'My dearest love, your father isn't dead yet,' said Balazar, wrapping his arm around his wife's waist. His eyes were a little unfocused from the wine but he had sobered his mood.

Jezebel watched as Esther walked beside the couch, her father's limp hand in her own, Balazar cradling her.

'I apologise,' she said, turning back into the banqueting hall. 'Ahab has been unwell for some—'

But Jehu had gone and the hall was empty.

Jezebel rested her hands on Ahab's chair for a moment, seeking some residue of her husband's warmth in the cushions. But the chair was cold as if he had never sat there.

Chapter Twenty-Nine

Boaz thrust open the Council Chamber doors.

'My Lords, the Queen Consort. Rise up!'

Reuel and Tobiah, smart in their robes and caps, entered ahead of her bearing their ebony boxes of scrolls, and Jezebel followed them through the Council Chamber to Ahab's throne. The Chamber was packed with noblemen, even more than it had been for the petitionary court the previous day. Jezebel felt the hair stand up on the back of her neck, beneath the high collar of the Queen Consort gown that Raisa had given her when Ahaziah was born. The gown was heavy, with wide stiff sleeves that made it impossible to sit in any position other than upright on the throne. But this was to be an extraordinary Council of Nobles to discuss whatever issues Jehu had brought from Judah and her brother from Tyre, and she hadn't even considered dressing more comfortably. Jehu's blatant warnings over Elijah last night had kept her awake, not out of trepidation but out of anger at how readily he still sided with the so-called prophet. She had risen this morning with a determination to show her former lover that she ruled Israel with not just her own confidence but that of Ahab too.

Her husband had sensed that resolve for himself when she visited him in his chambers shortly before the meeting.

'Don't let Jehu rile you, Jezebel,' he had mumbled, his face still slack and deformed. 'He knows his own mind but it's Jehoshaphat who holds the throne of Judah.'

'Don't worry yourself,' Jezebel had said, kissing him on the forehead. 'Just enjoy Esther and your grandchildren being here, and concentrate on getting well. I'll take care of matters in the Council.'

But as Jezebel reached the front of the Chamber she found that Jehu still sat on his couch, ignoring Boaz's proclamation of respect, and she noticed Balazar grinning without restraint – her brother seemed to be anticipating the meeting with some glee. He gave a florid bow, waving his arms wildly, but as soon as Jezebel sat on the throne, Jehu leapt up from his seat and strode away from the table.

'Do you decline the audience of the Israelite nobles?' said Jezebel. Jehu stopped but he didn't turn round. 'It was a long way to ride if you no longer need their help.'

'I came to speak to Ahab,' said Jehu, 'not to his wife.'

'I speak for the King of Israel and have done so for a long time.'

'And surely you remember how clever she is,' added Balazar, settling himself on his couch before any of the nobles had sat down. 'Even our father says so, and you know he is no fool.'

Jezebel shot him an irritated look – couldn't he take anything seriously? – then turned back to Jehu.

'Please, Jehu, accept the audience of the nobles. If there are matters you feel I haven't resolved to your satisfaction, then perhaps if Ahab feels better tomorrow he may be able to see you. But you will find that I run the Council fairly for all who come to it, and the presence of so many of Israel's noblemen is a sign of their confidence in me.'

'Well said,' declared Balazar.

Jezebel held back a second furious glance at her brother as Jehu silently took his place at the table again. After the other nobles seated themselves, Jezebel glanced at Boaz who gave her an almost imperceptible nod of approval as he laid down the gavelstone before her. Tobiah coughed discreetly, wetting his reed pen in the ink, and Reuel smiled his encouragement.

'Your Highness, if I could just have a word before we begin?' Jezebel turned to find Naboth standing beside the throne, leaning over her. His face was flushed and taut with worry. 'The full moon is tomorrow and Meir's land, the land I wish to buy for my vineyard, falls into the King's estate.'

'I said I would give my decision in nine more days.'

'But it will be too late, the right of purchase—'

'The land will still be there,' said Jezebel, 'but this is neither the time nor the place to discuss it. This is a diplomatic Council, not a petitionary one. Please accord our guests from Judah and Tyre the respect due to them by not confusing political and financial gains.'

'But Your Highness . . .' Naboth dropped clumsily to his knees, grabbing the arm of the throne and catching his ring on the sleeve of the Consort gown. It tore the cloth, scattering a spray of pearls that rang against the stone floor. Naboth gasped in horror and tumbled back on his heels. 'Your Highness, forgive me!'

'You've torn the gown of office,' said the noble Achidan,

207

who sat on the other side of Jehu. 'Was it not enough to blunder through the Council seeking favours you are not entitled to?'

'It can be mended,' said Jezebel.

'The significance should not be overlooked,' said Tobiah quietly from beside her. 'It is the gown of office and marks your status in the kingdom, especially before our visitors.'

'I think our visitors are quite clear about my status,' said Jezebel, irritated by Tobiah's patronising tone.

'I will pay for the restoration of the gown,' said Naboth. His face had drained of colour.

'Please return to your seat,' said Jezebel.

'Money won't help you now,' said Achidan amid the murmuring of his peers. 'You have shown disrespect to the throne.'

Naboth lurched forward and clung to her arm, bringing a gasp from the room. 'Please, Your Highness—' he began, but two guards swooped down on him and hauled him away. 'Unhand me!' he cried. 'I'm no assassin!'

The other noblemen began a chorus of ugly jeers as the doors closed on Naboth's cries. Jezebel grabbed the gavel-stone and slammed it down. The Chamber fell quiet. 'It was clearly an accident. Now, please, let us get on with business. Boaz, open the session.'

'Jehu of Judah, do you request the audience of the Council of Nobles?'

Jehu gave a dismissive wave. 'As you wish. I've no need for such ceremony. It only leads to unnecessary tension.' He rocked forward on his couch and pointed at Balazar. 'The kingdom of Tyre and the kingdom of Judah are in agreement that the death of Ben-Hadad of Aram-Damascus now puts our three kingdoms under threat. Ben-Hadad the son is known to be an aggressor but, despite that, Aram-Damascus is a weak state. The succession won't be popular among his father's supporters and the kingdom is bound to become unstable while the new king establishes his rule and wins over the army.'

'It is the perfect time to strike,' said Balazar.

'You want to go to *war*?' said Jezebel. She wondered how long he and Jehu had been in communication. Until that moment, she'd thought of her brother as a petty nuisance, trying his best to make up for years of their father's disapproval. Now she saw he might really be trying to undermine her. And for what – to play at being a general?

'We should take advantage of the Damascan army commanders' anxiety about the succession and take them by surprise,' said Jehu. 'That stretch of plain on the other side of the River Jordan is absolutely crucial for the safety of the King's Highway, the passage of river traffic, and the fertile lands you farm there. Judah cannot afford for that region to fall into Ben-Hadad's hands.'

'And there is also the matter of the neighbouring Kingdom of Ammon,' said Balazar. 'They're virtually a vassal state to Aram-Damascus, their King is a puppet who did exactly as Ben-Hadad the father told him to, and if I were Ben-Hadad the son I would march straight into Ammon and claim the entire territory as my own before my crown was on.'

'Aram-Damascus can't be permitted to extend to the south,' agreed Jehu. 'If they then make an alliance with the Moabites the entire Gilead plain will be encircled by our enemies, and before we know it you will lose the land, and half the length of the river will be under their control.'

'I don't need a lecture on the strategic importance of Ammon,' said Jezebel. 'But Israel has kept deliberately peaceful and mutually advantageous relations with the Ammonites for many years now. They cross the plain to use the River, and farmers along the border trade goods with each other, goods that find their way to Jezreel, Samaria, and even to Jerusalem.' She sat back in the throne, trying to ignore the way the torn sleeve of the gown flapped at her wrist. 'If I may be so bold, our two royal visitors seem intent on war.'

Jehu and Balazar exchanged a glance across the table. 'If we miss this opportunity,' said Jehu, 'we will always regret it.'

'I would point out that you refer to "we",' said Jezebel. 'And therein lies our strength. But war is expensive. Not only am I unwilling to divert money from improving our water systems towards a war we are not certain to win, but then if we do win the war, we will need a great deal of money to secure Aram-Damascus permanently.'

Jehu leant forward. 'With the three nations fighting together—'

'And furthermore,' said Jezebel, 'with a concerted and collective effort of negotiation and diplomacy rather than combat, plus some thought about how to manage Damascan access to the Great Sea across the border between Israel and Phoenicia, we can show Ben-Hadad that it isn't in his interests to invade Israel, nor to threaten Phoenicia and Judah. He cannot possibly control the amount of land it would require for him to do so, no matter how aggressive he feels towards us. Finally, if he sees all three kingdoms acting together in diplomacy, he will know we *would* act together in war. Even coercing the Ammonite army to help him, he could never hope to win.'

'She has a point,' said Balazar.

Jezebel sat forward. 'I invite responses from the Council.'

'Despite my commercial interest in a war,' said a noble named Ido, whose tannery supplied leather to the army, 'it is difficult to disagree with the reasoning of the Queen Consort. After the long drought, this kingdom now feeds itself well, trades with its neighbours, and—'

'*And* that life is under threat and weakened by your complacency,' said Jehu, his face growing dark.

'If you had let me finish you would have heard me say that though we are ready to go to war, this time we don't actually gain anything by doing so. The fight for Gilead last time enabled the very prosperity in the plains that literally kept our people alive during the drought.'

'A drought,' observed Achidan, 'during which the Judeans ignored our every plea for help.'

'But this time it sounds like you propose we declare war on Ben-Hadad not to gain his lands,' said Ido, 'but just to frighten him.'

'Gaining Aram-Damascus would give our combined nations an enormous strategic advantage in the region,' said Jehu.

'The Judean Prince is right,' said Balazar, causing Jezebel to look at him in frustration. 'To take control of both banks of the river over such a distance as that, and then sweep south through Ammon—'

211

'I believe the Phoenician mastery of the sea has deluded you into believing your small nation can control the land as well,' said Jezebel.

'You were once Phoenician too,' said Balazar.

'I don't deny my past, but I believe we must be realistic about our future. We cannot possibly take permanent control of so much land between us at this time.'

'You err in favour of cowardice then,' said Jehu.

'Is that how the Council of Nobles wishes to see it? Are we cowards?' said Jezebel, stung as he surely wished her to be.

'I say Aye to the Queen,' proposed Ido.

'Aye to the Queen!' chorused the other nobles.

'It seems that either we are all cowards,' said Jezebel, 'or we are all wiser than Judah.'

Jehu pushed himself up from the table. 'A strategy reliant on appeasement won't protect you for long. I will take your decision back to Judah but I don't expect their approval. I'm comforted that Israel will know the onslaught of Ben-Hadad the Second long before either Phoenicia or Judah do.'

He pushed past the nobles and threw back the curtains, and moments later she heard him yell for his horse to be brought from the stables.

'That ended well,' declared Balazar, rubbing his hands together.

Chapter Thirty

Jezebel carefully removed the Consort gown before going up to see Ahab. Tobiah was still fussing over the tear and Naboth's insult to the kingdom, but Jezebel agreed with Boaz that it was better to make as little of it as possible until the decision about the land had been made.

Ahab was sitting up in his bed when Jezebel peered round the curtain, surrounded by his mother, his daughter and all three of his granddaughters, and he looked a little better, though his eyes were hollow and his cheek still sagged.

'I hope you haven't brought the business of the Council up here,' said Raisa. 'Ahab needs to rest, though he is very poor at it.'

'Ignore my mother,' said Ahab, 'I want to know everything. I refuse to sit here like a badly stuffed doll while everyone else makes the decisions.'

'Come along,' said Esther, levering herself up off the bed. 'Let's leave Grandfather in peace. Athaliah, can you carry Kitra if I bring Nurit?'

Athaliah planted a kiss on Jezebel's cheek, then she swept up the little toddler in her arms and bundled her out of the room, followed by Raisa and Esther with the other child.

'Did Jehu give you trouble?' asked Ahab when they were alone.

'Now what makes you say that?'

'He is a hothead, prone to argument and hostility where sense and patience would be better. His father Jehoshaphat is far easier to deal with. We hunted together when the negotiations for my marriage to Leah were taking place. He could spear antelope with his eyes closed.'

Jezebel thought of Jehoshaphat's visit to Tyre with Jehu and Asa all those years ago, of his meanness and his constant bad moods. At least Jehu's fury had focus.

'We are at odds with Judah though,' she said. 'Their instinct is towards combat while ours is towards diplomacy. My brother was no help at all, for he shifted wherever the sun shone. My father would have cringed to see it.'

'I wish I'd been there,' said Ahab. 'Did the nobles support you?'

'Yes,' said Jezebel. 'They're nervous of the war that Judah wants with Damascus, and still hold a grudge over Jehoshaphat ignoring us during the drought.'

'Judah is a nation driven by fear,' conceded Ahab, 'be it over Elijah or Ben-Hadad. They fear the worst, so they constantly act in defence.' Dribble seeped from the corner of his mouth and he flapped at it ineffectually with his limp hand.

'Let me,' said Jezebel, wiping his mouth with a cloth.

'I hate getting old,' barked Ahab. 'Why does my body fail me?'

'There's nothing wrong with your mind though.'

214

Ahab snorted. 'I wish we could say the same for Jehu. That man's memory must be short. To snub us in our hour of need and then seek our help.'

'He is in a difficult position,' said Jezebel, remembering the roof of the Palace in Tyre, that sunny morning so long ago. 'He carries the burden of being the second son, with much to prove. I suspect Jehoshaphat favours him over his brother Jehoram; it's always Jehu who's sent on the diplomatic missions.'

'A marriage would do much to remind Judah that we consider their alliance important. Two generations of this House have strengthened ties with Tyre, and Leah's departure from Israel did not please Jehoshaphat.'

'But who will be married? Ahaziah is still only eleven,' said Jezebel.

'I was thinking of Athaliah,' said Ahab.

'What?' cried Jezebel. 'She's only ten, five years younger than I was when I married you. She is far too young.'

'But we could promise her to Jehoram, Jehu's older brother, for when she is ready. The prospect of a marriage would give them time to decide how they're going to strengthen their relations with us. And it would give you time to prepare Athaliah—'

A wretched cry pierced the room and they both looked towards the door. Jezebel pulled back the curtain and saw Athaliah running away.

'Darling, wait!' called Jezebel, running after her, 'wait for me.' She reached the girl quickly enough but had to drag her into an embrace to stop her running off. 'Come now, Athaliah, nothing is worth such sorrow.'

'I won't!' howled the girl. 'I just won't!'

'You won't what, darling?'

'I won't leave you,' she hiccupped, 'I won't go away to Judah to marry some old man.'

'But one day you might want—'

'I never want to leave you, I never, never will!' Athaliah stamped her foot and convulsed in tears.

'But you only know the palaces, my sweetheart, and there is a whole world out there, a beautiful, wonderful world full of people who will want to befriend you and love you. Think of how much you have enjoyed having Esther here and the little ones. One day you will want to see Tyre and Jerusalem, and have children of your own.'

Athaliah's answer was a wretched sob. Jezebel drew her tightly into a cuddle and breathed into her daughter's hair, rocking her gently. 'Then I will never make you do anything you don't want to.'

'Never?' came the muffled response.

'Not if you don't want to,' said Jezebel.

But she knew it was a lie, for Jehu had reminded her of how painfully love entwines with sacrifice.

Chapter Thirty-One

Jezebel made a great fuss of Athaliah that afternoon. They ate a midday meal alone in Jezebel's own room, and then she played with her daughter's hair, combing and curling and plaiting it until the girl fell asleep on her bed. Perhaps Jezebel had been infected by Athaliah's own anxiety, for she felt restless and impatient and she kept thinking back to the Council meeting. What had possessed Naboth to plead so inappropriately when he should have known better? Balazar too had annoyed her with his constant changing of sides. It was difficult to know if war with the Damascans was really what Tyre wanted, or just Balazar trying to find favour with another king's son. Whatever the case, discussions had been taking place about Israel behind her back. Her father must be very unwell indeed for Balazar to have gained so much authority. She went to the window, looking out towards the north-west and Tyre.

The Phoenicians were not a warring people, at least not any more. They lived in relative harmony with the world around them and yet Balazar seemed keen to abandon that principle in favour of alliances with nations who wanted

Phoenician trade but didn't respect their customs. She couldn't help but think again of how Jehu had mentioned the influence of Elijah; just how far would Balazar go to keep the Judeans' favour when he became King?

Her thoughts turned to her father, and she wondered if Balazar had spoken to Daniel about him. She hesitated for a moment, knowing that if she were to seek out Daniel, then she must be ready to apologise for her rather terse manner in recent days. She picked up her stole from the couch, kissed her sleeping daughter on the forehead, and left. *If I'm to lose the loyalty of my brother,* she thought, *then I can't afford to lose a friend too.*

Jezebel went to Daniel's quarters in the east wing of the Palace and knocked rather nervously at his door, belatedly aware that he might well not be alone. But there was no answer, nor the muffled giggling of those who would prefer not to be disturbed, and she turned away unsure where to look next. Ahab was sleeping, so he would not be up there either.

She went down into the gardens, retracing the route she, Raisa and Esther had taken when they discovered Daniel. But of course he was not in the doorway with Hemen – *he surely wouldn't make that mistake again,* she thought ruefully. Even the birds sounded fractious, chirping at each other and flying endlessly from tree to tree.

There was another sound too, a distant clanging. Swords, she realised. The precise whistle of sharpened bronze was unmistakeable. It came from the stableyard and as she drew nearer, the swish of slicing air suggested a determined battle.

As she turned the corner into the stableyard she heard a terrible groan and the clang of a sword falling to the ground. Jehu lay slumped against a stable door, clutching at his chest, his lips drawn back in a rictus of pain. Jezebel screamed and ran across the courtyard. She crouched beside him. 'In the name of El,' she murmured, 'who did this to you?'

'Got you!' cried a joyous voice. 'Mama? What are you doing here?'

Jezebel looked over her shoulder to find Ahaziah peering out from behind a cart, a bronze sword in one hand, a shield drawn across his body.

Jezebel stared from her son to Jehu and back again. Jehu rubbed at his chest, then let his hand fall away. There was no blood. He jumped up nimbly and clasped the boy's forearm in the warrior greeting.

'You thought I could be bested by a boy?' he said, grinning at her. He took her hand and helped her stand up. 'He fights well for his age, certainly, but he's not quite my match yet.'

'You shouldn't be practising with real weapons,' said Jezebel, primly removing her fingers from his. 'He's too young.'

'I'm eleven,' protested Ahaziah, 'and almost a man. Jehu was using a proper sword by the time he was seven so I'm at least four years behind in my training.'

'He has some good habits and some bad ones,' said Jehu to Jezebel, glancing at her as he picked up his sword from the ground. 'But he won't develop strength, nor will he understand how to use the true weight of the weapon to defend himself if he continues to play with wood.'

'And why would he need to defend himself?'

'He is the heir to Israel,' said Jehu. 'And soon he must show his strength on the battlefield as well as the throne.'

Ahaziah had become bored with the discussion and was hopping from foot to foot, the blade glinting as it arced above his head. Jehu stepped forward and tapped the blade with his own, and Ahaziah sprang into position, the sword wobbling slightly as he extended it.

'Now lift!' said Jehu. 'Turn the blade – that's it. Then you have your weight balanced to your advantage. Try that again.' Jehu was grinning at the boy as he frowned, practising the move over and over, his blade ringing like a bell each time it touched his tutor's. Jezebel could see that each time Jehu moved his own sword a little further back to make Ahaziah work harder, and within a few minutes the boy had perfected the move and was begging for something new to learn.

Jezebel retreated to the edge of the yard, watching her son play with his true father. They looked alike, she thought, and yet it was only seeing them play together like this, enjoying themselves, that it became so obvious. When had Jehu lost that enjoyment of life, she wondered.

Or did I steal it from him when I married Ahab?

Ahaziah sprang forward, combining moves, and touched Jehu in the chest again with the tip of his sword. 'Got you!'

Jehu groaned horribly and sank to his knees, and Ahaziah raised his arms aloft in celebration, dancing round his father with innocent delight.

If only she could tell Jehu the truth. How proud he would surely be that his son was a warrior in the making.

'Get up, get up!' cried Ahaziah. 'I want to go again!'

'Perhaps you would teach my other son as well,' said Jezebel as Jehu picked up his sword. 'Joram is only seven, but if you were old enough to take up a sword then perhaps—'

'Joram is a little girl,' said Ahaziah with contempt. 'He will be playing his harp or fussing with clay.'

'I can try him with a wooden sword,' offered Jehu. 'Then he would not hurt himself.'

'Don't bother,' said Ahaziah. 'I'm a far better pupil.'

Jehu gave Jezebel a sidelong grin that acknowledged there was something in the boy's arrogance, then he offered the blade again and the battle resumed. Jezebel slipped away.

Ahaziah's disdain for his younger brother had given her an idea about where Daniel might be found, and she went down to the small orchard, listening for the sound of her youngest child practising on Daniel's nevel. But instead she found him sniffling sadly at Daniel's elbow as they bent over something in the grass.

'What is it?' asked Jezebel gently as she approached.

'A peacock chick,' said Joram. 'Its wing is broken.'

'How did it happen?' asked Jezebel as Daniel fingered the soft brown wing gently. The bird cheeped and pecked at Daniel's palm.

'The nest is on top of that woodpile,' he said, nodding towards the corner of the orchard, 'but normally it would be in the grass. It's safer to be high up with the dogs roaming in the orchard at night, but I think the bird must have fallen out.'

Joram grabbed at his mother's skirts. 'Can you mend it?' he asked the physician forlornly.

Daniel shook his head. 'When we touch them, we leave our scent on them and the mother doesn't want it any more. She would know its wing was broken and leave it to die anyway.'

'I don't want it to die,' said Joram. His cheeks reddened and his eyes filled up with tears, and suddenly he bolted for the Palace.

'It is probably better he doesn't see me put the chick out of its misery,' said Daniel. He turned his shoulder to Jezebel and moved his hands swiftly, and the bird's cheeping stopped. He pulled his pocket knife from his tunic and began cutting out a piece of turf. 'Joram will be back later to ask what happened. It is better to have something to show him.'

'You are very kind to him,' said Jezebel, aware that she had let Daniel speak for a good while without answering him. 'I don't think I've ever thanked you properly for how much you do for all of us. For me.' She chewed her lip. 'I should not have been so mean to you about Hemen. I apologise.'

'I accept your apology,' said Daniel, glancing up briefly as he dug down into the soft earth. He pulled back the grass then laid the bird carefully in the hole. 'You must be worried about your father.'

'Seeing my brother has been more difficult than I thought it would be,' said Jezebel. 'And Ahab seems to fade with every day, even though he clings on like a limpet to the bottom of a galley. But none of that is any excuse for the way I spoke to you.'

Daniel stood up and brushed the soil off his hands. 'There's no need—'

'I was absorbed for so long by giving up Jehu to come to Israel and marry Ahab,' said Jezebel, 'that I never thought about how much you, Beset, Amos and all the other Tyrians must have given up as well. I don't mean to be so selfish and seeing Balazar has reminded me of the worst of myself.'

'I should not have embarrassed you,' said Daniel, his forehead creasing in faint lines. 'I should have been more discreet. Hemen was very pleased to see me. We met by accident . . . she grabbed me and it surprised me . . .' He stuttered to a stop, the frown deepening. 'She does not mean anything to me any more. It was just . . .' He sighed. 'Reminders of home. They have unsettled us both, but otherwise we are unchanged.'

There was something inscrutable and unfamiliar in his expression, but Jezebel was thinking of poor Hemen, no doubt weeping in a corner somewhere, knowing that the love of her life no longer wanted her.

Chapter Thirty-Two

The Palace felt empty after Balazar and Esther returned to Tyre, and for several days Jezebel could hear only its echoing silence. Jehu had ridden back to Jerusalem the evening of his swordplay with Ahaziah, having tried once more over dinner to persuade Jezebel that war should be declared on Damascus. Their fleeting friendliness in the stableyard had been lost in his angry pleas; she was saddened but not surprised when he stormed away from the table, leaving Jezebel alone with her brother.

Ahab improved in health after the departure of the guests, buoyed by the affections of his daughter and grandchildren. Within a couple of weeks, Daniel determined that the King had recovered as much as he was going to. Ahab's mouth still drooped a little and he couldn't feel all the fingers in his left hand, but he was able to walk with a stick and had even attended a Council session, though he had let Jezebel manage proceedings.

'But do you feel well enough to travel to Samaria?' Jezebel said that same afternoon as they sat in his room. 'There has been rain every evening for days and I don't think you should camp out in the cold.'

'Then we will travel all night,' said Ahab. 'It is the first Spring Council in Samaria in five days and I cannot allow people to believe I'm not fit to govern.'

'Very well,' said Jezebel. 'Then I shall stay in bed all day and be waited on like a queen so that you may take all the glory of your return.'

Ahab kissed her hand. 'You have managed the affairs of our people very well. It was clear in the Council that everyone trusts your judgement.'

'I think they're relieved not to be going to war, not least because we won't raise a war tax.'

'It costs the Palace far more than it costs any of the nobles—'

'Please!' shouted a voice beyond the door. 'You must let me see the Queen!'

'Who is that?' asked Ahab.

'I don't recognise the voice.' Jezebel went to the door and pulled back the curtain.

In the corridor two personal guards grasped a boy between them as he wrestled to free himself, his face grubby and tear-stained. Seeing Jezebel he lurched forward. 'You must come now!'

'Greet your Queen with the proper respect,' barked one of the guards.

'You have to come!' His expression was terrified, but his eyes were huge and pleading.

'Who are you?' Jezebel asked.

'I'm Ner, from the—' he gulped, 'from the estate of Naboth.'

'Let him go,' said Jezebel sharply. The boy shook himself free of the guard. 'Why does Naboth not come himself?'

'A mob has taken him.'

'A mob?'

'They came after lunch, the master was still on the verandah, they came from everywhere like ants.'

'What is going on?' Ahab appeared behind Jezebel in the doorway, leaning on his stick. The boy dropped to his knees.

'She has to come, sir, she has to help me find Naboth. He was shouting for her as they took him away. The mistress sent me—'

'Who?' Ahab shook his head in bewilderment. 'Who took your master away? Was it members of my guard?' He gestured at the soldiers.

'No, sir, it was everyone.'

'Everyone? Did you recognise—'

But instead of answering, Ner grabbed Jezebel's wrist and tugged her along the corridor.

The soldiers instantly seized him, but Jezebel quickly said, 'No, it's all right. I will go with him.' She turned to Ahab. 'I will ride out to Naboth's estate and see if I can talk some sense into these people.'

'I'm coming with you.'

'You are supposed to rest.'

'I'm travelling to Samaria in three days,' snapped Ahab. 'Now let's go.'

The royal carriage set off alone but by the time they reached the plain, a large retinue of Ahab's mounted guard had joined them. At Ahab's insistence, Ner was sitting in the carriage with him and Jezebel. As the carriage turned to the west below Jezreel's plateau, Jezebel saw a dreadful dark cloud hovering above the vineyard owner's land.

'The house!' screamed Ner, jumping up.

'You won't get there any more quickly if you run,' said Ahab, restraining the boy and glancing at Jezebel with great concern.

'Faster please,' shouted Jezebel to the driver. But it was all too clear that the estate house was thoroughly ablaze, and as the carriage finally stopped on the edge of the estate, the sky was clogged with smoke.

'You should stay here until I know what is going on,' said Jezebel to Ahab as Ner leapt from the carriage and she ran after the boy through the rows of vines towards the house. They were halfway up the hill when the air was cut by the most dreadful keening wail that made Jezebel's blood turn cold.

'Mistress!' shouted Ner, following the sound and disappearing through a row of vines. The boy was small and Jezebel couldn't follow him, so she pulled her stole over her face against the smoke, and ran towards the burning house.

The shell of the building was still visible amid the scorching yellow glow but there was something in the way Naboth's wife stood with her back to the house that terrified Jezebel. Breathless from the climb, she pushed her way through the knot of servants that stood around her.

'Is Naboth in there?' she asked.

But the woman curled in on herself, shuddering as she fell to her knees, and the servants stepped back. Behind them, against the low courtyard wall lay the broken corpse of a man. Hundreds of stones, some small, others rocks as big as a first, were scattered on the bloodied ground around him. Tufts of his curly grey hair shimmered and shook in the heat from the fire.

'Naboth . . .' she muttered, grabbing fistfuls of her skirts to stifle her shock. The old man's face, half covered by his robe, was virtually unrecognisable. 'In the name of El and all the Gods, who could do such a thing?'

The Gods seemed to answer in a great thundering, and Jezebel looked round to find Ahab riding up the slope on a horse, followed by six of his guard. The horse reared at the sight of the body but Ahab yanked on the harness, his face white.

'Who did this?' he bellowed. Naboth's wife let out a wretched howl.

Ahab slid down off the horse and approached a man on the edge of the group, his waist bound in an apron. Jezebel recognised him as Naboth's vineyard manager. 'Ari?'

The man fell to his knees. 'Forgive me, Your Highness. I couldn't stop them.'

'What happened?' demanded Ahab, dragging the man to his feet.

'A crowd came for him,' sobbed Ari, 'some nobles, some farmers, the cousin of Meir.'

'This was about the *land*?' said Jezebel. 'They killed him for that?'

Ari shook his head and drew a scroll from his apron. 'They came with this.' Ari finally looked his King in the eye and Jezebel saw such doubt there, such fear, that she took the scroll herself from Ari's hand and snatched it open.

'Breaking religious laws?' she muttered in disbelief as she read. 'Naboth, of all people?'

But Ahab didn't care for what was in the scroll. 'Give the names of everyone who came for Naboth to the head of my guard. I want them rounded up and brought to the Palace immediately.'

Jezebel laid her hand on her husband's arm. 'You should read this, Ahab.'

'Ari will give me the names.'

She shook her head, barely able to bring herself to say what she had learned. 'This is a Royal Decree. The scroll says you and I ordered Naboth's death.'

Chapter Thirty-Three

Though night had long since fallen, the Council Chamber was stiflingly hot as man after man was brought into the hastily convened court. Ari was right, for not only were there landowners and Meir's cousin among the mob, but also the nobles Achidan and Yonah. More than twenty men had been rounded up by the time Ahab decided that the trial must begin.

Jezebel stood back as her husband assumed his throne, sitting instead on a couch placed by Boaz nearby. For once she was glad that Ahab assumed responsibility for the outcome of the Council, for she couldn't imagine how she would retain her composure as the truth came out. It wasn't the sight of Naboth's damaged and disfigured body that she kept remembering, but how irritated she had been with him the last time they met, and how she had let him be dragged from the Chamber more like a criminal than an old friend.

Achidan and Yonah, his main opponents in the Council, now sat with their heads in their hands, while other members of the mob exchanged terrified and bewildered looks with each other. Each of the accused was flanked by a pair of guards, their swords drawn.

Boaz closed the doors at the far end of the Chamber and Ahab banged the gavelstone, his face as white and hard as the granite. He read the names of each arrested man, then he pushed himself unsteadily to his feet, his knuckles taut around the arms of his throne.

'You are accused of the unlawful murder of Naboth, noble of—'

A shudder of horror rose up from the accused and Yonah got to his feet. 'Your Highness!' he exclaimed. 'Why say you unlawful? You have the scroll before you. Your own seal is present.'

'That is my seal but I didn't make it,' shouted Ahab.

Yonah stared. 'In the name of Yahweh—'

'Yes,' said Ahab. 'In the name of Yahweh. That is what this decree claims as the basis of his crime. But what did you believe Naboth had done that I might order his execution, this man that you had known for so long?'

'But the decree clearly says he has cursed the name of Yahweh—'

'Naboth liked the fine things in life, but he was a devout and charitable man—'

'He was greedy!'

'Who interrupts me in this court?' he demanded, scanning the crowded room.

'I do!' A shabbily dressed man stood up, his hair matted beneath a farmer's cap, a rough woven jacket hanging from his bony frame. 'I'm Cherut, cousin of Meir, and rightful heir to his land. Naboth knew I was trying to get the money together to buy the land from my cousin before he died.'

'You are not a direct heir,' said Ahab.

231

'This man told us Naboth tried to bribe him not to buy the land,' said Achidan.

'Naboth could be persuasive,' said Ahab, 'but he never acted unfairly.'

'He tried to steal my land!'

'Silence!' Ahab's shout stilled the room. 'It is clear to me that your collective envy of Naboth combined into an intoxicating dislike of him, and under its influence you were easily persuaded of his crimes. But I make it very clear to you now that this decree did not come from my hand, and that to my knowledge he had never broken any religious strictures. Besides, as nobles of this land, you surely know that punishments for those particular transgressions are never exacted by a man's peers but by the King alone.'

Yonah and Achidan exchanged startled looks across the flanks of guards that stood around them. Then they glanced at Boaz.

'What is it?' asked Jezebel, turning to her closest aide.

But it was Yonah who answered. 'The decree came from the Palace and was delivered to me at my home.'

'By Boaz?' She studied her adviser's face for some sign of culpability but all she saw there was a deep anger. 'What did you do?' she began to ask, but behind her the door opened.

'Who disturbs the court?' barked Ahab.

'He's gone!' said Reuel. 'My apologies, Your Highnesses. Boaz sent me to look for him, but he's disappeared.'

'Who?'

'Tobiah,' said Achidan in a hollow voice.

Reuel nodded. 'His rooms are empty and I can't find him anywhere.'

'It was Tobiah who delivered the decree this morning,' said Yonah. 'He said the King had called him to his chambers to write and witness the decree and it was to be acted on by sundown.'

Jezebel stared at Boaz. 'You suspected him? Why did you not bring this to me?'

'Pride, Your Highness,' said Boaz, lowering his head. 'I thought that soon you would think of Tobiah as more valuable than me and that if I mentioned it, it would only hasten my departure from your service. I knew a seal was missing from the office, but when it reappeared the next day, Tobiah convinced me I was a mistaken old fool. Reuel was sure I was right but I didn't listen to him.'

'We have all been fooled,' said Jezebel.

'But why Naboth?' said Ahab, sagging down onto his throne. 'What threat could Naboth have been to Tobiah?'

Jezebel unrolled the scroll. Cursing the name of Yahweh. Defacing the Temple of Yahweh. Using pagan rituals to pray for a good harvest. She let it roll closed. The charges were absurd. Naboth was the last person in the kingdom to whom such charges could be laid. They were the crimes of an infidel, and she knew exactly at whom they were really levelled.

And, in that moment, she realised that Tobiah was only the executor of the plot.

Guiding his hand was a greater enemy.

Chapter Thirty-Four

In the days that followed Naboth's death, the mood in Jezreel was dark. There was always sadness in the city before the King's departure to Samaria, as though the citizens resented relinquishing their leader. Even the Spring Banquet that marked his last night in the city held no prospect of joy, and Jezebel was relieved when Ahab decided to cancel it as a mark of respect to the vineyard owner. Jezebel spent that night looking across to the north, wondering where Elijah was now. He must have left Damascus if he was in communication with his agent Tobiah.

Jezebel arranged and paid for Naboth's burial herself, and she had been to the vineyard every day to monitor the clearing of the burned building. Naboth's wife had refused to move from the land and was living in a tent, so Jezebel had made arrangements to ensure that the entire household had everything it needed. Though the woman didn't blame anyone other than the men who had thrown the stones for her husband's death, Jezebel bore a terrible guilt she couldn't shed, not only for her last words to Naboth but also for failing to see Tobiah in his true light.

Elijah's influence was a mystery to her – and she asked herself again and again when Tobiah had turned from a loyal clerk into a plotter capable of such an horrific misdeed. Or perhaps she been deceived all along – maybe he was planted long ago, like bad seed ready to ripen?

As she and Beset walked to market the following morning, Jezebel tried to remember everything Tobiah said to her. The way he spoke, the way he looked at her, that neat script with which he took notes. She tried to imagine what his real thoughts must have been, how he must have felt about her, about the King, about all of them. Was it money which swayed him to treachery, or simply the sincere belief that he was doing Yahweh's work? She would never know. She had overlooked him, certainly, thinking him a harmless bureaucrat, but now she saw he was much cleverer – much braver, even – than Obadiah had been.

Jezebel glanced at the cadre of Ahab's personal guard who were walking a few paces behind them. *Is it really necessary?* she wondered. Surely the people would know her remorse over Naboth was genuine.

'Ahab was right to insist,' said Beset, as if reading her thoughts. 'While rumours circulate amid the truth, there will be uncertainty. I'm sure that Meir's cousin will have tall tales of his own to tell about the court, if his claim about the land was anything to go by.'

Jezebel frowned. 'I hope that they remember the Queen I have always been to them.'

The marketplace was busy and Jezebel took care to greet as many by name as she knew. But people were nervous of the soldiers and in the narrow passageways between stalls and carts, it was becoming impossible for anyone to go normally about their business with the bulky royal retinue passing through.

'Just wait on the west side of the square,' Jezebel told the guards. 'We'll look at the pots here and the silks over there, and then we'll return.'

'I'm sorry, Your Highness, but the King's orders were specific,' said the commander.

'Very well,' said Jezebel, 'then just one of you.'

The commander surveyed the market, then nodded to his team, who retreated to the edge of the market, while Jezebel moved towards a stall selling assorted tableware. In the centre at the back of the stall was a display of small bowls made out of lapis lazuli, their deep blue cut with sparkling veins of beige and so deeply polished that they glowed in the sun. But among them was a bowl of paler blue, flecked with white, that reminded Jezebel of the sea at Tyre, and she asked to see it.

'Isn't it beautiful?' she said to Beset. 'I will buy this for Daniel, to soften the blow of going to Samaria.'

Beset smiled. 'He does dislike the upheaval of moving every six months.'

The stallholder refused to take any money, claiming that royal patronage would do his business nothing but good, but when Jezebel pressed three silver coins into his hand, he grinned and told her she was his best customer.

'You overpaid him,' murmured Beset as they went to the silk stall on the opposite side.

'I can buy loyalty, can't I?' said Jezebel. 'Talking of which, you will need some new stoles for Samaria. That red one I bought you last year is looking very shabby around the edges because you will insist on polishing my earrings with—'

Beset shrieked, but as Jezebel turned to see what had happened, her cheek was smacked with wetness as though she had been caught by a wave. Her eyes stung and she saw Beset's hands fly to her blood-soaked face.

'Beset!' As Jezebel reached for her maid, she smelled something familiar. Tentatively she licked her lips. 'Wine?'

Beset, her shoulders soaked through, was staring over Jezebel's shoulder. She turned and found Elijah, a flask dripping in his hand, its pottery neck slashed open.

'The blood of his body and the blood of his land is on you!' he shouted, his voice cracked with age. The guard beside Jezebel stepped between them, but hesitated to lay his hands on Elijah.

Jezebel's heart thudded. 'Whose blood?' she demanded.

'The blood of Naboth. You have claimed that farmland at the cost of his life. In the name of Yahweh—' Elijah raised his staff as far as his decrepit arm could manage, but Jezebel jumped forward and grabbed it with both hands before he could drive it into the ground. The staff shook between them, the old man surprisingly strong, but Jezebel's grip was firm and fuelled by anger.

She looked around at the people in the marketplace. 'Naboth was murdered by a wicked mind and weak hearts,' she shouted. 'His land will be given by the Palace to all the people of Jezreel to farm.'

'It isn't Ahab's to give,' shouted Elijah.

Jezebel pulled the staff from Elijah's hand and threw it to the ground. A murmur of shock rippled through the crowd. 'Arrest this man for assaulting the Queen of Israel.'

But the soldier simply stared at Elijah, his sword still sheathed in his belt.

'Arrest this man,' insisted Jezebel. 'He has defamed your King.'

Elijah shuffled round. 'I am the emissary of his God.'

He drove his fists towards the sky. 'Let it be known,' he cried, 'that while Ahab would own your hearts, your souls and your land, it is Yahweh who gives you life. But the House of Omri will rot from the canker within. Its offspring will sicken and die. Ahab and every son of Ahab who follows him will be cut down by the God they have spat upon. The House will fall!' Elijah turned to Jezebel, his eyes blazing. 'And the whore who fouled these lands, who prostituted her Gods within your temples and invaded Yahweh's sacred borders with her army of infidels, she—' Elijah stabbed his finger at her, 'she will meet her death from these very walls at Jezreel! Her blood will soak the land she infected and her flesh will feed the dogs of the Palace she has seduced. Her death will be spoken of wherever men have tongues.'

Jezebel's breath died in her chest and it took all her poise to face Elijah. His eyes glittered deep within his face and his jaw quivered with the relish of his proclamation. Then anger surged through her and she inhaled deeply.

'If you are Elijah then I am Jezebel,' she shouted, summoning down all the wrath of Anat, the Goddess of war, to steel her heart. She snatched the commander's knife from his belt, and slashed the air in front of Elijah's face. 'Be gone, or I will kill you myself!'

For a long terrifying moment, Jezebel thought she would

have to plunge the knife once more into the old man. As she held his venomous gaze she remembered the top of Mount Carmel. Perhaps Elijah recalled it too, for he stooped to pick up his staff and shuffled away without another word, soon lost in the crowd.

Chapter Thirty-Five

Athaliah grabbed her mother tightly, sobbing into Jezebel's neck, her whole body shaking with misery.

'Why do you have to go to Tyre?' she wailed. 'I don't want to go to Samaria on my own with the boys.'

Jezebel looked into her daughter's eyes. 'Do you remember uncle Balazar saying that my father is very ill? Think about how sad you would have been if you couldn't have cheered up your father when he was ill. I haven't seen my father since before you were born, and this may be my last chance.' She kissed her daughter on the forehead and squeezed her tightly, her own eyes stinging with tears she knew she couldn't shed in front of the child. 'I'll miss you so much.'

Athaliah wriggled free of Jezebel's embrace. 'I don't believe you!' She ran away, back into the Palace.

Jezebel turned to Ahab, who stood by the carriage. Torchlight lit one side of his face, and the shadows thickened his frown and deepened the hollows in his cheeks.

'This is absolutely wrong,' he said.

'But it's the right thing to do,' replied Jezebel. 'At least until the situation becomes less volatile.'

Ahab leaned forward and kissed his wife on the forehead. 'Perhaps when Naboth's wife has begun to rebuild her house,' he said, 'people will begin to forget.'

They will never forget what they heard in the market today, thought Jezebel, wrapping her hands around her arms to suppress a shiver.

'Take care of yourself,' she said.

'It will be harder without your physician.'

Jezebel glanced at Daniel, who was stacking his chests on the cart. Given his dislike of moving, she hadn't wanted to ask him to join her, but as soon as she told him that she was going back to Tyre, he asked permission to come with her. Jezebel had made Beset promise not to tell him all the details of what had happened in the market, but she must have told him something, for he had barely left her side since they returned. He tightened a strap and turned to her with a smile

'Since he came to Samaria with you,' said Ahab, 'it is I who've taken up the majority of his time.'

'Nonsense,' said Jezebel.

'He's a good man,' said Ahab, placing a hand on Jezebel's shoulder. 'You'll need people you can trust if . . .'

'If what?'

His hand slipped away. 'I may not be here to protect you always. Elijah is a powerful man.'

His tone was so laden with doom that Jezebel felt a shudder. 'And you are a king. Don't let his words eat away at you; that's half his power.'

Daniel was helping Beset up into the carriage.

'It's time to go,' said Ahab, holding out his own arm to help Jezebel in too. But she simply bent to kiss his ring,

241

then climbed in unaided. Soon the small procession of carts, soldiers and the carriage was on its way out through the gates.

'I wish we didn't have to travel at night,' murmured Beset as the gates swung open to let them through.

'It's the safest time,' said Daniel. 'We'll be far from the city by daybreak.'

Silence fell over the carriage, and Beset was soon rocked to sleep by the motion. As she mumbled something Jezebel looked across to Daniel. 'Thank you,' she whispered.

His eyes stayed locked to hers for a moment, then he bowed and rested his head against the seat. Jezebel turned her face to the window and stared out at the dark. If she listened hard, over the night winds, she fancied she could almost hear Elijah's curses still.

The slowing of the carriage jolted Jezebel awake.

'Get out of the way!' bellowed the driver

'What is it?' muttered Jezebel. Daniel had already pulled aside the curtain to look, and Beset was rigid with fear in the corner of the carriage.

'Someone lying in the road,' said Daniel, pulling his head back inside.

'Dead?' asked Jezebel.

'In the name of Yahweh,' rose up a quavering broken voice.

Jezebel drew her shawl around her as the carriage stopped. Daniel half-climbed out and a swirl of dirt blew in around their feet.

'You should stay in here,' whispered Beset.

'There's a man in the road,' said Daniel. 'He's begging

for water. I cannot pass by without helping him.' Daniel took one of the skins of water from beneath the seat then disappeared up the road. Jezebel guessed it must be well after dawn for the sun was already quite high.

A few moments later, Daniel returned. 'I think you should see this.'

'Let the soldiers deal with it,' said Beset, nervously.

Daniel shook his head. 'This man is no threat to you, not now.'

There was a strange hollow tone to his voice, and Jezebel accepted his hand to get out of the carriage. Some distance beyond the horses a man did indeed lie in the road, one ankle trapped in a rusting manacle that had worn a festering scar into his heel. He wore shreds of a tunic tied with a hemp rope, his hair was long and matted with dirt, and from the smell of him he had soiled himself where he lay.

'Help me,' he muttered. 'Water.'

Jezebel peered at him, holding her stole up to her nose against the awful stench. 'Why did you—'

'Look closely,' Daniel murmured. 'He is blind so he won't know you.'

Jezebel stepped forward. The man must have heard her for he turned his face towards her. But it was not the hair or the cut of the jaw that gave him away, but the way his eyes stared vacantly at her, as though he knew only himself.

'Obadiah,' she said.

'Jezebel?' he wailed, reaching for her.

'You will address your Queen correctly,' demanded one of the soldiers from the party who had come to join them, his sword unsheathed.

'There's no need,' said Jezebel.

Daniel helped the banished adviser to sit, raised the water skin to his lips, then steadied it as Obadiah drank greedily, rivulets of dirt washing down his chin and neck. Jezebel felt a confusing mixture of pity and anger at seeing him again. And as though he could see himself as she did, he lowered the water skin and felt for the manacle around his ankle.

'Someone took pity on me and cut the others off, but this one would not be broken. I might have thought you forged this yourself.'

'Have you been blind for long?' asked Daniel.

'Time does not pass in the same way when you cannot see.' He hesitated then turned to Jezebel. 'I sought out Elijah after I lost my sight. Many people told me of the miracles he could perform.' Obadiah's lips bared in a tooth-less grin, but there was no humour in it. 'He wouldn't even see me.'

'Is there anything that can be done for him?' Jezebel asked Daniel.

He stood up and brushed his hands on his tunic. 'There's nothing.' The wind whipped at the scarf around his neck and sand was spitting and stinging at their faces. 'Can you drive around him?' he asked the soldier.

The soldier nodded. 'We should get moving before this storm hits.'

'Then his fate is in the hands of any God who is watching,' said Daniel.

He tramped back to the carriage, pulling his scarf around his mouth against the rising wind, and Jezebel ran to catch up. They climbed in, then pulled closed the doors and dropped the shutters against the biting flurries of grit and dust.

The carriage jolted forward and Jezebel opened her mouth to say something, but she recognised in Daniel that same weary fury at she had felt the night before when they left Jezreel. So she closed her eyes, settled her head against the wall, and listened to the wind cry its desert song.

Chapter Thirty-Six

As the carriage turned onto the causeway at Tyre, Jezebel shielded her eyes against the glare. But it wasn't just the blazing white of the city, nor the intense blues of the sea and the sky melting together in a shimmering haze, but the sheer riot of colour from all the ships dotted around the harbour. Cranes lifted fat brown trunks of cedar and fir from the galleys, and carts nudged past on their way to Sidon and Acre, stacked with black and white slipware from Ashkelon, and soft rolls of cloth in ochre, turmeric, and *qirmiz* red.

Jezebel banged on the roof of the carriage. 'Stop!' she shouted, grabbing the door. 'I'm walking the rest of the way.'

Daniel and Beset scrambled out of the carriage behind her and they stood on the causeway, breathing deeply.

'I'd forgotten just how rich the air is. Even the sun smells sweeter.'

'It's the salt,' said Daniel. 'It makes everything smell better.'

Jezebel tore off her headscarf and unpinned her hair, running her fingers through it to dispel the dust of the plains.

'No one will realise you are the Queen of Israel if you try to get through the city gates looking like that,' said Beset.

'Let her,' said Daniel, his eyes sparkling at Jezebel. She caught the intensity of his gaze and realised how much bluer his eyes seemed in Tyre than against the dull landscape of Israel. 'It will do no harm for her to be just Jezebel for a while.'

As they climbed the causeway with all the other traders and citizens come home to Tyre, the carriage train dawdling behind them, new scents drifted to them on the breeze, the sour stink of the snail vats, the sweetness of honey caramelising in the bakeries, the bitterness of roasting wheat, and by the time they reached the city gates, Jezebel was breathless with all the joy of being home.

'Name and business?' demanded the gatekeeper as they reached their turn in the long queue at the gate.

'I'm Jezebel, come home to Tyre.'

'What kind of . . .' The gatekeeper gazed at her, frowned over the details of her face, glanced at the carriage and the Israelite soldiers behind her, then spluttered and dropped to his knees. 'In the name of Melqart, Your Highness, we welcome you!' He scrabbled to his feet again and shouted, 'It is Princess Jezebel! Come home to Tyre!'

Murmuring in the crowds of citizens around them turned to cheering and Jezebel squealed as she was hoisted up onto the shoulders of two fishermen to be borne through the gates. Behind her, the Israelite soldiers protested, but their demands for respect fell on deaf ears and Jezebel laughed and waved as her bearers spun her slowly through the gates above the heads of her delighted people. Daniel and Beset were soon lifted aloft too, Daniel shaking hands with old friends, Beset squeaking crossly at the indignity of it all, and in this boisterous procession they were borne through the streets to the Palace.

The joyous party wasn't permitted to pass through the Palace gates however, and Jezebel felt rather abandoned as they wandered alone into the stableyard.

'I'd forgotten no one was expecting us,' said Jezebel as the soldiers began unpacking the chests from the cart. An elderly man emerged from the colonnade, resplendent in the robes of a senior court official, his beard clipped neat but as white as the Palace walls.

'Philosir?' Jezebel ran to greet him, taking his hands in hers.

'I heard the crowds calling your name,' said the old councillor, but your brother didn't think a formal welcome appropriate.' He frowned. 'I'm afraid your father is dying, Jezebel.'

'I hoped he might have improved,' said Jezebel, a lump forming in her throat.

'He's an old man, my dear, we both are, and you should be glad as I am that you've come home in time to see him. Mot must be looking kindly on his old rival Melqart not to have taken your father from the city before your return.'

'Is there anything that Daniel could do for him?'

Philosir looked at the physician. 'Your old friend Eshmun has become the Royal Physician.'

'He's a good man and as learned as anyone,' said Daniel. 'If there's something that could be done for the King, Eshmun would already have done it.'

248

Jezebel tucked her hand in the arm of her former adviser and they moved through the Palace towards her father's chamber, Daniel and Beset following behind. As they went, the corridors grew darker and quieter and Jezebel realised that the windows had all been dressed with fine Egyptian gauze.

'He complains the light is too bright, so we have shrouded this wing,' said Philosir.

They paused outside the door to the King's suite. 'Let me tell Eshmun you are here.' As he opened the door it was pulled from his grasp and Balazar strode through.

'Oh. There you are, Jezebel.' He brushed her hand with his lips. 'The fuss in the streets disturbed Father and he has only just gone back to sleep.'

'I'm sorry,' she said, peering past his shoulder into the gloom. 'I had no idea we would cause such a commotion.'

'Why didn't you send a messenger ahead to say you were coming back?'

'Why didn't you send a messenger to tell me to come home?' said Jezebel, keen not to disclose the reason for her sudden departure from Jezreel. 'I'm only glad that Astarte spoke to me in a dream and told me to come.'

'Don't you start. Father keeps saying he can see Mot in all his black sepulchral majesty.'

'Visions are not uncommon,' said Daniel quietly, 'especially when eyesight is failing. It is as though the eyes—'

'Yes, well,' Balazar stepped out into the corridor and pulled the door closed. 'Why don't you go to your old bedroom and I'll call on you when he has woken up.'

Jezebel stepped around him and opened the door again. 'I haven't come all this way not to be with him.'

She ignored Balazar's irritated protests, and slipped through the curtain into her father's bedroom. A soft grey light from the gauzes suffused the room, and in the middle stood the grand oak bed, canopied in heavy swags of Tyrian purple cloth. Eshmun was bent over a chest on a low table, and he bowed as he saw her.

Within the bed, frail and so much smaller than she remembered, lay Ithbaal, his white hair almost invisible against the white silk pillows, his slight frame barely lifting the embroidered counterpane. Until that moment, the dozen years of their separation hadn't seemed all that long. Jezebel swallowed hard to retain her poise.

A small wooden step had been placed beside the bed for the physicians to use so that they might reach their patient more easily. Jezebel shed her cape and climbed it so she could settle herself on the bed beside her father. She curled up near his shoulder and reached for his face, stroking the papery skin with the tips of her fingers. He didn't stir, and with every rasping breath she could see tiny bubbles of spittle form at his lips. She offered up a prayer of thanks to Astarte for allowing her to arrive in time.

'Thank you for everything you've done for him,' she murmured to Eshmun, her eyes damp with tears.

'He's had a long and healthy life, Your Highness,' said Eshmun. 'It's only age that wishes to claim him, and he has outlived his predecessors by many years. With the blessing of Mot he'll pass peacefully.'

Perhaps Mot didn't agree, for Ithbaal began to shake with coughing and Eshmun leaned past Jezebel to dab a cloth to his mouth. 'There may be some blood,' he murmured, 'but don't concern yourself. He's in no pain.'

Ithbaal turned his face a little and his eyelids fluttered. Jezebel slid her fingers beneath his cheek to cup his face in her palm. After a moment his eyes opened and he blinked, as though trying to force their cloudiness away.

'Jezebel?' he murmured. 'Does Astarte bring me Jezebel?'

'Dear Father,' breathed Jezebel, bringing her face closer to his.

His hand shook beneath the counterpane and he lifted it towards her face. Jezebel took it in her own and pressed it to her cheek, drawing his fingers around her face and kissing the tips of his fingers.

'Leave . . . us,' he muttered.

'Your Highness—' began Eshmun.

'Leave.' Ithbaal exploded with coughing, and Jezebel grasped his shoulders to steady him, then dabbed at his mouth with the cloth.

'Just a moment or two?' she asked.

Eshmun and Daniel exchanged glances, then they nodded and retreated from the bed, clearing the room. Balazar, standing near the door with his arms folded across his chest, muttered angrily at them, but perhaps his father's opinion still held sway for he left too and the door was closed.

'I'm tired of all the fuss,' Ithbaal murmured, his eyes flicking back and forth across Jezebel's face.

'Then I'll see you're not plagued by it any more,' said Jezebel. 'Philosir can manage things for you.'

'Balazar is keen to take office but,' he coughed, 'I make him come in here every day to give an account of everything he does. He says I sleep through his reports but in truth he has no gift for rule. He's more interested in spending

251

money than making it, and I fear he will bankrupt the kingdom by sending us to war.'

'I tried to talk him out of it.'

'Bah!' Ithbaal weakly waved his hand. 'Let's not bore each other with Balazar as well. I'm sure he'll be a perfectly dull King, numbed by his own taste for luxury and content to sit in Tyre and not see the world.' He let his hand fall on Jezebel's arm. 'It is you I'm proud of – you who should lead Tyre.'

Jezebel blushed. 'I'm happy with my lot, Father. Ahab is a good man, our children are strong.'

'You've learned how to make yourself happy,' murmured Ithbaal, 'and Ahab too. He knows he was lucky to have a bride with courage who has grown into a queen of wisdom. I'm sure you think we are stuck away here on this island, out of touch, but I make sure that I'm kept aware of all the challenges that face Israel.' Ithbaal closed his eyes, his fingers weakly squeezing hers.

Jezebel sat in silence, watching the shallow rise and fall of his chest. It wouldn't be long, she knew, and she had no intention of burdening him with Elijah's latest curse. The threats were empty, she was sure: grandstanding to the people by a man fuelled to self-righteousness by the sound of his own voice.

So why, she asked herself, could she not forget them?

Chapter Thirty-Seven

Two days later, Jezebel stood alone on the roof of the Palace, watching the smoke drift up from her father's funeral pyre. The Royal Galley had been anchored in the heart of the harbour, its heart stripped out and the redwood carcass lined with slate, on which the pyre had been built. The priests lined the harbour promontory, a black line in their funeral robes which would be ceremonially burned on the last flames of the cremation. The smoke was thin now as though Ithbaal's soul had long gone and his frail body offered nothing left to feed the flames, but still the streets below echoed with the mourning wail to Mot for the life and death of the King.

Everything looks the same, she thought, *and yet everything has changed.*

Balazar appeared at the top of the stairs to the roof garden, dressed in his coronation robes. 'I've sent word to the harbour that I'm going to begin the crowning ceremony,' he said. 'This has already dragged on too long.'

'I'm sure Father didn't wish to be an inconvenience to you,' said Jezebel.

In the harbour, the priests were removing their black

vestments for burning as was the custom. Shortly they would don white robes to symbolise the coming of the new King. Balazar clapped his hands gleefully and galloped down the stairs, and Jezebel followed at a discreet distance. Esther was waiting at the bottom, the amethyst-studded coronet of the Queen Consort sitting on top of a mass of neat curls, the skirts of her gown splayed around her. She looked stiff with nerves and Jezebel smiled warmly at her as she took her husband's hand and accompanied him through the Palace.

The great harbour bell rang out and a peal of smaller handbells chimed through the streets marking the end of one reign and the start of the next. Prayers to Melqart for blessing of the city's new King began to float up among the ringing but it was hard to detect a shift from the sombre tone that had infected the city while Ithbaal was dying. Balazar must have sensed it too, for he lingered behind the balcony.

Jezebel glanced at Philosir, who stood to one side. 'There are many in this city who were too young to remember the last coronation,' he said. 'They don't know what to expect. Your father himself lit the pyre at the funeral of Phelles, the last King—'

'That's because he killed the thieving bastard himself,' said Balazar from across the room. 'He lit the fire to be sure he was actually dead!'

'My point, Your Highness,' said Philosir, 'is that your father walked back through the streets from the harbour and brought his people with him, as it were. There are many who may not realise they must gather at the Palace—'

'They'll be here soon enough,' said an eager young man named Mazzer, whom Balazar had chosen to be Philosir's replacement. Philosir bowed to the enthusiasm of youth and Jezebel suppressed a smile.

'I'll return to the roof,' she said, 'so I can see how matters are progressing at the harbour. Then you'll know how long you'll have to wait for the priests.' She bowed to her brother and retraced her route, wondering how Esther put up with him.

'Jezebel?' Beset ran to keep up with her. 'I came to see how you are. Balazar wouldn't let me join the funeral procession.'

Jezebel frowned. 'He has been rather petty today. He says he doesn't want to be morbid, but I think he's still unsure of himself.'

Beset squeezed her mistress's arm. 'With good reason, I hear. I don't think it has anything to do with morbidity.'

Jezebel didn't like Beset's mischievous tone. 'What do you mean?'

Beset lowered her voice. 'Many people have asked me how long you plan to stay. People see how you have ruled in Israel – they still love their princess.'

'Enough of that,' Jezebel scolded lightly. 'It's been twelve years since I left.' She felt the urge to change the subject. 'What about Daniel?' she asked as they climbed the stairs to the roof. 'I haven't seen him since Father died.'

'He has gone to be with his family on the mainland.'

'Oh,' said Jezebel. 'I didn't know.'

'He tried to find you after your father died but that guard dog Mazzer wouldn't let anyone not connected with Balazar's new court enter the Palace. I only managed to get in through the kitchen because I was carrying your new undergarments from the seamstress!'

They emerged back into the rooftop sunshine. 'It will be good for Daniel to spend some time with his family. Renew old acquaintances.' She hesitated. 'Perhaps he will see Hemen again.'

'I don't think so,' said Beset. 'There was no hope for that young lady.'

Jezebel could feel her friend's gaze upon her, and stared resolutely out over the harbour, shielding her eyes.

A great shout surged up from the streets. 'That's the sound Balazar wanted to hear,' she said, going to the corner and peering across the face of the Palace towards the balcony. 'In a moment he'll come striding out—'

'Jezebel! Jezebel! Bless the reign of Jezebel!'

Jezebel's hand flew to her mouth in surprise and she glanced at Beset. Her maid was staring wide-eyed down into the streets, but she was grinning broadly and nodding.

'It's not right,' said Jezebel as the cry spread across the Palace gardens and Jezebel saw a large number of citizens below with their hands raised towards her.

'I told you,' said Beset. 'They want you to be their ruler, not Balazar.'

'In the name of Melqart,' cried a man ringing a bell at the foot of the Palace walls.

'We bless the reign of Jezebel,' answered the crowd around him as they gazed up towards her. 'In the name of Melqart, we bless the reign of Jezebel.'

Jezebel lurched back from the edge of the roof.

'Jezebel! Jezebel! Show us our Queen!'

'It's you they want,' shouted Beset above the din. 'I told you!'

Jezebel's heart was pounding. What must Balazar be

thinking, how angry and embarrassed he would be behind the balcony. A chaotic peal of bells rang out across the gardens and the line of priests in their celebratory purple robes hastened through the streets. Still, she could hear her name being shouted every way she turned.

'Let them see you,' said Beset.

'My place is not here,' Jezebel replied. 'Balazar is heir. He should go out on the balcony. They're just confused. I shouldn't have let them see me.'

The bell rang on the Palace gate and the first of the priests entered, clearly calling Balazar's name. But they looked as one towards the roof, and Jezebel knew she had to retreat if the coronation were not to descend into mayhem. Balazar would be bursting with indignation.

Looking out towards the Great Sea, she realised this was the exact spot where she once sat with Jehu. It was here he first tried to kiss her.

'Jezebel! Jezebel! Show us our Queen!'

Mazzer came to her side, pale and stuttering. 'Your Highness.'

'Yes?'

'You will have to come down to the balcony, quieten the crowd. They won't accept His Highness as the King until you do.'

'It will make matters worse.'

Mazzer shook his head. 'His Highness insists.'

'Very well,' said Jezebel. 'But no king I've ever heard of was crowned by his sister.'

Chapter Thirty-Eight

For more than a week, Jezebel remained inside the Palace grounds in deference to her brother. She'd managed the succession with considerable grace, silencing the crowd so that she could announce herself as daughter of Tyre and Queen of Israel, and then offering her brother to the people with her blessing and that of her father. But for a short while as she listened to Balazar's coronation she wondered what life might be like were this kingdom truly hers, were she able to leave Israel to Ahab and stay here well out of reach of Elijah, among the people, the life and the sea she loved so much.

Daniel was due back any day, and she looked forward to his calming presence and advice. She adopted a routine, sleeping late and going to bed early, and always eating in her quarters with Beset or with Esther. The children were frequent visitors when Esther had to meet visiting dignitaries with Balazar, and Jezebel realised how much she had missed simply being with her own children. She wondered how Ahab was coping in her absence as there had been no messengers.

She didn't bother to dress formally for her role as

glorified nursemaid, for it meant she could move around the Palace more inconspicuously, and so she was in a plain linen shift dress when Mazzer knocked at her door one lunchtime and told her that Balazar wished to see her.

Her brother was sitting on his throne, well supported by cushions in bright colours, a large table covered with food to his left, and a smaller one with a few scrolls on it to his right. A pile of different coloured marble slabs lay in a heap at his feet.

'I rather like the red one,' he said. 'What do you think?'

The red was garish and she much preferred the blue. 'For which room?' she asked.

'The bedroom, of course. We have taken over the Royal Chambers now.'

'Which colour does Esther like?'

'She chose the white, but she has no real grasp of opulence.'

'Your wife does have good taste.'

'She is married to me,' grinned Balazar, and Jezebel smiled. For a moment he drummed his fingers, then, 'I was wondering how long you are going to stay with us.' He wriggled off his throne to pile up a plate with slices of meat. Without his tight-fitting ceremonial armour, his belly protruded some way. 'Esther tells me the children are growing fond of you.'

'I'm fond of them. They have the blessing of being both attractive and intelligent.'

Balazar grinned again. 'I tell all of them they're my favourites.'

'I'm sure that's wise.'

He spoke while chewing a mouthful of food. 'So?'

'Perhaps another month. I'd forgotten how much I missed Tyre.'

'A month.'

'Yes. Ahab left for Samaria the day I came to Tyre and he will be busy with matters there.'

'I'm sure he needs you, Jezebel. He looked worse than Father when he had that funny turn at the table in Jezreel. Besides, you practically run his kingdom now. What will happen to the place if you aren't there? They'll probably declare war on the Judeans or something daft like that.'

'I'm not the only one who has come home,' she said. 'Beset and Daniel have missed their families; Rebecca is delighted to have Beset with her every day.'

'You can go back without them.'

'I could,' she said, 'but Israel is a home for them too. Besides, who will advise me if Ahab *has* declared war on the Judeans?' she said. 'I shall need Daniel to cut open a chicken and read its innards for me.'

'It's unlike you to be so fatuous.'

'And it is unlike you not to be direct. Why don't you tell me why you want me to leave? I've kept well out of your way since the coronation.'

Balazar dumped his plate on the table. 'You might as well have been sitting on the throne,' he snapped, 'for the number of times these idiots have been asking for you.'

'I see.'

'You shouldn't have so much influence.'

260

'I wasn't aware I had any at all.'

'You've got Jehu eating out of your hand.'

'Hardly. You saw him storm off just as well as I did when I told him again we would not join his war against Ben-Hadad.'

Balazar gave her a sly smile that both rankled and frightened her. 'He could have pushed harder, but for some reason he didn't.'

'You're very perceptive all of a sudden.'

'A mere lovers' tiff.'

'I beg your pardon?' said Jezebel, her pulse quickening.

Balazar picked up another piece of meat and crammed it into his mouth, not bothering to turn round. He chewed, grabbing at a handful of nuts, then wiped his hand on a linen cloth and slumped back on the throne. 'He always comes back, doesn't he, like a puppy dog? Probably wants to see his boy grow up. The question I have is whether Ahab knows Ahaziah isn't his firstborn son?'

Jezebel knew she had to leave the insinuation untouched but her cheeks burned and Balazar licked his lips as he studied her.

'You can't keep secrets from me, sister dear. As you say, I'm very perceptive.'

'I don't know what you mean.'

Balazar cocked his head. 'Really? I suppose all those nights Jehu stole to your room were innocent.'

Jezebel fought to regain her composure. 'If such a ridiculous notion were true—'

'The months add up too, don't they?' said Balazar.

'You speak out of turn, brother,' said Jezebel.

Balazar waved a hand. 'I might be wrong, but he even looks like Jehu in certain lights.'

'Really,' Jezebel said, turning for the door and almost choking with shock, 'your imagination has become almost as gaudy as your taste.'

Chapter Thirty-Nine

Jezebel left the throne room, her chin held high, but she stumbled down the stairs almost blind with panic, her face still ablaze.

She blundered into the courtyard, followed by the curious looks of the household staff.

Dear Gods, do they all know?

As she ran down the colonnade, the sound of laughter cut through the desperate tangle of her thoughts and she looked around to see where it was coming from. A number of the advisers were gathered together in a corner of the courtyard, Daniel and Eshmun among them, and when Daniel held his hands out beyond his belly, making a curved shape, the other men fell about giggling.

Not him too . . .

Another of the men mimicked Daniel's gesture, then cradled his arms as though he were carrying a baby. The men wailed with laughter again.

Fired with indignation, Jezebel marched towards the group but Daniel saw her before she could summon him and he crossed to intercept her, guiding her away from the group with his hand gently beneath her elbow.

'What is wrong with you?' he whispered. 'You look fit to burst.'

'You'd know all about that!' she said, mimicking the gesture he had made with his hands. 'Since when was having a baby so hilarious?'

'Since Rubesh the blacksmith thought he was pregnant,' said Daniel, frowning. 'He called Eshmun and I to see him but of course—'

'Don't you dare lie to me!'

'Jezebel, what *is* wrong?'

'It's *Your Highness* to you!' she said, snatching her elbow from his hand.

Daniel shook his head in disbelief. 'I would never lie to you, Your Highness. What are you talking about?'

Her voice cracked. 'Ahaziah,' she mumbled. 'Balazar knows who his father is. So someone must have told him.' She looked past his shoulder to where the men were still laughing.

Daniel's head was still shaking. 'And you thought it was me?' He sighed and stepped away from her, turning the corner into the privacy of the gardens. 'I've served you my whole life,' he said as she joined him. 'I gave up everything to come to Samaria with you and even when my own father was dying, I never left your side.' He gazed at her, his eyes grazing her face with such tenderness, but behind it was a vein of hurt that stung Jezebel. 'Do you really believe I would betray you?'

'I don't know what to believe!' she said. 'You've been avoiding me ever since we got back to Tyre, I've hardly seen you—'

'I haven't seen my family for years! Surely you don't

begrudge me that?' He looked deep into her eyes, searching for an answer, but she could only shake her head, stupid with misery. Daniel frowned, his hand fumbled for hers, his fingers threading through hers, drawing her palm to his.

She glanced down, surprised by the intimacy of his gesture, but as she looked up he snagged his hand back.

'I'm sorry,' he said. 'I shouldn't have done that.'

As he stumbled away in silent embarrassment, Jezebel saw a servant girl watching from a doorway. She turned from the gardens and went quickly to her rooms.

The last of Jezebel's travelling chests was carried down from her room the following morning. She had passed the long afternoon alone outside the Palace, hiding from everyone on a boat that zigzagged up the coast to Sidon and back, piloted by an old fisherman who had taught her to sail as a child. But for all her fury at Balazar, for all her confusion about Daniel, she knew she could no longer escape her responsibilities, and that morning she had announced to Balazar and Mazzer that she had received word from Samaria and would return home. Balazar had accepted the lie without remark and Jezebel had only fleetingly visited Esther to say that she felt her place was with Ahab.

With Beset she was more honest, and when her maid tried to suppress her sadness at the sudden prospect of leaving her mother and Tyre, Jezebel said guiltily, 'You should stay a while longer. Rebecca is elderly, she needs you. I've kept you away far too long.'

But Beset shook her head, her lips narrow with anger.

'They're driving you out. Elijah drove you out of Jezreel and now your own brother is doing the same.'

'Then I will travel these lands until someone wants me,' she said. 'My heart will always be in Tyre, but my head tells me that I cannot stay.'

'But what if Daniel—' began Beset.

At that moment the soldiers arrived to collect Jezebel's belongings. She followed them down to the stableyard, trying not to think that this might be the last time she saw the island she loved so much. The sky was blue and the air soft with the sea breeze and Jezebel took a last few breaths of home. As she rounded the well she found Daniel waiting by the carriage, stroking the neck of one of the horses.

He bowed rather formally. 'Beset told me of the return to Samaria, Your Highness. It is regrettable.'

'We are all accustomed to departure,' said Jezebel. 'Are your things already on the carriage?'

Daniel chewed his lip and his gaze fell to the floor. 'I would like to ask your permission to stay.'

Jezebel tried to stifle her surprise but a tiny moan of shock still escaped. 'Of course,' she said, 'I should have thought of it myself. I think Beset tried to tell me. And besides,' she added, trying desperately to smother her disappointment, 'after the way I accused you yesterday, I shouldn't be surprised. It was wrong of me. I was upset by Balazar and I should not have inflicted my misery on you.' Her eyes fell to his hand, the one that had reached out for her, and he moved it out of sight behind his back as if it were dirt-stained.

'It's not about yesterday,' he said. 'I've missed my family

very much, I miss the sea, the air here, talking with Eshmun . . .' He trailed off.

'Is there any other reason you want to stay?' asked Jezebel. She tried to sound gentle, but the question came out as brittle and abrupt.

Daniel dropped his eyes. He seemed about to say something, then didn't.

'We were close once,' she said, trying again to find a voice that did not betray her dismay. 'You know everything about me, but you won't tell me—'

He looked up at her, his gaze so intense that for a moment she thought she understood. But as soon as she tried to catch the thought it vanished and he looked away again.

An attendant came to her side and bowed. 'Your Highness, excuse me,' he said. 'Everything is packed, and the horses are ready to harness.'

She thanked him and, after a moment of hesitation, reached out and laid her hand on Daniel's arm. 'I would never force you to come with me,' she said. 'Stay in Tyre and build yourself a proper life.'

Daniel nodded, at last meeting her gaze again, and he smoothed his hands down his tunic. His shoulders sagged and he turned away.

The last of the horses was yoked in and Jezebel climbed into the carriage beside Beset.

'Are you all right?' her friend asked.

Jezebel wiped away a tear. 'Just sad to be leaving again,' she replied.

The soldiers gave the cry to depart, and as they jolted forward Beset linked her fingers through Jezebel's. Seabirds swirling above the Palace gave mournful cries, as the carriage rattled along its slow silent descent through Tyre.

As they passed beyond the city gates, Beset released her fingers and reached inside her cape, taking out a tiny bag of *tekhelet* cloth.

'This is for you,' said her maid, the corners of her smile tugged down with melancholy. 'From Daniel.'

Jezebel took the bag and untied the leather strings. A ring rolled into her palm, a silver band inlaid with lapis, the same pale blue of the bowl she had given him in Jezreel.

She slid the ring onto her finger, so unlike the fat gold of the Queen's jewellery, so simple and yet so beautiful, like the sea and the sky at Tyre.

'It's beautiful,' she said.

'He was going to give it to you himself,' said Beset, 'but he couldn't.'

Jezebel stared at the ring, then rested her head on Beset's shoulder. Tyre already felt a long way behind.

Five years later

854 BC – Regent

Chapter Forty

From the banks of the River Jordan, the encampment of tents looked tiny against the endless peaks of the Judean mountains that rose up behind it. The morning air was freezing, made ghostly by the shimmering mist of the whickering horses' breath. Soldiers stretched and yawned and stomped to warm themselves, and from the centre of the circle of tents rose a hesitant column of smoke as the fire struggled back into life. The January sun was so weak that it sucked warmth from the land, dulling the mountainside and turning the glittering river black with cold.

After four days on the road out of Jezreel, and just one more from their destination of Jerusalem, Jezebel longed for a bath. The river waters weren't enticing, though; they'd surely freeze her blood and drag her to an early grave. She already felt as though she were following the path to Melqart's underworld as the river sank its way south to the shores of the Sea of the Dead.

Ahaziah and Joram had begun their bickering before breakfast even, arguing over a broken harness for one of the horses. Ahaziah towered over his brother, tall and broad like Jehu, his sword always sheathed in his belt, even when he slept. At eighteen he was older than some of the soldiers who formed the cohort of the Royal Guard that was accompanying them, and they looked to the warrior-like prince as much as they did to their own commander. Joram was dwarfed by his brother, not just in age and build. But his movements were quick and tidy, and he was up on the horse and circling the camp before Ahaziah had even mounted.

'If you are the great horseman you always boast yourself to be,' Jezebel heard Joram shout to his brother, 'then you can easily ride without a full harness. I'm such a fool in the saddle I need all the straps I can get.'

Jezebel concealed her smile, for part of her had grown irritated at how relentlessly the brothers had fought since they left Jezreel. In the Palace they could avoid each other, Ahaziah almost permanently in the company of his military friends while Joram spent hours with his tutor, or reading to Ahab as the King lay in his bed. Ahab had protested that he was well enough to join the caravan, but the protestations had been feeble and easily overcome by advice to stay put.

Jezebel doubted whether her sons would have been any better behaved if their father were present. Out here on the road they couldn't escape each other, and their differences had distilled into competitiveness over every small detail, from the number of times their mother smiled at them from the carriage, to how much they made their sister Athaliah laugh, to how many rabbits they could fell with their catapults from horseback.

As the soldiers dismantled the encampment, Jezebel returned to the tent she had shared overnight with her daughter. In the gloom, the huge bundle of furs and blankets on the other bed was moving and she pulled back a shawl from near the top.

Athaliah squawked and pulled the shawl back. 'Brrr! Go away!'

Jezebel laughed. 'You can't stay here. They'll pull the tent down around you and either you'll be left sitting alone on the river bank, or you'll be wrapped up in a boarskin canopy and we will never find you again.'

'Either way I won't have to marry Jehoram of Judah,' Athaliah mumbled from beneath her shrouds.

Jezebel wrapped her arm round the mound. 'You were restless in the night, and murmuring to yourself.'

Athaliah pulled back the shawl and peered out at her mother, two beautiful dark eyes that sparkled a little too brightly. 'Was I saying Gefen's name again?' she whispered. Jezebel nodded. 'I don't know how to stop myself. When I go to sleep it's as though he's there, waiting for me in my dreams, on the roof of the Palace, or down in the winter gardens, or on the verandah of his father's estate house. He begs me not to go to Judah but every time I have to leave him.'

She sounded so desperate that Jezebel sat down on the bed beside her, weaving her hand through the layers to find her daughter beneath. But it brought no comfort, for Athaliah choked down a small sob. 'Ahaziah told me that Jehoram is so sickly he never sleeps, and instead he will just lie there and watch me. But what if I mumble Gefen's name and he hears me? The marriage will be over before it has begun!'

Jezebel thought of that first night almost twenty years

ago in her chambers in Samaria, how she had squashed Jehu's name deep beneath her heart, how she had winced when Ahab kissed the soft skin of her belly beneath which Jehu's baby already grew.

'I will see to it that you are given your own quarters, and that your privacy at night is preserved.'

'But Jehoram has no other wife to distract him and Ahaziah said that means he will never leave me alone.'

'I would remind you that no girl has yet chosen to tolerate your brother and so he has no idea what constitutes respectable behaviour for a husband. I should ignore him if I were you.'

Jezebel knew that her words would do little to soothe the anxiety of her daughter. If Ahab had been here, perhaps he might have found a way to comfort Athaliah, but he was almost beyond being able to comfort himself as his mind slid around between lucidity and confusion. It was as well that he remained in Jezreel with Raisa, the son watched over by his mother once more. It would only weaken his power among his rivals if his vulnerabilities were exposed to his neighbours. Yet it was ironic, thought Jezebel, that the forthcoming marriage reflected that same frailty in Judah. For the arrangement to marry Jehoram wasn't merely of political alliance but, Jezebel suspected, a last hope to secure the line of succession from King Asa through the firstborn son of the firstborn son. It had been sealed for three years since Jehoram became co-regent with his father Jehoshaphat and took effective control of the Judean Kingdom.

Regardless of its political purpose, in all that time Jezebel had never found the right way to explain to her daughter how she had learned to do her duty in similar circumstances. Even though she could see so much in Athaliah that reminded her of herself, the vulnerable little girl who'd cried that she would never leave her mother's side was still buried somewhere beneath all these blankets and Jezebel wished she didn't have to be surrendered.

The warming sun lifted her spirits a little, as the caravan of carriages and carts loaded with wedding gifts from Jezreel continued slowly up through the foothills of the Judean mountains towards the plateau of Jerusalem. Athaliah stared listlessly out of the carriage, as though every turn of its wheels drove her sadness over Gefen deeper into her, and the brothers only kicked up more and more dirt as they rode their horses fast across the mountain paths. Jezebel was about to stick her head out of the window to shout at them to stop when the carriage itself pulled up.

'What is it?' she asked, calling up to the driver.

The commander of the soldier troop jumped down and came to the window. 'There are a lot of people gathering on the road and it's going to be difficult to get through.'

'Where are my sons?'

'Somewhere behind us, still chasing game.'

'Where are they when we need them?' muttered Jezebel.

'Don't concern yourself, Your Highness,' said the soldier, 'I'll walk with the carriage, just until we get through here.'

'Are we in any danger?'

The soldier shook his head as the carriage set off again. 'They look harmless enough. It seems to be some sort of priest. There's a spring not far from here and given how little water there is in these parts, he's probably making a few coins from blessing the water. But seeing as we're carrying a bit of gold ourselves,' he nodded towards the chest at the rear of the carriage in which Athaliah's wedding jewellery was locked, 'it pays to be cautious.'

'Perhaps bandits will capture me and sell me to pirates on the Great Sea,' said Athaliah quietly as the soldier left.

'Be careful what you wish for,' murmured Jezebel. 'I hoped that Kesil the archer would come down from the sky and steal me away too,' she continued, 'but he just sat up there, winking, and no help at all.'

'But you love Father, don't you?'

'I learned to,' said Jezebel. 'But until we meet Jehoram and know him for ourselves, we won't know if there is a man there to love.'

'Perhaps he will be like Jehu,' said Athaliah. 'Handsome, even if he is sickly.'

Jezebel was sure she coloured at his name, but a voice interrupted them.

'Make your offering in the name of Yahweh!' Coins rattled somewhere ahead.

'In the name of Yahweh!' chorused voices in reply.

'Should we just pay so we can pass?' asked Jezebel, reaching for a purse beneath the seat.

'That may help,' said the soldier, putting his hand through the window and taking a few coins from her. 'There are two of them, one with a bowl, another giving blessings. I'll take this money and see if we can clear the path. I don't want to get stuck here.' He disappeared up ahead and in a moment they heard him shout, 'Make way for the Queen of Israel, make way!'

'The Queen of Israel?' bellowed a cracked voice that still made Jezebel shudder after all this time. 'Yahweh does not make way for the whore of Israel!'

'Stay in the carriage,' said Jezebel to Athaliah, 'pull your veil down over your face and don't get out unless I tell you.'

Athaliah's eyes widened, but Jezebel got out before her daughter could argue, and she drew her cape around her as she marched up the road.

Elijah's cloak of stitched hides hung raggedly off his shoulders, and he was doubled over with age and decrepitude. His staff was as grey and gnarled as the distorted fist that clung on to it, while his other hand waved vague blessings over the heads of the travellers who gathered around him. He stood on a pile of rocks that raised him up above the road while a younger man, his bald head shining in the winter sunshine, shuffled among the gathering accepting coins and food in a bowl.

'For a blessing from Yahweh?' muttered the younger man as he sidled in front of the commander, his head lowered as he offered him the bowl, but Jezebel took the coins from the commander's hand.

'I'm given to understand that Yahweh does not recognise the Queen of Israel,' she said, 'so He will surely not accept my money.'

'Elisha,' shouted Elijah to the younger man, 'see how the harlot's daughter now prostitutes herself to Judah! Judah will soon fall to all the same temptations that have withered the soul of Israel and their corrupted issue will span the borders of Yahweh's once-great kingdom.'

The younger man glanced sidelong at Jezebel, and as

their eyes met, she had the strangest sensation of familiarity. *Carmel*, she thought, suppressing the shiver at the way he looked right through her. *He must be one of Elijah's acolytes from that dreadful day.*

But Jezebel was too weary of the road to stay and argue with Elijah, and she wanted to get Athaliah safely to Jerusalem. So she turned her back on the prophet and his pupil and, remaining on the road, waved the caravan of carriages and carts through the narrowing of the road. Only when her sons had ridden through, staring down on the prophet from their horses as they passed, did Jezebel return to her carriage.

'You should not have defied him like that,' said Ahaziah, leaning from his horse to peer through the carriage window as they climbed on up towards the plateau. 'Word will have reached Jerusalem by the time we arrive that you have insulted their prophet.'

It wasn't the first time Ahaziah had spoken down to her, but Jezebel ignored the brief pain. 'Have you learned nothing from Ahab?' she asked. 'When you rule Israel you will only succeed if you are your own man. Many will claim your ear, be they priests or politicians, or even your wife, should you be lucky enough to find one.'

'Besides,' added Joram from the other side of the carriage, 'you should be defending Mother against Elijah, not the other way around.'

'How dare you!' barked Ahaziah. 'At least I can defend myself and don't have to go running to Father every time someone waves a sword at me.'

'At least I will be ready to govern when my time comes.'

'Boys!' said Jezebel. 'Elijah need not poison you when

you succumb so easily to your own brilliant wisdom. Now dismount from those horses and get into the carriage so that we can arrive in Jerusalem as one family.'

'But Mother—' said Ahaziah in dismay.

'We have come in peace, not to conquer,' said Jezebel, remembering Daniel's advice to her not to ride into Samaria that first time. Then she thought of Elijah, of how he had somehow known of the purpose of their journey, and his dark vision for Athaliah's reign as Queen of Judah.

She took Athaliah's hand in hers and squeezed it firmly.

Chapter Forty-One

Through the archway of the Court of the Priests, Jezebel could see the two enormous bronze pillars of the Temple of Jerusalem, glowing in the midday sunshine as though brushed with fire. They reminded her, unexpectedly, of the pillars that adorned the facade of the great Temple of El in Tyre, though this was on a scale Jezebel had never seen before. Indeed the Brazen Sea, the purification bath in the centre of the Court of Priests, was as large as some of the smallest temples in Tyre itself, a great copper bowl on the back of twelve oxen that shone like a divine cup. It wasn't just the size of this holy place that was breathtaking but the elaborateness of the wedding ceremony. Athaliah had been shaking as Jezebel kissed her daughter for the last time, so overwhelmed was she by the number of people gathered to witness the union. The enormous Outer Court of the Temple, where the ceremony was to take place, was dressed with canopies woven of flowers and foliage, swags of silk and embroidered pennants, and beneath them gathered hundreds of people, almost all of them strangers to the small delegation from Jezreel.

Jezebel had been reluctant to leave her daughter alone

beyond the Temple's outer entrance, shimmering in her beautiful ivory wedding robes, but protocol demanded that, as the most senior representative of the Israelite Kingdom, she accompany King Jehoshaphat. They had walked in complete silence through the assembled crowd, elderly Jehoshaphat wobbling with the aid of a gold sceptre, followed by Ahaziah and Joram, each carrying a small chest containing deeds and scrolls from Ahab. In front of two ceremonial thrones they had stopped and, seeing Jehoram already installed on one of them, pale wood elaborately carved and inlaid with gold and ebony, Jezebel had taken the chest from Ahaziah and offered it to Jehoshaphat.

'The King of Israel offers his respects to the King of Judah and his Co-Regent and, with the offering of his daughter Athaliah in marriage, pledges co-operation for the war against Aram-Damascus—'

'Let us not do business here,' said Jehoshaphat, lowering himself in an ungainly fashion onto a well-stuffed couch. 'Let the children marry first.'

Age had softened the irascible King, or perhaps it just wearied him, for he stamped his foot rather ineffectually and two courtiers appeared to take the Israelite chests away.

'Sit down.' He waved at a couch on the other side of the aisle on which Jezebel settled. She watched as hundreds of priests filed out of the Temple and through their court into the wedding arena. A blast of trumpets rose up from atop the outer walls, drums pounded from behind, and the procession began, Athaliah walking alone at an agonisingly slow pace through the crowd towards

281

the second throne, a mirror of the first but of dark wood inlaid with ivory.

It wasn't until Athaliah installed herself on the throne that Jezebel realised just how small and sickly Jehoram really was. She had assumed the size of the throne to be enormous, like everything else in the wedding and the Temple, but Athaliah filled her own throne and Jezebel realised that her husband-to-be was shrunken with a painful distortion of his skeleton that made him look as old as his father.

Athaliah must have noticed too, but her face was a mask of dignity and respect. Her daughter had eschewed the heavy cosmetic paints favoured by the Phoenicians for a more elaborate headdress and Israelite styling of her curls. She looked like a Temple sculpture, smooth and perfect.

The Judean wedding rituals were unfamiliar to Jezebel and even the rites of Yahweh's Temple which she knew well seemed foreign and difficult to understand. Athaliah though grew in beauty as the wedding went on, the priests bowing ever deeper, her gown shining ever more. At its close, she was showered with flowers to mark the end of the formalities and the start of the wedding feast.

Jehoram barely moved during the ceremony, and brushed off the assistance of a courtier when the banquet began, waiting until his bride had been led down to meet the Judean King before he slid off his throne, clumsy but unnoticed. Jezebel felt a pang of sympathy for him as the nobles of Judah gathered around Athaliah, eager to pay their respects.

'She looks so much like her mother,' murmured a voice in Jezebel's ear, soft breath against her cheek that made her heart jump. It had been five years since she last heard him, but for a moment she was further back still, in those first days at Tyre with a young man whom she thought she loved. Whom she did love.

She stood up gracefully and turned to face him.

'Your Highness,' she bowed low.

Jehu shrugged. 'Save that for my father.'

'He has been most hospitable to our delegation. Jerusalem is a glorious city and we are honoured to be here.'

Jehu looked past her to Athaliah, who stood like a pearl amid a swirling ocean of well-wishers and officials. Ahaziah and Joram flanked her like a pair of Royal Guards, so that even her husband couldn't get near to his new wife. A band of pipes and drums began to play, a troupe of acrobats spun and turned round the edges of the crowd, and several roast antelope were borne in on spits. All the solemnity of the rituals evaporated and a great rush of talk and laughter echoed through the Outer Court. Athaliah and her brothers were swept away by Jehoshaphat in a procession towards the feast and Jezebel saw that Jehoram stared at her from the foot of his throne, as though she was somehow responsible for her daughter's popularity.

'I should join them.'

Jehu glanced at his brother, then said, 'Walk with me.'

'I hardly need directions to the feast.'

'In the gardens.' He offered his hand but Jezebel felt unnerved by the transformation in the face she thought she knew so well. The body of the man remained intact, broad and strong, his dark curls shot with the occasional silver strand, his face furrowed with lines of thought and anger in equal measure. But his eyes had lost all their sparkle and passion, all the depth and warmth that fuelled that fire within him.

'I should stay—'

'We are practically brother and sister now. We have argued over the fate of our kingdoms and, as you observe, you are a guest of my father.'

'But I really should—'

'What is it you should do?' he said so quietly that she had to strain to hear above the noise of the celebrations. 'It would do me great honour if you would join me.'

She remembered the last time they'd spoken, while he tutored her eldest son, his own child, with a sword. In those moments, she glimpsed the man she had fallen for as a girl and now she thought again of how life might have been if politics and Gods had not intervened. In his earnest, hopeful expression, she could see the man he was then and the man he perhaps still wanted to be.

He bowed low, offered his hand once again, and this time Jezebel took it. Her stomach was tight with nerves as she realised this was the first time in almost twenty years that they had touched one other. Jehu led her through the crowd, people stepping back and bowing as the couple passed.

The gardens were quiet after the noise of the Temple, and they walked silently for a while down a long colonnade of marble columns and low hedges, water bubbling musically in pools and fountains on either side. Jezebel waited for Jehu to release her hand now they were alone but he didn't, and so as they approached a low stone bench, she moved to sit down. He held her hand until she was seated, then stood beside her looking down.

'My condolences on the passing of your father,' he said, his eyes darting across her face.

'Thank you. It's been almost six years and I still miss him.'

'Tyre continues to be a strength commercially.'

Jezebel smiled. 'Father feared that Balazar would spend more money than he earned, but in truth I think it is your cousin Esther who manages the finances of both the Palace and the kingdom.'

'She is a fine woman, dignified and intelligent. Ahab must be very proud.'

Jezebel nodded, wondering where the conversation was leading. 'He misses her. But such are the lives of the daughters of kings.'

'Yes.' He was silent for a moment. 'Perhaps the beauty of Tyre is consolation for absence from her home.' He glanced around the gardens, an unmistakeably bitter look in his eyes. 'I spend so much time in the borderlands now that I forget how much splendour there is in Jerusalem.'

'Are you away very often?'

'I command the Judean army. We have been engaged on the southern front again with the Edomites and the bandit forces, and of course soon we will ride north to Damascus with your own army – if a strategy can be agreed.'

'Then I'm honoured you came home for Athaliah's wedding.'

Jehu frowned as though he thought nothing of the effort, and Jezebel remembered what a lonely figure he

285

had sometimes seemed all those years ago in Tyre, desperate for someone to talk to, good at conversation when he enjoyed the company. For while they had drowned easily in the pleasures of each other's bodies, they had also lain for hours talking of the worlds they knew and imagining those they did not.

He's still lonely now, she realised. *He has achieved everything he can and yet—*

'What else is there for a second son to do but leave the city to lead the army?' said Jehu suddenly, as though he had stolen the thought right out of her head.

She laughed with surprise. 'You could marry.'

Jehu sat down and took her hands in his, drawing them into his lap. 'Tell me, Jezebel, how long is it since you've known passion as deep and as strong as we once had for each other?' Jezebel gasped as Jehu drew her hands onto his breast and laid them flat over his heart. 'I dream of you every night,' he said, his eyes warming as they gazed into hers. 'I have done since the night your father sold you to the Israelites.'

'Jehu—'

'It was a trade, Jezebel, there was no love in it, not like we had.' His heart pounded beneath her fingers, his head moved a little closer to hers, his voice fell a little lower. 'Wherever I am, on the dry plains or high in the winter mountains, whether I sleep in the saddle or in the deepest goosedown beds of the Palace, my last thought at night is always of you. Tell me you haven't forgotten how it felt to lie down with me.'

He reached for a curl of her hair that hung down against her cheek, rested his thumb on her lips, and Jezebel realised her hands now rested against his chest of their own accord, that her fingers moved unbidden seeking his skin beneath the folds of his robe.

His face moved close to hers, his lips almost touching. 'Tell me, Jezebel, have you ever known again what we had?'

Jezebel closed her eyes, willing her head not to move any closer to his. Her hands fell from his chest to her lap, her fingers entwined with each other, and she felt with her thumb the smooth silver and lapis ring that she had worn on the index finger of her right hand every day since she left Tyre, just as Daniel had surely wanted.

'I'm married to Ahab,' she said, knowing that he inhaled her breath, seeking the taste of her in his mouth.

'I've never forgotten you.'

'Nor I you.'

'Then let me know you again as I once did—'

'I can't.' Jezebel opened her eyes and dragged herself away from the intoxicating reach of his feelings. He stared at her, his face as still as though she had slapped him. 'Your brother . . . Athaliah . . . Ahab . . .' She sighed. 'I can't betray that which I am now.'

'The Queen of Israel,' he said.

Jehu held her gaze in his for a long moment, then he let her go and stood up. But he didn't walk away and simply stood there, his arms limp at his side. When he spoke next, there was a hardness to his words, as though their conversation just moments before had never happened. Jehu's impenetrable defences were back in place. 'This union between our kingdoms will have to be strong to withstand the different temperaments of the groom

287

and the bride. My brother is better known for his weakened body.'

Jezebel sighed inwardly. 'Then it is as well that my daughter has strength enough for them both.'

'Jehoram is a devout man, not disposed to tolerate the pleasures of other cultures.'

'Must you be so direct one moment,' said Jezebel, leaping up in frustration, 'and so oblique the next? If you believe the marriage has no political or diplomatic value then simply say so.'

'I do indeed say so,' snapped Jehu.

'The love we felt for each other might have survived had we not become different people, and our nations changed too. Things are not as they were, and Israel and Judah—'

'The arrogance!' he scoffed. 'Judah and Israel have not grown apart because you rejected me.'

'I claim no such thing!'

'They've grown apart because it is the will of Yahweh and so, as the prophets tell us, they will be reunited only when Yahweh wills it.'

'Once, you believed in love and common purpose, in the meeting of minds, in the benefits of trade and common security.'

'It was you who would not go to war with us against Ben-Hadad when he was first crowned and now we are paying for your reticence.'

'We are paying with five good years of peace during which we have rebuilt our supplies of food and water, supplies which you will no doubt wish to share should another drought begin.'

'It will be the will of Yahweh if we suffer another drought. As it is, He punishes Jehoram for his union with Israel.'

Jezebel stared at him, recalling her meeting with Elijah on the way to the city. 'Some would call your words treasonous, wouldn't they?'

'They are not my words,' said Jehu.

'Of course not,' said Jezebel. 'They are the prophet's. But you repeat them like a child.'

'We are all Yahweh's children.'

His quick answers, uttered with such conviction, drained Jezebel's resolve.

'Your father and brother obviously don't fear Elijah's pronouncements.'

'And yet my brother suffers.'

'Because he's married my daughter? Do you really believe that?'

'My brother was fit and well until the marriage was agreed,' said Jehu. 'But since then his body has failed him and he cries out from constant pain. He was only able to attend his own wedding after taking a strong potion from his physician. The prophets have decreed that this punishment is his alone for a decision that prized diplomacy above the will of God.'

'And I suppose you believe Elijah when he says I brought down the curse on Israel.'

'You ignore the prophets at your peril.'

Jezebel shook her head, struggling to find some way to get through to him. 'You used to know your own mind, but now you swallow all their opinions without thinking.'

'I judge their prophecies on whether they come true. So far I have no reason to doubt them.'

'Then how is it that Yahweh has not struck you down for lying down with me?' asked Jezebel. 'If Jehoram's punishment is so severe for marrying my daughter, then surely you should be dead by now for wanting me back.'

Jehu reeled, and for a moment Jezebel thought she had got through to him. But then he folded his arms across his chest and said, 'If Yahweh wishes me to suffer for my choices, then so be it.'

Jezebel turned away towards the Temple. 'Then it is just as well that I've saved you from yourself.'

Chapter Forty-Two

Though it pained Jezebel dreadfully to leave Athaliah behind in Jerusalem, she didn't wish to linger after the wedding. Jehoram and his father had given her a brief audience the following day to discuss Ahab's plans for the campaign against Ben-Hadad of Aram-Damascus, but Jehu was thankfully not present. It was rumoured – and with good reason, Jezebel suspected – that Ben-Hadad II was sponsoring bandits operating in the foothills to the north of Gilead. No doubt Jehu would have said they should have struck pre-emptively years ago, but Jezebel stood by her decision to hold back and Jehoshaphat told her, rather condescendingly, that he agreed she'd made the most prudent choice. Now, however, war could not be avoided.

Jezebel hadn't seen Jehu since she left the gardens, and she hadn't enjoyed the wedding feast either, fearing he would suddenly fix her with his stare across the Temple Court. Perhaps he felt as she did that they had nothing further to say to each other now she had rejected him, for he stayed out of her way.

Furthermore, it seemed imprudent to remain so far

from Ahab's side when both kingdoms were preparing for war. Ahaziah was itching to return and Joram was eager to discuss strategy with his father now he had met the Judeans.

Athaliah tried to put a brave face on it, and Jezebel attempted to lighten the mood with good advice.

'Always listen, never gossip, and learn patience,' she said. 'You must be above reproach if you are to win the confidence of your husband. And once you have done so, let him defend you rather than the other way around.'

'I don't believe you followed any of that advice yourself,' Athaliah smiled.

'If I had, you would have been married five years ago. Though you might have married a rather different man.'

'I don't believe Jehoram to be cruel at least,' Athaliah said, 'or unkind. In fact he was rather—' At that she blushed. 'I believe he's only so bad-tempered because he's in great pain. He was a different man when we were alone.'

'Then I hope he does not come to rely on you as much as he does on his physician,' Jezebel replied.

But as the carriage began its slow descent from Jerusalem, she regretted not mentioning what Jehu had said about Jehoram's punishment. Better that Athaliah hear the rumour from her than through a loose tongue in the household.

They were to take a different route back, cutting north through the mountains towards Samaria rather than following the river. Jehu would be setting off with Jehoshaphat and the bulk of the Judean army to Jezreel and so were already crossing the plains to the west. She had tried to pass the journey in sleep but was woken by the pounding of hooves beside the carriage. She blinked into the lowering sun as Ahaziah called out for her.

'Where are we?' asked Jezebel through the window.

'Bethel,' he replied. 'Near the border.'

'Then we are stopping here tonight?'

'You may not wish to,' he said. 'I rode into the town to let them know of our arrival but I found the people in mourning.'

Jezebel's first thought was of Jehoram. Great El, had he died? As quickly as the thought occurred, she dismissed it. Such news couldn't have overtaken them.

'If I were as sensitive as Joram,' scoffed Ahaziah as he dismounted, 'I would say I can smell trouble. But it was obvious even to me that something peculiar has happened here. No one would look at me as I rode into town, and I've never heard such a dreadful wailing.' He shuddered. 'I for one don't wish to sleep in such a cursed place as this.'

Jezebel got out of the carriage. They were on the outskirts of the town but though it was late in the afternoon, there were no farmers' carts on the road or children playing, and all she could see were two old women draped in black, walking slowly towards the town.

Jezebel told the retinue to stay together, and she went with Ahaziah and Joram to catch up with the two old women.

'Where are your townsfolk?' she asked.

'At the Temple,' muttered one of them in reply, reddened eyes set into her deeply creased face.

'What happened here?'

'Was it the plague?' asked Ahaziah, his hand over his mouth.

The women exchanged glances, then the one who had spoken looked over Jezebel's attire, from the simple silver and lapis diadem woven into her hair, to her heavy white woollen travelling cape edged with Tyrian purple. 'Who asks the fate of Bethel?'

'I'm Jezebel, Queen of Israel. My daughter has just married Jehoram, Co-Regent.'

'Then we know all about you.'

Jezebel shivered; it wasn't the welcome she'd hoped for. 'We are on our way from Jerusalem to Samaria and had hoped to stay the night in your town.'

'You have inflicted the curse of Elijah on Bethel,' said the second woman, her ash-grey hair scraped back from a bony profile.

'I would wish the curses of Elijah on no one,' Jezebel replied. Out of the corner of her eye she saw Ahaziah rest his hand on the hilt of his sword, and she laid her hand on his arm to still him. 'Tell me what curse befalls your town?'

'We have been robbed of all but a very few of our youngest children,' said the first woman.

'Were they stolen?' asked Joram.

'Their lives were stolen on this accursed day,' snapped the second, her eyes glistening with the agony of loss. 'Every family here has lost a child and you have brought it down on us—'

'Rabiah,' warned a voice nearby. A priest approached and Jezebel bowed respectfully. 'Your families are waiting at the Temple,' he said to the elderly women. 'I will see to our guests.'

'She isn't welcome here!' cried the second woman, waggling her bony finger at Jezebel. But her friend took her elbow and drew her away.

'I apologise for Rabiah, Your Highness,' said the priest. 'This tragedy has torn the heart out of this town and I only wish you could have visited us on another day.'

'What happened?'

'It is the strangest tale,' replied the priest, walking Jezebel and her sons back towards their caravan. 'Our children like to play in the caves on the western slopes when the weather is very hot for they are cool. We use the stone caverns to store our dried and salted foods during the winter, as many towns do. The slopes of the mountain can be very slippery with frost though, and the children are forbidden from playing in the caves during the winter; it's dangerous and wild animals have been known to hibernate there. We cannot watch over them . . .' He tailed off, his voice catching in his throat.

'But the children went to the caves?' prompted Jezebel.

'We don't know why,' said the priest, wringing his hands. 'They had no reason to go. They knew it was dangerous; they knew it was forbidden!'

'Did they slip and fall?' asked Joram.

But the priest shook his head. 'They were mauled to death by a family of bears,' he said. 'Every last one of them.'

'Why didn't they run away?' asked Ahaziah, but Jezebel shook her head warningly.

'How many children did you lose?' she asked.

'Every child who could walk, forty-two in all.'

Jezebel couldn't stifle a wail of shock. Ahaziah shook his head in disbelief, and Joram reached for his mother's hand. 'It was a massacre,' she whispered.

No wonder the women blame me . . .

She drew herself up and bowed again to the priest. 'Every one of your people has my prayers,' she said. 'We won't trouble you for hospitality on this dreadful day. You should be with your people.'

'But Your Highness, we had our instructions from Jerusalem—'

'We will draw water from your wells, if you permit us.'

'Don't go near the caves,' insisted the priest. 'You must take the route further to the west.'

'We will take good care,' said Jezebel.

The priest seemed so grateful to be released from his duty towards them that as they parted, Jezebel couldn't help but wonder if he shared the views of his people.

Ahaziah shuddered as they walked back towards the caravan. 'I will be glad to leave this wretched place.'

'It is simply their misery you can feel,' said Joram. 'You might know it yourself one day on a battlefield when losses are bad.'

Ahaziah sneered at him, glad to be distracted by how much his brother annoyed him. 'You are a fool to hold with such notions. All I will know is the smell of the blood of my enemies.'

But Jezebel was thinking about the old woman's hostility towards her, so unbidden and yet so clear to the old woman herself. Surely it was just coincidence, she thought, that she was passing on this particular day.

Joram squeezed his mother's hand, perhaps sensing her

anxiety. 'Angry, frightened people are likely to blame an outsider for their problems,' he said.

'Mother's reputation precedes her,' said Ahaziah. 'We all have to live with it. The best thing to do is show strength. We should seek out the bears and kill them.'

'We will do neither,' said Jezebel, unsettled by Ahaziah's frankness. 'We have nothing to prove in Judah, so let us cross the border tonight and be glad that we are going home.'

Chapter Forty-Three

The plains around Samaria were almost unrecognisable, so thick were they with the tents of Judah's army, gathered ready for the surge to the plains of Gilead to the east. Among them, Jehu would surely be brooding, tense with readiness for war, but Jehoshaphat was the one who rode up the mountain to meet with Ahab. Jezebel marvelled. Was it so simple that a marriage could yoke two kingdoms who for so many years had viewed each other with suspicion? Where a common enemy was involved, she supposed so. While the Kings discussed the war alone, she sat with Boaz and Reuel, discussing what had taken place while she was in Jerusalem.

'And how did the King manage in Council?' asked Jezebel, finally addressing the issue they had been avoiding all morning.

Reuel looked nervously down at his slate, but Boaz smiled sadly. 'It was a struggle for him, Your Highness, I won't lie to you. We tried to dissuade him from attending, saying that it was simply mundane matters, but he insisted.'

'He did his best,' said Reuel.

'As Your Highness knows,' nodded Boaz, 'he becomes

particularly attached to one issue over all the others, and it can then be difficult to convince him that it's unimportant.'

'He kept talking about the war,' said Reuel. 'Achidan was trying to get him to agree that the new silos at Shechem should be built as soon as spring comes, but he only wanted to talk about attacking the plains of Gilead.'

'Then at least the King of Judah will find him in the right frame of mind.'

'Only if he isn't now thinking about the silos at Shechem—' began Boaz.

'It's all your fault!' Jezebel heard Ahaziah shout from the corridor. 'Why couldn't you just pretend to be a soldier for once?'

'Excuse me,' said Jezebel, getting up from her couch. Her advisers nodded and buried themselves in their work as she left the office. In the corridor she found Ahaziah holding his brother up against the wall by the neck of his tunic.

'Put him down!' demanded Jezebel. 'This isn't the training ground.'

Jezebel grabbed her elder son's arm and dragged it with all her strength until he freed Joram. 'In the name of El, what's wrong with you both?'

'I was going to war until this stupid runt opened his mouth,' barked Ahaziah. 'You know how stupid Father gets these days.'

Jezebel slapped Ahaziah's hand and he reeled in surprise. 'Don't you ever talk about your father that way again. He is your King and you should not even have been in the meeting with Jehoshaphat.'

'Father would have made a fool of himself if I had not

been there to steady his mind,' muttered Joram, still flushed from Ahaziah's rage.

Gradually, Jezebel got to the bottom of the matter. It seemed that Joram had asked to attend the war party as a strategy adviser – proving himself 'both an idiot *and* a coward', according to Ahaziah. The upshot was that Ahab in his confusion had said that neither of his sons was to accompany him this time.

Ahaziah looked pleadingly at Jezebel. 'Can't you ask Father for me?'

'You won't be going to Gilead,' said Jezebel. 'You're too young—'

'I'm eighteen!'

'And old enough to know that if Ben-Hadad gets news of the King of Israel and both his heirs on the battlefield then he will surely seek you all out with one blade.'

Joram sneered at Ahaziah. 'You didn't think of that, did you?'

'Enough!' snapped Jezebel. 'Why can't either of you think of your father and your kingdom instead of yourselves?' She strode away, her fists clenched at her sides, trying to shed the image of Ahab demeaning himself in bewilderment in front of Jehoshaphat.

But when she finally located Ahab in his chambers, she was shocked to see him being fitted with new armour.

'I missed you,' said Ahab, reaching for her.

At least he still knows who I am, she thought as she crossed the room and took his hands in hers. 'Leave us please,' she asked his attendants.

But Ahab grabbed one of them by the arm. 'Send for Micaiah,' he demanded.

The servant bowed and hurried from the room.

'Who is Micaiah?' asked Jezebel, but Ahab was back in front of the mirror, admiring his breastplate.

'What do you think of it?' he asked. The straps dug into his scrawny shoulders and it was at least a size too large, banging against his chest every time he moved.

'Ahab?'

'It looks well on me,' he said, running his palm over the beaten metal. 'What do you think of it?' he repeated.

'I think you should not be going to Gilead,' she said softly, drawing him down to sit on a couch with her.

He sat down, puffing with the effort, the breastplate riding up to cover his chin. Jezebel undid the straps and lifted the armour off. 'I don't know how you can wear even this one piece,' she said, laying it on the floor, 'let alone ride in the whole outfit.'

'I must fight with my men,' said Ahab, his attention still caught on the abandoned breastplate. 'When a king stops leading his people from the front, then Yahweh won't look kindly on his army. Israel needs me.'

'Yahweh will not ride ahead of you with a shield though, will He?' she said, turning his face tenderly towards her.

He looked confused for a moment, then his eyes sharpened. 'You fear for me.'

'Of course I do.'

'Five years ago,' he said, 'you were right to avoid a confrontation with Ben-Hadad, for we were still rebuilding our prosperity, but now it cannot be put off. He must be shown he has no right to the plains and I must be the one to show him.' His face clouded. 'Besides, what use am I in Council? I see the characters on the scrolls but I cannot

301

make sense of them. Boaz talks in circles and the nobles despair of my confusion.' His voice rose up in frustration. 'You've been protecting me for too long; you've been shielding me from myself!'

'Then we can lead Council together.'

'I must lead my kingdom to war! That is all that is left for me.'

'Please don't go,' said Jezebel, squeezing both his hands in hers. 'If something were to happen to you, Ahaziah isn't ready to rule—'

There was a sharp knock at the door.

'Who is that?' Ahab looked confused, his eyes staring wildly.

'Come in,' called Jezebel, frightened at the unpredictability of Ahab's bewilderment.

'You asked for me, Your Highness?' A thin young fellow in an army tunic entered the chamber, a dagger strapped to his waist.

'Are you Micaiah?' asked Jezebel, standing up. 'What place have you in the household? Were you appointed during my absence?'

'I am a priest in the service of Jehoshaphat.'

Jezebel looked him over once again. He was muscular and strong like Ahaziah, and the only sign that he was not a warrior was the distinctive signet ring of the priesthood on his finger. 'You are not dressed like a priest.'

'I'm trained to fight as well,' said the young man. 'I counsel the King of Judah, but I'm also prepared to protect him should I need to.'

'It seems your entire kingdom is ready for war,' observed Jezebel.

Ahab grasped Jezebel's arm and she helped him to his feet. 'Who is this man?'

'You asked for Micaiah and he has come.'

'Yes, yes,' Ahab nodded vigorously. 'You are worried about what will happen to me at war, so we will consult Micaiah. He is said to be very wise.'

'What about your own priests?' asked Jezebel. 'If it is their blessing you seek—'

'She wishes to know the will of Yahweh,' interrupted Ahab, flapping his hands tiredly at Micaiah.

Micaiah glanced in surprise at Jezebel, no doubt aware that she didn't share her husband's singular worship.

'Please do whatever it is that is necessary to fulfil my husband's request,' she said, gesturing at the small shrine in the ante-room.

But Micaiah shook his head. 'Yahweh knows you seek His Word.' He adjusted his dagger in his belt. 'I was just on my way from the Temple to see the King of Judah.' He hesitated. 'I've been blessed with a prophecy already.'

'I'm perfectly accustomed to proclamations from the mouths of priests,' said Jezebel, but she felt sick with fear at how Micaiah's demeanour had changed.

'I should tell my own master first,' murmured the young priest.

'No,' said Jezebel, her anxiety building. 'For it is our fate you hold, is it not?'

'The armies of Judah and Israel will be victorious over Ben-Hadad on the plains of Gilead,' answered Micaiah quickly, 'but the King . . .' He faltered.

'The King of Judah?' asked Jezebel.

Micaiah swallowed hard. 'The King of Judah will lead

the armies home, for Ahab, the King of Israel, will die in battle.'

'You wanted to know,' said Ahab, picking up his breast-plate from the floor. 'And now the prophet has spoken.'

'All the more reason not to go to war,' pleaded Jezebel.

'The loss of one man against the gain of the kingdom is the correct accounting,' said Ahab, stroking the beaten shell of armour in his lap.

'Then let Ahaziah come with you and protect you as Micaiah does Jehoshaphat,' she said.

'You would sacrifice the future of this kingdom in favour of its past? Now who has lost their mind?' Ahab stood up and began fiddling with the straps of the breast-plate, and Micaiah stepped forward to help him. Ahab turned his back on Jezebel as he was strapped in.

'You have managed the affairs of the Kingdom of Israel to our great prosperity for many years,' he said to Jezebel, 'and now you will remain in Samaria and continue to build for our future until I return. But if the prophecy holds, then you will lead Ahaziah until he is fit to rule.'

Micaiah tightened the last strap of the breastplate, then handed Ahab his helmet, and the King slid it on over his thinning white hair.

And so at dawn the following morning, the senior cohort of the Israelite army gathered in the courtyard of the Palace, waiting for their commander, the King. The horses shifted from hoof to hoof on the stone, the dogs whined and strained at their chains. Soldiers thumbed the hilts of their swords and brushed dust from their breastplates, and beyond the Palace walls, Jezebel could hear the troops and wagons beginning their march down the mountain-side to join the Judean army on the plain. Ahaziah stood behind Jezebel, dressed in armour even though he would not be joining the battle, while Joram watched from the balcony, his hair still untidy from sleep.

'His Highness the King of Israel,' went up the cry from inside the Palace, and the troop snapped into salute.

Jezebel swallowed down a twist of pride and sadness as Ahab walked unsteadily out into the courtyard, his helmet already on his head, soft strands of white hair poking out over his shoulders. Beside her, Raisa gave a satisfied bob of her head to see her son. It was a cruel irony of Ahab's decline that he now looked almost as old as his mother, and considerably more frail. For Raisa did not seem to age, only to become a little smaller with every passing year.

'I wish you'd been able to talk him out of going,' murmured Jezebel to her mother-in-law. 'I'd hoped he would listen to you.'

'He listened to me because I agreed he should go,' said Raisa. 'It's the right thing for him to do, Jezebel, and I believe you know that.'

'The kingdom before everything?' she murmured.

'Indeed.'

Jezebel stepped forward, a terrible weight of foreboding in her heart, and took Ahab's beard in hers. She kissed it with reverence, then she let it fall against his breastplate and stood back as he was helped up onto his horse.

'The King!' cried Ahaziah.

'The King!' shouted the cohort.

'May Yahweh bless this mission!' proclaimed a voice

from the far end of the courtyard. The dogs began to bark and howl, and Jezebel glanced at Raisa.

'Is that Micaiah?' she asked, but Raisa shrugged, unable to hear her in the din.

And then, as though Yahweh Himself had silenced them, the dogs fell quiet and dropped to their bellies. Jezebel recognised immediately the wretched cloak of tattered animal skins still barely held together, but the man who wore it was tall and upright, his head bare of cap or hair, and he walked through the crowd without the stick of oden wood. Jezebel was curiously reminded of watching Ahab don his war garb for here was the armour of Elijah, but on the narrow shoulders of the acolyte who had passed round the prophet's bowl on the mountain pass near Jerusalem. And he was clearly at home in his master's robes for he looked around the courtyard and the gathered cohort with all the calm appraisal of a man who knows his purpose.

'Where's Elijah?' asked Jezebel.

'My master has ascended to God,' said the man, his voice clear and steady, without the brittle fervour of Elijah.

Jezebel frowned, trying to recall this younger man's name. 'Elijah is dead?'

A murmuring spread across the troops.

'The heavens opened in a great whirlwind,' said the bald man, 'and a chariot of fire drawn by horses of flame came down. Elijah cast off his mantle onto my shoulders and rose up to meet his God.'

Jezebel couldn't stop herself glancing at the flat and winter-grey sky. Could it be true? Was the dark shadow of Elijah's menace gone at last?

'I am Elisha, and I have come to bless this mission,' said the man, holding his hands up in benediction. 'May the Kingdom of Israel know victory on the plains of Gilead.' Then he turned his back on the King and walked out of the courtyard and the troops followed him, just as though he was their leader.

Jezebel went to Ahab's side and touched him on the arm. 'Please be careful. I know that you have now heard two prophets speak in favour of victory, but Micaiah said—'

Ahab reached for her hand, his eyes glistening within his helmet. 'You never normally take heed of the prophets of Yahweh, so why do so now?'

'It isn't the prophets I'm thinking of. You are bound to be a target for Ben-Hadad. Let others do the fighting. You can win this war just as effectively from a position of safety.'

'I'm twice the man Ben-Hadad the father was, so his son will be but a quarter of me.' He twitched the reins and his horse rode on, bearing its frail leader to the rear of the army.

'That may be,' she murmured. 'But you are not the soldier you once were. And all the words of all the Gods won't repel the arrows of men.'

Chapter Forty-Four

A prophecy was just a set of words, Jezebel told herself. Elijah's vitriolic predictions of her own death had come to nothing, and it was he who'd met his fate first. In the first days of the campaign, Jezebel imagined Ahab falling victim to Ben-Hadad's sword, but those days passed and no news came from Gilead. She allowed herself to believe that Micaiah's prophecy too was false, and prayed daily for her husband's safe return.

But spring was slow to come to the high plateau at Samaria, the grey sky enveloping the whole city. Several times Jezebel thought of going to the Palace at Jezreel, so strange was it to be in Samaria in the late winter, but she was comforted by the ludicrous instinct that Ahab's return was more likely if he could find her exactly as he had left her. Not that Samaria felt to Jezebel much like a city; it was so empty since the garrison had gone to war, and she found herself thinking often of Bethel, that miserable town near the Judean border, where the soul of the people had died with their children. News rarely came of the combat in Gilead, only occasional administrative reports dribbled in from Jezreel, which were talked over in Council by the few nobles who had not taken up places in the army. Jezebel began to think that there was no kingdom left for her to govern. With every afternoon she went up to the Palace roof, wrapped up against the bitter winds, searching the skyline to the east for any signs of life.

Beset had returned from another visit to Tyre the day after Ahab had led the army to Gilead, and Jezebel was glad of her company in a way that made her feel girlish again. Since Balazar's coronation, she had encouraged her maid to make more frequent trips home. With the children grown up, and Jezebel's position as regent of Israel settled, she had felt less need to keep her Tyrian companions close. She was confident that the priests of Yahweh within the city no longer viewed her with suspicion and since Tobiah's deception and disappearance, she was more careful about those she allowed within the inner circle. She'd earned the respect of a loyal cadre of councillors and took a diligent interest in the promotion of new ones.

She suspected Beset had seen Daniel in her home city, but her friend never mentioned it and spoke only of her elderly mother, and Jezebel hadn't the courage to ask after him. She wondered if her maid had told him that his ring never left her finger; Beset couldn't have failed to notice.

In these empty days of waiting, the silence of the Palace broken only by tempestuous arguments between Ahaziah and Joram, Jezebel realised how much she missed those early days in Samaria, when there was so much to do and learn and talk about with Beset and Daniel.

Then, one afternoon around a month after the army had ridden out, she saw a horseman riding across the plains. In that moment, she realised how complacent she'd become about Ahab's safety. As the dark figure of the messenger drew ever nearer to the Samarian foothills, Jezebel's stomach twisted in fear at what news he brought, and she was at the Palace gates waiting for him when he arrived, his horse sweating.

'What of the war?' she asked him between the peals of the Council bell as they walked swiftly through the court-yard. 'Is Ben-Hadad defeated?'

'It was a rout, Your Highness,' said the messenger with a grin, unwrapping a boarskin pouch to release the scrolls of report. 'Ben-Hadad had underestimated the numbers of troops in the combined armies, and the Judeans were able to control his army's movements to the north and south while the Israelites pushed them back from the River Jordan.'

'And the Ammonites? Jehoshaphat feared there may be trouble from the south.'

'They stayed within their own borders. Their peace with the Damascans is one of convenience at best, and I imagine when they saw eight hundred angry Judeans on horseback they thought better of an incursion.'

'And our King?' asked Jezebel, pausing before the doors of the Council Chamber.

'He is in good spirits, Your Highness.'

Jezebel's hand flew to her mouth but it couldn't stop the gasp of relief that burst from her. 'You saw him?'

The messenger grinned again. 'He was riding his chariot, waving the remnants of Ben-Hadad's pennant. His seal is on the scrolls, if you wish to see them.'

Jezebel nodded, unable to speak, and led the messenger into the Council Chamber where he unrolled the scrolls on the cedarwood table. The cloth was littered with notes and diagrams, troop movements, lists of casualties, and finally an inventory of the spoils of war claimed from Ben-Hadad's army in defeat. Jezebel sank down on a bench and let the words swim before her eyes.

Though she knew it was her duty to allow the messenger to read through the reports in full, she could only sit through the first few minutes of the formal Council meeting before she excused herself. Ahaziah and Joram could guzzle down the information between them, no doubt fighting over the triumph at a distance, but Jezebel couldn't settle to the idea that the war was over so easily. She couldn't sit down to eat, and the harp Daniel had left brought no comfort. Finally, after darkness had fallen, Beset came to her with a bowl of strange-smelling liquid.

'I don't know why good news should trouble you so,' said Beset, 'but if you are as tired of it as I am of watching you suffer, then you will drink this and give us both a good night's sleep.'

'I've grown so used to the fear of losing him,' said Jezebel. 'I cannot get used to the idea that I have not.'

'But you seem to fear much more than merely his death,' said Beset, lowering the bowl into her mistress's hands.

Jezebel shrugged. 'I fear his life too, I suppose. The weakening of his mind causes him great distress. I'll be glad for him to return triumphant, but it will have lulled him into the belief that he's invincible, and that'll make it even harder to reason with him.'

'Are you afraid you'll no longer have control over the kingdom you have enjoyed for so long?'

Jezebel glanced at her maid. 'You have become almost

as direct as Ahaziah. The only thing he has not yet said to my face is that he believes he should be Ahab's co-regent and not me, like Jehoram is with Jehoshaphat.'

'Well?'

Jezebel shook her head and sniffed the liquid in the bowl. 'I suppose I dread the moment he begins to demand his right. In truth,' she lowered her voice, 'the best ruler would have Ahaziah's courage and Joram's intelligence. Ahaziah is poor at taking advice from those who are more experienced, and he sees trade and diplomacy only in terms of combat strategy.' She rubbed her forehead wearily. 'It's never bothered me that I'm not a warrior, for I have an army to fight for me should I need it. But Ahaziah will allow no one else to think for him, and that worries me.'

'Then let's hope that a victory has invigorated Ahab and he will come home refreshed of mind and body.' Beset tapped the edge of the bowl. 'Drink up.'

Jezebel winced as she swallowed the bitter wine, but she was relieved to feel its stupor in her limbs as she lay down in bed, comforted by the way it dulled her mind. But the unease that had plagued her ever since she saw the messenger galloping across the plains would not entirely leave her, and as she fell asleep she sensed it rise up into a cloud above her chest. Several times as she slept she felt herself try to push it away with her hands, but each time it sank back around her like a great dark smothering fur, cold and damp and sticking to her face, like the cool dark of a cave.

Even in her dreams, Jezebel was sure she had been in this deep, desolate place before, but no matter how many times she turned around she couldn't see outside to the daylight.

Is it Carmel . . . the caves at Carmel?

Instead of the comforting whispers of the sea she could only hear the whimpers of children crying, round and round her, their voices swaying until they were lost one by one.

The smothering fur fell on her.

'Behold the harlot Queen!' The fur shimmered before her, drawing her deeper and deeper into the cave, her legs growing heavier, every breath harder to draw. Out of the odorous miasma of noise and damp crawled not a bear but Elijah on all fours scrabbling to reach her, blood pouring from the wound in his groin, the knife Jezebel thrust into him dragging against the stone floor, chink-chink, chink-chink—

Jezebel lurched out of the dream, forcing herself upright in the bed, gasping for breath that didn't smell of that wretched cloak of skins. But she couldn't rid herself of the stench and she blinked herself awake, her eyes darting across the dark in search of familiar shapes, her couch, Astarte's shrine.

A man stood at the end of her bed.

The scream stuck in her throat.

Elisha.

She fumbled at her face, sure her hair was stuck across her eyes, but her arms were so heavy.

I'm dreaming, I'm still dreaming.

But she blinked over and over and still he stood there, the moonlight gleaming on his naked scalp, the cloak around him, that feral smell of the cave seeping out of him.

She forced herself to think, her tongue thick with the sleeping drug, breath still sparse.

This cannot be. How did he get in?

And then the figure turned his head and pulled up a sort of hood, two strange corners like ears.

Jezebel forced down a great gulp of stinking air and rubbed her eyes and this time she saw the man for who he was, for with his head covered right down to his ears and the neat profile looking just as it had in the Council Chamber day after day—

'Tobiah?' Jezebel shuddered, hauling in awakening breaths as she pinched herself to wake herself up. 'You're not Elisha, you're Tobiah. You stole the royal seal. Naboth . . . You killed Naboth!' She tried to struggle onto her knees, flailing at him as all the memories collided into the truth, but he simply stepped back and pulled off the hood.

'I didn't kill Naboth,' he said. 'The nobles were foolish enough to do it for me.'

'His blood is on your hands,' gasped Jezebel.

'And I'm not Tobiah,' said Elisha, running his hand over his scalp. 'He was merely a myth who served his purpose.'

Jezebel felt in the dark for something to defend herself with. 'You shaved off your hair . . .' she said, trying to distract him.

'The last to make fun of me paid with their lives,' he hissed, spreading his fingers like claws.

And then her dreams drove rifts in memory and Jezebel saw clearly in the dark, the ruthless swipe of revenge.

'You killed those children at Bethel?' she whispered in disbelief. 'You were the bear?'

'They had been told not to go to the caves and they disobeyed,' he said. 'They found me feeding on the fruits that were hidden there. They taunted me, called me a leper because of my hairlessness.'

'And you killed them for that?' she whispered, the smell of the caves flooding in waves from her dream.

'My hair is removed to signify my devotion to my God,' he said. 'It was my God who killed them.' He smiled. 'I let them feed first, for they were as greedy as I was,' he said, his hand falling to his hip where a short dagger glinted darkly. 'They would have run away otherwise.'

'What possessed you?'

'Those who mock Yahweh's prophets must pay for their disrespect. How else will they learn?'

Jezebel snatched the candlestick from beside the bed and swung it at him, rocking forward onto her knees as she did so. But it took all her effort to control the heavy iron stand and Elisha grabbed it easily, pushing it back at her. She fell back in a heap.

'What do you want from me?' she demanded, feeling a sharp spike of terror. She pulled her robe down over her legs.

Elisha laughed, a dry screech that cut the dark. 'Don't flatter yourself. Elijah was vulnerable to your charms, but I am not.'

Jezebel remembered her dream, Elijah crawling towards her, the knife deep in his groin, and for a dreadful moment she wondered if Elisha did indeed have the power to read the minds of mortals as well as to hear the voices of Gods.

'So you know the so-called prophet of Yahweh couldn't control his lust,' she spat.

Elisha looked surprised, but then he smiled. 'Elijah had become a liability, too beholden to his arrogance, too determined to write myths of himself that were told more widely than the messages of his God.'

'You killed him,' breathed Jezebel, suddenly sure of herself.

'Let us say the flames of his ascension were entirely from my own hand.'

'You're a common murderer.'

He walked slowly around the side of the bed, speaking in a low voice. 'Yahweh has not forgotten this kingdom. The House of Omri will fall, your children's reigns will be cut short by their own foolishness, and you will end the wretched line below the walls at Jezreel as food for dogs, just as Elijah prophesied. This kingdom will return to Yahweh under the hand of another ruler.'

'Those are words of insurrection and hatred, not of any God.'

'What makes you think the two are so different?' asked Elisha. He glanced up at the window, lifted his hand, and a veil of cloud moved across the moon.

The room fell into shadow and Jezebel held her breath, terrified that he would slice her throat in the gloom. But when she thrust out with her fists to push him away, his face was no longer there and when the moon emerged and flooded the room with silvery light, she found she was alone.

Chapter Forty-Five

Jezebel called for Beset, who summoned the commander of the Palace Guard, but even after a thorough search, Elisha was nowhere to be found anywhere in the city. Jezebel shivered to think he must have had help to escape.

Despite the commander's assurances of their safety, sleep was impossible, and Jezebel and Beset lay side by side until dawn.

'His behaviour is strange,' murmured Beset after the dawn bugle had sounded. 'Prophets like to be heard, but he appeared to you only.'

'He wanted to frighten me,' said Jezebel. 'If he'd come before all the people, I would've identified him as Tobiah and ordered his arrest. He's too clever to move out of the shadows, when he can let rumour spread the word for him. It only serves to increase the mystery of his prophecies.'

Beset grumbled about her mistress's reasoning, and protested noisily at breakfast that she should have a permanent guard to assure her safety, but Jezebel just wanted to be alone, so she took herself up to the roof to escape. It was still and quiet up here and her fingers played over the ring Daniel had given her as she walked slowly around, surveying the whole land around Samaria. How she missed the peace his constancy brought her. It wasn't that he didn't have opinions – it was difficult to be a Tyrian in Israel without them – but his first concern had always been with her as a person, not a princess or a queen. As she stared out towards the north-west, wondering what he was doing on a cold morning in Tyre, she realised she longed to be somewhere where prophecies were irrelevant, where kings didn't fight over territory or sons over power.

But Ahab would be home soon and the business of the kingdom would resume. She glanced towards the north-east, guilty for wishing for any other life, and her breath caught in her throat. A rider was galloping across the plain towards the city, a cloud of dirt dragging in his wake. A dark feeling enveloped her and she grabbed the wall, dizzy with fear.

She made her way down the stairs through the Palace, all the way to the gates, her feet heavy.

The guards looked at her strangely as they let her through, but still she walked down the mountain road to meet the rider. And as the horse slowed to a canter, fifty paces away, she recognised the solid cast of the rider in the saddle and the black stallion beneath him. Jehu. She hesitated on the path.

He halted the horse and slid down from the saddle, tugging a rough scarf from across his mouth. Jezebel noticed how his hands were chafed from riding and his forearms were smeared with blood from the battle, and sweat and dust from the road. She knew she should say something but it took all her will to stand upright before him and when he dropped to his knees before her, she could barely hold herself still and not sink to the ground, so weighed down was she with dread.

'Your Highness,' he said in a hollow voice. 'I come to offer my condolences.'

'Ahab?' His name already felt dead in her mouth. 'I don't understand. A messenger came, he told me Ahab was safe, he had seen him on his chariot . . .'

Jehu looked surprised. 'I didn't know about the messenger. I only know that it was Ahab's own idea to send another man in his armour on his chariot, while he took the place of an infantryman and marched into battle with his own troops. He insisted on leading from the front, rousing the morale of his men.'

'The kingdom before everything.' Jezebel stared out past Jehu towards the plains. 'How did it happen?'

'He was shot by a retreating Damascan marksman. Ben-Hadad's men were angry, humiliated, they were still firing off volleys of arrows as the Israelites were pushing them back. Ahab fell quickly and of course the men around him knew it was him, but it would have been disastrous for the Damascans to realise they had wounded the Israelite King. The double in the chariot had to maintain the deception all the way to victory.' Jehu stood up. 'I am sorry, Jezebel.'

She dragged her eyes to his, and saw he felt no triumph or malice.

'Where is he?' she asked emptily.

'At Jezreel.' Jehu offered her his hand to guide her up the path. 'He has been mortally wounded—'

'He still lives?' Jezebel snatched up her skirts and began running towards the city gates.

'Surely not by now,' said Jehu, jogging to catch up. 'The arrow caught him in the neck. You will be too late, I saw the wound myself.'

'He isn't your King,' said Jezebel. 'My place is at his side whether he lives or dies.'

Jehu slowed at the Palace gates and she pressed on inside. Her only thoughts were of Ahab, on his couch in his room in Jezreel, pale and weak and bleeding to his death. She shouted orders for a horse and provisions as she ran through the courtyard, and Beset came quickly at the sound of Jezebel throwing open chests in her room in search of clothes.

'What is it?'

'Ahab is dying in Jezreel. I'm going to him.'

'Oh!' Beset sank down on the bed.

'Find Boaz,' continued Jezebel, slipping out of her dress and into an old riding habit. 'He should break the news to Ahaziah and Joram. But he must convince them to stay here until I return.'

'You cannot ride to Jezreel alone.'

'No doubt the commander of the Palace Guard has already thought of that,' muttered Jezebel as she tied her hair into a scarf. 'But I don't want to dawdle in a carriage when I can ride a horse at my own pace.'

'It isn't dignified for a queen in mourning—'

'I'm not yet in mourning,' said Jezebel. 'Go and tell Boaz.'

She softened immediately, and crossed to her maid, kissing her on each cheek. 'I've known for so long that it would end this way.'

'Is it the prophecy?' whispered Beset.

But Jezebel shook her head. 'It was his own foolishness that took him, his pride and his refusal to grow old with dignity. It was not the hand of an angry God.'

But as she ran through the Palace and down to the stableyard to find her horse, she couldn't help but remember Elisha's words in the night. *The House of Omri will fall.*

But what made her shudder was an entirely new thought that gained sudden clarity in her mind: Ahab only went to war to prove her wrong.

Chapter Forty-Six

Down in the stableyard, several horses were already harnessed and saddled for the journey, but when Jezebel asked the commander of the Palace Guard how many of his men would accompany her, he looked instead at the Judean prince.

'I will ride with you to Jezreel,' said Jehu.

'You have already had a long journey,' said Jezebel. 'You should stay here and rest. My Palace and its staff are at your service for as long as you remain.'

She bowed to him and took the reins of her horse, but no sooner had she swung herself up onto the animal's back than she found Jehu's eyes level with hers once more, from the back of a fresh animal among those already harnessed.

'You won't ride alone,' he said.

'Can you spare the men to ride with me?' Jezebel asked the commander.

'They would be better remaining here,' said Jehu. 'If the King has died, then Ahaziah will become regent.'

'I will make the decision about accession should it be required,' said Jezebel stiffly.

'And should Ben-Hadad hear that his men have killed the King of Israel,' continued Jehu, 'then it would be foolish to leave the main city garrison even less guarded than it already is. The Damascans are angry and would no doubt enjoy a sudden reckless attack on a vulnerable enemy capital.'

Jezebel turned her horse on the spot, for it sensed her impatience and was tugging at the reins. She looked down at the commander, and then at Boaz, who had joined them in the stableyard.

'I believe the Prince of Judah may be right about the motives of the Damascans,' said Boaz.

Jezebel turned the horse once more and glanced at Jehu. 'Very well. But you ride to my pace.'

'Your Highness,' he said, nodding dutifully.

They stopped only once on the way, to water the horses and eat a little themselves, but Jehu barely spoke to her beyond offering her food, perhaps respecting her mourning, perhaps simply unsure of what to say now they were alone. In all he didn't say, she sensed echoes of their bitter argument in the gardens at Jerusalem. For here was another prophecy come true, and therein Jehu surely found his proof of Yahweh's power.

But now wasn't the time to fight over it.

They took a longer route skimming the edge of the western plains to spare the horses the mountain riding, but every bone in Jezebel's body ached by the time they reached Jezreel in the dusk, and the darkness forced them into a slow and frustrating ride up the final twisting stretch of road to the gates.

'Does the King still live?' she asked the astonished army commander in the stableyard as she slid down off her horse.

'He does, Your Highness, but—'

'Then I'm not too late,' she said to Jehu, handing him the reins.

The Palace was flooded with torchlight as she ran on leaden legs to Ahab's rooms, quite the opposite of her father's own passing in the shadows. Outside his door, she peeled off her scarf and shook out her hair. She rubbed her hands quickly over her face, brushing the dirt from the creases around her eyes. She glanced briefly through the windows towards the stars, casting up a prayer to Astarte that he might be blessed with a painless passing, then she pushed through the curtain and into Ahab's room.

Two physicians stood at Ahab's bedside, and two junior officials from the Council Chamber who were present to take down any last instructions from their King. A pallid nephew of Boaz's named Teom came to meet her in the middle of the room.

'Your Highness,' he bowed low, 'my condolences.'

'Where is everyone?' murmured Jezebel. 'Their King is dying.'

'There are fears of a spy in the Israelite army, someone who let the Damascans know that the King was among the infantry and not in his chariot. Therefore as few people as possible are to know of the King's situation until it is absolutely necessary. Ben-Hadad must receive no encouragement.'

'Then it must have been the King's own idea to send a messenger to Samaria with news of his survival.'

Teom nodded sadly as one of the physicians approached them, a man of about Jezebel's age with long straight hair, who reminded her so much of Daniel, she had to blink in the shadows to be sure it wasn't him.

'I'm Yaphet, a physician in the Judean army,' he said. 'Prince Jehu ordered me to accompany the King of Israel back here, as I understand the King's usual physician is in Tyre.'

Jezebel frowned at how much Jehu knew about her household, and at how much responsibility he had taken personally for her husband.

'How is the King?' she asked, glancing down at him. He looked peaceful enough, his eyes closed, his chest lifting and falling faintly beneath a thin linen gown, a silk coverlet drawn across him.

'He wakes because of the pain,' said Yaphet, 'and he is very weak.'

Jezebel crossed the room to sit beside her husband, though it was not until she reached the far side of the bed that she saw what was killing him. There was a deep wound in his neck from which protruded part of an iron arrowhead, its long fin cutting into the flesh, the skin already festering.

'It cannot be removed,' said Yaphet quietly, 'for it will kill him instantly.'

'Do you . . . discuss me . . . even though I'm not dead?' Ahab's whisper was barely a breath but the room was so still that all of them heard it, and Jezebel sank down on the bed beside him, taking his hands in hers.

'Leave us,' muttered Ahab, and the four attendants scuttled away.

The room felt huge and dark around them, and Jezebel knew that she held the most fragile remnants of a life in her hands.

'It was the right thing to do,' whispered Ahab.

'I haven't ridden all this way to scold you,' said Jezebel, her eyes stinging with tears.

'The kingdom—'

'—before everything.' She kissed his hands. 'I know.'

Ahab's eyes opened a fraction. 'You have been a far greater queen than I deserved.' He coughed and the arrowhead glittered in the lamplight as his head moved.

'Only because you allowed me to be.'

He looked directly at her. 'Jehu won't . . . Jehu would not have done what I did for you.'

'Now isn't the time to talk of Judah—'

'But you bore his son . . . and now that son . . . will become King of Israel.'

Jezebel couldn't stop her fingers from tightening around Ahab's, and she chewed on her lip to keep herself from crying out.

'I have always known,' he gasped, 'Ahaziah . . . was not mine.'

Jezebel's cheeks flared in the shadows, and her whole body sweated with the hot waves of guilt she had suppressed for so long. For the moment she had dreaded so much had passed not in fury but only with the kindness Ahab had always shown her. 'But you raised him—'

'—as my own boy. Jehu will become King. So will his son. Born with Jehu's strength. Raised with my wisdom—'

'Then we have all been blessed.' Jezebel swallowed down the tears, of remorse, of relief, of loss, and leaned forward to kiss Ahab's forehead. 'It is I who didn't deserve you,' she murmured into his ear.

'Tell our children I died bravely.' But his face contorted in the most dreadful agony, and his body tensed.

'Ahab,' sobbed Jezebel.

But the King closed his eyes and set his jaw against the pain, and Jezebel knew that only the most merciless God would make him suffer any longer.

She kissed him on the lips, then she rose from the bed and went to the door, asking for Yaphet. The physician came quickly, and Jezebel noticed a vial in his hand. She nodded.

'End his misery,' she said quietly.

Chapter Forty-Seven

Messengers were dispatched to Samaria, Tyre and Jerusalem to spread the news, and Ahab's funeral took place at first light the following morning. It was a soldier's funeral, rather than a regal one. Eight infantrymen carried him down the hill to the burial caves. Jezebel ensured the rites were conducted in strictest accordance with Israelite traditions. She was sure that somewhere Elisha or his followers would be watching.

She knew Jehu and Jehoshaphat too had observed her during the funeral, and she was not surprised when Jehu drew her to one side afterwards.

'You were right to return to Jezreel,' he said. 'I shouldn't have doubted you.'

Jezebel couldn't think of what to say, and made a vague gesture of acknowledgement with her hands.

'Will you return to Samaria now?' asked Jehu. 'We can escort you.'

'Do you really believe the Damascans will mount an attack now Ahab's death has been announced?'

'It depends on how quickly you arrange Ahaziah's coronation.'

Jezebel looked sharply at him. 'You are making quite an assumption.'

'He is the eldest son.'

'And I have been co-regent for many years.'

Jehu frowned, a faint smile of disbelief playing on his lips. 'Unofficially. You have no legal status without a king at your side, and you surely can't be thinking of ruling yourself?'

'The future of the Kingdom of Israel is the business of the Kingdom of Israel,' said Jezebel, turning away.

'And what of Jezebel of Tyre?' he asked.

Jezebel heard a hint of wistfulness in his voice that still haunted her when she knelt to Astarte soon after in her chamber, trying to complete her own mourning rituals. His curiosity about Ahaziah's accession had reminded her how lonely she was in Jezreel, without her sons or even Beset. She remembered how important the rite of passage had been in her own father's death and the passing of the Kingdom of Tyre into the hands of Balazar, even if her own presence had confused things. But here, just as there, that passing had meant Jezebel's own passing into the shadows of the kingdom, and it was with a weary heart that she blew out the candles on the shrine.

'It's what Ahab wanted,' she murmured to the statue of Astarte. 'I must prepare Ahaziah to meet his destiny as King of Israel.'

The following evening, Jezebel rode through the gates of the Palace in Samaria and went straight upstairs to find her eldest son. She expected him to be deep in grief, but when she entered his chamber he was sitting on a couch in his quarters having his hair dressed by the Palace barber. The bedroom was already half empty of his possessions, servants bustling in and out with crates. The coronation robes lay on the bed, almost abandoned as though Ahaziah had tried them on then shrugged them off, and he was regarding himself impatiently in the mirror.

'Your Highness,' bowed the barber on seeing Jezebel. He snapped his fingers, and the room cleared in an instant.

'You can always see where the true power lies,' Jezebel said. 'Any man who carries a blade as deftly as he does . . .'

She tailed off as Ahaziah picked up his sword from the bed, glancing down its length and wiping its hilt with a corner of his tunic. He handled it lightly these days and the blade glittered in the lamplight.

'And now my son is to be King,' she said. 'Your father would be very proud,' she added, thinking of both Ahab and Jehu.

'You should have taken me to Jezreel,' Ahaziah said. He didn't look at her as he spoke and his words were clipped.

'You speak to me like a councillor,' said Jezebel in a rush of hurt. 'I'm your mother.'

Still he didn't look up her as he sheathed the sword. 'I could've been crowned there and then we wouldn't've had to put up with the Judeans for so long. I hear Jehu and his aides are to be given quarters in the Palace for the coronation.'

'They've just helped us win the war,' said Jezebel. 'It isn't prudent to push away your friends.'

'They're not friends,' said Ahaziah, dropping his sword down on the robes, 'they're merely temporary allies.

Anyway, I still don't understand why you made me wait to be crowned.'

His words revealed the young man within the soldier's strong body; he might have been eighteen years old, but his petulance showed a heart not yet mature.

'Because the rites insist on the completion of the funeral before a coronation, and because it would have been disrespectful to Raisa to crown you King with her son barely cold in the ground.'

'I don't even understand why Raisa is still living in the Palace. She serves no purpose, though I suppose it will give you someone to talk to now that—'

There was a knock at the door and a young man stuck his head round the door. Jezebel saw with a certain relief that it was Nissim, eldest son of the noble Achidan and one of Ahaziah's childhood friends. Yet Nissim only glanced at Jezebel and when he raised his eyebrows enquiringly at Ahaziah, the King-in-waiting briskly shook his head and Nissim disappeared again.

'When did your friends become so rude?' asked Jezebel.

Ahaziah glanced at the doorway, then back at his mother. 'When I decided that I don't want you living in the Palace any more either.'

Jezebel reeled. 'I beg your pardon?'

'At least Raisa knew when to step back and let Father get on with ruling on his own.'

'King Ahab was ten years older than you when his father died and vastly more experienced in matters of state.'

'Nissim and I agree that—'

'What has Nissim to do with this?'

'He is my chief adviser. Chanan will be his deputy.'

'You are all just boys, barely finished with your military training, barely educated in the ways of the world and only you have ever left Israel's borders.'

'A king decides who to listen to!' shouted Ahaziah.

'At least let Joram advise you.'

'Joram hates me.'

'He doesn't hate you, but he does disagree with you. That is a good thing. Part of what made your father's reign so successful was that because so many disagreed with him, he was forced to analyse every decision thoroughly.'

'If I allow Joram to advise me then every decision will take weeks. You can't win a war if you chew over every troop movement for hours.'

'We are no longer at war.'

'Nor will we ever be if Joram has anything to do with it. He understands nothing about the roots of a kingdom's strength.'

'And you wish me to retire to a distant corner of the Palace so that I'm no longer visible to our people.'

'That's the point, Mother. They're no longer *our* people.'

He sounds more like Balazar's son than Jehu's, thought Jezebel, her heart racing with shock.

'You will be a distraction to them,' Ahaziah continued, 'they will defer to you instead of looking to me for leadership, and you still carry the aura of Father's principles. How can I lead this kingdom in my own way if your shadows still hang over me?'

'Power is learned and earned, Ahaziah, it isn't bestowed or taken. You will need to win the confidence of the people of Israel before they listen to you, and you will need to

332

win their trust before they follow you blindly. You may have been young during the great drought, but you will surely remember how hard your father worked to keep water and food flowing into his kingdom, just to keep his people alive, let alone to enjoy their loyalty. Before you dismiss me so readily, think about all I have seen and done in Israel.'

'You're still a foreigner.'

Jezebel's fingers flew to her face as though her son had slapped her for he looked at her with an arrogance she had never seen even on Jehu's face at his most dogmatic.

Her head throbbed with anger, but she fought down the urge to tell Ahaziah that his blood contained not a single trace of Israel.

'What happened to my dear son?' she asked.

Ahaziah looked at her at first with sorrow, but his expression hardened to a sort of pity. 'I became a king.'

Chapter Forty-Eight

The coronation was set for the following day, and from first light the city echoed with bugle calls and the ringing of bells. The Palace was noisy with the bustle of preparations and the air grew sweet with the smells of all the rich foods of celebration. But Jezebel dawdled in her room unwilling to leave it for the last time, even though several of her couches and chests had been removed on Ahaziah's orders even before her return from Jezreel. Perhaps this was how Leah felt, she thought ruefully, when she saw that young Phoenician princess sweep into this very Palace all those years ago.

All around the city walls the horn-blowers began ceremonial fanfares, and cheers rose up from the crowds who had gathered in the streets around the Palace. Jezebel let Beset silently arrange the Queen Consort's gown on her shoulders for the final time, then she walked silently out onto the balcony corridor and along to Ahaziah's old quarters. Down below in the courtyard as she passed, she saw Jehu and Jehoshaphat standing with the senior Judean officials among dozens of Israelite nobles, dressed in all their robes of state. In a small chair beneath a palm tree sat Raisa, still in her mourning clothes, the only mark of celebration an opulent diadem of gold and pearls nestling in her thin hair.

There is only one diadem for the Queen Mother, thought Jezebel sadly, *and one robe too. I don't want to ask her to give it up—*

'Get off me! You have no right! I'm the King's brother!'

Jezebel looked round to see Joram at the other end of the balcony, outside Ahaziah's room, being pinned back against the wall by two soldiers of the Palace Guard.

Jezebel strode to join them. 'What's going on? Put him down,' she ordered the Guard.

Joram struggled free of their restraint, but he had to grab on to one of them to steady himself, and Jezebel could smell wine so strongly on his breath, his blood might as well be running with it. His robes were askew and he looked as though he had not sat down with the barber himself for days. She grabbed him and pulled him close to the wall.

'What is wrong with you? Today of all days!'

'I wanted to see Ahaziah,' burbled Joram, 'but these goons won't let me anywhere near him.'

Jezebel turned to the Guard. 'On whose orders do you prevent the King's brother from saluting him on his coronation day?' she demanded.

'By the order of Nissim, the Chief Adviser,' one answered.

'Nissim has the wits of an ass,' muttered Joram.

'All armed men are to be prevented from greeting the King,' added one of the soldiers, pointing to the ceremonial dagger sheathed at Joram's hip.

'Then will you stop the Royal Family of Judah, not to

mention all the nobles of Samaria and Jezreel from greeting the King also?' asked Jezebel.

'What seems to be the problem?'

Nissim and Chanan approached together, and beyond them Ahaziah standing in his doorway, just out of sight of the crowd in the courtyard. He was looking at Joram, a strange defensive look on his face.

'I thought my son wanted to rule like a warrior,' said Jezebel coldly to the young advisers. 'Surely he can fight his own battles with his brother?'

Nissim leaned forward. 'There is rumour of an assassination attempt,' he murmured. 'The prophecy.' He looked knowingly at Jezebel, who felt the last of her patience evaporate.

'As Joram isn't yet of age to rule, he would also have to kill me to get the throne,' she said. 'He has not yet seized that opportunity.'

Nissim glanced over his shoulder to his King, and Ahaziah strode towards them, swelling visibly within his new robes.

But Joram spat on the floor. 'You cannot shame me and then embrace me,' he said.

He stalked off just as the processional fanfare began. Jezebel knew it was pointless trying to call him back. Ahaziah gestured towards the courtyard and Jezebel moved between Nissim and Chanan to lead the way. But she was too angry to let it go and before she set off down the staircase she turned back and looked at Ahaziah, her voice thick with bitterness.

'Your father would be *so* proud of you now.'

336

Chapter Forty-Nine

Throughout the coronation ceremony, Jezebel kept looking around the fringes of the formal audience of nobles, priests and foreign dignitaries, hoping that Joram would return to see his brother assume his birthright. If Ahaziah cared for Joram's absence he didn't show it and, as soon as the ceremony was over, he swept through the courtyard and out into the streets of Samaria to greet his people, the Guard keeping them at a safe distance.

Jezebel looked around again for Joram as the guests began to mingle, taking bowls of wine and nuggets of roast meat from silver platters, but he had apparently had his fill of that too. She found herself alone in the crowd of people who knew she no longer mattered to them.

This is how it will be, she thought, *I'm just an onlooker, pushed out of this role of queen as abruptly as I was pushed into it.*

Even Raisa was being attended by a number of elderly nobles from Assyria, and Jezebel glanced at the Palace above her. It had changed little, really, in all these years; her impact on its fabric was negligible.

Jehu came to her side, a drinking bowl held out towards her. 'You look lost.'

'I'm looking for my other son,' she said. She was still irritated with him for his remarks after Ahab's burial, even though it all seemed so long and so far away.

'I noticed he was not at the ceremony.'

Jezebel sighed. 'He and his brother have exchanged words, and bad feelings with it.'

'I know it well,' said Jehu smiling ruefully, and Jezebel remembered that young man in Tyre, struggling to find his way as the second son.

'Perhaps you could talk to Joram,' said Jezebel, in spite of herself, surprised by Jehu's softened manner. 'He might believe the things you tell him.'

'And not you?'

'I've lost my crown and my influence today. You're wasting your time talking to me now, for if you want the ear of the Kingdom of Israel, you must cut through the maze that is Nissim and Chanan to reach Ahaziah.'

'I will be sure to learn my way,' said Jehu. He offered the bowl again, and Jezebel took it, drinking from it to avoid having to say anything else.

'That was a fine horse you rode to Samaria,' he said after a moment.

'I brought him down from Tyre after my father died, just broken in.'

'He has an excellent line about him.'

'Balazar wants him back for breeding, but I've refused to let him go.'

'I would not have given him up either,' said Jehu.

'Balazar thinks me selfish when he knows I don't have

338

the time to ride as much as I want to. But I suppose that will change now too, for the Israelites need not fear a Queen Mother who rides among them.'

Jehu smiled, guiding Jezebel to one side as the crowd surged past them in the wake of the King, eager to be part of the extended procession. Jehoshaphat was now talking to Raisa, and Jezebel suppressed an ironic smile.

'I would like to apologise to you,' Jehu said, 'for my manners at Athaliah's wedding in Jerusalem, and because I think you misunderstood me when we spoke the day before yesterday about ruling Israel. I did not mean you would be unfit . . . I didn't express myself appropriately and I fear I offended you.'

Jezebel frowned. 'The past is always difficult to reclaim.'

He smiled gently. 'Perhaps I *should* talk to Joram, for I'm an expert myself at dark moods and foolish words.' Jezebel struggled for something to say in response, but Jehu didn't seem to notice, and continued, 'I wanted also to say that you were right about the need for unity between Judah and Israel. I shouldn't have brushed your argument aside so clumsily.'

Perhaps he wasn't such an unthinking brute after all. 'The marriage between my daughter and Jehoram has brought contentment to both sides,' she said.

'And it need not stop with marriages that are arranged.' He set his bowl down on a nearby table then did the same with hers. He took her hands in his, and Jezebel glanced around anxiously; no one seemed to notice.

'You needn't be shy,' Jehu said. The eyes that searched hers had become transformed and shed of their deep cares. 'You are now a widow, and there is a reason I do not want you to stay in Israel. I would like to make you my wife.'

'Marry me?' She couldn't hide her shock and stared at him dumbly for a moment. 'But . . . but we see the world so differently. And the world sees us differently too. I'm still Jezebel with my pantheon of Gods and the curses of the prophets on me, who will be as unwelcome in Judah as I was in Israel. You are a leader in your kingdom, head of the army, brother to the King—'

'I've never taken a wife,' interrupted Jehu. 'Why do you think that is?'

'Because no woman in her right mind would live in a boarskin tent on the edge of a battlefield,' she suggested, struggling for levity to calm her nerves.

Jehu smiled but his gaze rested deep in her. Though the fire had returned to his eyes, there was a fervour too that she did not recognise.

'I've never taken a wife because no woman could take your place,' he murmured. 'I gave up a part of myself when you were given away to Ahab, and now he has relinquished you again, I hope . . .'

Jezebel blushed deeply and looked away, unable to bear the clarity of his feelings, the startling simplicity of his love for her, so constant, stretching back through all the women she had since become. Could his love really have remained unchanged, despite the infrequency of their meetings, through all their disagreements and the twisted logic of his beliefs? He had put his faith in the poison of the prophets, paid lip service to their vicious assessments of her rule and of Israel's sufferings. And yet, his love for her still overcame everything else.

'At least I can see I haven't offended you this time,' Jehu said, his fingers caressing hers. 'I will of course respect the period of mourning before expecting an answer from you. Your fondness for Ahab did you great credit as his Queen and his wife, and I'm not so clumsy as to pretend that does not exist. But I hope you will remember me now as you did once before?'

And it was only then, his voice lifted in hopefulness rather than certainty, that Jezebel understood the depth of his delusion. He mistook her dumbfounded shock for fear of returning to the past. And she realised that all of their conflicts, over alliances, over prophecies, over Gods and borders, had been something quite different. All that time, his heart had harboured the flame she thought extinguished years ago when her father married her to another man. She didn't have words to withstand the fire of his passion, or to douse it. Instead, feeling wretched and full of pity, she sought refuge in formality and smiled.

'I'm honoured by your offer of marriage,' she said, 'and I will give it the fullest consideration during the period of mourning.'

'I will be away on campaign for at least three months in the south again, so you won't have to suffer my anxious presence.' He grinned foolishly, all the shadows of age and responsibility stripped away. 'You could visit Jerusalem again in my absence, to see Athaliah perhaps. It would show you what our city would be like as home.'

'You told me once it was like an island in the land, just as Tyre is an island in the sea.'

'You remember that?'

'Of course.'

341

'Until the summer then.'

'Until then.'

He bowed low then he retreated, and after a brief word with Jehoshaphat, he disappeared into the crowd behind Ahaziah.

'That was an intimate discussion.'

Jezebel found Raisa standing at her elbow, both hands grasped on her walking stick.

'A proposal, perhaps?'

Jezebel blushed deeply. 'You think it premature.'

Raisa frowned and lifted a finger to nudge at her diadem. 'I think he has been extraordinarily patient, given how he feels about you.'

Jezebel nodded, hoping that if Raisa was that observant, she had not seen the resemblance between her suitor and her elder son.

'Of course,' Jezebel said, 'if I went to Jerusalem, I could see Athaliah every day, and you would not have to share that beautiful crown or the robe.'

Raisa gave a toothy smile. 'And it would further strengthen ties between the kingdoms. The north and the south would be closer to becoming one again.'

And I would not be trapped here or in Jezreel, stuck in the palaces, unable to go out for fear of unsettling my son.

'But you are in no rush,' said Raisa.

'The mourning period—'

'I was thinking more of the time the heart needs to make up its mind,' added the Queen Grandmother. And then she hobbled away and Jezebel stared after her, no wiser as to what she should do.

Chapter Fifty

The Palace was full of noise that evening, but Jezebel retired early to her new quarters in the annexe at the rear of the Palace, along the corridor from Raisa. She felt as she had when Ahab was away at war – so far removed from the heart of the kingdom, even though it was just yards away, that she might have been alone on the face of the earth. Beset's bustling welcome roused her from her thoughts.

'Look, see, I've done the best with your couches, but these rooms are very poky,' tutted her maid as she lit another lamp against the evening gloom. 'Really, Ahaziah had no right, after all you've done for him.'

'He fears my popularity.'

'He fears his own shadow, that one. What fool wears a sword to bed? He's downright disrespectful.'

'Well,' said Jezebel, sinking down on the end of her bed, and untying the straps of her sandals, 'we may not have to suffer it for too long.'

Beset stopped in her tracks, peering at her mistress over the top of an armful of cushions. 'What do you mean?'

'I've had an offer of marriage.'

Beset rushed to her side, dumping the cushions on the floor. 'You've seen him?'

'He came to me at the coronation.'

'I thought he would wait for a better moment. He's only just got here.'

'It was public enough as it was, Raisa saw us—'

'Public?' Beset shook her head. 'Daniel would never do that—'

'Daniel?' Jezebel stood up. 'He's back in Samaria?'

'Who were *you* talking about?'

'Jehu.'

Beset nodded slowly. 'Of course. I should have thought of it.'

'But you didn't,' said Jezebel. 'You thought only of Daniel.' She hesitated. 'Why has he come back?'

'Why do you think? He heard that Ahab had died and . . .'

'Is he in the Palace?' she asked. 'Joram at least will be pleased to see him.' She studied her fingernails. She could feel her heart beating all the way to the tips of her fingers.

'Never mind Joram,' said Beset, sitting down on the bed beside her. 'Ahaziah will likely be much less welcoming, but Daniel is intelligent enough to know that his position here has changed. Besides,' Beset cupped Jezebel's chin in her fingers and drew her face round so she could look her mistress in the eye, 'he wasn't sure what reception he'd get from you.'

Jezebel blushed. 'Why on earth would he say that?'

'Why indeed?' Beset laughed and released her mistress

from her grasp. 'I have never seen you look so pleased about anything.'

Jezebel was already kicking off her sandals and pulling off the black mourning robes. 'Find me something plain to wear so I can go out without being noticed.'

'What about the banquet?'

'Ahaziah has made it clear he has no need of my wisdom, so he hardly has need of my presence.'

Jezebel left the Palace by the servants' passage, and no one seemed to notice her pushing through the bustle of attendants and slaves organising the celebratory banquet. Huge platters of food were being shepherded from the kitchens to the dining hall and a steady procession of wine jars flowed in each direction. As she passed one of the entrances to the Great Hall she saw Joram sitting with a group of his friends at a lower table, all of them red in the face from drink and bawdy laughter, while Ahaziah sat elevated and distant on the dais with his advisers and senior guests.

Jezebel quietly let herself out of the garden gate and ran through the dark streets towards the artisan quarter of the city where Beset had told her Daniel was staying. Her heart still pounded and her palms were damp with nerves. The ring he had given her had been a constant feature, but she had never allowed herself to dwell on what its constancy represented for either of them. All she knew now was that in the turbulent seas of recent weeks, he was a safe harbour.

The lanes were narrow in the artisan quarter and the residents were having parties of their own, music spilling from lamp-lit windows, people dancing and sharing food around small fires. She threaded her way among them, looking for the house marked with a beehive for the waxmaker where Daniel was lodging. But when she finally found it the door was open and no one answered her tentative calls.

'In the name of Astarte,' she murmured, 'where *are* you?'

'Can I help you?'

Jezebel turned round and found Daniel, a loaf of bread in his hand, and her breath caught in her throat at the sight of him. He had barely aged in the six years since they'd said an awkward farewell in Tyre, but a narrow stripe of silver hair fell long and straight among the black and seemed to glow in the scattered light from the other doorways. But his eyes were as deep and dark as ever, and his eternal generosity of spirit still showed in the enquiring tilt of his head, and the slow dawn of recognition.

Jezebel flung her arms around him and pulled his head close to hers. 'I missed you, I missed you so much,' she breathed into his neck, sobs surging up within her.

His arms enfolded her, the unfamiliarity of his embrace tempered by the sweet scents of herbs and sea and home, and they stood like that for a long time, the music sparkling around them in the night. And then slowly, a little embarrassed at first, Jezebel pulled herself away and looked up at him, searching his face for any sign that she had misjudged him, misunderstood the ring she had worn all this time. Just as if he heard her thoughts, he unlaced her fingers from his neck and studied them, kissing the ring and then the finger, and then the hand. Then he smiled shyly at her, and looking deep into her eyes, he tilted his head towards hers, moving his lips to hers. And Jezebel knew what her answer to Jehu would be.

'I'm so sorry,' she murmured to Daniel, between their tentative first kisses, the sweet softness of his breath in hers, his touch so tender. 'I'll never leave you again.'

Two years later
852 BC – Queen Mother

Chapter Fifty-One

The spring sunshine brought a light breeze with it, and the panels of fine pale muslin fluttered at the windows. In Jezebel's old suite in the main Palace, the high windows were screened by wooden shutters and heavy woven drapes that made the huge rooms dark. By contrast the small annexe that had become her home since Ahaziah's coronation was constantly flooded with light, and she'd become used to living her life behind the soft screens that filtered out the bustle of the Palace grounds.

She no longer travelled to Jezreel with the royal party and now spent her winters in Samaria as well as the rest of the year. It had been long and bitterly cold this year, but with Beset, Daniel and Raisa around her, the days had passed pleasantly enough in bracing horse rides among the foothills, followed by evenings in front of the fire playing highly competitive games of *senet* or Dogs and Jackals. They played on boards Raisa had brought from Egypt years ago when she married King Omri. The Queen Grandmother liked to keep her mind sharp and insisted on playing alone against the others in twos or even altogether, scolding them for dithering over strategy and shouting at herself on the rare occasions that she lost. The evening would always end with Daniel playing a tune for them on the nevel, and the women would take it in turns to choose a song.

It was one of these tunes, a blessing chant from a Tyrian birth rite, that Jezebel was trying hopelessly to master on the nevel that afternoon, plucking clumsily at the strings while Daniel refreshed the contents of his medicine chest beside the hearth. Though her fingers were smaller than Daniel's she lacked his light, precise touch, and she would no sooner pluck the right string than her fingers would catch its neighbours and the tune would be spoiled.

'I spent all the time you were at market today learning that,' she said ruefully.

'You've been practising?' said Daniel, teasing her. 'I never would have guessed.'

'Huh!' Jezebel flounced round on the bench as though insulted, then laughed, and laid down the instrument. She joined Daniel by the hearth, kneeling carefully so as not to disturb the small piles of dried flowers and leaves in front of him. 'The Artemisia is so pretty,' she said, nudging the tiny yellow flower heads with her finger. 'You wouldn't think it could be so poisonous.'

'It has many beneficial uses, though the stallholder was telling me today that he has heard of the extraordinary visions people have when they drink an infusion of it. Some unscrupulous priests have started using it to enhance their reputations as messengers from God.'

'I think I should come to market with you one day, so I can hear what really goes on in Israel. I am told so little these days,' she said.

Daniel glanced up at the regret in her voice, then picked up one of the piles of herbs. 'You hear all sorts of tall tales,' he said. 'Apparently, some fellow had his farmhand bury him in the ground up to his neck for a day, just because Elisha told him his herd would double in size if he did so.'

Jezebel stifled a shudder at the prophet's name. She'd never told Daniel about Elisha's terrifying visit to her room before Ahab's death, and she tried to think of him as little as possible. But occasionally some story or other would filter through to her, and she could easily imagine him holding court in that awful cloak of skins, the sun beaming off his head.

'What happened to the man?' asked Jezebel.

'He nearly died of thirst,' said Daniel, the beginnings of a smile playing on his lips. 'He chose a spot in the middle of his pasture land, believing it to be at the heart of his herd, then sent his farmhand away. By the time he was rescued the following say, he had terrible wounds from insects burrowing into his flesh.'

Jezebel winced and went back to her nevel.

'What I find so ridiculous,' said Daniel as she began to play again, 'is that he believed the prophecy so absolutely that he was prepared to put his own life at risk. There is no sound reason behind the notion of burying yourself in the land, for it surely has no bearing on whether two animals will mate to produce two more.'

Jezebel didn't answer, because she was frowning at the strings, willing her fingers to behave as they should, but they struck two strings together and she let out a wail of frustration.

353

'Here,' said Daniel, straddling the bench behind her. He sat close, his thighs against hers, his arms curved in embrace, his fine hairs brushing her skin, his hands resting on her fingers. 'Begin again.'

Jezebel felt his breath on her neck as the warmth of his legs seeped through her skirts, and she fought hard to concentrate on the tune. She began to play, slowly, following his fingers as they moved from string to string, but she could feel his heart beating hard into her back. He smelled of fresh spring sunshine and lavender oil.

And he must have felt it too, for as they reached the end of the tune his lips brushed her bare shoulder with the tenderest whispering kisses and she arched her neck and let her head roll against his, twisting so that she might meet his mouth with hers—

A sharp knock at the door interrupted them and Daniel leapt up from the bench just before a servant entered. Jezebel twanged at the instrument but her cheeks flared with embarrassment. The servant was standing before her.

'Madam?'

'Yes?'

'The King has requested you join him in his office.'

'I will attend him in the hour before dinner,' she said, her heart still thumping from Daniel's presence.

'He asks you come now.'

'Does he?' Jezebel laid down the nevel with deliberate slowness. The servant lingered and she said, rather irritably, 'I don't need to be escorted.'

The servant retreated from the room.

Daniel was carefully wiping the corners of his cedar-wood box. 'We should be more careful,' he said.

Jezebel glanced to the door, sure that the servant loitered outside. She tidied her hair in the mirror and left the room. Before she'd made it to the end of the corridor she heard the soft strum of the nevel again. It bothered her that she must treat Daniel so distantly in public. She was free to do as she pleased, so long as it was invisible to King and kingdom alike. There was no telling how the people would respond to a relationship between two of such different status. But Jezebel suspected it would be her son who would disapprove the most.

Ahaziah stood at the window in his office, his back to the door, but Jezebel knew from his hunched shoulders and the wide spread of his feet that he was angry. Nissim and Chanan sat pinch-faced at small tables either side of Ahaziah's desk, while Joram lounged on a couch on the far side of the room. Jezebel gave a polite nod to her son's advisers and glanced at her younger son, who rolled his eyes then buried his nose back in the scroll he was reading.

'You asked to see me,' said Jezebel to Ahaziah.

He didn't answer and Jezebel eventually glanced at Nissim. 'Or was the servant mistaken?' she asked.

Nissim frowned, his narrow features grown mean with power, and Ahaziah looked at her for the first time.

'King Mesha has refused to give Israel his tribute.'

'Has he indeed?' said Jezebel. Ahaziah's grandfather, Omri, had led a war against the Moabites, whom Mesha ruled, some forty years before. Since that time, the tribute had been paid each year in the spring. 'Did he give a reason?'

'He's doing it to test my resolve,' said Ahaziah.

355

'Your father kept good relations with him,' said Jezebel. 'As far as I can see, you have not.'

'He didn't bother to send a gift to my coronation either,' said Ahaziah.

'He is flexing his muscles,' said Nissim. 'He's a heathen and blasphemer.'

'He thinks I'm weak,' said Ahaziah, turning from the window.

'I'm sure he thinks no such thing,' said Jezebel, keeping her expression neutral.

'We have word one of his cousins has been leading raids on our river settlements,' said Ahaziah.

'Reports from whom?' asked Jezebel.

Ahaziah looked to Nissim, who coughed. 'Sources we trust.'

'I've sent a message, demanding twice the normal tithe.'

Jezebel rolled her eyes. 'Are you sure that was wise?'

'I told him not to,' said Joram from across the room. 'But he treats it like a game of Dogs and Jackals. Moab takes his piece, he sweeps all Moab's off the board.'

'That is a crass allegory, even for you,' said Nissim.

'You invited me here,' said Joram, shrugging as he got up from the couch. 'You asked for my advice. As I see it, Moab has prodded Ahaziah to see if he will go to war. Ahaziah is too frightened to do so, and instead he makes a ridiculous and insulting demand that demeans his opponent.' He picked up a drinking bowl from the floor, drained it down, then wiped his mouth on the back of his hand. 'Your idea of war, brother of mine, is to send Moab's ambassadors home with fleas in their ears, and yet only two years ago you couldn't wait to saddle up and ride out to slay the Damascans. Have you lost your nerve, or are you paralysed by the decision now it is finally only yours to make?'

Jezebel expected her elder son to fly into a rage at her younger one, but instead he just stared across the room.

'It's always easier to follow orders than give them,' said Joram, refilling his bowl from a wine jug on Ahaziah's desk.

But Jezebel had caught the exchange of looks between Nissim and Chanan. 'And then there is the new fashionable inner diplomacy of Israel,' she said, 'where men who are not brave enough to speak communicate with sidelong looks and frowns. I've sat in enough meetings with both your fathers to know when something is being kept from me. What is it?'

Nissim blushed. 'Elisha has prophesied that any war with the Moabites won't be looked on favourably by Yahweh unless the malign influences in the kingdom are purged.'

'By that I presume you mean me,' said Jezebel.

Chanan looked with annoyance at his co-adviser for his clumsiness, but Jezebel continued, 'I have suffered the intolerance of this kingdom since you were babies.'

'It would be foolish to ignore the prophet,' said Nissim.

'There is more to this than you're telling me,' she said to Ahaziah. 'Mesha would never suddenly decide to stop paying the tithe—'

'Our brother decided he couldn't spare a few soldiers to help with Mesha's Edomite problem,' said Joram.

Ahaziah jerked round. 'Will you shut up!'

357

Jezebel sighed. The Edomites held the balance of power to the south-east, for while Judah could keep them in check to the west, Moab was all that stopped them from sweeping north, encircling the Sea of the Dead and threatening the plains of Ramosh Gilead. Forget about Ben-Hadad of Damascus. The Edomites were by far the greatest threat the region faced.

'This is basic politics,' she said to Nissim and Chanan. 'Your fathers learned this at their nursemaids' knees and yet you believe you can let other kings fight among themselves while Israel pretends that everything will continue as normal. It won't be a hundred thousand lambs you lose if Mesha cannot hold Moab against the Edomites. It will be control of the Sea of the Dead, the food we produce in the plains of Gilead, secure trade routes to Assyria—'

'We don't need a lecture on our kingdom from a foreigner,' said Nissim, standing up. 'Why don't you just go back to bed with your Tyrian lover?'

'I beg your pardon?' said Jezebel, sickness rising in her throat.

'Don't you dare speak to the King's mother like that,' shouted Joram. 'You accuse *me* of crassness—'

'Get out!' yelled Ahaziah.

'Are you going to let your guard dogs snap at Mother's heels?' demanded Joram of his brother.

'Just get out! All of you!'

Nissim and Chanan threw furious looks at Jezebel, but she stood her ground, refusing to move until they had left, and she shook her head when Joram shot her a

358

pleading look to intervene so he might stay. She heard him bickering in the ante-room with the advisers, but only then did she turn to Ahaziah.

'It isn't too late to send troops to help Mesha fight the Edomites. A victory would help erase all—'

'Do you share a bed with Daniel?' demanded Ahaziah, snatching a fresh wine jar from a rack behind his desk and slopping its contents into a drinking bowl.

Jezebel lifted her chin slowly so that she could look her son fully in the eye. 'I don't see that it is any concern of yours.'

'Everyone is talking about it.'

'You keep me locked up here like an exotic bird, so people are bound to speculate. I've done my very best to keep out of sight so that you may have your kingdom to yourself.'

'It only feeds the poison of men like Elisha.'

Jezebel touched her son very gently on the arm. 'I'm glad that you see that it is indeed poison.'

Ahaziah stared at her for a moment, then drank down the bowl of wine. 'He mocks me too, doesn't he?' he moaned. 'He doesn't think I have the nerve to go to war with the Moabites.'

'Then help the Moabites. That is the sensible thing to do, and then Mesha will learn to trust you again.'

'And if I do, will you keep your lover out of sight?'

Jezebel released Ahaziah's arm. 'You would make a deal with me about this?'

'Will you keep Daniel out of sight?'

Jezebel studied his face. He looked so like Jehu, the dark

curls around the face, the deep angry eyes, that it was impossible not to think of Ahaziah's demand as spoken in Jehu's voice.

'Do you believe I'm sharing a bed with Daniel?' she asked.

'It doesn't matter what I think,' Ahaziah said. 'The people of this kingdom only listen to Elisha.'

'Then whatever I say or do will fall on deaf ears.'

Chapter Fifty-Two

Beset dropped her spoon on the platter, a dull thud in the silence that smothered the room. She sighed crossly but didn't say anything, stabbing a knife into a piece of meat so viciously the table shook.

'Why don't you speak your mind?' said Jezebel. 'It would be less hard on the plates.'

But Beset only glared at her, then at Daniel, then she got up from the table and went to poke angrily at the fire.

Daniel stared at his plate, his food barely touched. She wanted to slide her fingers among his, but they had promised they would not show any physical affection in front of Beset, for even though she knew and blessed their relationship, Jezebel didn't want to exacerbate what were surely her maid's own feelings of loneliness by seeing the pleasure of others.

He must have felt her eyes on him, for eventually he looked up. 'I should not have come back to Israel,' he said.

'You've been back more than two years.'

'I think it's just plain wrong,' sniped Beset, clanging the

poker against the hearth. 'If Ahaziah hasn't the guts to stand up for you then why doesn't he just let us all go back to Tyre?'

'Balazar does not want me there,' Jezebel reminded her.

'Then what about Sidon, or Mog'dor, or even Egypt? Why does he insist on keeping you here?'

'Perhaps he doesn't,' said Jezebel. 'Perhaps it's my reluctance to leave Israel that is at fault.'

'After all the support you have given those wretched nobles,' said Beset. 'Nissim's father for one, I never did like Achidan—'

'What I fear,' said Daniel, looking at Jezebel, 'is being a reason for people to turn against you. Perhaps we should no longer spend time together alone and then people cannot imagine the worst.'

'It isn't the worst,' said Jezebel, reaching to take his hand. 'And I refuse to change the way we live.'

'I don't know why you don't just publicly admit your relationship,' said Beset. 'It would stop all the gossip and spite. Let the people see their Queen being happy again.'

'But if people believe I have so easily taken another lover after their King's death—'

'Then they will speculate about the parenthood of the new King,' murmured Daniel.

Jezebel nodded. 'I'm trying to protect Ahaziah. He feels vulnerable enough as it is.'

'He is vulnerable because Nissim and Chanan tell him he is,' said Daniel. 'I wonder who is really ruling Israel sometimes. He used to be so clear-headed about everything.'

'I don't see any way to improve his situation,' said

Jezebel. 'He believes giving Moab support against the Edomites is weak, but that going to war against him would also be a mistake. Defending me is weak but letting me leave Israel shows he is afraid of my influence.' She put her head in her hands. 'I just don't know how to help him.'

'He doesn't deserve your help, if you ask me,' said Beset. 'This situation is entirely of his own making and I for one—'

A scream cut through the night, a dreadful howl as though the Great God El himself had reached down to the underworld and yanked Melqart from his realm. Jezebel's blood ran cold, for there was something in the scream that she knew as well as the sound of her own voice. She threw back her chair and ran after Beset to the window.

'Oh! Oh, in the name of the Gods!' cried Beset, her arms flailing at Jezebel to keep her away. 'No, no, don't look, you mustn't—'

But Jezebel could still hear the scream ringing in her head and she stumbled past Beset, drawing aside the veil. Torches were scything through the dark onto the terrace opposite, and up above on the roof of the Palace more torches gathered, stinging the blackness with their glare.

But it was the clustering light on the terrace that snagged her attention, as one by one the torches lowered over the dark mound between them, a body, a man, dressed in the ceremonial robes of the King.

'Ahaziah.' His name tore apart on her breath. She dragged her eyes up the Palace walls and saw in the flickering torchlight a great gash in the fence of the roof gardens. 'He fell . . .'

Her head shook in disbelief, its shudder resonating through her, and only slowly did she sense Daniel's hand on her shoulder, and the dreadful wailing of Beset.

Chapter Fifty-Three

Shadows from the lamp danced on the walls of Jezebel's room as she lay on her bed in the small hours that followed, staring at the dying embers of the fire. She knew their outlines well, the couches, the nevel, her shrine, a bowl of wine softened with a sleeping potion that Daniel had made for her. But every shape reminded her of Ahaziah's body slumped on the terrace, every howl of the dogs or screech of the nightbirds seemed to call after his dreadful scream. The Palace rustled with nervous whispers beyond the muslin screens at her windows, but no one called on Jezebel.

Not that she could have faced them. Her body felt so heavy she couldn't raise her arm to drink down the drowsy embrace of the bowl of wine, yet her thoughts raced and spiralled in her head until they made her dizzy. Daniel had offered to sit with her, but she could not rouse herself to reach out for him. Besides, Beset had much greater need of his care, grown hysterical at the thought she had somehow been responsible.

'The Gods heard me cursing him,' her maid had sobbed

on her knees in front of Jezebel, 'and they punished me for my disloyalty.'

'No,' Jezebel had answered, helping Daniel haul Beset to her feet. 'It is me they are punishing.'

Daniel had looked at her in disbelief as Beset shook in his arms. 'Surely you don't believe this was the hand of any God?'

Jezebel shook her head. 'This was a man's doing. Someone weak enough to let Elisha guide his hand against me.'

Now, in the hours before dawn, she lay on her bed and dragged her thoughts back to Ahaziah's office, to how her son had stood at the window, so embattled, so trapped, unable to distinguish good advice from bad. For a moment Jezebel had thought she had got through to him, that he did understand how dangerous Elisha was. But then his clarity had crumbled around the stupid fear of the rumours about Daniel.

He came to her now, a lamp in one hand, his fingers gently resting on her shoulder.

'What is it?' she mumbled, rolling over to face him.

'The Council of Nobles is being convened.'

'By whom?'

'Joram.'

Jezebel sighed and struggled to push herself upright. 'I suppose he wants them to confirm his succession,' she said numbly.

'I tried to talk him out of it.'

Jezebel glanced at Daniel with surprise. 'He didn't listen to you then.'

'He might have done had I told him my suspicions.'

Daniel put down the lamp and sat down on the bed. 'I saw his brother's body. The other physicians – well, they seemed unwilling to take responsibility for it, so I offered.'

'Did he suffer?'

Daniel glanced down. 'I don't think so. Not much. His neck was broken by the fall. It would have been quick after that.'

'But?'

Daniel sighed and looked up at her again, his eyes sharp and clear in the shadows. 'His body shows all the marks of falling through the fence, but there was a deep knife wound on his arm, as though someone had attacked him. And his eyes looked very strange.'

'He'd been drinking. He opened a jar when I was in his office.'

'That wouldn't have been enough. His mouth smelled peculiar, bitter. I think he may have been drugged too. There would have been a struggle, perhaps he was threatened . . .'

Jezebel scrambled off the bed as though she could not keep company with the revelation. 'Who else knows?'

'I didn't say anything because I wanted to tell you first. But the other physicians will see the same signs I did.'

'But you didn't tell Joram.'

'He could be in danger too.'

'Only from himself. With that evidence and the argument they had, it will not be long before the nobles make up their minds that Joram killed his brother to take the throne.'

Crowds of nobles were still jostling for space when Jezebel walked into Council soon after in the long black

367

cloak that she had worn for Ahab's burial. They were arguing among themselves, but studiously ignoring Joram who stood before them by the throne, his hands raised, shouting for their attention. But at the sight of Jezebel they fell silent, lowering their heads as she passed. Joram stared belligerently at her. Jezebel could muster nothing more than a sad shake of the head and he reluctantly retreated to one side so that she could sit.

The nobles immediately burst into a barrage of questions and accusations.

'Has the assassin been caught?'

'There have been Damascan traders in the city this week.'

'There must have been at least three of them, for the King was strong and should have been able to defend himself.'

'It was a trick, he should not have been up there alone.'

'He *couldn't* have been alone.'

'Of course, jealousy, the oldest motive for murder.'

'They had been arguing about the Moabites—'

'Enough!' Jezebel slammed the gavelstone down on the table.

The Chamber fell silent.

Jezebel cleared her throat. 'Examination by the physicians shows wounds on the King's arms and legs –' *Why do I call him the King, instead of Ahaziah?* – 'scratches on his feet, bruising to his hands, as though he stumbled and fell through the fence. It was dusk, the roof torches had not been lit—'

'Then what was he doing up there?' demanded Achidan, Nissim's father. 'Joram tried to force his way back into the office before dinner—'

'Only his brother could have convinced him to meet in secret,' agreed Ido.

'Do not talk of me as though I'm not here!' shouted Joram, slamming his fists down on the table beside Jezebel.

'Joram had no need to meet Ahaziah in the shadows,' Jezebel said, without looking at her son. 'Your own son can tell you, Achidan, that Joram has always disagreed publicly with his brother. Their biggest problem was that they had no secrets between them and didn't know when to take their battles out of sight.'

'Then who killed him?' demanded Ido.

'It was just a dreadful accident.'

A murmur of disagreement swelled around the table and the nobles looked at each other. 'Our kingdom is under threat from malevolent forces,' shouted Achidan above the noise. 'They would do well to know whom they threaten,' he added, looking straight at Joram.

'They threaten me,' said Jezebel rising quickly from the throne. 'For now at least. I will resume my position as Regent.'

The nobles fell silent and for a long moment they glanced furtively at each other, waiting for one among them to say something. Joram shifted at Jezebel's side, but as the silence drew on he suddenly pushed past her and stormed out of the Council Chamber.

'Aye to the Regent,' said a quiet voice from among the crowd.

'Say Aye to the Regent,' added Achidan. The nobles chimed in their assent, but as Jezebel sank back onto the throne, she felt only the cold embrace of Ahaziah's shade and saw his last furious look at her in his office.

Chapter Fifty-Four

A terrible pall of silence had fallen over Samaria after Ahaziah's death, as though his awful scream had snatched the breath of the entire city. Jezebel hadn't slept since the close of the Council meeting, and at first light she led the burial procession out of the city and down the mountain path. Beside her Joram scuffed along, staring at the ground, while Raisa, draped in black, was borne down the hill behind her on a mahogany litter, weeping silently over the first of the grandsons she had helped bring into the House of Omri. Far above, crows circled above the city, their piercing cries cutting through the mourning bells.

In the bright, unforgiving daylight Jezebel retreated in on herself, the robes of state concealing the grieving mother. She stifled the flood of tears that constantly threatened, but she couldn't listen to the rapid prayers of the priests, their brows furrowed with fear, nor the responses of the crowd that gathered like a dark cloud behind her. *Father. Ahab. Ahaziah.*

She jerked at the touch on her elbow and saw Joram was trying to guide her towards the grave to pay her last respects. The mouth of the burial cave of the House of Omri yawned in a great gloomy chasm before her, and she felt its cold damp brush her face, as though the dead somehow exhaled. Somewhere in there lay Omri, Ahab's father, surely horrified at how his line stumbled and fell in his wake.

Beset and Daniel stood a discreet distance away among the crowd of Palace staff, but though Jezebel longed to be with them, longed for Daniel's kind patient gaze, she knew she must keep her distance, at least in public. Ahaziah's words still stung her and now, in temporary control of the kingdom, she knew she must be more flawless than ever before the people who would look to her for guidance.

But she was not blind to the way that the priests, nobles and citizens around her studied Joram suspiciously as they passed the grave, and Jezebel laid her hand protectively on her son's arm until the last note of the prayers had been sung. Joram must have seen it too, for he guided her away from the crowd around the tomb, their backs turned to them.

'Everyone thinks I killed him,' he muttered. 'I suppose I should be flattered they think I have the strength, when everyone was always telling me I'm the weaker brother.'

'So did you?' she asked.

Joram jerked angrily and hissed, 'No, I did not.'

'You always had your father's wisdom. So you know that if I'm to defend you I need more than my instincts. Someone will surely demand of me whether I've asked you.'

'You don't have to lie for me.' He hesitated. 'Or to me. It wasn't an accident, was it?'

'And because you have your father's wisdom,' she said, 'you will understand why we should delay your coronation.'

Anger flared in Joram's face again. 'Caution is ridiculous. The kingdom needs to know that its ruler won't be cowed by threats.'

'We have no idea who killed him,' said Jezebel, 'and I won't risk the kingdom on such an uncertainty. The assassin could still be in the city, he's probably among this very crowd.'

'All the more reason for me to show courage. It is what Father would expect.'

'Your father would say that the security of the kingdom was more important than the lives of any of its rulers.'

'Exactly,' said Joram, slapping his fist into his palm. 'The kingdom won't be secure if we dither over my coronation.'

'Which is why I declared myself Regent—'

'You simply won't let go!' snapped Joram. 'Ahaziah was right. You spent so long running things while Father was ill that you've never got used to letting others get on with it.'

'That isn't true.'

'Isn't it? I've lived my whole life in the shadows, first Father, then you, then Ahaziah, and now you again,' he shouted. 'When am I to claim my birthright?'

Jezebel glanced over her shoulder. A group of nobles stood watching them, and she knew Joram had been heard. She gripped his elbow firmly and moved him a little further away, but he shook her off.

'*You* don't guide *me*,' he said.

'I'm trying to keep you alive,' said Jezebel. 'Don't you understand that I would rather die myself than lose you as well? If an assassin means to destroy this kingdom, then he will surely take me while I'm Regent. And then at least you would be more sure of your foe.'

Joram shrugged sulkily. 'Then I will earn my crown the way my grandfather did, through the conquering of the Moabites again,' he said. 'I will fight the war that Ahaziah feared, and write my own history in this land.'

Jezebel shook her head. 'You damned Ahaziah for dithering, but you know that war is not going to solve the dispute with the Moabites.'

'But today it brings me the throne,' said Joram, wrapping his hand around the hilt of his ceremonial dagger. 'Send word to Judah. We call on them to fight the Moabites. And when I return you will crown me King.' Then he stalked away, a lonely figure marching through the crowd towards the mountain path.

That night, Jezebel sat for a long time in front of the fire, alone. She'd dismissed Beset, and Daniel had taken his leave too. He seemed to understand that the situation had changed and that she could no longer be seen informally in his company. He insisted on doubling the guard outside her room but she had sent them away as soon as he'd gone; their presence made her more uneasy than the threat of any danger. Nonetheless, she jumped with nerves at a knock on her door, and was relieved to find Raisa standing outside.

Jezebel glanced down the corridor. 'Did you send your guards away as well?'

'They're better guarding Joram, perhaps even from himself,' said Raisa, with a bitter smile.

Jezebel nodded and gestured for Raisa to enter. She settled her mother-in-law before the fire. 'There is talk that we too are in danger,' she said.

Raisa snorted. 'I'm no threat to anyone. I merely linger on like the taste of rotten grapes.' She grinned, accepting a small cup of warmed wine. 'Forgive me, my dear, for a little dark humour is always useful in these times.'

'Do you think we are being hunted by a madman?'

'If the killer is someone in the Palace, bent on destruction of the House of Omri, then he would need an obvious base of power behind him. But there are no rumours of insurrection in the army or the nobles.'

'Elisha's handprints are all over this. He wishes to fulfil his predecessor's prophecy because the sight of me sticks in his gullet. He's probably persuaded some fool to do his bidding.'

'Much as he did when he wished to dispose of Naboth,' said Raisa, sipping the wine.

Jezebel felt that old sadness at her friend's name. 'Too many people have died because of me.'

'Too many people have died because of the deeds done in Yahweh's name.' Raisa put down the bowl and laid a papery hand on Jezebel's. 'You think me blasphemous, though you know I don't deliberately offend. But that God has become an excuse for the actions of men who have shed tolerance in favour of arrogance.' She paused for a moment. 'But we might rid ourselves of that knife in the back of the kingdom.'

The old woman peered meaningfully at Jezebel over her drinking bowl.

'You mean . . .'

Raisa leaned forward, beckoning Jezebel closer with a gnarled finger. 'My spies have found the place where Elisha sleeps when he is in Samaria. He hides in plain sight, as all arrogant men do. But it wouldn't be hard to make sure he doesn't wake up tomorrow.' She snapped her fingers, a hard dry sound that cracked the shadows. 'Hmm?'

Jezebel tried to imagine a kingdom without the prophecies and malice that had dogged her since her arrival in Israel. 'It tempts me,' she murmured. 'I've little doubt that he was somehow involved in Ahaziah's fall. He's so blinded by the idea of revenge that he'd act first, and claim Yahweh raised his hand afterwards.' She glanced back at Raisa. 'How would it be done?'

But Raisa shook her head. 'The less you know, the better.'

'But you can't just—'

'If you give the word, I will see to it. There are enough men in this city loyal to me alone. I mean no insult by that.'

Jezebel smiled. 'And none is taken.'

Though the thought of ridding the world of Elisha's poison was intoxicating, though she need only say 'Yes' and it would be done . . .

'That would make me no better than him,' she muttered.

'Besides, he rose up in Elijah's wake, and surely another more vicious, more powerful prophet would rise up should Elisha die, whether that be the will of their God or simply the desire of men to make their mark on the world. We might pull out the knife, but the wound will still fester.'

Raisa shrugged. 'I leave the thought with you. And Ahab's own words.'

'The kingdom before everything.'

Raisa struggled to her feet and hobbled towards the door. 'Indeed. Goodnight, my dear.'

'Goodnight.'

Chapter Fifty-Five

'It's too dangerous,' said Daniel, as Jezebel stood on the Palace roof at dawn a week later, watching Joram ride down the mountain path at the head of the army. The horses' tails swished and their heads jerked, impatient at the slow pace of the procession down to the plain. 'If you think that talking to Elisha will make any difference at all, then you're as mad as he is.'

But Jezebel only pointed to the gap in the fence where Ahaziah had fallen to his death. 'I can't stop Joram riding to Jericho, I can't call back the request to Judah for troops, nor can I design a strategy for war that will help the army defeat the Moabites. But I can confront Elisha. Every man has his price and his weakness.'

'And you are Elisha's weakness,' said Daniel. 'He will stop at nothing to destroy you, and you'd make it easier for him?'

Jezebel looked out across the plain, pink beneath the sunrise, charting the route that Joram would take south-east to Jericho. Word had come that Jehu and Jehoshaphat were bringing a large cohort of troops from Judah, and they would cross the River Jordan together and push south in a wide flank to attack the northern Moab border. Jezebel had stared at the maps as the Samarian soldiers assembled in the barracks, trying to find a flaw in Joram's plan, but the war itself was so flawed she knew that arguing with him over tactics was irrelevant. The army commanders, to their credit, had rallied behind their King-in-waiting, but Joram's lack of leadership and camaraderie with the soldiers was evident, for he rode out alone, a great pannier of scrolls sagging from his horse. Jezebel wondered who would be leading the army by the time they reached Jericho. She had secretly attached two ambassadors to the troop herself, with orders that should an opportunity arise for negotiation with King Mesha, they were to take it.

But she couldn't sit around doing nothing. She sent Beset on a minor errand later that morning, and announced she was having a bath and didn't want to be disturbed. Once alone, Jezebel pulled some old robes of her maid's out of the wicker towel chest and changed into them, tucking her hair up inside a brown scarf. She could hear Daniel in an adjoining room, so she eased open the shutters and peered out. The terraces were utterly quiet in the absence of the troops, and so she clambered onto a fig tree and slithered down to the ground. It was undignified, but she felt a thrill to be doing something so un-queenly.

She walked swiftly through the streets that fringed the marketplace, the voices of traders calling for custom. Raisa had given her an address not far from the forge, in one of the ramshackle buildings that rose up like fungus among the warehouses. The streets were wide enough for carts, but they were scattered with debris and filth. Feral cats fought over scraps of meat from a food stall and the workers who picked flesh off a boiled chicken catcalled as she passed. Perhaps they were surprised to see a woman so well covered in this part of town.

The house Elisha was staying in was sturdier than those around it, and above the door hung a tile etched with the sign of the whetstone. She glanced up and down the street, but the place was deserted. She wiped her clammy palms on her skirts and nervously tucked a strand of hair back into its scarf. There was no one to see her arrive, no one to miss her if something happened . . .

She raised her fist to hammer on the door, and almost fell forward as the door swung open before she had even struck it.

The youth who opened it was tall, muscular, and beautiful. For a moment, Jezebel was sure she'd come to the wrong place. 'I'm sorry to disturb you.'

But he yanked her by the wrist, and she stared at him, shocked by his strength. 'Let me go.'

'But you have come to see Elisha.'

Jezebel jerked in surprise. 'How did you—'

'His God is all-seeing,' declared a familiar voice from inside the house. 'Welcome, Jezebel, welcome to my humble home.'

Jezebel shook off the youth's hand, and he gave an ironic bow and gestured her in. But he bolted the door behind her and stood, his arms folded, barring her exit. Jezebel cast a casual glance at the youth, but her heart was thundering against her ribs. There was to be no turning back, and no quick escape like there had been on Carmel when Elijah turned on her.

Daniel was right. This was a stupid idea.

Elisha sat at a rough oak table at the back of the room, lit by a small window that opened onto a shabby courtyard. The knifegrinder's equipment stood out there, and a neat array of knives and daggers glinted in the sun. The room was gloomy, and Jezebel thought of the caves at Bethel, the caves of her dream, the dark of her room he had invaded.

'You hide in the shadows,' she said, trying to keep her voice steady.

'Perhaps because you dislike the sight of me.' He licked his fingers slowly and dropped a bone onto a pile on a wooden board, from a half-eaten bowl of food beneath his hands. 'And yet you come all the way over here to find me.'

He gestured at a stool. 'Sit. Gehazi will pour you some wine. It's a good vintage, from the vineyard Naboth once owned.'

Jezebel forced herself to stay calm. 'Your hospitality would be wasted on me.'

'And yet still you seek it. Or perhaps you came to see if my throat had been slit in the night.'

'Why would I—'

'Or maybe you came to slit it yourself.'

'I was not brought up that way.'

'No,' he said, gnawing on a rib, dripping with a spiced sauce that scented the room. 'Although desperate circumstances can drive a person to do extraordinary things.'

'You should know.'

Elisha sucked his fingers then washed them in a bowl of water. 'What is it you want of me?'

She inhaled, trying to remember the speech she had

been practising all night. 'All my children have been raised in worship of Yahweh, which was my choice out of respect for Ahab and this kingdom. Ahaziah was innocent.'

'You give me credit for his death?'

'It was murder.'

Elisha rocked his head from side to side, considering it. 'When a man acts in the will of Yahweh, then it is hardly murder.'

'Then you admit it.'

Elisha laughed. 'I do no such thing.'

'You ordered it.'

'Men do strange things when they're compelled by the will of—'

'Men do more sensible things when they're compelled by chests full of gold and silver.'

'Oh come now, you would bribe me?'

'What price to leave Joram alone?'

'Your son has gone to war. If Yahweh wills the battle lost—'

'No!' said Jezebel. Behind her, she heard Gehazi shift, but she was suddenly more angry than afraid. 'What price Joram's life?'

'I have no need of money. Men open their doors to me because I'm the prophet of their God. Besides, unlike Elijah I cannot be seduced by anything you offer.' His eyes trailed over her body.

'I would have slit my *own* throat before I lay down with Elijah.'

'You poisoned his mind with desire and the earthly wants of men who must taste the rotten fruit just to see if its sweetness still lingers. Besides, if I wanted you, I would have taken you already.' His gaze flickered past Jezebel to Gehazi. 'Anyway, the fate of your second son has already been determined.'

'You speak of fates,' snapped Jezebel, 'but you only use your words to twist the lives of the innocent. You think you can terrify people with dreadful visions of death and destruction, you think you can control kingdoms and shape borders with subterfuge and terror.'

'I make no such claim,' said Elisha, his voice turning cold. 'I am simply the messenger of God.'

'Then let Him come down, right here, right now, and show me for Himself that this is His will!'

Elisha didn't answer for some time, nor was the building rent apart by the smiting fist of a God. Jezebel feared she had said too much and her fate would come from a more earthly hand. She could hear Gehazi shifting his weight behind her, the knives glinted out in the courtyard, and the rush of anger was receding beneath a rising tide of fear once more.

Elisha stood up and spread his palms wide. 'By now Ben-Hadad of Damascus has already died at the hand of Hazael, the head of his own army, and set that kingdom on a course to destroy the Israel you have built. Yahweh deplores this decaying city, corrupted by the hollow images of foreign Gods. He has ridden out in His chariot with Hazael, and he will crush the Moabite shadow-God that is Chemosh. But then he will take Israel too.'

His spoke quietly, without the fervour of Elijah, but his words carried such strange weight that Jezebel could almost see the great plains of Gilead and Moab and the blood pouring across them.

'You really mean to bring me down.'

Elisha came round the table to face her, and she felt Gehazi close in behind her. She tried to swallow down her fear, but it rose in waves and made her shake.

'It isn't me who will bring you down,' said Elisha. 'It is the will of Yahweh as told to Elijah. Your flesh will be food for the dogs of—'

The door shuddered behind them and light flooded the room. Gehazi stumbled as four of the Palace Guard blundered in, shields to the fore, shouting for admittance in the name of the House of Omri.

'Are you safe?' Daniel pushed through the soldiers to Jezebel's side.

'Has the loyal puppy come to rescue you?' asked Elisha. 'I would have given her back when I had finished with her, Daniel.'

Daniel grabbed Jezebel's hand and pulled her to the doorway. 'What did you think you were doing, running down here in secret?'

'I fight my own battles.'

'Not against this man.'

'You see,' said Elisha, 'even your physician believes in me.'

A ripple of laughter ran through the soldiers.

Jezebel snatched up her skirts, picked her way out of the broken doorway and up the street. She knew Daniel was behind her but she didn't look back.

Chapter Fifty-Six

Jezebel's melancholy was infectious. She and Raisa sat for a long time in the dark after dinner without speaking. Daniel was no doubt sulking in his quarters, probably in the company of Beset, for neither of them had sought the other out since their return from Elisha.

Eventually Raisa pointed at a jug of wine that stood on the tray. 'Perhaps a drop will help us sleep.' Jezebel poured out a bowl wordlessly. 'None for you, my dear?'

'I doubt I would sleep if my head were cut off,' Jezebel said. 'I can't get his face out of my head.'

Raisa smiled. 'We don't hold with prophets in Egypt. Our rulers are also our deities, so we have no need of mortal intermediaries.'

'My father had a great friend from Egypt when he was a young man,' said Jezebel. 'He sailed all the way along the coast to Tyre and stayed for a year and a day. He told my father everything he had seen and fostered in him the love of discovery.'

'Those are exactly the sort of tales that made our kingdom what it is. I miss the stories of home.'

'Did you ever go back?'

Raisa shook her head. 'I wasn't as lucky as you. Besides, the tales told at home were far more exotic than the reality. And I had no desire to share my uncle's fate.'

'What happened to him?'

Raisa reached for the drinking bowl and nestled it in her lap. 'Osorkon was a great Pharaoh, and very handsome too. All his nieces were in love with him, and it was easy to believe he was a God. He led successful wars against Israel and Judah, and he built three of the most beautiful temples our kingdom has ever known. Yet he died not in battle, but choking on an apricot stone. Gone in an instant!' She chuckled. 'A ridiculous death for a deity, I'm sure you would agree.'

Jezebel smiled wanly. 'I've always believed that the Phoenician Gods have a sense of humour, but they rarely show it.'

'You've been brave, clinging on to your own Gods in the face of such opposition. It would've been easy to give them up.'

'My Gods would hardly be pleased if I did. But perhaps I was stupid not to.'

'You were far stronger than all of us.'

'I brought many of my own people with me. You were alone, weren't you?'

Raisa cupped the bowl in her hands. 'It was worse after Omri died. I don't mind admitting that I sought out a new lover, or two, after he had gone. The bed seemed so empty and I quickly grew bored of my own company.'

Jezebel felt her mother-in-law's penetrating gaze, and she blushed, fiddling with the grapes in her hand.

'Another lover does you no harm,' said Raisa, eyeing

her knowingly. 'Someone close to you, for example, who cares for you instead of being foisted upon you.' She drank some wine, and sucked on her teeth. 'It's been two years since Ahab died and it was hardly a love match.'

'Raisa,' said Jezebel, seizing her courage, 'I should probably tell you that the rumours of Daniel and me—' Raisa gasped, and Jezebel dared not look up. 'I thought you knew . . .'

The bowl fell from Raisa's hands and smashed on the floor. The old woman gave a strange moan and Jezebel glanced across to see she was doubled over, coughing, wine staining her garments.

'Raisa!' Jezebel crouched beside her, rubbing her back, but the old woman had begun convulsing and shuddering and filthy-smelling spittle was dribbling from her mouth. 'Beset!' screamed Jezebel. 'Get Daniel now!'

Raisa gulped and shook in Jezebel's arms, her eyes rolling and her fingers scratching at her throat. Beset flung open the door, took one look at the elderly woman, and ran down the corridor, shouting for Daniel.

'Water!' cried Jezebel. 'Swill your mouth out.'

She snatched a finger bowl from the tray but she couldn't get it near to Raisa's mouth, and even as she offered it, she knew it was too late. Raisa's face had sunk in on itself and turned deathly pale, and her mouth was bubbling with vomit.

'Don't give up on me!' she demanded. 'Don't you dare leave me, not you as well.'

Raisa's body shuddered, then sagged in Jezebel's arms. Her eyelids twitched, but she could only gurgle, her angry spirit trapped inside her paralysed body. As the sound of

387

rapid footsteps came to the door, she gave one last choking hiss and fell quiet.

'No . . .' Jezebel jolted against the chair, Raisa's tiny frame rattling in her embrace.

Daniel peeled her away from Raisa into Beset's arms, but though the maid quickly draped a shawl around her, she couldn't stop trembling.

Daniel laid Raisa on the cushions and felt for a pulse in her neck. Jezebel saw him swallow, then lay a cloth over her face. He knelt down and picked up the bowl.

'Was she drinking from this?'

Jezebel trembled a nod.

'Did you have any?'

Jezebel's eyes opened wide, staggered by the understanding, and she shook her head, unable to speak.

He sniffed at the wine. 'Monkshood, I think. She didn't stand a chance.'

'It could have been you,' cried Beset, 'in the name of the Gods, someone was trying to kill you!'

'But Raisa . . .' whispered Jezebel, 'what had she done?'

'This was meant for you both,' said Daniel. He put down the bowl. 'Pack a few things for her, Beset, we will leave tonight.'

'I should stay,' muttered Jezebel, 'for her burial . . .'

'And for your own?' said Daniel. He put an arm around her shoulders. 'I will make arrangements so Raisa is properly laid to rest.'

Jezebel pulled away from him, and went to the body. She lifted the cloth from Raisa's face and gazed down at the features of the dear old woman. Raisa had been the first person to welcome her in Israel, a lone kind stranger in a foreign land. She'd been a constant in Jezebel's firmament from that first day. Her spirit had infused the House of Omri, her strength had fired Ahab. In many ways, she'd become a second mother to Jezebel.

'Jezebel,' said Daniel. 'We should go.'

Jezebel replaced the cloth and swallowed bitterly. 'It wasn't her time.'

Chapter Fifty-Seven

Even after a month, Jerusalem still felt like a foreign city to Jezebel though, like Samaria, it was a city whose heart had been wrenched out by having an army at war. The combined forces of Judah and Israel were still engaged on the Moab border, but Jezebel no longer had access to daily updates from the front, so her fears for Joram could only fester. Though she was still regent in name, on leaving she had ceded power to a council of nobles, and she had little doubt their loyalty lay with her son. She was in effect an exile from her own city.

At least the Tyrian merchant's house in which she, Daniel and Beset were staying was comfortable and well appointed, with a pleasant courtyard pond and a good view of the river valleys to the south. They lived in anonymity, guests of a ceramics dealer known to Daniel's family, but they weren't confined to the house, so Jezebel spent much of every day in the Palace enjoying the opportunity to lavish time and attention on her daughter Athaliah and her grandson, Ahaziah. The little boy was already two, and there was a passing resemblance to the dead uncle for whom he had been named, not least in his fondness for jumping about and poking at furniture with a short stick.

Athaliah had grown even more beautiful since marrying Jehoram, blossoming into an assured and confident young woman even as her husband withered away in his bed. Unlike her mother, Athaliah had no interest in the politics of the kingdom into which she had married, turning her hand easily to the running of its Palace household instead.

'Don't tell this to anyone,' Athaliah murmured, leaning closer to her mother, 'but I find these royal men as easy to manage as my son. Jehoshaphat is now so old, he likes everything to be done for him; Jehoram is in too much pain to offer any resistance to any of my ideas; and Jehu does not care for any of my arrangements as long as his breakfast and dinner are served at the same time every day!'

'That comes from a life in the military,' said Jezebel, smiling.

'I suppose I should count myself lucky he does not wake Ahaziah with a bugle call at sunrise every morning.'

There was a loud yell as Ahaziah the younger came running into the room, waving a bit of blue cloth like a pennant, then a wail and a thud as he tripped over and fell flat on his face at Jezebel's feet. She scooped him up, smothering his face in kisses to stifle his tears.

'There, there! You will have to be steadier on your feet if you are to run around like an infantryman,' she said, rubbing his nose and his palms to soften the bruises.

Athaliah ruffled her son's hair. 'They've developed their own parts. Jehoshaphat is older than Father was when he died, but he still takes a lively interest in all the decisions and likes to be seen out and about in the city, because Jehoram cannot. Jehoram rules with his head, of course, he is clever despite all his agonies, and Jehu is the man who puts their thoughts into actions. Somehow it works, and my input isn't required.'

'I suspect I pushed my nose in where it was not necessarily wanted,' said Jezebel. 'And now I'm paying for that impudence.'

Athaliah squeezed her mother's hand. 'You miss Samaria, don't you?'

Jezebel frowned. 'I'm trying to think of this as an extended holiday. Besides, I love spending so much time with you. I suppose when Jehu and Jehoshaphat come home, it won't be as easy to come to the Palace every day.'

'They would understand.'

'I very much doubt it,' said Jezebel, wondering what Jehu would have said to how brazenly she had confronted Elisha. 'I'd prefer they didn't know I was here. If I'd wanted this to be a formal visit, I wouldn't be hiding out of sight.'

'I'm only cross that Joram has forced you out.'

Jezebel hesitated, for the web of half-truths and omissions from which Athaliah had woven her own understanding of her mother's situation was too fragile to bear examination. 'Joram is ignoring his good instincts just because he wants to be seen as different from his brother.'

'Perhaps I should talk with him when he returns,' said Athaliah. 'I was always closer to him than to Ahaziah.'

A slow and sombre bugle call interrupted the peaceful afternoon, and Athaliah went to the window. In the corridor outside her room, shouts rang back and forth, and the bell rang in Jehoram's suite next door. Jezebel shivered at the familiar portent of doom. She set Ahaziah back on his feet, but as though he sensed his grandmother's anxiety, he didn't run off again but slipped his hand into hers.

'That is the Burial Call,' she said. 'That is the sound of a dead king or a defeated army.' Athaliah frowned and hurried out to the corridor, and Jezebel swept her grandson back into her arms. 'Let us hope you never know that sound,' she murmured into his soft brown hair.

Athaliah returned shortly after and sat down on the couch beside them. 'The combined armies have been defeated,' she said. 'I can't believe it. They sent so many men.'

Elisha was right, thought Jezebel. 'Is there news of Joram?' she asked.

'He is safe and well in Jezreel, with Jehoshaphat. Jehu is on his way back to Jerusalem.'

Jezebel set Ahaziah down on the floor again and stood up. 'Then I will return to the house.'

'But he could tell you about Joram—'

'He will tell you, and you can send me a message. It's better he doesn't know I'm here.' She kissed Athaliah on the cheek.

Better he does not ask questions I don't wish to answer.

Chapter Fifty-Eight

It wasn't Athaliah who called on Jezebel the next day. She'd spent the morning in the courtyard, trying to read a scroll of poetry from the Tyrian merchant's extensive library. The pale stone walls had ceased to be elegant facades draped with climbing plants, and now only held her fast in the grip of a strange city. The noises in the streets were unfamiliar, the harsher accent of the Judeans more difficult to decipher, and she longed for Daniel and Beset to return from the market even though the food they brought didn't taste the same as in Samaria. So when she heard a quick tread in the colonnade behind her, she looked up impatiently and was shocked to find Jehu striding towards her. He was dressed in ceremonial military attire, a stiff linen tunic beneath a rich red cape that hung across one shoulder, a highly polished leather belt and harness holding his sword to his hip.

She lowered the scroll, but her cheeks reddened with embarrassment at being discovered, and in such an informal state. Her last words to him had been a handwritten message sent south the day after Daniel returned to Samaria, declaring that she had thought carefully about his offer of marriage but felt their time had passed. He had not replied and only now did Jezebel realise she had never really expected to see him again. Besides, he should have called ahead.

'I asked Athaliah not to reveal that I was in Jerusalem.'

'Your daughter is blameless. Her nursemaid, however, is not.'

Jezebel stood up and bowed low as befitted a visitor. 'I beg leave from the Prince of Judah to stay in the city of Jerusalem. I apologise for not making a formal request sooner.'

'Do you think I have come to chase you out?' Jehu sat on a couch, leaning forward, his elbows on his knees. 'There's no need to stand on ceremony.'

She forced herself to study his face. 'Then to what do I owe your visit?'

'I rode down by way of Samaria but was told you were no longer in the city.'

'No.'

Jehu frowned but he only said, 'It was a rout. We lost thousands of men.'

Jezebel lowered herself onto the couch opposite him. 'I'm sorry. I'm sure it is no reflection on your command.'

'I don't need your sympathy.'

'Then what—'

'I want you to listen, for once. You are too accustomed to the sound of your own voice when it comes to matters of state.'

Jezebel reeled, stung by his tone, and perhaps he noticed, for he raised a mollifying hand.

'It may be that it is a reflection on my command. And

395

yet it was clearly not the will of Yahweh that Israel and Judah should defeat King Mesha.' Jezebel sighed, and he looked up at her sharply. 'My strategy was sound enough. The armies were fit, strong, prepared. But word came the night after the first phalanx had moved south from our mustering point that Mesha had made a sacrifice – of his own son – for victory.'

'Rituals for the God Chemosh have never included human offerings,' said Jezebel.

'It was not a sacrifice to Chemosh. We heard later that Mesha had received word from Elisha that such an offering would draw decisive favour from Yahweh.'

'Mesha surrendered the religion of his entire kingdom on the basis of a message sent by a stranger?' asked Jezebel.

'Elisha is no stranger to anyone in these lands. Tales of his miracles abound wherever you go.'

'But our armies?'

'Mesha's personal offering to Yahweh struck utter fear into the hearts of our men. They believed that an enemy who would give up his son to God must be divinely guided. Their spirit was broken before we even called on it.'

'And you?' asked Jezebel. 'Was your spirit broken by this ridiculous gesture?'

'I was disappointed to see so many men flee the field of battle. Many of them were Israelite—'

'It is always easier to blame your allies than your own people.'

'—*but* enough of them were Judean. They might have fought men like themselves, but they would not fight the will of Yahweh.'

Jezebel rose angrily from the couch. 'And Joram? Ahab

and I brought them up to worship Yahweh. Why did you not look favourably on the Kingdom of Israel when its last remaining son pledged himself to the cause?' she asked. Jehu didn't answer and, profoundly irritated, Jezebel added, 'You must be able to see that Elisha is simply manipulating all three kingdoms to his own ends. Moab would have lost the battle in the face of a combined army more than twice its size, and yet King Mesha was so desperate not to lose he would have done anything if he thought it would help him win. It was the news of such an extraordinary gamble that terrified our armies. That isn't the will of God, it is the frailty of men.'

'You shouldn't be so cynical,' said Jehu.

'Almost overnight Elisha has stripped an entire people of a God they have worshipped for generations. What right does he have to do that?' She put her hand up to stop Jehu speaking. 'You will tell me it is Yahweh's right and nothing to do with Elisha. But who is this man who passes himself off as the messenger of a God?'

'*The* God.'

'He's just a bald-headed soothsayer. Such men can be bought for a few coins in any land.'

'He has foretold much that has come true.'

'He is a good judge of weak character.' Jezebel thought of Elisha's prophecy in the gloomy knifegrinder's hut. 'I won't fall under the spell of his illusions,' she said. 'I don't share his madness.'

Jehu stood, shaking his head. 'You won't see the truth, will you? He has never been wrong. Just as Elijah was never wrong.'

There was one prophecy that hadn't come true, for she

still lived, safe from the slavering jaws of the dogs of Jezreel. Three times she'd heard it, once from the mouth of Elijah, and twice from his successor, echoing through her life, but never fading. But Jezebel could see this argument was pointless. She looked at the face she knew so well, framed in an expression of utter faith she just didn't recognise. She couldn't bring herself to say another word to him. It felt as though she fought not only the words of Elisha but the blind faith of thousands of people she'd never met.

Chapter Fifty-Nine

Without the protection of her anonymity in Jerusalem, Jezebel found herself drawn back into affairs of state between the two kingdoms. Two days later she reluctantly answered Jehoram's invitation to an audience, hoping that she would have the opportunity to see Athaliah and little Ahaziah also. Jehoram had risen from his bed in her honour, though he could barely hold himself up on his throne, and Jezebel felt a strange sympathy for this man, a crippled, deflated contrast to his brother.

Yet the Co-Regent's eyes were sharp enough. As Jezebel settled herself on a couch opposite him, he said, 'You needn't feel sorry for me. Your daughter has given me a fine son, and my brother has the enthusiasm for combat that I never cared for myself. I rule more than adequately as I am.'

Jezebel bowed her head. 'I mean no disrespect. We have not met since your wedding, and I was troubled to see that you are still unwell.'

'Pay no heed to the prophets,' he said. 'My failing body isn't the price I pay for marrying your daughter. I would sooner believe that one of my own staff is slowly poisoning me because I once struck him, than some distant God has picked me out from hundreds of thousands of men for such a particular punishment.'

Jezebel stifled a smile at this unexpected oasis of sanity. 'Your ailments have indeed not dulled your wisdom.'

'Or my tongue,' agreed Jehoram. He winced as he shifted his position in the throne. 'Now, with Ben-Hadad's passing—'

'He's dead?' interrupted Jezebel.

'You hadn't heard? He didn't merely die. He was killed. Some ambitious fellow named Hazael –' he waved a hand dismissively – 'formerly the commander of the army. He wielded the knife and now has crowned himself King.'

'Elisha was right,' murmured Jezebel. How could he have known, unless he himself had been the cause?

'We are expecting the Damascan ambassador at any moment,' Jehoram was saying.

Jezebel shook herself, caught on his words. 'What interest does Damascus have in Judah?'

'I ask myself the same question, so I will wait to see what form that interest takes. Do you wish to be present?'

'It would probably be unwise. I'm not in Jerusalem in any official capacity.'

'Your younger son was indeed too quick to proclaim himself King in the wake of defeat.'

'He'll only be crowned on my return to Samaria.'

Jehoram shook his head, his eyes widening frankly. 'He has already taken his crown in Jezreel. Word came today from my father. Your son took Jehoshaphat's presence as sufficient impartial witness and without you there . . .' He spread his hands, a gesture of surrender and yet of commiseration too.

Jezebel grasped the edges of the couch. She thought quickly. Hazael's accession to the throne in Damascus was not simply a worrying fulfilment of Elisha's prophecy, but his ambassador's arrival in Jerusalem so soon was a sinister indication of the new ruler's view of his neighbours. Joram would be too desperate to establish his authority to want to consider another warring neighbour, and Jezebel realised she would have to stay and find out what the Damascans were up to, even though the thought of it sickened her.

'Perhaps I will remain to meet the ambassador, if you don't mind,' she said, standing up. 'I think it wise to be able to take news back to Israel that may strengthen Joram's position.'

'Under the circumstances, that is the prudent choice,' said Jehoram, ringing a small bell that summoned an adviser from an ante-room. 'Is the Damascan here?' he demanded.

The adviser nodded and Jehoram waved to a low couch beside his throne. 'You may sit here,' he said to Jezebel.

She crossed the room and was settling herself on the couch when the doors were opened again and the Damascan entered, followed by four servants dragging a massive wooden chest. They were red with the strain of moving it and Jezebel wondered what could be inside.

'Ambassador Hul of Aram-Damascus,' said the adviser.

The ambassador was looking around him, taking in the splendour of Jehoram's chamber, though it was not with admiration but a supercilious contempt that was only fractured by the arrival of Jehu through a door to the rear of the chamber. A look seemed to pass between them and Jezebel wondered fleetingly if they had met before. But Jehu looked only briefly at Jezebel, his expression cold, his demeanour stiff in his formal clothes. He stood on the other side of Jehoram's throne, his arms crossed.

'We were surprised to learn of your defeat to the Moabites,' the Damascan said in his thick accent. 'It was a clever bluff though. Our new King Hazael sends compliments on your strategy.'

'Our strategy?' said Jehoram.

'Your brother allowed Israel not only to humiliate itself, but to destroy itself too. A weakened army, a naïve youth clambering onto the throne. Your allegiance was intelligent for its impermanence.'

'What makes you think it only temporary?' asked Jehu.

'Because King Hazael has long respected the wisdom of the Judean royal house. He has also admired Jehu of Judah for many years, as one military man to another. The father and two sons have long lulled the Israelites into a false sense of security. Losing together in battle took nerve, for you could easily have turned against them there and then.'

Jezebel's head was pounding, and she felt sick at how stupid, how blind she had been. Jehoram had sounded confused at first, but the Damascan was speaking of years of manipulation that she had never even sensed. Neither she nor Ahab had ever taken the Judeans' co-operation for granted – it had been difficult enough to secure as it was – but it was humiliating to realise that everyone else had seen their motives so clearly.

'And now you need a new ally,' the Damascan was saying.

There was a yawning creak of wood and the two servants lifted the lid of the chest. The ambassador reached in and the air was filled with the unmistakeable music of rivers of precious metal. 'King Hazael imagines your coffers will be swelled by this humble offering. Forty thousand pieces of gold.'

Jehoram shifted on his throne and Jezebel turned to see him exchange glances with Jehu, but neither of them looked at Jezebel. She might not have been there at all.

'Of what is this the price?' asked Jehoram.

'Of using your intimate knowledge of the weaknesses of Israel to our collective advantage. The time to strike is now, with the young King smarting from his defeat, and his army in tatters.'

Jezebel stood up, unable to keep her silence any longer. 'It takes a certain kind of arrogance to believe that a man is worth his weight in gold,' she said. 'But I am not surprised that the Damascan Kingdom cannot survive without buying the loyalties of others.'

'You allow your wives to speak on matters of politics?' the Damascan demanded of Jehoram.

'You have been misinformed,' said Jehoram. 'This is not my wife.'

'This is Jezebel,' said Jehu, 'Queen Mother of Israel.' His voice was brittle and Jezebel knew he was angry that she had spoken, angry to have his machinations laid bare. But she didn't care, for if he consorted so casually with other nations, if he let the Damascan speak so dismissively of Israel, then what could he expect but her anger too?

The ambassador looked her over, his flat features

403

crinkling in contempt. 'Only a harlot would slide unseen into chambers that were not her own.'

'How dare you!' snapped Jezebel. 'You insult my kingdom and then—'

Jehu moved to stand before the ambassador. 'You would be wise to watch your tongue in our court.'

The ambassador raised his eyebrows and puffed out his chest. He glanced at Jezebel. 'You must offer them far greater riches, for they rush to stand up for you. But it has never been your kingdom,' he said, 'any more than its new King is truly an Israelite. He is one half Tyrian and one quarter Egyptian.'

'You have already shown how carefully you do your calculations,' snapped Jezebel. 'But forty thousand gold pieces is much too little to buy a couple of kingdoms.'

'Indeed,' said Jehoram. 'Hazael cannot know Judah so well if he believes a chest of gold would buy off years of alliance in an afternoon. I believe you have allowed your ambition to influence your intelligence. The situation is not as you would wish it to be.'

'I told His Highness not to think so highly of you. For you,' the ambassador stabbed repeatedly at Jehu's chest with his finger, 'are clearly under this harlot's spell. Do you enjoy her in turns, a night each, Judah as crippled as her King—'

Jezebel was slow to realise what she was seeing. The air flashed in front of the ambassador, silvery light cut with an icy hiss, and the room suddenly swelled with a primitive howl of agony as the ambassador sank to his knees. Only then did she understand what Jehu had done. She screamed and stumbled backward against the couch, as

404

blood gushed onto the floor from the Damascan's severed elbow, his arm flapping uselessly in search of itself.

Jehu stood over him for a moment, then he sheathed his sword and walked past the shocked servants from the room. He left the wounded man writhing and screaming on the ground. Jehoram was retching into the scroll on his lap. The ambassador's servants swarmed uncertainly around their master.

Jezebel staggered away, blundering through the confusion, dull with shock. But what she remembered most clearly was Jehu's expression as he drew the sword.

Was he defending his own honour, she wondered, *or mine?*

Chapter Sixty

Five days later Jezebel received word that Joram had returned to Samaria and expected her to join him. She had been trapped in the Tyrian merchant's house, unable to visit Athaliah in the wake of events at the Palace. The evening of Jehu's attack on the Damascan ambassador, Jezebel had dispatched a messenger to Tyre, hoping to find sanctuary there, but Balazar had not even responded himself, the note from Mazzer concisely rebuffing her request: *His Highness does not think such a journey would be conducive to his sister's health.* There it was. As oblique as ever, yet somehow so final.

Athaliah had visited her once and vaguely suggested that arrangements could be made for Jezebel's more permanent residence in Jerusalem, but Jezebel had grown nervous rather than envious of her daughter's blissful ignorance of the political goings-on at court. And besides, it was out of the question to remain within reach of Jehu. She had accepted an insistently worded invitation to see Jehoram at the Palace, but her meeting with him was brief. Jehoram had refuted the Damascan claim of an alliance and she believed him. He'd also apologised for his undignified response to all the blood, and told her that the chest of gold had been more intact than the Damascan ambassador when both were returned to Hazael.

Joram's message was more of a surprise, given how swiftly he had declared himself King, but with Jehoshaphat expected back in Jerusalem at any day, Jezebel convinced herself that her son still required the wisdom of a more experienced ruler at his side. She wasn't looking forward to telling him about the Damascans, and no matter how she rehearsed, she could not find a way to relate the facts without the prospect of inciting him to pursue another war.

'I can't believe Balazar refuses to let you go home,' said Beset on the eve of their departure. 'He can't still be afraid of you after all this time.'

'Perhaps he is afraid of the prophecies,' said Jezebel. 'After all, I drift about these lands watching Elisha's announcements come true one after the other. Perhaps I'm condemned to be a spectator until the last of his prophecies fulfils itself and all the kingdoms from Phoenicia to Egypt are rid of Jezebel.'

'Surely you don't believe that?' asked Beset, her eyes darting between Jezebel and Daniel. 'You know Elijah only said it to begin with because he was afraid of you.'

'And what is there to be afraid of now?' demanded Jezebel. 'What power do I wield?'

'Can't you go to Egypt, or even across the Great Sea? I'm sure that Balazar could be convinced to furnish you very comfortably if you promised him you'd stay away forever.'

'My brother is easily swayed,' said Jezebel, 'but Israel is

my home and I've no wish to stray so far from Athaliah and her son. They'll have to come to Samaria now if I'm to see them, for I'll never return here.'

'I am surprised by how welcoming Jehoram has been,' said Daniel as Beset stood up and began stacking the platters.

'He is one man of three, and hardly in a position of strength. Besides, how much influence does he really have? Athaliah told me today that Jehoshaphat has overruled him to make Jehu the commander of the combined Israelite and Judean armies. I'd never have agreed to a military alliance of that sort, and I struggle to believe that Joram has, so soon after becoming King.'

'I suppose it puts to rest any hint of betrayal,' said Beset.

'If Joram wishes to show strength,' replied Jezebel, 'he must continue to show independence, and not cling to his nearest neighbour.'

'Do you have to tell him what happened?' asked Beset.

'If I don't, someone else will.'

Beset sighed and left the room, her arms laden with the detritus of their evening meal. Jezebel turned back to Daniel. 'I haven't said anything to Beset, but I fear we may not be long in Samaria. Joram has only invited me back out of duty.'

Daniel tucked curls of Jezebel's hair behind her ear, and caressed her cheek. 'Wherever you go, I will follow,' he said. 'I could make a living anywhere as a physician, and you and Beset could learn to be my nurses.'

Jezebel smiled. 'But I have no stomach for blood. I thought I would be sick when Jehu . . . when he cut off . . .'

'Then you can learn to mix potions and try not to poison my patients.'

Jezebel leaned forward to kiss him, but she was interrupted by a nervous cough from the doorway. Beset was standing there, wide-eyed with panic, and gesturing furiously behind her. 'Jehu is here!'

Jezebel frowned. 'I didn't hear the bell.'

'He just walked in—'

'Again?' Jezebel was strangely reminded of that first night he came to her room in Tyre, also unannounced, but there was no time to send Daniel away on this occasion. Jehu strode in just as he had a few days ago, except that his breastplate now sat between his tunic and his red robe, and both his sword and dagger were strapped to his belt.

'You are leaving for Samaria tomorrow,' he said, without bothering to bow or make greeting to Daniel and Beset. 'I am sending a cohort of my guard with you.'

'There's no need,' said Jezebel, surprised by the offer, though not by its brusqueness. 'Daniel drove us here. He can drive us back.'

'He's useless with a weapon.'

'We're not in any danger, surely?'

'Only from him,' said Beset, pointing at Jehu's armour.

Jehu glanced at her then at Daniel, then he gestured to the door. 'Don't you have something else to do?'

'These are my closest advisers,' said Jezebel.

'Then that is how far you have fallen, that you would take the thoughts of a physician and a maid and pass them off as wise counsel.'

Daniel took a step forward, but Jehu simply laughed at him. 'Remember your place.'

'It's all right,' said Jezebel. 'You can go. I will be safe.'

'When he thinks so little of you?'

'That probably assures my safety,' said Jezebel, nodding to the doorway. But while Beset stomped away, Daniel left only with great reluctance while Jehu watched, his arms folded across his chest.

'You can see his point,' said Jezebel after the others had gone. 'You barge into a stranger's house unannounced, dressed for battle, and demean me in front of my friends.'

'With someone as stubborn as you, only direct remarks are worth the effort.'

'And I was about to congratulate you on your promotion,' said Jezebel.

'And yet you feel no joy on my behalf.'

'Do you feel joy? I'm surprised you want the responsibility when you clearly think so little of Israel.'

'I defended you to that brute from Damascus.'

'Is that what you call it? Or were you angry because he humiliated you? Another man would have taken the money and the credit for a brilliant deception.'

'Hazael will be defeated soon enough. An alliance with Damascus is worth less than the casket the gold was brought in. But an alliance with you—' He reached for her wrist, closing his fingers around her, and pulled her swiftly to him.

But his voice had neither the softness nor the gentle dignity of his proposal at Ahaziah's coronation, his eyes were narrow and heavy as they bored deep into hers, and his grip was unyielding.

'Surely you don't need me to confirm your authority at the head of our armies,' said Jezebel.

'But where else can you go if you don't stay here with me? Your son does not want you, your brother—'

'Spare me the litany of my isolation,' said Jezebel, peeling his fingers away. 'And spare me your pity. Isn't that why you offer yourself again when I've already turned you down?'

But Jehu's fingers remained entangled in hers. 'I would save you from yourself.'

'The arrogance!' said Jezebel. 'If only you knew me so well. For if you did,' she tried in vain to steady her voice, 'you would already know that I cannot marry you when I love someone else.'

Jehu snorted with bitter laughter, and nodded towards the door which Daniel had left through. 'Him? There is no one else in your sorry court.'

'It doesn't matter who it is, only that there is someone.' She snatched her fingers out of his and wrapped her arms around herself. 'When I promised myself to you we were both young. But we're not the people we were then, time and circumstance have changed us both, and not necessarily for the better.'

'I'm still the same man.'

'Look into your heart and ask yourself if that is really true.'

'You've brought nothing but grief to your kingdom. Since you turned Ahab's head, Israel has staggered on like a wounded antelope, limping from disaster to failure. And your sons are no better, weaker than they should be with neither the wisdom of their father nor the fire of their mother.'

'Ah! Now we get to it. Does your brother know you have your heart set on the Israelite throne?'

Jehu's eyes blazed, but he said nothing.

'A less intelligent man than you would have denied that,' she said, her head spinning as she tried to see what was surely in front of her. But though she stared at him, tracing the creases in his face for signs of the truth, it eluded her.

'Joram has no fear of me,' snapped Jehu with contempt, 'when he is already terrified of the world. You should have seen him on the plains of Moab, sobbing his eyes out beneath the carcass of a dead horse when men were falling around him, their breasts pierced by Moabite arrows, choking on their own blood.'

'What did you all expect?' she demanded, her heart breaking at the thought of her son, so lost amid the carnage. 'Ahaziah was snatched from Joram's side long before he was ready to learn the ways of a ruler. Which of you stepped forward to earn his trust and show him the way? Instead you let him blunder on.'

'He should have learned caution from the fate of Ahaziah.'

Jezebel jerked at the hollow sound in Jehu's voice. 'What do you mean?'

But Jehu reached for her again, his hand sliding beneath her hair around her neck. 'Everyone else knew it was a warning.'

'I don't understand.' Jezebel tried to release herself but he held her firmly.

'Anyone but you would have seen the prophecy coming true and sought a way to protect themselves. They would have looked for friends with whom to shelter instead of ploughing on, so sure of themselves,

412

ignoring all the warnings. But not you. Ahaziah even told me that you would never be driven by fear, but it was too late . . .'

Jezebel shook her head, transfixed by the madness that was swirling in Jehu's eyes, aware of the great horror that was drawing itself together before her. 'What do you mean? When did you speak to Ahaziah? What do you know of his fate?' she whispered.

Jehu's face darkened and he threw her off. Jezebel gasped as she sank to her knees, the underworld surely cracking open to accept her in Ahaziah's wake, all her will draining out of her. 'No . . .'

'Why didn't you come to me when he died?' Jehu asked, his voice cracking. Not since the night in Tyre had she seen him so distraught, so torn by emotion. 'I could have kept you both safe – you and Joram.'

'I'll ask you again,' she said. 'What do you know of Ahaziah's death?'

He turned wretchedly to face her and stumbled down, grabbing her shoulders. 'Why do you turn me away when all I've ever done is love you?'

Jezebel was hardly listening. For so long she had seen Jehu as the young man she'd known in Tyre, thrust this way and that by forces beyond his control – his father, his brothers, his simple soldierly devotion to his God. Even when he declared his love for her at Ahab's funeral, she had seen the boy in him. Now she realised that he had deceived her, and maybe himself too. That young man was dead or at least deeply buried within someone more ruthless and conniving.

'You killed my son, didn't you?'

'I wanted you.'

'You don't deny it?' Her words tumbled out. 'Why, Jehu? Why?'

'For you,' he said. 'Ahaziah didn't want you. He wouldn't *look after* you. He said you were working against him, against the interests of Israel. He said—'

'You bastard,' she screamed, driving her fists into him, over and over, 'you thieving bastard, you stole my son.'

'I did it for you!'

'You did it for yourself!' Her voice heaved with anguish as she pounded at his breastplate, his shoulders, his arms. 'Get out of here!'

'Jezebel. I thought—'

'Get out! Never,' she sobbed, 'never *ever* show yourself to me again!'

She hit him with every word, his armour smearing with blood from her knuckles, and she hardly knew the gentle arms that pulled her back until she had folded in on herself, howling. She saw the strange sight of Beset hauling Jehu to his feet and pushing him out of the house.

For a long time, she knew only the sound of her own grief pouring out of her, the lightest touch on her shoulder, and the paralysing echo of her own thoughts. *He killed his son, I should have told him he killed his own boy—*

Slowly she realised that her hands were being washed and salved, and she lifted her swollen face to Daniel as he looked down on her with tenderness. He sat down beside her and took her hands in his and for a long time he simply breathed into her hair as her head rested against his shoulder. She felt his even pulse beat calm into hers as his stillness embraced her.

And when he scooped her up into his arms and carried her up the stairs, she let herself lie against him, her eyes closed, blocking out the hard corners of the world. And when he lowered her onto her bed, she reached for him, sliding her hands beneath the sleeves of his tunic, drawing him to her. He watched her carefully, doubtful that she would want him when her misery was so raw, but she pulled him down and kissed him, her tongue fluttering against his, and she fumbled for the belt of his tunic, suddenly aware of his skin against hers as though this was the very first time they had lain down together. He pulled off his tunic, then he gently unpinned her brooches and drew the folds of linen from her shoulders, softly kissing her throat and her shoulders, until she began to shed the dreadful weight.

Ten years later
842 BC – Jezebel

Chapter Sixty-One

The tiny stone house in the corner of the Palace orchard in Jezreel was mercifully cool in the late afternoon sunshine. The summer had been hotter than any Jezebel could remember. Since returning to Jezreel, she'd planted and tended the gardens over the years, but the air was too still and stifling to be outside today. She had dozed fitfully all afternoon, soothed by the sound of Daniel patiently picking leaves from the herbs she grew for him, and then awoken by his tender kiss.

'You wanted to pray before dinner,' he murmured, the lines around his eyes deepening as he smiled at her.

Jezebel pushed herself up from the couch and drew her loose hair into a twist over her shoulder. The long dark curls were peppered with grey now, stronger, coarser, curlier hairs that sprang from any plait or headdress into which they were entwined.

'I don't know why I bother,' she said sleepily, 'except that I feel somehow it would be worse if I didn't.'

'Baal surely hears your thoughts even if you are not kneeling at his shrine.'

Jezebel stood up and kissed Daniel on the cheek. There

419

was one small Phoenician temple on the edge of the city which Joram had quietly allowed to be built for her, with just a single priest to lead the worship. After so many years at odds, she and Israel had fallen into a kind of truce.

'I don't know that Baal is any more bothered than I am. We're like an old married couple. He must be tired of my entreaties over wars on the plains of Ramoth Gilead.'

'Well, someone in the great Pantheon is listening to you.'

'About time,' said Jezebel, pinning up her hair.

It was true that Hazael's army had been heavily depleted by the latest attack from the south. Once more, a combined force of Israel and Judah were fighting the Damascan invaders.

In the report of that morning, it was predicted that Joram would be home in the following days, bringing his triumphant army with him. For Jezebel, soon wasn't soon enough. She sighed, drawing a stole over her shoulders. 'What is to say that war won't come again in two years or five or ten? Perhaps Israel is doomed to fight the Damascans for all eternity.'

Daniel put his arm around her waist. 'Joram has developed into a good ruler. He's learned his lessons well and brought his intelligence to bear where his strength is absent. If you don't wish to trust the Gods, then you can trust him, I'm sure of it.'

'I don't doubt Joram,' said Jezebel. 'I just long for the burdens of the past to be lifted from this kingdom.'

'Then the proposed marriage between young Ahaziah and this Damascan princess Hanina is surely the best option.'

Jezebel smiled at Daniel. 'Don't be such a politician.' She hadn't travelled to Jerusalem for ten years – the place held too many painful memories of Jehu and the past – but she saw Ahaziah once a year when Athaliah brought him to Israel. 'He's only thirteen,' she added. 'I think he'd run away!'

'I've heard she's a beauty,' he said.

Jezebel laughed, then said more seriously, 'It would bring joy to both Judah and Israel particularly as Joram seems to have no interest in finding a bride of his own. But speaking of marriage, I've been thinking it is time that you and I rendered ourselves respectable. We may not cause a scandal any more, but a woman likes to be assured of her place, in case you take a second wife.'

'Ah!' Daniel kissed her on the forehead. 'So after thirty years you finally have sympathy for poor old Leah, shoved from the marital bed by your glamorous arrival in Samaria.'

Jezebel looked down at her plain dress of *tekhelet* blue, the fine necklace of lapis beads and the only ring she still wore, the silver and lapis band Daniel had given her all those years ago when she left Tyre. 'My glamour has faded, but you would make a good second husband.'

Daniel grinned. 'Very well. I will speak with the priests of Astarte tomorrow. You may have given up on the Gods but I have not. If we are to marry, we will do it properly.'

Jezebel embraced him softly, breathing deeply of the sunkissed skin of his neck. 'You have done so much for me,' she murmured.

'Then why do you sound so sad?'

'Think nothing of it. I'm sure I will feel content again when Joram has returned safely.'

421

'And perhaps when he has, we might think of leaving Israel?'

Jezebel pulled back a little so she could see his face. 'To go where?'

'I have been exchanging letters with Eshmun. He lives in Sidon now, and says that a middle-aged doctor, his wife and maid would be very welcome in one of the seaside villages near the city.'

'I had no idea . . .' she tailed off.

Daniel frowned. 'I shouldn't have mentioned it. I just thought that if we are to marry . . .' He too fell silent, but Jezebel kissed him tenderly.

'I'd given up all thought of leaving,' she said, 'but you're right – there's no reason for us to stay here any more. Joram is well established, he doesn't need me. And young Ahaziah has never been to Phoenicia. He will reach Judah's age of accession next year and he should have seen more than just his nearest neighbour before he has to take the throne.' She nodded, warming rapidly to the idea. 'As long as we give Tyre itself a wide berth, my brother should have no objections. When Joram is home again we'll tell him. And you can write to Eshmun and ask him just which village he has in mind.'

Jezebel settled herself on a rough wooden stool in the stableyard and watched as Ahaziah dodged and ran among the rows of Palace Guard, trying out his fighting skills. It was his first trip from Jerusalem alone, without Athaliah, and he was enjoying the company of the soldiers and Daniel, spending as much time outdoors as he could. His blunted iron practice sword looked comfortable in his hands, for at thirteen he was already tall like Ahab, with a stockiness about the shoulders from his other grandfather, Jehoshaphat. He would grow to be a handsome young man, for his hair was pale brown which made his suntanned skin look even darker, and his face was cheerful and attractive like Athaliah's.

As Jezebel watched, Ahaziah's practice became more intense. The soldiers moved around him, their swords arcing as he blocked and jabbed, and soon he was whirling this way and that, the tail of his tunic stuck out behind him like a jackrabbit.

'I don't understand how they can enjoy themselves so much when they're fighting,' said Beset as she approached. These days she no longer wore the sombre dark tones of the household staff, but her own clothes in pretty blues and greens. Her hair was still dark, a miracle she claimed, considering the years of service to Jezebel.

'I would rather he knew how to defend himself,' answered Jezebel. She raised her hand to shield the sun from her eyes. 'What brings you out here? You hate the smell of the horses.'

A cry of aghast surrender shattered the rhythm of sword on sword, and the women looked at Ahaziah.

'You should not be distracted by a pretty face,' one of the guards was saying, pointing at Beset.

Ahaziah blushed heavily and raised his sword with a great flourish.

'And don't show off to her either,' reprimanded the guard.

'Ahaziah has always been fond of you,' said Jezebel.

'No, well, quite enough of that,' stuttered Beset. 'You have a visitor.'

Jezebel frowned. 'Can Reuel or Boaz not see to it?'

'He asked for you personally.'

Jezebel pushed herself stiffly to her feet and followed Beset into the house. It was gloomy inside compared to the bright stableyard and she had to blink several times before she could make out the man in a hooded cloak, fingering a statue from the small shrine to Astarte that stood in the corner.

'I told you not to touch anything,' said Beset.

'And I told you I wanted to see Jezebel.' The stranger's voice was cool and smooth and Jezebel shivered as he pulled back his hood.

'Elisha,' she said. The hall seemed to darken with his presence.

He gave an ironic bow, his head tanned and slick with sweat. Oddly, in the ten years since she'd last seen him, his face seemed not to have aged. She self-consciously touched her own greying hair.

Ahaziah appeared at her elbow, and demanded breathlessly, 'Who's this?'

'I'm an old acquaintance of your grandmother.' He glanced back to Jezebel. 'The resemblance to his namesake is striking.'

Jezebel slid her hand protectively around Ahaziah's shoulder.

'What business do you have here?' demanded Beset. 'You defile our shrine, you make the whole place smell bad—'

'I've come to tell you what you surely dread, that the

end of the House of Omri is upon you. Yahweh has proclaimed your days are numbered to the next full moon.'

Ahaziah whipped his sword forward and stabbed its point precisely over Elisha's heart. 'How dare you threaten the Queen Mother of Israel!'

'You would pledge yourself to their fate as well?' asked Elisha. 'Being a prince of Judah may not be enough to save you.'

Ahaziah sliced into the front of Elisha's cloak, then he jerked the sword tip beneath Elisha's chin, forcing his head up. 'And if I cut your throat?'

'Yahweh cannot be silenced,' said Elisha, his Adam's apple bobbing.

'Be gone!' Ahaziah lowered the sword and pushed the blunted blade into Elisha's solar plexus, nudging him backwards. The prophet turned and scurried away. Ahaziah pursued him at a few paces all the way to the gates.

'I'm so sorry,' said Beset. 'I'd never have let him in had I realised who he was.'

'Elisha can find his way into anywhere,' murmured Jezebel. The odious smell of his cloak still lingered, and her mouth was dry. Her heart was beating so hard she felt dizzy and she lowered herself onto a seat.

'You need Daniel,' said Beset.

'I'm fine, I don't want to worry him.'

'Elisha's appearance will be all over the Palace before long. He should hear of it from you.' Beset stuck her head through a doorway and called for Daniel.

Ahaziah reappeared, examining the tip of his sword. 'I made sure he left,' he said.

'At least your bravery isn't in doubt,' Beset observed, ruffling his hair. Ahaziah grinned shyly at her.

'What's going on?' Daniel came running in.

'Elisha,' said Jezebel.

'He's an emissary of the serpent-God Lotan that one, not of Yahweh,' muttered Beset.

Daniel placed a silencing hand on the maid's arm. 'We should leave the city soon. He will stir up trouble.'

'No,' said Jezebel firmly. 'I am not running away again.'

The chill that Elisha had brought with him couldn't be dispelled, and though the sun shone on all afternoon, Jezebel shivered and she found no comfort in Daniel's embrace or Beset's nervous teasing. It was only eight days until the full moon. She doubted that Yahweh had the power, or the inclination, to take all three of them – herself, her son, and her daughter's child. But there were always men who called themselves loyal to the God who might get carried away and cause trouble. Athaliah would never forgive her if something happened to her only child while he was in Israel. Jezebel insisted Daniel accompany Ahaziah everywhere, she had his chamber moved into the garden house next to theirs, and despite all her grandson's protestations, she insisted he was not to leave the Palace until Joram returned home.

So it was with great relief that Ahaziah came running down from the roof the next morning, shouting that a messenger had been sighted. But the joy was shortlived when the messenger, sober-faced and bloodied, knelt before Jezebel in the Council Chamber.

'I bring news of the King.'

Jezebel's throat tightened. 'Yes?'

'He has been injured and is being brought home—'

'To die?' mumbled Jezebel.

'There was much blood,' said the messenger.

Jezebel rushed out of the Chamber and into the garden, staring up into the sky. The hollow white ghost of the moon, three-quarters full, hung to the east of the sun.

Chapter Sixty-Two

Jezebel rode out to meet the carriage that brought Joram home, Ahaziah and Daniel beside her. The procession had been moving swiftly across the plains to Jezreel but it drew to a halt so that Daniel could climb aboard. Jezebel hung back, her imaginings almost suffocating her after the long day and night of waiting since the messenger's arrival. But eventually she steeled herself to peer over Daniel's shoulder, and she found Joram wincing, his leg shrouded in mounds of bloodied bandage, as the physician inspected the wound.

In the shadow of the carriage, Joram looked thin and pale, and Daniel explained that it was partly from having lost so much blood. But Joram would barely meet his mother's eye and said nothing until he had been carried to his room and Daniel had stitched, salved and redressed the wound.

'It looks worse than it is,' he murmured to Jezebel as he passed her in the doorway of Joram's room. 'He was caught in the leg by a chariot spur. It would fell a horse and he was lucky.'

'But he will live?'

'This won't kill him.'

428

Jezebel cast a grateful look heavenwards on the whisper of thanks to Baal, then she slipped into Joram's room and sat down on the end of his bed. But even in the bright room, he looked like a ghost, broken and lost, and Jezebel knew that it was not the agony of Daniel's brief operation on the wound.

'I should have stayed in Ramoth Gilead,' he said, his eyes closed.

'You weren't meant to.'

'I'm the King – it's my duty to stand at the head of the army.'

'Then better to be alive and have the opportunity to do your duty once more.'

Joram shook his head, his jaw slack with resignation. 'I've never seen anything like it. The sheer carnage, every man for himself. Ruthless violence.' A tear swelled in the corner of his eye but he made no effort to brush it away.

Jezebel laid her hand on his good leg, but she thought of what Jehu had said about Joram in Moab, how the combat had petrified him and reduced him to a miserable coward seeking shelter behind a dead animal.

And perhaps Joram thought of Jehu too, for he said, 'They call him "The Invincible One", you know? He always leads his corps from the front and he can see the weak points in the enemy in an instant. I knew that my brother was a good soldier, but I've never seen anyone fight like Jehu.'

'He has many years of experience,' Jezebel said briskly. 'How goes the war?'

'In our favour,' said Joram, opening his eyes, though he looked past Jezebel to some distant plain. 'The night before I was injured, Jehu drove a wedge into the Damascan troops. It broke them in two and we were able to spread out and enclose each half.' He dragged his eyes to meet his mother's. 'I couldn't even have imagined such a manoeuvre and yet it will probably have won the war for us.'

'And yet it is you who kept this kingdom at peace for ten years, you who fed its people, increased the water flowing to its farms and traded with kingdoms we had never heard of when your father was alive.'

'What is the point of that when Hazael would ruin us?'

'Well he won't ruin you now,' said Jezebel. 'Your leg will heal, and your kingdom is strong in itself.'

Joram shook his head. 'The full moon is coming—'

'You saw Elisha?' she said.

'He stopped my carriage, a dozen miles east of here, crowing at my fate.'

'East?'

Joram nodded, confused. 'Does it matter where he fore-tells our doom?'

'He must have been on the way to Ramoth Gilead – why?'

'Yahweh doesn't care for borders,' said Joram.

Jezebel stood up. 'Yahweh had His chance to take you,' she said, 'yet He did not. Sleep while you can.' She smoothed Joram's hair across his forehead. Her son lifted his hand to brush hers away, but his fingers caught among hers and he squeezed them fleetingly.

'You can only be the man you are,' said Jezebel. 'And if Jehu is so eager to drive home his sword then we cannot stop him. You are still a better man than he is.'

Her thoughts were so full of all the possible trouble Elisha could cause that she was several paces into her room before she noticed it was full of flowers. The small shrine to Astarte in the corner was wound with vine leaves and tendrils, and bowls of water were sprinkled with white petals. Jezebel looked around her in puzzlement, her attention finally falling on the bed behind her, where a white dress edged with Tyrian purple lay arranged.

'Beset?' she called.

'Ah, there you are!' The maid bustled in, herself dressed in a fresh pale blue dress trimmed with ribbons.

'What is all this?'

'The priest is here.'

'The priest?'

'Do you not recognise a Tyrian wedding dress when you see one?'

'Oh!' She looked again around the room.

'I cannot believe this is my first opportunity to decorate the bridal suite,' Beset was saying. 'After all these years!'

Jezebel watched her maid, her cheeks pink with the fun of it as she fussed at the flowers and brushed imaginary dust off Jezebel's best sandals. 'Come along,' said Beset, gentle but firm. 'Joram is home and you can enjoy your wedding day without worry. I won't let anything spoil this, including you being late.'

And so Jezebel slipped out of her clothes and Beset anointed her skin with fragrant oils, and proceeded to dress her in the white gown. But she refused the ceremonial painting of her face, protesting that Daniel already knew the lines and creases and loved her regardless.

So when Daniel came into the room with the priest, and he took her hands in his as they knelt before the shrine, she knew she was marrying him not out of convenience or duty, not because it would strengthen one kingdom or weaken another. No one would be displaced by their union, nor would children be required to bless it and preserve its purpose.

'In the name of Astarte,' the priest said, 'between Shalim and Shachar, from dusk to dawn, I marry you in the bonds of eternal love.'

'From Shapash and Yarikh,' said Daniel.

'From the sun and the moon,' answered Jezebel.

'In Molech and Yam.'

'In fire and in water.'

The priest continued. 'How blessed are this couple who make their pledge to each other before the Pantheon. In the name of the Great God El, may they know all the strength of Baal and all the wisdom of Astarte.'

Daniel released her hand and reached into his tunic, and Jezebel felt a ring slip onto her finger beside the old lapis and silver band. She glanced down and saw another band, purely silver this time, engraved with Astarte's vine tendrils in the most traditional style.

As Daniel gazed at her, a quite distant memory sprang to mind, the ceremony she had witnessed from the promontory in Tyre thirty years ago. Though just a girl then, she remembered thinking such a simple fate could never be hers.

'And yet now it is,' she murmured.

Chapter Sixty-Three

Once again it was Ahaziah who spotted the arrival of the messenger. He ran breathlessly into the small courtyard outside the garden house where Jezebel and Daniel were having breakfast with Beset. The marriage was only two days old but already the sheep's curd tasted a little sharper, the honey a little sweeter. Nothing had changed and yet everything felt different.

'The messenger brings the pennant of the Damascans!' shouted Ahaziah, leaning against Beset to catch his breath.

'Is it victory?' asked Daniel. 'So soon?'

'He's riding up the path now,' said Ahaziah. 'I will fetch uncle Joram.'

'I will come with you,' said Jezebel, putting down her bowl of fruit. 'If this is a great victory for Israel then we should celebrate it together.'

Joram was in the Council Chamber with the messenger, a crutch abandoned by the throne and several scrolls unrolled across the cedarwood table.

'Is it over?' asked Jezebel.

'Were they routed?' shouted Ahaziah in expectation.

Joram nodded. 'These are the treaties of peace.'

The messenger bowed low. 'Your Highness,' he said to Jezebel. 'I bring news that Hazael of Damascus has conceded defeat. He presented his sword to Jehu on the banks of the River Jordan.'

'At what price?' asked Jezebel.

'Don't be so cynical, Mother,' said Joram. 'The victory is significant. Jehu would not have accepted it were Hazael not in earnest. His troops must be severely depleted for him to seek out Jehu with such a gesture. You'll no doubt be pleased to know that the treaties include concessions on travel taxes, return of rights to river tributaries that the Damascans had deprived us of, and a share in the food tithe. I drew up the terms myself on the eve of battle and would have settled for nothing less.'

Jezebel sank down onto a couch. *Then I can go home,* she thought, *Daniel and Beset and I can go home to Sidon and leave Joram to rule Israel.*

'I will ride out to the Jordan,' said Joram, grabbing his sticks from the floor.

'Are you fit enough to go?'

'I will be fine on horseback.'

'May I go too?' asked Ahaziah. 'Oh, please! There's no danger now the war is over, and I want to show Jehu how much I have improved with my sword.'

Jezebel shook her head, but Joram put his hand on his nephew's shoulder.

'We will take good care of him, and it's only right that he should join in the official delegation.'

'Is there mention of Hanina?' asked Ahaziah, pointing to the treaties.

Joram gave him a sly look. 'Now that you come to mention it, there is mention of a pretty girl.'

Ahaziah grabbed at the scroll but Joram was too quick for him and he mussed his nephew's hair with his hand. 'Get yourself ready, pack a light bedding roll and we will leave immediately.'

Jezebel placed a restraining hand on Ahaziah's arm. 'You may be King, Joram, but I'm by far the most sensible person in this room. Ahaziah can only go if Daniel agrees to go with him. You'll be engaged with further negotiations with Hazael, no doubt, and my grandson should not be allowed simply to roam around the Kingdom of Damascus unaccompanied, following any fancy that takes his eye.'

'Very well,' said Joram. 'You'd better ask Daniel, though.'

'I'll go!' said Ahaziah. He dashed out of the Chamber.

'It's over,' said Joram.

'The Gods have been kind to us,' said Jezebel. She stood up and went to the table, casting her gaze over the scrolls and treaties. 'Do you think we can trust Hazael?'

'His pride will have been wounded by giving himself up to Jehu, and he'll be ready to listen to reason.'

'Then use your reason wisely. And don't stay away from Jezreel any longer than you have to.'

Jezebel returned to the garden house to find Daniel putting a few clothes into a boarskin pouch. His harp lay on the bed as though he had picked it up and then thought better of it, and his medicine chest lay open, a few cloth bandages and salves removed from the compartments.

Jezebel slid her arms around him from behind and laid her head against his shoulder as he folded clothes into the pouch.

435

'You gave me up easily enough for a life on the road,' she murmured as he turned to face her. 'Two days of marriage and already you want to run away.'

'I wouldn't leave you for anyone else but a young man who needs a watchful eye.'

'I rather think he should keep an eye on you, for all those Damascan beauties will pick you out of the crowd in an instant.'

He lowered his lips to hers and kissed her, gently at first and then with such passion that she felt weak at the knees.

'If that is what I'm going to miss,' she said, 'then you had better come home soon.'

'I'll think of you every moment.'

When he had put the final few possessions into his pouch and tied up a bedding roll, they walked out to the Palace gates together, hand in hand. Jezebel felt as she imagined the youngest of couples must feel, swollen with all the blind joy of love that knows no darkness.

Joram was being helped up onto his horse but Ahaziah was already mounted, turning the beast impatiently in circles around Beset, a new sword strapped to his waist.

'I don't think you will have any need of that,' said Jezebel.

'It was a gift from your Palace Guard,' said Ahaziah proudly, 'as befits the Prince of Judah.'

'The Prince of Judah.' Jezebel and Beset bowed low, concealing their smiles.

'And with the sword comes my responsibility to look out for the subjects of our allies,' declared Ahaziah. 'That includes Daniel, Grandma.'

'I will watch out for myself too,' grinned Daniel, mounting his own horse.

'Ride safely, ride swiftly, ride home,' said Jezebel in the old Tyrian way.

Ahaziah gave a great whoop and kicked his horse to a canter through the gates, followed by Joram at a steady trot, finding his balance with his leg heavily strapped. Daniel gave Jezebel a last wave, then he urged the horse forward and they were gone.

'If we keep ourselves busy,' said Beset, brushing the dust from her skirts, 'they will be back soon enough.'

'I have in mind to plan a feast for their return,' said Jezebel. 'Not one of triumph over Hazael, for that would be foolish, but simply one of peaceful celebration at the state of our kingdom. We will have tables of food in the streets, and the people can share in my good fortune.'

Beset squeezed her arm. 'And it is your good fortune, isn't it?'

Jezebel nodded. It was as though the weight of the last thirty years – all the hostility that greeted her arrival in Samaria, the defacing of the Temple, the slaughter of Amos and the priests at Carmel, Naboth's murder, the misery of all – had at last been lifted. The borders were secure, alliances made. From now on, they could only grow stronger and more content.

'And what of you and Daniel?'

'What of us and Daniel, you mean. We're going to Sidon,' she said suddenly, turning to Beset. 'That is, if you'll come with us. I was going to wait until Daniel returned to tell you, but it is too good a secret to keep any longer. We will make our arrangements once they have returned.'

Beset's face broke into a smile of such utter delight that

437

Jezebel felt guilty at having kept it from her at all. 'The sea!' she cried. 'Think of it!'

'It won't be all fun,' said Jezebel, tugging playfully at Beset's sleeve. 'Daniel will need to work as a physician to keep you and I in food and colourful clothing. We must learn to be his nurses and earn our keep.'

'Is it too late for me to run after them?' Beset pointed at the gates. 'If they don't go to Damascus, we could leave tomorrow!'

Jezebel laughed but her eyes grew wet and she stopped walking. 'You've stuck beside me all this time, suffering as I have done.'

Beset's cheeks went pink. 'Come now,' she said, wiping a smudge of tears from Jezebel's cheek. 'In a way I've enjoyed far more freedom than you. I used to think of you as a sack of grain,' she said, 'always being traded about. I'm sure Jehu thought no better of you than that.'

'Well,' said Jezebel, as they walked through the archway into the small courtyard, 'he has his victory and I hope it makes him happy. I'm glad not to have to consider him any more.'

'Aye to that,' said Beset, clearing the table. 'What about if we go through your clothes this afternoon and see if you have anything remotely suitable to wear as a physician's wife?'

Jezebel smiled. 'I cannot think of a better way to plan for my future.'

Chapter Sixty-Four

Jezebel blinked in the darkness, unsure at first what had woken her. She stretched out her hand, searching for Daniel, then remembered that he was east in Ramoth Gilead with the victorious armies. This was the fourth night since he had left, and perhaps he too had woken and was looking at the stars, thinking of her.

She rolled over in the bed, drawing the sheets to her face and breathing deeply of his scent. She closed her eyes and tried to imagine him here with her, but on this side of the bed it was strangely light, and she realised that the moon was shining in through the window, casting a silvery sheen across the place where Daniel should be lying.

Jezebel sat up and looked around her. Somewhere in the stableyard a dog howled, another answered it, and she shivered at how near they sounded.

She sipped from a cup of water beside her bed, then she lay down again and pulled the covers up to her chin. The room felt huge and empty around her, and she realised she wouldn't be able to sleep again easily. The fire hadn't been lit, for the summer nights were not cold, so she draped a stole over her nightgown and went out into the main room, looking for a candle or a lamp to bring a warm glow to her room. A strip of light glowed beneath the front door. It was odd that a torch had been lit. She pushed open the door and heard the hum of voices in the courtyard.

Beset was there, wrapped in a cloak, her hair loose over her shoulders, arguing in heated whispers with a messenger who carried the torch.

'What is it?' asked Jezebel from the doorway.

But Beset wouldn't meet her eye and Jezebel knew immediately something dreadful had happened. Her legs went weak beneath her and she clung on to the door. Beset rushed to steady her, but the messenger stayed in the courtyard, his torch shimmering waves of yellowish light around them all.

'Forgive me,' he was muttering, 'forgive me!'

'The prophecy . . .' The words choked Jezebel as she uttered them and she lifted her eyes to the sky. The moon was almost round, its cool silver chilling the dark. 'The King is dead, isn't he?' she whispered.

Beset's features were contorted, her cheeks streaked with tears and Jezebel felt deathly cold. She grasped her maid's face between her hands, twisting it to and fro. 'What is it?' she asked. 'Tell me!'

'Don't punish her!' said the messenger, approaching. He fell to his knees before her. 'The King is dead,' he said. 'And Ahaziah, Prince of Judah.'

From somewhere deep in the stableyard, the dogs let out a wretched howl.

'The Damascans?' Jezebel whispered.

The messenger made no response and Jezebel grabbed

his hair and thrust back his head. Only then did she see how young he was, barely older than Ahaziah himself, and her hand fell from his fine hair, her fingers catching against his soft face, the memory of her grandson snagging on her heart.

'Tell me,' she begged, in the voice of the dead. 'Was it Hazael?'

The messenger slowly shook his head. 'He is to blame, but . . .' He struggled to his feet and stepped away. 'It was Jehu. He killed them all.'

The next question was almost impossible to ask, but she managed to utter the words. 'And Daniel?'

'Daniel too,' he said.

Jezebel reeled against the doorway, staggering against Beset. Her shoulders heaved up and down. She knew the messenger was still speaking, trying to explain, but she couldn't hear his words. She frowned and peered at him, as though the blackness that closed in around her would clear.

'We have to leave!' Beset was shouting, piercing her mistress's stupor. 'Jehu will surely come for you next.'

Jezebel lurched forward. 'Tell me what happened,' she demanded of the messenger. 'Tell me what he did!'

'The treaty was a ruse,' mumbled the messenger, struggling to his feet, 'between Jehu and Hazael. Unite to conquer, divide the spoils—'

'*Herem*,' whispered Jezebel. 'Slaughter your enemy and steal what is his. All in the name of Yahweh.'

'Jehu knew that news of the treaty with Hazael would bring the King back to the plains to claim the victory,' said the messenger. 'He was not expecting the Prince of

441

Judah too. Or Daniel. For a moment, I thought perhaps he might not . . .' The youth's eyes shimmered with tears like deep black pools. 'Jehu made no secret of Hazael's visit,' he continued. 'In the King's absence he behaved as if he were the King. None of us dared defy him. We knew he would kill us where we stood. So when the King returned, got off his horse, we could only watch. The King limped across the sand to Jehu. Jehu opened his arms. In greeting. Welcome to your River Jordan, welcome to your Gilead—' His arm jolted forward and his gaze flicked onto Jezebel's.

'He killed him in the embrace,' muttered the messenger. 'His dagger, thrust into the King.'

Jezebel felt the dagger had pierced her too, but felt only the agony of betrayal.

'And what of Ahaziah and Daniel?' she asked, feeling a shell hardening around her grief.

The messenger's face fell. 'The Prince of Judah understood the treachery immediately. He shouted for the King. Watched him fall. He cursed Jehu, drew his sword, ran towards him.' The youth rubbed his eyes as if he could wipe away the memory. 'Daniel ran in front of him, trying to stop him. Grabbed him, trying to hold him back. Jehu saw them and drew his sword.'

Jezebel closed her eyes. 'Go on. I must know.'

'He took the Prince first,' said the messenger. Somewhere the Gods were surely roaring, for a sound like distant thunder was building in the night. 'Daniel tried to stop him. He tried to reason, even as Jehu murdered your grandson. Soldiers pulled him back. They held him while Jehu spoke with him. I couldn't hear what they said.'

'And then Jehu killed him too,' said Jezebel.

The messenger nodded and told her how it happened.

'Go,' she said, 'get out of here.' The dull thunder that had surely been the fury of her Gods had grown too earthly loud and the sky hung clear and cloudless above them.

'Leave the city,' she cried, shoving the messenger towards the gates. 'You aren't safe with what you know.'

The messenger staggered away.

'You aren't safe either,' said Beset, clinging on to Jezebel. 'Jehu will come for you too.'

A single searing stab to the heart, Jehu's breath hot on Daniel's face, his fist hard and cold around the hilt as it drove home his revenge.

'He already has,' said Jezebel, looking up and around her. The thunder echoed off the city walls and she knew the sound of chariots on the mountainside. She felt the rage of Baal surge up through her and she ran across the terrace and into the Palace, her whole body burning with the God's fire.

The noise was dulled within the walls, but the torches of the raiding party already threw a dirty tinge through the shutters as Jezebel hurried up the main staircase.

'Where are you going?' asked Beset behind her.

'The moon turned full tonight,' said Jezebel.

'You should leave with the messenger, together you might make it!' shouted Beset, but Jezebel stopped and shook her head.

'Why?' she said. 'Daniel is dead.'

A flood of misery made her bend double. He had died without her, so far away. Beset grabbed her, tugging her back towards the stairs. 'Go! Go before they find you!' she hissed.

But Jezebel grabbed the balustrade and drew herself upright again. Her eyes were clear as though Astarte herself had blown her tears dry. 'He's come for me. Let him take me at last.'

She strode into the chambers she had once used when she was Queen. She lifted the lid on the grand chest, then she slid out of her nightdress and stood naked in the moonlight. Outside, she could hear hammering on the city gates and the dogs barking frantically in the stableyard.

'Dress me, Beset,' she said. 'Dress the Queen of Israel for the last time.'

Beset's head twitched in denial, but Jezebel held her gaze, and slowly the maid stumbled towards her, dragging the heavy ceremonial gown from the chest and hauling it over Jezebel's shoulders. The fabric felt heavy and stiff against her bare skin, the golden clasps as cold and sharp as arrows. Beset carried the headdress, proud and gleaming from the chest.

Jezebel shook her head. 'I must paint myself first.'

'No—'

'I will not cower before him. He will see the proud face of Tyre.'

Beset chewed her lip, tears pouring down her face once more, but she scuttled to the corner of the room and returned with a box of kohls and powders and henna, unopened in more than a decade.

Her maid's hands were unsteady at first, but Jezebel softly touched her face and they stilled. With every caress of the brushes, Jezebel willed Astarte to breathe dignity into them both. Beset painted first her feet, then her hands

444

and last of all her face. Beyond the Palace, the heavy city gates were being dragged open, wood shrieking against stone. Soon the clatter of horses' hooves and the judder of wheels filled the streets. Beset glanced out in terror as the howl of the dogs surged up beneath the window. Jezebel grasped her shaking hands and brought them back to her face.

'Quickly now, dearest friend.'

'I won't leave you to that . . . that . . .' Beset said, her head falling forward onto her mistress's shoulder, and Jezebel wove her hennaed fingers through the maid's hair, breathing calming words like benedictions over her oldest friend.

'If you don't leave me, then who will tell of my fate? You must tell them, Beset. You must speak for me otherwise he will have won.' Beset pulled her head upright, nodding fitfully, her face sodden with tears, and Jezebel saw how they made the stones on the ceremonial robe glisten. 'You see? I will carry you with me,' she said, lifting the brush in Beset's hand back to her forehead.

As Beset drew the final lines on the Queen's face, there was a great hammering at the Palace gates.

'Now go,' said Jezebel. 'Ride safely. Ride swiftly.'

Beset glanced reluctantly at the side-door, but with another great beating on the gates, she gave Jezebel one last agonising glance and then fled. Jezebel took a deep breath, then grabbed the leather strap on the side of the ceremonial chest and hauled it across the room to barricade the main door. She pushed across the bolts. None of it would stop anyone intent on breaking in, but it would buy a little time and a little dignity. For already she could hear the snorting of a single horse in the street below.

She walked slowly to the central full-length windows, holding herself tall, the robe trailing behind her. Then she lifted the headdress and placed it on her head.

She reached for the shutters and pulled them back. Moonlight flooded the room. She looked out over the plains, where a great army was already gathering, torches puncturing the flat shadowlands. Beneath in the street, the horse neighed pitifully, and a voice rose up, that voice she knew so well and had once loved so much.

'Jezebel.'

She didn't look down. 'Who calls on me?'

'Jehu, Prince of Judah, Commander of the Judean-Israelite forces—'

'And traitor,' said Jezebel, casting her eyes downwards. He sat on his horse, fatter than she remembered, his jaw heavy, his hair untidy and long, his hands darkened around the reins.

'You are stained with the blood of my son, my grandson and my husband!'

'You can still save yourself,' he shouted.

Jezebel stared at him. 'And give you the throne?' she said. 'Why would I do that?'

'I have the throne already.'

'On whose authority?'

'With Yahweh's blessing.'

'With Elisha's blessing, you mean.'

His chin sagged to his chest for a moment, then he lifted it again. 'You're nothing unless you marry me. You'll lose everything you have ever had—'

'I've already lost it!' she screamed. 'And you stole it from me! The man I love is dead, slain by you. What could possibly possess me to marry you now?'

'It's the only way to save yourself.'

'Yet I only wish to be saved from you.'

'I've gouged out the rotten line of Omri,' growled Jehu. 'I have earned Israel.'

'Listen to yourself!' she said, her voice louder. 'Israel's people cannot be bought and sold.'

'I will join Israel with Judah as it should always have been.'

Jezebel moved closer to the edge of the window, her bare toes now over the edge of the stone sill, its sharp edges digging into the balls of her feet. The moment of revelation was upon her. 'This kingdom has already had a king that united Israel and Judah,' she said.

'That's ancient history—'

'No!' she shouted. 'It's barely a decade old. But you killed that king with your own hands.' She drove her gaze deep into his, his eyes so black in his silvery face. Jehu frowned, the fragments of the truth swirling before him, and Jezebel gave a bitter laugh. 'You see it now, perhaps. *Our* son.'

His eyes flashed. 'You lie!'

'As the Gods are my witness, I do not,' she said. 'The son was born to me eight moons after I left Tyre. The boy you killed. Speak his name, Jehu.'

Jehu stuttered wordlessly. His hands fell to the neck of the horse and he seemed to cave in on himself. 'You never told me.'

'You hated Israel so much, you belittled everything I

447

brought to this kingdom, how could you ever have accepted him?'

'But I loved you, all that time—'

'You loved me enough to kill my son!'

A sudden gust of warm air touched her skin and she gripped the window ledge. There was nothing left now, nothing to keep her strong.

'I loved you,' he repeated desperately. And then something seemed to pass over his features, creasing his face with fury and sinister shadow. 'You denied me *my* son!' he screamed.

The dogs barked and howled in horrifying chorus, snapping at the walls beneath Jezebel, and Jehu raised his sword. Through the locked door, she heard dozens of feet thundering through the courtyard. Jezebel pushed herself onto the balcony rail and swung her legs to the other side. Her robes swayed as though Mot, the God of Death, tugged at the hem, enticing her towards his deep dark realm.

In the sky, the faint sparkle of stars clustered in so familiar an outline.

'The archer, Kesil,' she said. 'He will live on long after both of us.'

Behind her the door shook with the hammering of fists, then the steady thud of an axe. She lowered her eyes towards the street, not to Jehu, but to the glistening stone that shimmered before her eyes like the ebb and flow of the waves against the harbour wall in Tyre. She felt dizzy, as though the ground was coming up to meet her, and she clung on to the balcony to steady herself. Then the axe shattered the door. Jezebel looked back one

448

last time as the Guard who had once been so loyal to the House of Omri forced their way past the chest, their swords glinting.

For a moment, she smelled the tang of salt and felt the sweet western breeze on her cheeks. Then Jezebel spread her arms wide, inhaled deeply of all the memories of the sea, and, as the soldiers' hands snatched for her robe, she pushed herself away.

Epilogue

Who will stop and drop a coin to hear the stories of Jezebel? Yes, I see it in your face, you know her name. Perhaps you heard of her beauty. Perhaps you drew comfort from her wisdom. Perhaps your fathers and grandfathers survived the Great Drought and were fed by her when she brought food down from the temples to the streets for the starving. I went with her, you know.

My name? Beset.

You speak a little Phoenician then? Yes. It means protector. I'm not sure the name was well earned for a time, but now . . . Well, I do what I can.

A silver piece? Some bread too. Your kindness won't go unnoticed by your God. Sit here – that cushion is the most comfortable. Your bones don't shake you the way mine do, but still you'll be glad of its feathers.

From your high forehead I think you come from the north. A merchant of cloth – really? My mistress would have been interested in your wares. Oh yes, I was her loyal maid for more than thirty years. And now all that is left of those days are this old woman before you and a sacred flowerbed in the Palace gardens at Jezreel.

I know, it surprised me too. I thought when Jehu discovered where I had buried her, he would dig her up and cast her out of his kingdom altogether. Not that there was much left of her when the dogs had finished. Just her hands, her feet, and her head. I see it sickens you, but at least she died at her own hands, spared the worst of the executions. Yes, those were dark days.

I buried her husband's nevel with her— You play too? Of course, neat small fingers you have, a weaver's fingers. Ah, I see it now, that is how you got into the cloth trade. And the faint stains of blue around your nails. Her husband? He was her second husband, of course. A good marriage that one, well blessed. No, he must be buried somewhere else, at Ramoth Gilead, I suppose. A Tyrian would tell you they sit together on some soft couch in Melqart's underworld, playing and singing and laughing.

Am I Tyrian? Once I was. But I've lived in Israel for sixty years and now I'm just an old woman who doesn't care to belong to any kingdom. Yes, it's true, I've seen a great deal of Israel, and I've seen the reigns of five kings. But none of them has really been my ruler, shall we say? How could they be beside a queen like Jezebel?

Jehu? I hesitate to speak ill of the recent dead. Let us just say he was not the king that Ahab was. Oh, yes, that was long before your time. Ahab looked outwards to far horizons and other lands, while Jehu looked only inwards. Ahab had the courage to open the kingdom to the influences of other nations while Jehu sought counsel only from the same God and the same prophets. I mean you no insult, whoever you worship, but after Jezebel had died, Jehu drove out the last of her priests from Israel and hauled down her last temple in Jezreel. And perhaps the Phoenician Gods stirred themselves long enough from their couches to be offended, for Jehu's truce with Hazael crumbled within a year. I see you know that story and how badly it ended.

I agree. He had no choice but to turn to the Assyrians to bolster his borders. Their vast armies make our own look like trifling gangs of children. Jehu was little more than their puppet king, and how he would have hated that. In the end, neither Israel nor Judah were proud to call Jehu king.

You think that is what drove him mad? No, I think his madness was there long before.

And Jehoahaz? Well, it would surely anger Jehu to know that his own son permits the discreet worship of Yahweh's consort Asherah.

Yes, you see it too. Jezebel's influence lives on in Israel. Her memory lives on in the hearts of other good women of these lands too. Her daughter Athaliah was a great queen to a crippled land and a crippled king. And Esther was much loved in Tyre, long after that sloth of a husband of hers had drunk himself to death. They were shadows of Jezebel, of course, but better women, better queens, for having been loved by her.

She does live on. Even this blighted kingdom couldn't know such a queen as her for as long as they did, and then destroy forever all she was. Jehu might have tried, but—

Jealousy, you say? Revenge?

Darker motives pollute even the most open of hearts. And if it happens early, before the love has come to know itself. And yet . . .

She still remains even now in the gardens of the Palace, yes, there, just up the hill from here. He never cast her out completely. He all but pushed her to her death, but he never let her go.

A good horsewoman, you say? Yes she was. I remember once, watching her ride the long sands of the coast at Tyre . . .

Samson's strength
made him a legend.
But even he was
powerless to resist her...

Delilah
ELEANOR DE JONG

Eleanor De Jong • Delilah

Maligned as the courtesan who revealed the mighty Samson's secret for money, Delilah has become synonymous with treachery. But behind the myth is a tale far more tragic . . .

In the ancient Holy Land, the Israelites and the Philistines are locked in bitter conflict. Samson – a seemingly unbeatable adversary – has come to symbolise Israelite defiance and the dominant Philistines are desperate to uncover the secret of his power.

Delilah – desirable, headstrong and reckless – is tired of living the demure life of a demure maiden. She wants more, and tempted by an offer she can't refuse, is persuaded to make a bargain. But this is no easy game of win or lose.

Instead, Delilah makes an astonishing discovery, one that she could never have imagined. But a sequence of events have been put into motion and only a miracle can change the course of history . . .

Allow yourself to be seduced by a novel as alluring as Delilah herself. The perfect treat for fans of *The Borgia Bride* and *The Red Tent*.

Gillian Bagwell • The Darling Strumpet

She sold her innocence . . . and captured the heart of a king.

London, 1660

Growing up in the bawdy atmosphere of 17th century Covent Garden, Nell Gwynn is little more than a girl when she enters the world of the courtesan. But Nell learns the hard way that to be at the mercy of unscrupulous men is no life at all.

With London's theatres flourishing, Nell seizes an opportunity to change her luck and takes a job selling oranges at The King's Playhouse on Drury Lane.

It isn't long before Nell takes centre-stage herself and her saucy wit and ambitious temperament soon catch the eye of the young King Charles II. But can she keep him enthralled when the country's finest Ladies are vying for his attentions at court?

Nell Gwynn was a darling of the people and the most famous courtesan of her age. You too will find it impossible to resist her in The Darling Strumpet.

£7.99
ISBN 978-1-84756-250-0
Out now

AVON